THE WORLD
WASN'T READY
FOR YOU

THE WORLD WASN'T READY FOR YOU

STORIES

JUSTIN C. KEY

HARPER

An Imprint of HarperCollins*Publishers*

HarperCollins books may be purchased for educational, business, or sales promotional use. For information, please email the Special Markets Department at SPsales@harper-collins.com.

FIRST EDITION

Library of Congress Cataloging-in-Publication Data has been applied for.

ISBN 978-0-06-329042-6

23 24 25 26 27 LBC 5 4 3 2 1

TO ALL THE BLACK WOMEN IN MY LIFE.

CONTENTS

The Perfection of Theresa Watkins

EVERYTHING HAD TO BE PERFECTLY IMPERFECT. A LIVING ROOM COUCH THAT didn't quite align with our centrally hung wedding picture. The entertainment console's unbalanced arrangement of rimmed diplomas, family photos, and assorted snow globes. The half-filled kitchen trash can, scant dishes in the sink, and a bathroom that was clean but not spotless.

If everything wasn't just right, I'd lose her again.

My arms were trembling tuning forks as I twisted off the medicine cap, popped a Xanax, guzzled water from the kitchen sink, and counted.

Onetwothree, onetwothree, one, two, three, one . . . two . . . three. My heart slowed. Fragments of worry gradually became coherent thoughts.

I hated medication, but Resurrection, Inc. advised against the electronic limbic treatments that usually eliminated my anxiety attacks altogether. They'd prescribed me a short-acting sedative to take "as needed" until things at home resembled normal. Despite warnings of the medication's addictive properties, I found myself taking more and more lately.

And then, a voice: "It took me long enough."

I straightened, banged my head on the bottom edge of the wall cabinet, and gripped the counter to keep my balance. The ceiling lights split into dancing stars. One special pair shone bright among the rest. Eyes I'd feared I'd never see again.

A White woman stood in the dining room. I had spent the morning agonizing over this first moment, formulating the perfect greeting and gestures and phrases. Now my dead wife was here, and I stood clutching my head, my mouth leaking water. What's more, I was unprepared to hide the shock. With her loose-hanging curls, defined neck, and coy smile, she looked like a distant relative of the wild-haired prisoner from the body-donor pictures. She looked nothing like the wife I knew. The one with tight black coils, full lips, and deep mahogany skin the same shade as mine.

Except for the eyes.

She spread her arms. "I'm White, Darius. Only in America." The voice was wrong; Theresa's had been lower. "Ian'll have a field day with this."

"Life lasts a lifetime, our love lasts forever." The phrase I rehearsed had sounded a lot better that morning in front of the mirror.

She laughed. My skin went down a size. This wasn't going well. I turned to busy my hands with another glass of water.

"I've missed the shit out of you," she said, suddenly beside me. Her mouth fell over mine. The lips were thin. Her taste was sweet, different from what I was used to; I had kissed the same pair of lips for almost a decade.

Theresa and I had always been eye to eye. Now, I bent a little to embrace her. This woman's hips were wider than Theresa's, her back muscles firm and tense. I pulled away and touched her cheek. The skin was rough and pink beneath the makeup, where Theresa's had been smooth umber.

"Do you see me?" she asked. "I see you."

"You have her eyes," I said. "Your eyes, I mean."

Before she died, my wife's features had kept their soft benevolence even at the height of her cancer's hunger. Long and thin with sunken cheeks, she now had the face of a woman who had been through a lot, but a long time ago. This new refined body was without menace— Resurrection, Inc. had gone to great lengths to reverse the effects of decades of incarceration—yet somehow frightening in the history still visible along its edges, the shadows of a past life lingering like erased pencil markings.

Whether I knew it then or not, this new body had its own memories.

Nine Years Before Resurrection

My first panic attack came the same day I met my wife. As Ian Cole pulled up to New York-Presbyterian Hospital, a hand—perhaps God's—gripped my heart as I gripped the door handle. What if my body couldn't take this round of chemo? What if a clot formed in the line and went straight to my brain? Every muscle in my body twitched to run.

"Bruh," Ian said, his hand on my shoulder. "Your forehead shiny as hell right now. You good? Should I call Jerry?"

"I'm fine," I said as I opened the door. He and Jerry Brown, old college roommates turned business partners, helped me through treatments the best they knew how. Ian made sure I made my appointments, and that life still had laughter. Jerry the Christian visited to pray over me. He continued silently even after I told him to stop, and I resented him for it. The last thing I wanted was help from Jerry the psychiatrist. "See you in two?"

I was out before he could answer. I hurried through the lobby and up to the oncology floor.

During those months of treatment, I went from being a young computer engineer with a budding 401(k), stock options for three different tech start-ups, my own business, and a vibrant online dating profile to a shadow of a man voluntarily pumping poison into his veins. The chemo had eaten everything else—my hair, my energy, my digestive system, my hope, and my faith. Why not feed it this new sensation, too? I willed myself into the treatment chair; the toxins mixed with my blood while I was still on the verge of a breakdown. It ate at me—all of me—and I found sleep.

I dreamed chemo-torn dreams, my weathered mind left to reconstruct splinters of cognition. I was back in my childhood bedroom, only my twin-size mattress had become a deathbed. My legs dangled over the edge; my feet scritch-scratched, scritch-scratched against the wood as I trembled from the drugs.

My dead mother tended to me. Bits of blackened flesh dropped from the rotting hole in her neck into my tea. She somehow saw my fear with her cold eyes and began to sing. The whites of her spinal cord were visible through the shreds of her throat. More bits fell into the cup.

And then I felt God's hand on mine. I tried to pull away. Didn't He know we were done?

My dreams broke under His touch. I looked down, curious to see the Hand of God. Thin, spotted skin stretched pale over straining knuckles. The slender fingers were strangely delicate. My laughter came out as a painful cough. God was Black. God was a woman.

I looked up, ready, and saw not God, but instead someone broken like me. Her eyes and mouth were tight lines under a domed head capped with a purple polka-dot scarf. Dark patches stained mahogany skin that lay lazily over her skull. Orange lines shuttled treatment from hanging bags into her swollen arm. She wasn't the most beautiful thing I'd ever seen.

She woke some time later to me watching her. After a brief, orienting smile, she sat up and pulled her hand into her lap.

"You're not going to get weird on me, now are you?" She spoke slowly, as if parts of her were still dreaming.

"You were holding my hand," I said.

"I'm Theresa. Ovarian cancer. What you got?"

"Uh, Darius. Lymphoma. I've got three more sessions."

She nodded, closed her eyes, and laid her head back against her seat. I thought sleep had reclaimed her when she spoke again. "Same, more or less. See you Thursday?"

No, I didn't think so. The sessions had taken their toll. Even with them, my chances were slim. The quick flick of a knife across my wrist would offer a much cleaner death. A lot could happen before Thursday.

But I didn't tell her that. "Yes. Definitely," I said.

And I did. That Thursday and many times after.

That was the worst of the chemo, and in some ways the best.

Remission, like our relationship, had its expected highs and lows. I often thought of chemotherapy as a kind of first death. The hopelessness, the fear, the exhaustion, spiraling down to a forfeit that finally ushered us into a second life of recovery and relationship.

We had found love in poison. We had found life in death.

...

We sat facing each other on the living room couch. Theresa had spent the last hour retelling what she remembered of how we first met. Resurrection, Inc. stressed the importance of these drills to further cement her memories. I relived many of them as she did, only correcting small details and filling in a few blanks. Besides the occasional confirmatory eye contact, her gaze was off interrogating the past. Theresa's new White skin competed with the memory sewn in her words. She caught me staring and touched my hand. I calmed in her eyes.

Thank god for the eyes.

"This is hard," she said. "I know."

"They offered to let me remember you as you are now." I pulled out my remnant card. "I still can."

"I want you to remember me like I remember me."

I reached over to brush away an intrusive strand of hair and found myself trying to curl it with the tip of my finger. Theresa placed her hand over mine. Her face flushed in a way that wouldn't have been possible before.

"I hate it, too," she said. "They tried—Lord knows they tried—but the curls wouldn't hold. I looked like a weeping willow. Not cute. Brain transplant? Piece of cake. Transracial hair? Who do you think we are? Miracle workers?"

We shared a laugh. It felt good.

"I almost broke up with you when we were both out of the woods," Theresa said, still smiling.

"Yeah?" This was news to me. I considered telling her to save the story for another time. Her brain was still unraveling itself. How would I know if the memory was accurate or some scrambled perspective? Instead, I said, "Why?"

"We met dying. It didn't seem like a smart foundation. You never thought of it that way?"

I hadn't. In the weeks before meeting her, my nights were spent in a bathroom reeking of vomit, a chef's knife hovering over my wrist, waiting for the courage to end it all, to take back control. After Theresa, when I found myself back on the bathroom floor, it wasn't cowardice that kept the blade from doing its work, but the want to make it to Thursday. To see her again. The chemo had saved my body, but Theresa had saved my life.

The doorbell rang. Thank God. "That's the food," I said.

"I'll get it," Theresa said, rising. "I need to stretch my legs every few minutes anyway. I have to keep the neurons firing."

"You got to sleep, though, don't you?"

"Didn't they tell you? I don't sleep."

"Really?"

"Joking, babe," she threw over her shoulder. Her hair went the opposite direction whenever she moved. It was distracting. "Sleep's the easy part. That's where all the magic happens. At least, that's what they told me."

I admired Resurrection's work. Despite the company's assurances, I'd expected the worst from her donor body. Years of incarceration doesn't look good on anyone. But a month of training both mind and body between neural implantation and family presentation had given her toned legs with little blemish and buttocks that sat high atop her thighs. Nearly caught up in the illusion, I fully realized the magnitude of what Resurrection had accomplished. They'd cheated the grave. Fear grazed my heart.

I went to clear the dining room chairs and table of the clutter I'd artificially planted and began to set for dinner. When I came back out of the kitchen with our guest plates, I frowned. Theresa was sitting in the wrong place. I saw the problem and plucked a piece of mail from the seat directly across from her. The correct seat.

"If I remember this right, this smell is a good smell," she said as she pulled out cartons of food from a brown bag.

"Sorry for the mess," I said, waving the piece of mail. "You can sit here."

"I'm fine, it's not a problem. Champignon makes catfish?"

"They do now, yes." I sat, then stood. My fingers twitched against my thigh. "You sure you don't want to switch? Facing the kitchen means you see all the dirty dishes, and that means bad mood bears . . . remember?"

"Of course I remember. The kitchen's clean, though. So, no worries, right?"

"Right. Sure. It's just . . . you sit here, and I sit there. You know what? Never mind, it's not important."

Theresa rose. "Trade with me," she said.

"Really, it's fine."

"I'm serious. Looking into the kitchen is depressing. Reminds me that I need to learn to cook all over again."

My thumbnail picked at my pinkie knuckle. Had I already taken today's Xanax? Yes, earlier. Before she came.

I smiled. "Perfect. Let's eat."

...

"Where did I propose?" I asked. We lay in bed, continuing the talks that were supposed to be like exercise for a resettling brain.

"Under a willow tree in . . . Marcus Garvey?"

"Central Park. It's okay."

"Shit, yes, Central. You were such a hopeless romantic. Didn't you say you wanted us to be buried under that tree?"

"I was high on love. What can I say? Okay, next question. First kiss?"

But Theresa was staring off to the side, her smile barely hanging on. Her eyes darted within their sockets; her mouth grew thin.

"Theresa."

"Hmm?"

"You looked . . . distracted. You okay?"

"Yeah, I was just thinking about something."

"No voices?"

She smiled. "No voices."

Soft vibrations through the sheets. Theresa frowned, reached under her pillow, and pulled out her phone. She stared at the screen for what seemed like a long time.

"Everything good?" Resurrection, Inc. had issued her a private, restricted line for her probationary transition period.

"Yeah. Just a reminder of my next appointment." She slid the phone back under the pillow. "What else you got?"

"What was it like?"

"What was what like?"

"Dying."

"Ah, that," she said. Her expression went serious. Her lips scrunched up toward her nose. The arrangement nipped at a corner of my mind until I recognized it as a pirated version of the old Theresa's thinking face. She probably didn't even notice she was doing it; her muscles simply weren't in sync with the neural networks controlling them yet. I imagined thoughts wandering around her brain, bumping into things like someone taking a midnight trip to the bathroom in a new home.

"Please," Theresa said. She'd stopped me from pushing the right corner of her mouth just a little bit higher, where it should be. "Be patient with me."

I tucked my hand away. "What was it like?" I said.

"Remember when we went bungee jumping in Ecuador? It's like that, but slower. A lot slower. I went down and down and down until I couldn't go down anymore. Then I was coming back up."

"Immediately?"

"No. Not immediately. There was some time. A couple hours, maybe?"

"A week. It took a whole week to get you back in a body."

"Wow. I mean, I had to be somewhere, right?"

"Yeah," I said. "Somewhere."

...

In the soundless night, she watched me. Theresa's gaze was so much a part of my past, from moments of love to rage to lust, that I felt it even before fully rising from my dream.

Thank God for the eyes. I thanked Him who no longer existed for me, as I had thanked Him when I first knew—really knew—Theresa was coming home. Sometimes it was just easier to have someone to thank.

Thank God for the eyes.

I should have sat up to share this moment with her, whatever this moment was. I should have asked if she was all right. I should have found out why the hell she was watching me in the middle of the night.

Instead, I pushed my face into the pillows to recapture sleep before it scurried too far away.

Thank God for the eyes.

Seven Years Before Resurrection

"It's blasphemy," Theresa said. She rolled up the plastic from our new coffee maker, shoved it in the trash can, and snatched the Resurrection, Inc. pamphlet from my hand. We'd just moved in together in a one-bedroom on the Upper West Side. While Theresa had been quick to unpack, much of my modest belongings remained haphazardly stuffed in reused cardboard boxes lining the short hallway. The hastily painted walls were bare except for a trio of placards instructing to LOVE, LAUGH, and DREAM.

"What's the harm in meeting with them?" I said. "See what they're all about?"

"I already know what they're all about. It says so right here. 'Be the master of your fate. Be the Captain of your soul.' God is the captain of my soul."

"I'll make an appointment," I said. "Just a consult. And if you don't like it, we don't have to do it. At all."

She leaned against the kitchen counter and sighed, long and heavy, as her eyes scanned the sheet of paper. The common whirr of an ambulance drew her gaze out of the barred window. I saw my chance.

"I don't want to lose you," I said when the siren dissipated into the background noise of a New York morning. "I don't want to lose us."

Resurrection, Inc. was located just a few blocks away, twelve floors above a busy Columbus Avenue. The elevator groaned in defiance the entire way up. A tall, thin man with a pin-striped suit, wavy black hair, and a metallic smile greeted us at the top. Theresa burst into laughter when she saw him.

"Ian?" she said, wiping her eyes. "You run this?"

"I'll take that as a compliment. You were really going to leave all the explaining to me, huh, Darius?"

"I thought you were out today?" I said. Ian led us down a dimly lit hall to double doors branded with Resurrection's logo: a generous hand cupping a brain, its neurons firing in excitement.

"I cleared my schedule. Did D tell you he helped invent this tech?"

" 'Helped invent' is a big stretch," I said.

"No." Theresa's laughter had come and gone like a midsummer rain. "I had no idea, actually. You told me you were part of a tech start-up."

"I was," I said. "Neurotech. Always good to see you, Ian. You mind putting on your business face and showing us around?"

At first, Resurrection's office seemed like a smaller version of the psychiatry suites I had come to know well. Books lined thin shelves in a waiting room meant for two. A white-noise box hummed from a chipped coffee table. Neutral and unimposing. Ian led us single-file back to the main procedure room, and any illusion of normal fell away. Here, the walls popped with shades of red and turquoise. Stenciled eyes tracked us from a flat-screen built into the wall. Meditation music hummed through my body. At the far end of the rectangular room was a computer hooked up to a long silver-and-black robotic arm with eager fingers. Theresa looked around as if the place smelled foul, then at me. I silently begged her to give it a chance.

Ian gestured to two nonmatching chairs—one green, the other pink—opposite the robotic arm. "Have a seat, make yourself comfortable."

Ian served us green tea as an assistant fitted me with a helmet covered with electrodes connected to the computer. Theresa refused to participate in this demonstration. Her gaze lingered uneasily over the contraption on my head.

"How is this better than the brain transplants?" I asked after Ian had explained their service. It had been very hard to take Ian's idea of neuro transplants seriously back when we were managing Continuum. Jerry, Ian, and I had built the lifesaving electronic limbic treatment clinic from scratch, originally to treat addiction. The noninvasive outpatient procedure targeted the emotional centers of the brain and rerouted their connections from substances to more sustainable coping mechanisms, like exercise or video games. When I got cancer and Jerry got saved, Ian's propensity for avant-garde endeavors took over. If emotional responses could be stored and rewired, could we do the same with a person's whole being and transfer it to a donor brain? He scouted out any potential investors with a foot in the grave. Mostly those with cancer, some with a life-long anxiety over a human's expiration date. Ian didn't need fancy promises to woo the desperate into seeing if wealth could translate to immortality. Hope and ambition were enough. Resurrection was born. Even then, despite my own hand in the coffin, I paid little attention to the details of how Ian's technology cheated death.

"A brain transplant is only the riskiest procedure known to medicine. Dr. Nduom pioneered the first twenty years ago while researching brain cancer. His own son, I've heard, and now they are in practice together. No one has been able to get it quite right since. Today, there's a fifty percent chance of rejection. Fifty percent. That's flipping a coin to see whether or not your new body attacks your brain."

"There's been some success," I said.

"In Japan, yes. But no one knows the long-term outcome. And you only have one copy of your brain. If something—anything—goes wrong: lights out. In a perfect world, the outcome would technically maybe be better. But we live in the real world. You have your remnant card?"

I did. I hesitated, glanced at Theresa with a nervous smile, and took out my keychain. The blue-and-red-striped piece of metal looked like a dog tag. My ticket into the ELT clinics, it held my past neural configurations, told the staff exactly what treatments I needed, and was always on me. Ian slipped it into one of the computer's sockets.

"And when's the last time you had ELT?"

"A week ago."

"Long enough. Pick up the can," Ian said, gesturing to the red-and-white-striped soda can sitting on the table. Its aluminum caught the light, reminding me of the moon.

"What's ELT?" Theresa said.

"Electronic limbic treatment," Ian said. "Targets the wiring in your brain that controls emotion, simply put. We call it 'limbic,' but in reality it's wherever your brain stores your emotional response, which is specific to each individual. No more getting addicted to benzos or alcohol just because you don't want to be a nervous wreck all the time. Continuum was the first to do ELT. We created, others stylized."

"So you're also a customer?" Theresa said to me. "What's next, you're going to tell me you're a robot?"

"Well—"

"Shut up, Ian." I turned to Theresa. "Look, honey, I didn't want you to freak out. But we—they—do good work. Remember how bad I was?"

"Just go on and pick up the damn thing," Theresa said.

I concentrated. Nothing happened.

"You're getting ahead of me," Ian said. "Pick it up with your hand. Like you normally would."

I did. The metal was warm. Despite the angle shift, the can somehow still caught the light. I placed it back.

Ian clacked away at the computer. "Do it again."

I did. The sliver of movement out of the corner of my eye could have been my imagination, but I knew it wasn't.

"I was just thinking," I said. "When I code, I can make a program on one computer and then use it on any other. They all share the same basic language. Our brains aren't like that. They're all different."

"Ah. But when I look at this can, I see red. You see red."

"My red may be different from your red."

"Does it matter, though, if we both agree it's red? In a sense, we don't talk to each other, our interpreters do. They take our complex network of unique electrical signals and turn them into a common result. If I thought of the word 'fruit' and stimulated the same firing pattern in your brain without the interpreter, you might think of the word 'meat.' Or it might not even be a word at all. You might see a certain color or smell a certain scent.

"The remnant card stores your neural connections. Resurrection stores your interpreter. Together, it's like packaging a novel with a universal translator." Ian turned the computer screen toward me. Thousands of lines connected dots in a virtual plane that took the crude shape of a brain. "See, here's a snapshot of you lifting the can. Here's a snapshot of the sensory input and output at that time. And here's the intersection of those two. The Interpreter."

Lines of code in an unfamiliar language scrolled the screen for five seconds before stopping.

"Unimpressive now, but it'll grow," Ian said.

"What happens to the donor?"

"All neural networks—memories, knowledge, Interpreter, every-thing—are erased. Once a wipe has been made on a consenting candidate, they are considered legally dead."

" 'Consenting,' " I said. "Is that real consent or prison consent?"

"We actually have a hefty waiting list. I've spoken to each donor myself. Many feel this is their chance at redemption. And of course their families get a comfortable sum of money, and criminal records are erased."

"I have schizophrenia," Theresa said. I had almost forgotten she was there. "Well controlled; I haven't had a flare-up in years. Would that mess with any of this?"

"Good point," I said. She was engaging, which was encouraging. "We probably don't want any of the schizophrenic donors, especially from prison. Should we edit it out, you think? Could be a dangerous window."

"All our donors are serving life sentences, yes. And likely for violent crimes. But those with psychiatric issues are more likely to be victims of violence, not perpetrators, even in this population. That said, yes, we'd remove any identifiable brain diseases for both parties so as not to interfere with compatibility matching."

"Does anything stay behind?" Theresa asked. "After the wipe?"

"No," Ian said, a little too quickly. I sensed Theresa didn't believe him. As the Interpreter's lines of code rolled across the screen, I realized I didn't either.

...

"Go." Theresa shooed me toward the door. We'd spent the day doing memory exercises and sifting through her wardrobe. After some convincing she'd tried on an old favorite: an oatmeal-colored matching loungewear set that made its debut in remission and returned in those last, hard months before we needed Resurrection's services. It fell differently now, but the way the new Theresa owned it made me smile. "It's Thursday night. Jerry and Ian won't know what to do without you."

"You remember Thursday nights?"

"Don't change the subject. Get out of this apartment. You need it."

My wife had seen a missed call from Ian on my phone. He was most likely at Jerry's in Brooklyn, watching the Giants game.

"You sure?" I asked again. Thursday-night drinks and football had been a pivotal tradition in getting me through the pre-Theresa chemo days. But I hadn't seen Jerry and Ian since before Theresa died. They'd have questions I wasn't quite ready to answer.

"It's hot outside." Theresa went to the kitchen and pulled out a can of cherry-flavored seltzer. She gave a cursory glance out the unbarred window as a vocal ambulance passed. Her expression remained unaffected. "Drink plenty of water and walk slow."

"What am I? Eighty?" But it was hot. I grabbed the can. "What will you do?"

"I'll get out. Maybe I'll find a 'Was Black, Now White' support group. Show off my new look." She stretched the relaxed fabric of her pockets and twirled in an awkward pose. She blushed—a new feature I allowed myself to enjoy—and adjusted herself. "Joking, babe. I'll probably pick up some wine for when you get home, so save some room."

"Avoid that stuck-up place on Amsterdam. That lady puts you in a bad mood. Remember?"

"I can handle it. Now go. Give the boys my love."

I took the 2 train down to North Brooklyn and picked up a six-pack of Heinekens on the walk over to Jerry's third-floor condo. He lived in a studio with his three-year-old cat.

A tall man twice my width opened Jerry's door. We both paused.

"My man, Ian," I said. "It's been a while." My memory-lane sessions with Theresa had me envisioning the Ian from college on the walk over, back when he'd been a buck-fifty after dinner. He could eat anything without gaining a pound. Jerry and I called him the "black hole." When the fantasy world of college melted away, we realized Ian was an alcoholic. Our journey to his sobriety led to us all becoming business partners. Off the poison, he gained what seemed like a hundred pounds in a year.

"You look like a new man!" Ian said. He slapped my outstretched hand away and brought me in for a hug.

"I feel like one."

Freshly painted red walls were decked with yellow-framed photos and Jerry's existential artwork, which had secured enough gallery sales to justify him leaving his psychiatry practice.

"A new boyfriend?" I said, touching the wood of a hanging picture of Jerry and another man.

"Who knows?" Ian said.

"Old boyfriend," Jerry said. Unlike Ian, he often approached unnoticed. He was a full head shorter than me, and his small frame moved around the room without making a sound. He wore a homemade blue-and-white Giants jersey with a red-highlighted depiction of himself catching a football in the end zone. "You've probably met him. He goes to our church."

"Your church," I said. Jerry had first come to Shiloh Church at my invitation. I never admitted that, at the time, I thought his love for men was pulling him to hell, and he never admitted that he only started going out of spite. In the end, God surprised us both. Homosexuality wasn't the biggest threat to faith, after all. Cancer was.

The couch sat in the middle of the living room under a yellow chandelier. As I settled into the custom-made furniture piece, I ran my hands over the artwork tattooed across its smooth fabric: Black bodies twirled over each other in a dance against the background of a fiery sunset that lit the length of the couch. Two fluff pillows made up the sun's golden eyes.

"I know this piece," I said. "Yours, right?"

"It is," Jerry said.

"You never cease to amaze."

"Neither do you." Jerry handed me a beer and sat at the other end of the couch. Ian pulled close a barstool from the marble-top island that separated the living room from the kitchen.

"Theresa's home, right?" Ian asked. Once Resurrection went mainstream, he'd jumped at the opportunity to sell and retire young. He remained on the company's board but was more than happy spending his time traveling the world. "You got a picture?"

"I do, actually," I said. I pulled out my phone. We'd snapped selfies her first night, when neither of us quite knew what else to do.

Ian swiped his thumb one way, then the other, and frowned. "You know this is a White woman, right?"

"Really?" I said. "She's not albino?"

"They couldn't find a sister? I would have found you a sister."

"You hadn't heard? The state only allows White donors. Keeps Black bodies in prison."

"You're shitting me."

"I am shitting you, actually," I said. "Though I wouldn't be surprised. Resurrection said it's all about compatibility. Brain compatibility."

"Who the hell told you that?" Ian imitated a balancing scale with his hands. "Black brain here. Black brain there. How doesn't that add up?"

"It's not about Black or White. It's about the wiring."

"So, you're saying Theresa has more of a White brain than a Black brain?"

Jerry raised his hand. "Excuse me, I'm sorry, but what is a White brain?"

"Ask Theresa," Ian said.

"Bottom line: whoever this woman is—was—her brain had just enough in common with Theresa's for this to work," I said.

"Question." Ian postured with an open hand, forecasting the

profundity of these next words. "Would you let Theresa—this new Theresa—say 'nigga'?"

"She doesn't say it anyway."

"Right, right. But what if she did?" When I didn't answer, Ian leaned slightly back to engage both of us, his solid cheeks rising in a grin. "This is going to revolutionize the way White people justify using the N-word. 'Well, my White friend who used to be Black says it, so . . .' "

"A fitting legacy for you," Jerry said.

"Fuck you."

But Jerry had shifted toward me. "Who cares about White people using a word they invented, anyway? It's just distraction from the real problem."

"What's the real problem?" I said.

"Nothing, D." He took my empty can and stood. "I was just talking."

"No. Speak your mind."

Jerry looked to Ian, who held up his hands. "I'm not in this."

"Really?" Jerry and I said together.

"I sold the company. Remember?"

"Whatever." Jerry turned back to me. His finger picked at the rim of the can. As a trained psychiatrist, Jerry's deliberate expressions offered only the emotions of his choosing. Now there was rare uncertainty in his wandering gaze and loose jaw. "Theresa . . . she's dead. Dead, Darius. You don't get to come back from that."

"It's no different from you hooking up a computer to someone's brain to make the crazy go away," I said. "It's science."

"It's an abomination, that's what it is. They made a copy of her. A copy. There's a Theresa lying dead somewhere. Just because we didn't have a funeral doesn't make that less true. How do you even know the transfer worked? These prisoners, they're resilient people. You think some simple brain-wipe could get rid of all of them? How would you ever know she's not just acting like your wife?"

"I'd know."

Jerry didn't seem to hear me. He was pacing across his condo. He pointed to my phone. "That's not Theresa. That's a computer program that acts like Theresa."

I sprang up and caught a startled Jerry midstride. His hands grabbed mine as I gripped his collar.

"Whoa, shit bruhs." Ian wedged between us. "What are we, in the club or something? Chill the fuck out, Jerry."

"I thought you were staying out of this?" Jerry said. And then, to me, "Get off me, Darius."

I jostled him. He tensed.

"It's time to update your beliefs," I said. "Dead isn't dead anymore."

"You can tell yourself that. But when you go home and look in her eyes, there'll be no soul there. I know it and you know it."

"I said 'chill'—You know what? Fuck it." Ian sat down. "Whoop each other's ass, see if I care."

I let go; Jerry nudged me away and straightened his shirt. I took the momentum and headed for the door. Ian urged Jerry to go after me, but I knew he wouldn't. Jerry and I would be good, we always were. Best friends knew when and where to walk away.

"Hey, D!" Ian called when I was halfway to the elevator. His breath was heavy from the short sprint. "Jerry's being an ass."

"Say less," I said. I nodded to the beer he'd been nursing all night. "You good?"

"What? This? ELT keeps me in check. This is just my sweet tooth. Don't worry about me." He squeezed my shoulder. "How are you, bro?"

"Good. It's tough without neurotech." Just the mention of ELT had me craving the service. The anxiety melted away so easy. My finger outlined the remnant card through my pocket. "But the Xanax works. When I need it."

"It's probably for the best," Ian said. "You don't want to be confused when Theresa is confused. How is Theresa? Is she adjusting okay?"

"Yeah," I said. "It's like she never left."

"I'm here if you need help with anything. I still have some connections. Keep me updated. We're rooting for you two."

...

Theresa was in the shower when I got home. Jerry's ridiculous notion of desperate inmates acting out a part echoed loud enough to nearly push me into the bathroom. I needed to see her. Those eyes would calm me. I resisted.

I changed into shorts and a T-shirt and checked the hamper before throwing in my day clothes. Theresa's loungewear lay atop the pile, turned inside out. Just like she used to leave it. I sat on the edge of the bed, found and then followed my breathing. Things were good. We would work out.

A flash of light caught my eye. Theresa's phone lit with a notification from the bedside table. I stared at it for a long time. Who was messaging her? Someone in on the act?

"Fuck you, Jerry," I said as I snatched up the phone. "You goddamn asshole."

Theresa had a text message. I tried my name as the password and, when that failed, considered my name plus my birthday digits, then stopped. Too many attempts, and the system would wipe itself. I had begun to put the phone back when I noticed what was beneath it. A hardcover book sported a female prisoner with both hands reaching from behind bars under the title *The Crisis of Women in the U.S. Prison System*.

I touched the cover, wondered, and went back to the shower door. Faint whispers coated the sound of falling water. I waited, and listened, trying to make sense of it. Was that weeping?

The water trickled off; any other sounds died with it. Curtains opening. The flap of loose cloth. I imagined her drying off. The door opened. Theresa started.

"Jesus, Darius!" She turned to wipe away tears with her towel. "Are you trying to win the Creepster Award?"

"What happened?" I said.

"You scared the shit out of me, that's what happened." She pushed past and sat on the bed.

"You were crying. I heard it."

Theresa mouthed a curse. "It's nothing, babe. Really. I don't want you to worry. Look, I got wine. We can play a game, watch a movie, quiz each other, whatever you like."

"Talk to me first."

She dried her hair in silence and stared at an old picture of us on the dresser. She bit her lip as her eyes welled. "I went to the wine and spirit store."

I couldn't help but smile a little. Was that all? The blond middle-aged manager there had always been cold to us, as if we'd accidentally wandered into her high-class establishment while looking for a corner store to buy lottery scratch-off tickets. "That woman'll mess up a wet dream on a good day. What did she say to you?"

"That's the thing. She was nice. Nice! Showed me the new wines they just got from Italy and everything. As if I belonged there. She never tr-treated me like-like that when I was . . ." She broke into sobs.

I pulled her close. She smelled fresh, like she always did out of the shower, but in a different way. "She's an asshole, babe. Fuck her."

"It's not just that. It's everything. I haven't even been back to the school to see my kids."

"We can go tomorrow, then," I said. "Get your job back. You'll teach. I'll code. It'll be like you never left."

"Don't you get it? I can't ever go back. Those girls looked up to me. Now all I'd be telling them is they can grow up to be a White woman!" She shook her head as she turned to look at our picture. "I never knew you hated my skin."

"What? Theresa, I—I didn't have a choice. I swear. It was either this or . . . I just wanted you back."

"I'm sorry. You're right." Theresa fingered my collar. "I'm scared, is all. I keep thinking you'll fall out of love with me—this new me—and send me back."

"Theresa, I would never. We have our second chance. That's all that matters."

She searched my eyes with hers. What lived behind those whites, now streaked with red?

I kissed her to drive the thoughts away, to stop my lips from asking about the phone or the book or when she would start being my Theresa again. When she kissed back, our mouths filled with salt and pain and fear.

We moved slow. Both of us were strangers to Theresa's skin. I'd married her mind; the rest of her was something else. Our bodies didn't mesh like they once had. I rammed her nose with my forehead as I positioned on top of her. She expelled me from inside her when she tried to squeeze me with her muscles. She burst into an infectious giggle in the middle of a kiss. I rolled to her side, laughing.

"We're like teenagers," she said. Moonlight through the window lit her face. "Old, stiff teenagers."

"You're going to love what I got, girl," I joked as I slapped her ass. "You ain't never had—"

At first, I thought I had slipped off the edge of the bed, and I was laughing even as the back of my head hit the wall, sparking stars.

Laughter died. Theresa knelt on the bed, her salvaged eyes wide and twinkling even in the dark. Her hand danced with light, as if encased in diamonds. I blinked, and saw it was a sliver of moonlight on a long blade. I knew that reflection; I'd prayed to it almost every night during chemo, before Theresa. "Honey. Baby," I said. "What is this?"

She stayed perfectly still. Had her body taken this stance before? A threatened inmate in a maximum-security prison, a different set of waves bouncing between her ears?

How different? a voice asked. It sounded like Jerry's.

I rose, careful to keep the moonlit blade in my sight. I'd let it sit atop the kitchen counter as a reminder of how low things had gotten, how far I'd come. When was the last time I'd seen it? I didn't remember it being so big.

I inched forward. Theresa was a statue. When I was close enough, I touched her shoulder. Her trembling body tensed; for a terrible moment I thought she was going to attack. Our second chance at happily ever after, sliced down with the same dull blade from which Theresa had originally saved me. I responded by continuing forward. This is my wife. This is my Theresa. It's all I had to combat the urge to run.

"You're home," I said. "You're safe."

All at once, her fire went away. She fell into me, sobbing. Her arm was limp at my side. The cold flat of the blade touched my stomach. I thought about gently taking it from her, but decided against it.

She continued to cry as we lay down on the bed, her body curved into mine. Her sobs carried her to sleep and, finally, silence. Despite a numb arm and a cricked neck, I waited another hour before sliding free. I gently pulled the knife from her fingers, crawled out of the bed, went to the kitchen, and returned the blade to the holder's open slot. I vomited in the sink and, when my stomach had nothing left, popped a Xanax.

I counted, meditated, traced the colored grooves in my remnant card as I waited for the benzo to do its job, and went back down the hall. Dark-bound whispers paused me at our bedroom door. I had heard these incoherent, private mutterings before, after Theresa's cancer came back and she decided to go off all her medications, including the antipsychotics.

I pushed on the door to cause a creak; the whispering stopped.

"Theresa?"

Silence. Perhaps she was asleep. Perhaps I was the one hearing things. I climbed into bed, considered wrapping my arms around her, decided not to, and closed my eyes.

...

"I only want to know what happened." I followed my wife out to the living room. I'd spent breakfast and much of the morning thinking about the night before, wondering how to address it. The topic fell out of me, clumsy and unscripted, while Theresa put away her clothes from the laundry delivery. "What were you thinking? Why were you thinking it?"

She sat on the couch, legs tucked under her, and looked up at me. "Can we just not talk about it? Please?"

What the hell was I going to do with her? Her schizophrenia at its worst bore crippling paranoia, but never violence. Had this been from that? Or was that something deeper? Resurrection's policy was clear: any psychiatric problems demanded reporting. But then what?

To the state of New York, Theresa was property. The original Theresa was dead, and the inmate donor had essentially signed away her right to live. Until the rapidly evolving technology of neurocomputing was regulated, if Resurrection thought Theresa was a threat, their only obligation was to offer a refund. They'd get rid of her.

"I can't fix this if I don't know what the problem is."

"Some things don't need fixing." She leaned forward to busy her hands organizing the coffee table.

"I'm a coder. Everything needs fixing."

"That's hilarious. Have you tried stand-up?"

"Do you think I want to hurt you?"

"No, babe, it's not like that."

"You're hearing voices, then? Is it her? Is it the donor?"

"What? No!"

"Then who?"

Theresa's mouth parted.

"I heard you whispering to them last night. Theresa would tell me."

She slammed her fist against the table. A coffee mug—one from Resurrection—cracked in half. "I am Theresa!"

"Okay. Let's just calm down," I said. My mouth went dry. "You came at me with a knife. A knife. I saw the prison book. Did you have some type of memory? A flashback, maybe, from the prison?"

She looked at me, and I knew. Dammit, I thought, what am I going to do with you?

"I got freaked out," she said. "That's all. Can we just put this behind us?"

"Sure."

Theresa leaned over and kissed me on the cheek. "Thank you. You want to rent a movie or something and stay in?"

"Yeah. Let's just stay in forever. I bet you'd like that." I stood. "I'll be back."

She looked like she was about to argue, but instead just said, "Don't be too long, then. And remember to drink plenty of water and walk slow."

Theresa would have fought. Theresa would have reminded me that I was her husband, not some boyfriend who could leave whenever things got hot.

Drink plenty of water and walk slow. She'd said that before. I googled it as I entered Central Park, scrolled past results showing portraits of George W. Bush with prison tattoos and random movie quotes, and tapped one. "Prison Maxims" stood bold over a list of phrases. One line read:

"Drink plenty of water and walk slow": Time moves slowly, but there are consequences to every action.

I slowed, found a bench occupied with lazy pigeons, and sat. My thumb bit at my other fingers as I read over the phrase, again and again. I took off my jacket. My armpits were cold with sweat. I rubbed my pocket: flat. I'd forgotten my pills. I did, however, have my remnant card.

I called Jerry. It only rang once.

"It's good to hear from you, D."

"Schizophrenia," I said. "How does it work? Is it in the body at all or just the brain? That's a thing, right? The brain-body connection? Can't you get depressed by having the wrong bacteria in your gut or something?"

"Whoa. Slow down. What's the deal?"

"I just need to know how it works. Do the voices ever come from . . . somewhere else?"

"What. Happened?"

"I think Theresa's hearing voices again."

"There's no reason to panic. She's had that before."

"No, you don't understand. I think the voices are from her body. Her prison body." The park lights blinked on as I told him about the phrase and the search results. "She said it twice, Jerry. Twice."

"Is everything else good between you two?"

"You think I'm being paranoid. I found her reading a book about prison." I took a deep breath and closed my eyes. I knew how I sounded. I'd just gotten my wife back and I was worried about random phrases and her reading habits. "She came at me with a knife."

Silence. The gravity of the situation was clear. I waited for Jerry to tell me there was only one thing left to do. I feared less the words and more what my reaction to them might be. That I might listen.

I opened my eyes. The sun was just dipping below the trees of the park. The once vibrant colors all faded to the same gray.

"You tell Ian?" Jerry said.

"He's still on the board and—"

"Say no more. Give me a second. There's something I—just give me a second."

I reached for my pills again, cursed, and ran my hands over my legs. Onetwothree, onetwothree, one two three . . .

An older couple walking a Labrador as gray as them slowed toward me. I gave a polite wave and a smile. They left me alone.

Onetwothree, onetwothree, one two three . . .

Jerry sighed. I straightened.

"I looked this up after Thursday," he said. "I just had to know."

"Know what?"

"I'll just read it: 'Cheryl McCarthy, Bedford Hills Correctional Facility for Women—McCarthy was convicted of killing Ricky "The Brick" Johnson, a heroin dealer, in July 2002. Johnson was stabbed nine times in the chest and the throat—'"

"Shit," I said. "Nine times?"

"Yeah." He continued, "'Authorities said McCarthy, who was known to have a long history of paranoid schizophrenia, killed Johnson and buried him in the woods. McCarthy's attorneys said she suffered years of abuse under Johnson, who had used her paranoia to isolate her from family and friends, create financial and emotional dependence on him, and force her into prostitution. The killing, they said, was in self-defense. The prosecutors argued that her hiding the body suggested pre-meditation. What's more, they made the case that she didn't have "true" schizophrenia. They pointed to a car accident in August 1997 that led to opioid and then heroin addiction. Her "schizophrenia," they said, was substance-induced and a result of her own negligence. McCarthy was sentenced to life in prison. She died in 2021 of unknown causes.'"

"You're sure that's her?"

"Positive."

"The voices," I said. The night crawled over me. "It's got to be this McCarthy woman."

"That's a reach, D. A big reach."

"But it's possible?"

"Anything is possible."

"Can you think of a way?"

"Schizophrenia doesn't hide out in the body. That's absurd."

"Forget that, then. Any way, at all?"

"Schizophrenia . . . it's a whole-brain disease. We used to think it was mainly caused by the malfunction of specific neurotransmitters. Many people swore by the dopamine hypothesis, but it just didn't explain what we were seeing on functional MRI. Hell, we even see changes in parts of the hippocampus—"

"The hippo-what? Jerry, you're losing me."

"The hippocampus is involved in memory. What I'm saying is, Resurrection's wiping algorithm looks for well-studied neural networks. But if both donor and client had similar brain chemistry in overlooked portions of the brain . . ."

"That could leave a door wide open for McCarthy," I said.

"Theoretically. Again, though, I don't—"

"Could we erase it? I have her remnant card. Fix her, you know?"

"You don't fix this, D. Theresa's gone. You need to let her be gone. Have you been doing ELT?"

"Resurrection said—"

"'You need to keep your mind clear,' right? Is your mind clear, though?" Silence. "Look. One session, and maybe you can start seeing things in a fresh light. Xanax is a shit medication. That ain't going to cut it."

"Got it. Thanks, Jerry."

"Bro—"

"I got to go, bye." I hung up and rose from the bench.

My phone vibrated as I walked across the park. I stopped in front of the 6 train, which would take me down to Brooklyn. I swiped through my phone apps without opening any, and then checked my messages. I had one unread. It was from Jerry: Stay woke, bro.

...

I frowned up at the two-story building. Its sleek metal skin stood out among the old brick shops and concrete apartment complexes with gray windows. The faded sign read NEUROPHORIA. What an awful name.

Ever since we founded Continuum, copycat neurotech clinics had been popping up all over the place. Whatever services they offered—electronic limbic treatment, memory manipulation, cognitive skills downloads—they all used the same neuro-network backup platform. All you needed was a remnant card.

I walked in and scanned mine at the nearest kiosk. Soon after, a young woman with thick purple glasses and neatly wrapped locs led me down a corridor that opened into a long room with high ceilings. We passed rows and rows of what looked like sleep pods until we came to an open one. I climbed in and instantly felt trapped. I was ready to ask for a larger pod when the padded cushions slackened. I shifted my weight; the pod shifted with me. Its walls maintained a constant but nonthreatening contact with my body.

"New design?" I said.

The woman shrugged. "I've been trying to get them to invest in the portable units. But what do I know?"

Portable ELT units were still years away, but I didn't correct her. She'd have access to my brain soon, after all. She quickly ran through my medical and neurotech history.

"Any history of memory wipes?" she said.

"I wouldn't remember, would I?"

I smiled. She was not amused. She reached for my ear. I recoiled. Tattooed on the back of my lobe was a hieroglyphic representation of all my neurotech. It was as intrusive as looking at my browser history.

"No memory wipes, okay? I guess you're not into jokes?"

"Been a long day. If you had a memory wipe—"

"I know the risk. I'm good. Seriously."

She considered me a moment longer, shrugged, and began to close the pod.

"No cap?" I asked. I scoped out the surrounding pods. A few down, a young man with golden curls pulled himself out. His expression was serene, his head bare.

"No need. Just lay your head back. You'll know when you're in the right place."

"How—" But she was right. As my body fell into an aural groove, twin heat beams started at the base of my neck and drew lines up my scalp, bathing my head in a warm tingle.

Theresa filled my mind. My wife, strong and full, an idea rather than a form, like the fragment of a dream. I struggled to hold on to her, to form an image of her in my mind. Sweat coated my brow; my fingernails clawed at one another.

The woman's voice drifted into the pod. "Relax. Every muscle in you is tense."

I released each muscle one by one; my mind followed. The machine mapped my brain from my remnant card and sent a cascade of electrical potentials through the neuronal network that regulated my anxiety. In doing so, it disrupted blockades Resurrection had put in place across select memory pools so that I could fully enjoy Theresa. So that we could start anew.

The anxiety flowed out . . .

. . . and the memories flowed in.

Three Years Before Resurrection

When the cancer returned, it didn't come for me.

The first time I missed one of Theresa's appointments, I had a job interview with PlaySmart, a three-person start-up working out of the corner of a coffee shop. While I sat opposite a thirtysomething millionaire in jeans and a hoodie, trying to pretend I wasn't having a panic attack, unable to trust my hands to control the cup of organic brew she'd offered, worrying if she noticed the sweat on my forehead, or worse, cancer's inscrutable shadow, Theresa was receiving the news that her CA-125 levels had come back elevated. They'd have to do more tests. I returned her missed call after the interview.

"Bad news," she said. I could hear the smile in her voice, and in some way that made it all worse.

"Are you at the doctor's?" I said.

"At the school." Her words crumbled at the edges. Rustling and static. When she spoke again, her voice was even. "How was the interview?"

"Terrible," I said. "I'll be there in ten."

There were no tears that night. Somewhere deep we had known the cancer would come back for one if not both of us. That our time together was borrowed.

"I don't want to do chemo again," Theresa said. She'd gained her weight back. "If it's bad . . ."

I touched her hand to let her know she didn't have to say any more.

"I don't want Resurrection, either."

"Let's get the results first."

She pulled her hand away. "When Ma's cancer came back, it was her brain. Near the end she'd look at me like she didn't know who I was. Like she didn't know who she was."

"Theresa—"

"We need to be clear about these things now. I don't want Resurrection."

"You want to leave me, then?"

"No. Just the opposite. I want to be here with you, fully, until the end. We all have to go down this road. The Lord gives us only one shot at death; I want to do it right. Promise me, no Resurrection."

"You don't have brain cancer. These tests, they're just to give the doctors something to do. But I promise. No Resurrection."

I was wrong. The doctor called us two days later. Metastases to her lungs and brain. She cried at the news. I couldn't cry. I was numb. Because I had made her a promise I knew I couldn't keep.

Instead of chemo, we traveled. Spain. Norway. Japan. New Zealand. We left the medications—all of them—at home. The voices weren't much of a bother when they first came trickling back. They brought Theresa a serenity I couldn't. Sometimes she said it was God, reminding her He'd be at her side until the end. She stopped telling me about what she heard, and eventually I stopped asking. Toward the end of our world tour, however, her questions gave me a glimpse into her internal suffering. Do you think I'm going to hell? There's no chance you caught your cancer from me, is there? Do you hate me because I'm choosing to die? When we came back stateside, sleep had completely abandoned her. She leaned to the left when she walked and often forgot to dress that side of her body. I couldn't tell where the schizophrenia ended and the brain cancer began. When I found her sleeping in the empty tub because she thought her room was haunted, I convinced her to come with me to an ELT clinic. They created a remnant card.

The neurotech sessions quelled the voices. For a while, things were stable. We didn't travel anymore. I inherited Theresa's insomnia and spent countless nights staring at her remnant card.

A month before Theresa died, I sat in Ian's Resurrection office. I'd come alone. The office halls had wilted from a once excited vigor to abandoned silence, as if the company were Lazarus awaiting its own Messiah. Donors had jumped ship after multiple failed resurrections. Jerry thought their friend a fool for not selling back when things were hot. But Ian had always seen his babies through, to success or ruin.

"It was a good run," Ian said. He poured himself a scotch, offered me a glass, and chuckled when he saw me looking at the clock. It was just before noon. "Don't judge me, D. How's Theresa?"

"Still dying." I cut right to it. "Remember you said schizophrenia could cause a barrier to the connection needed for a successful neurotransfer?"

"Your professional voice." He put his drink down. "I hate your professional voice. And here I thought you'd come by just to say hello."

"Do you remember?"

"Vaguely."

"What if it's the opposite?" Ian had kept me abreast of Resurrection's failures. They'd attempted almost two dozen neurotransfers. A few had gone terribly wrong; none had worked. "What if something like schizophrenia could create a stronger link?"

"You want my advice? Enjoy your wife, bro. When you think back on her, you don't want it to be with regret."

"That's exactly what I'm trying to avoid. Humor me."

Ian picked his drink back up. Sipped. Looked at me for a long time, then sighed. "Okay. I'll humor you. For each patient and donor we look at millions of structural, environmental, and genetic markers. You can't get more compatible."

"And yet it's still not compatible enough."

"Faulty logic there, D. Correlation isn't causation. Likely compatibility isn't the problem at all. Something else is. This isn't rocket science. It's harder than that."

"What if your markers are too specific? Too rigid. You can have twin brains but vastly different outcomes."

"Nature versus nurture. Biology one-oh-one."

"But with something like schizophrenia, nature or nurture, it doesn't matter. You know the end result is a fundamentally similar wiring. That Interpreter stuff you were spitting earlier, work that through the illness."

"Schizophrenia is a spectrum. It really should be several different diseases. Two patients with schizophrenia could have 'wiring' as unique as fingerprints."

"From what we know." I sat forward. Ian's belief that the human mind was science's final frontier had pushed him into the field. I needed to tap into that wonder. "But what if there are core commonalities in areas we haven't even discovered? Commonalities a strong algorithm could pick up on, easily. Tell me, when you're searching for a donor, how many matches do you get? Out of a complete pool of inmates?"

"One, if I'm lucky."

"If something like this works . . ." I let my old friend finish the thought. He didn't disappoint.

"Multiple matches. And multiple iterations, if need be. Shit. You son of a bitch." Ian paced the barren office. When he turned back to me, the smile that had crept into his voice was gone. "She needs to be willing."

I pulled out her remnant card. "She's coming around. Full backup, plus regular neurotech sessions."

"This is different."

"She thinks it's blasphemy, that she'll go to hell."

"There's a lot of people who believe in hell, D."

"Come on! She's a paranoid schizophrenic; she's not thinking right!"

"Jerry would trip if he heard you say that. Regardless, rejection is more likely if she's not willing."

"Can't we just edit it? After the fact?"

Ian's eyes narrowed. His head tilted. His lips parted. The way he looked at me then made me question a lot. My fingernail moved to scratch my palm. I swallowed the angst down and held his gaze. He had to know I was serious.

"I'll have my engineer run sims on your theory. Attica State is trying to back out of our contract after all the bad media. A prison scared of a Black man, ain't that something? I've been in talks with Bedford Hills for women. This could be a new angle. I'll work on that. You worry about Theresa. Get her in here, get her to consent, in person. If all that pans out—and that if's bigger than the suite in hell we just reserved—I'll consider it."

"One more thing."

"I'm afraid to ask."

"Can we keep her eyes?"

"We have a full cosmetic team, but that's way down the line."

"No. Not re-create her eyes. Keep Theresa's eyes. It's . . . it's important."

"Yeah, D. Okay, yeah. Sure."

The next time I took Theresa to her ELT appointment, she was too far gone to notice that the building was different.

"We're doing a new kind of treatment today," I said outside Resurrection's double doors. Fluorescent lights pulsed through the upgraded logo, bringing the brain alive. Theresa looked at it, confused, and then to me with a dull gaze. Her mouth hung at the corner. Somewhere in her failing cognition, realization took hold.

"Oh, no. No no no no no." Spittle dripped from her mouth.

"Babe," I said, taking her brittle hands in my rejuvenated ones, "you promised."

"I did?"

"After church. Bishop Reed had just preached on how God helps those who help themselves. You said that maybe this was God's way of telling you to help yourself. You said you didn't want to leave me." I squeezed her hands. "Remember?"

" 'For as in Adam, all die.' " She mumbled more to herself and looked from the logo, to me, to our clasped hands. I held my breath. "I said that?"

"You did. So that we could be together."

"Together," she repeated. Her eyes lifted with some life and what I thought was hope. "I trust you. For another chance, I trust you."

When Ian opened the door, he didn't look at me. I quickly wiped my eyes.

"Theresa—" Ian said.

"You're going to make me live forever?"

He smiled, relieved, and in that moment I saw that Ian and I were more alike than he'd care to admit.

"I'll sure try. Come inside. We'll get you scanned and go over some logistics."

Convincing Theresa that the cancer had erased her memory of agreeing to Resurrection's insurance was the hardest thing I'd ever done. But I did it, and when she entered the scanning machine she did it willingly. At least, that's what I told myself.

"She looks like me," Theresa said months later while holding up the photograph. Since Resurrection had secured a donor, discovering her features had become part of Theresa's bedridden routine. I was starting to see the resemblance, too. The mahogany skin—without makeup and surprisingly smooth—full lips, sharp cheekbones, strong jaw, and short-curled hair. The death-row donor could have been a first or second cousin.

"She is you," I said.

Before she died in home hospice, Theresa used her last breath to tell me something. I heard but didn't listen. My mind was already on the future—our future. Ian's crew came to retrieve the body and register it as part of the company's research protocol. And then, we went to work.

Theresa had lost her hope. With Resurrection, I rediscovered mine.

...

We never figured out how to make ELT compatible with past memory wipes. Apparently, no one else had, either: I remembered everything.

I let the warmth of the Brooklyn sun solidify the memories. Starting Continuum fresh out of college. The cancer, selling the company, Ian starting Resurrection with his cut. Protecting Theresa from her stubbornness, her paranoia. Her initial resurrection. The initial joy. The return of the whispering voices that turned her against me. Working with Resurrection for a host, and a memory, more conducive to happiness. For us both.

I called Ian.

"Bro! What's good?"

"You're still with Resurrection. You never left. Tell me I'm wrong." I held my breath. The memories were there, but fickle, like a silhouette in the heat of summer. If I was wrong about this, I wouldn't know what was right.

"How?" Ian said. His voice had changed. I gripped the phone.

"Neurophoria. Shitty place with a shitty name, but the neurotech works."

"Shit, Darius. I told you not to."

"Jerry suggested it."

"Of course he did. That fucker. How much do you remember?"

"Everything, I think." I shut my eyes against the pressure building behind my right temple. "How many times did we resurrect her?"

"Only two. And this second time was a favor. 'Third time's a charm' ain't going to fly with the board. I edited out my role in the company in your memory wipe just so you couldn't convince me again. Fucking Jerry. What. Happened?"

I took a second. I had to be careful. "Nothing. Nothing yet. She's freaking out a little. She's trying to find her identity."

"Let's bring her in."

"You sound like Jerry."

"I don't like this, D. The other trials are going well. Theresa's not an asset anymore. She's a liability."

"She's my wife. And you wouldn't have other trials if it weren't for her."

"Which is why I want you to bring her in. Before this ends badly."

I stood there, feeling the rumble of passing trains underfoot, thinking about what to do. The answer came to me sudden and clear, as if carried by the summer wind. Theresa wouldn't like it, but it was for the best.

"You're right. We need to fix this."

"So, you'll bring her in?"

"No. Portable ELTs: Are they out yet?"

"We've been equipped with those for months now. Why?"

"Could we do a reset in our apartment?"

"I told you there's no third time. And even if I had a body to give, you expect me to drag it through your front door?"

"Not a new body, Ian. A new memory."

...

Theresa came into the living room trailing energy. She wore her best red suit dress. It had been a week since she'd pulled a knife on me. Though it had stayed in its holder, the blade still hung between us. I slept on the couch in the living room and had fully replaced Xanax with neurotech clinic visits. My mind was sharp, clear. I closed the photo album I'd just finished and sat up.

"I know how to fix things," she said.

"I've been thinking, too."

"Just listen. Please." When I nodded, she began to pace. "I've been feeling lost. Very lost. What's my purpose? Why did God push me to this journey? Why did He bring me back like this? In this body? I think I've found out why. I talked to some people, and if I take half a year of classes, I can be a prison social worker. I can really make a difference."

She'd spit out the words faster than I could process them. She stood in the middle of the room, breath heavy, a life in her eyes I hadn't seen since before. But it wasn't right.

"Where did this come from?" I said. "You never talked about prison before. Not once."

"Every day I wake up and see another person's face in the mirror. Even though she's gone, even though I'll never know who she really was, I still feel like I owe her something. Like her history is my history."

"I'm glad you're excited about something. And we can certainly consider it."

"Consider?"

"I think something else might be better. I went by the school."

Theresa shrank a few inches and dropped onto the couch beside me. "You didn't."

"Those kids miss you. They understand why you haven't been by. I talked to the principal. She thinks we can work something out. You can pick up with the girls right where you left off. This will help."

I handed her the thick album I had compiled.

"What's this?"

"It's an album," I said. "I went through all the meaningful pictures I could find and photoshopped you in. The real you." I turned a page, excited. "See, this is you with your students. They saw it and love it."

"Darius . . . this isn't the real me."

"It can be."

She continued to flip through the album. I held my breath as she came to the end. She pulled out a slip of paper that advertised the wonders of portable ELT.

"Brilliant, right?" My gaze flicked to the clock staining the wall. Ian would be here soon. "They agreed to change both our memories so that we remember you like this. It's easier. And we can do it right here."

"You fuck. You fucking fuck. You want me to forget who I was? Where I came from? I didn't sign up for this."

"When you look in the mirror, you see someone who's not you. Not Black. Not Theresa." I lifted her remnant card. "This will make it so you just see you. Wouldn't it be better to forget this used to be someone else?"

"But I was someone else. At least this body was. She's a part of me. Sometimes I feel her . . ."

"When you hear the voices?"

Her eyes flickered. "You wouldn't understand."

"Help me to."

Theresa touched my face. Her hands chilled my skin. "I love you, Darius. I always have. I want this to work. I pray to God every day that you realize how much I want to just be here with you and love you."

"Then do this for us."

I held out the remnant card for her to hold and feel. She took it and hope crept into me. This would solve everything. Our perfect lives were just a—

She started, as if bitten.

"What is it?"

"Just my phone." She reached into her pocket and turned toward the corner.

"Who is it?" I said, annoyed.

Instead of answering, she sat back on the bed. Her grip tensed around the phone and remnant card as one. Suddenly I regretted giving it to her.

"Theresa—"

"One second."

Deep breath. In. Out. Patience. They were almost there. Onetwothree, onetwothree, one two three, one . . . two . . . three . . .

"When you said 'it's easier,' what did you mean?"

"Huh?" I said.

Theresa continued to grip the phone. "You said the memory reset would be 'easier.' Easier than what?"

"Nothing. I didn't mean anything."

"Easier than resetting me. Is that what you meant? If I don't go along with this?"

"Babe, you're sounding a little . . . well, paranoid."

"Don't you dare. Don't you dare! I'm not some broken computer program. How many times have you reset me already?"

The room burned hot. Something had gone terribly wrong, terribly quick. The image of Theresa poised on the bed, ready to strike, flashed bright as the blade she'd wielded. I had to be careful; those hands had killed. "Who texted you?"

"How many, Darius?"

"Only once. It wasn't a good fit. We both knew that."

"I agreed to it?"

"Yes," I said. "It was your idea."

"Yeah?"

"It was."

"Like going along with Resurrection was my idea? Or did you change that, too?"

"Where—where is all this coming from? Can I just see—"

I lunged for the phone. A mistake. Theresa whirled away, her arms tucked close to her body. In two quick strides she was at the door.

"Sorry. I'm sorry. I just want to talk. Me and you. Let's slow down. Wait, where are you going?"

"To get rid of this thing. Once and for all."

I followed my wife out into the hall. Her back was to me. She spoke rapidly with her hand to her ear as she went for the front door.

"Theresa!"

She broke into a run. I moved to intercept her. She cut to the right and turned as if to come toward me, a flash of light in her hand. The knife. Adrenaline sprang me forward; I pushed. The edge of the carpet curled up and entangled her legs. I watched her fall in slow motion. I saw her forehead connect with the corner of the mantel before it happened.

Theresa rolled to the floor, screaming and bleeding. I rushed to help; she kicked me away.

"Stop it!" I yelled. "Stop it! You're being unreasonable!"

I pinned her hands to the floor but she'd grown strong in her panic. I had to secure the knife. Her right hand yanked free and drove into my chest. I lost my grip on the other. I desperately tried to gain hold of them again, wincing in anticipation of the unseen blade slicing into my body. If she would just calm down. If she would just be like Theresa. If she would just shut the fuck up for a second and listen to me and not those goddamn voices in her head.

Her screams stopped. Sharp pain on the back of my hands; her fingernails digging into the flesh. My own fingers were tight around her neck. I didn't know how they got there. I'd let go as soon as she calmed down.

Onetwothree, onetwothree, one two three, one . . . two . . . three . . .

I released my grip and reeled back, as if the skin of her neck burned. Her eyes leaked pink, unformed tears; their lids hung halfway open. Splotches of red pressed into her neck. Her lips were fuller than before, distorted and lopsided. Blood decorated the carpet around her head.

"Theresa?" I shook her shoulders. Gentle at first, then with rising panic. "Theresa, hey, baby, wake up."

"What the hell, D?"

I turned to see Ian reeling toward us. He pushed me off Theresa and knelt beside her. His eyes grew as they took in everything. His mouth began to quiver.

"What did you do?"

"She had a knife. She would have killed me."

"This knife?" Ian handed me the cell phone.

"I swear she had one. She must have dropped it. You should have seen her, Ian. Is she . . ."

"She's breathing." Ian's fingers against her neck beneath the jaw. He tilted her head to the side. An unseen gash gushed dark blood from her head. "D . . ."

"She fell. I swear she did. I didn't do that."

"And this? Did her neck fall into your fingers?"

"I just wanted her to listen. I wasn't trying to hurt her. She was hysterical!"

"I wonder why?" The way he said it told me he wasn't wondering in the same way I was.

I started: Theresa's phone. I looked down at the vibrating metal, at first bemused by the green envelope blinking on the screen. A text message, from a private number. I thought, typed in a password, and grunted. After three failed attempts, the phone told me that security had cleared the device of all information.

I could see her breathing now. Slow and shallow, but there. The knowledge that she was alive dissipated some of the panic. This woman wasn't Theresa. Only the shell of a prisoner that Theresa had tried to inhabit. Tried, and failed.

"The voices came back," I said, as if that explained everything. "Strong, like last time."

"The voices didn't strangle her. You did."

"The schizophrenia link might have not been the best idea. She wanted to be a prison social worker. That's not Theresa."

"Prison social worker sounds pretty fucking good to me, voices or not. Would have made for a hell of a PR."

"We're a good team. We just have to find the right match."

Ian sat down beside me. He wiped his mouth. A wave of alcohol hit my nose, then was gone. "Things are different, D. Resurrection just signed contracts with three state prisons. We can't afford a mess right now. And this . . . this is a fucking mess. If it came out we covered something like this up . . ." Ian stood. "I have to call the police."

"Over property?"

Ian recoiled, as if I had just spat in his face. He went into the kitchen and leaned over the sink. Then he began to laugh. When he came back, he was holding a chef's blade. The chef's blade. He handed it to me, handle first.

"This what she came at you with? It was in the holder. Property or not, you're a Black man and this is a White woman." Ian turned to look at Theresa as if to confirm that this was indeed true. "Fuck. I—I have to think about the company, D."

"You're just going to throw me under the bus, then?"

"I gave you your second chance. You told me Theresa was the problem, and I listened. That's on me. But this fuckery? That's on you."

"Resurrect us both, then," I said. I held out my remnant card along with Theresa's. "New contract, new opportunities, right?"

"Even if I could, how would I justify—"

"We have to try! Take them, please. If the police get mine, they'll lock it away. Please."

Ian hesitated, then took them. Regretful eyes flicked to the knife. "I can't transplant someone who's still alive."

"Let me worry about that," I said. "You'll make it work. You can clean up anything."

His mouth went hard. The decision about whether or not to wrestle the knife away jumped between his eyes. Part of me wanted him to take it. The part of me that hated what I'd done to Theresa.

But that part was weak. That part could never do what was needed to make things right again. Could never have gotten us this far.

"This can't be her last memory of me," I said. "Please, Ian."

Ian cursed, low and fierce, then walked down the hall punching at his cell phone.

"Hi, yes. I need someone to check on my friend right away." Ian gave my address. "He called me, upset, said he was going to kill himself. I asked to talk to his wife and he started crying, wouldn't tell me what happened. They've had problems. Bad problems, but I thought things were getting better. I'm worried he . . . please, can you just check on them? I'm heading over there now. Yes, please, oh thank God. I'll be out front. Tall, Black, two hundred fifty pounds. Unarmed."

Alone again, I went to open the curtains. The full moon's milky blessing bathed the room. Now I could do what needed to be done. As I assumed my final position, the significance of the cold blade against my skin wasn't lost on me. Though she had never known it, Theresa had saved me from it before. Here she was, saving me again, but by leading me toward instead of away. The blade had always been consistent in its offering of control. Before, that meant avoiding a hopeless future. Now, it would usher me—us—into a bright new one.

I gave you your second chance. Would Ian resurrect us both? He had to. It was the only option. The current narrative wasn't right. "Man forces wife to cheat death, then kills her in a panic"? What if her body survived and remembered him that way? Made him part of her "overcoming adversity" Resurrection PR story? That wasn't me. I—we—could do better.

I sat there, under the moonlight. Sirens lifted from somewhere in the distance. I looked down at the prisoner's body, which was starting to stir. What had Theresa told me about death? You jump and feel yourself going down, and down, and then you come back up.

Could I take that leap?

Afiya's Song

Yes, I sure do remember the day Afiya come down to Ferrell Plantation. It was about ten years before the Union surrendered, in 1823 I recall, when us slaves still thought we was going to be slaves forever.

She come down from the Hairston Plantation in North Carolina. The scar on her cheek marked her a runaway. Her last master cut her tongue clean off. We only knew her by the sign around her neck, and even then only one of us niggers could read it. They married her to a woodchuck and put her in the fields. She won't that good at it.

We ain't know it then, but she was sent there to teach us her song. Yeah, I remember that day. You never forget when God put freedom in your life.

—Henry Ferrell, former slave, 1843

Hairston Plantation, Davie County, North Carolina, 1821

The fields didn't sing for Ole Mister Charles Hairston, who died choking on his own vomit during one of his whiskey fits in 1821. Not a single negro eye wept. He'd run his plantation of over one hundred slaves with a cold hand. His son, Louis Hairston, who had been living with his uncle Willy up the road, came home with his new bride, Beatrice, to take over the land.

Afiya, a young field slave who had flung rocks at trees and collected yellow leaves with Young Mister Louis as a child, took nine lashes on their second day running the plantation for sassing the new missus. As the whip cracked, she sang the song of Adesokash of the Sanain Empire to carry herself across the ocean to her ancestors' healing grounds of drums and wine and tea oil. Miss Beatrice, who most likely thought she had passed out, slapped her across the face and brought her back in time for the last crack of Harry the Overseer's whip. A pit of fire ripped open from Afiya's shoulder to buttocks. She didn't cry; all good negro girls knew not to.

Even though her ancestor's song healed her, Afiya usually took the given half-day's rest after a whipping to lay up in her cabin. This time, she had fire in her blood. She returned to the field two hours later.

"They touch you?" James said. Though they had been married for almost a year now, she hadn't told him about her healing song. He was a comely negro with acorn-colored eyes, full lips that sang against hers, and a belly just big enough to give Afiya something to hold on to. "I swear, if they—"

"You swears a lot," Afiya said. "Ain't no harm done." She exposed her back to him. "See for yourself."

James pulled her blouse down over her shoulders. "What they keep you there for, then?"

"To whip me. But I said, 'Please, Missus, don't whip me. I won't do it again. I'll be a good little negro.' They like stuff like that."

They laughed. When James turned toward the next cotton plant, Afiya looked back toward the whipping tree. She could just see its branches. She'd tell James about her gift one day. When she was ready.

...

The dry sky made for cotton stalks sharp as knives that left careless fingers bloody. Besides that, picking cotton was mindless work. Once a negro got into the rhythm of breaking the stalk, turning it over, plucking the bow of leaves off the back, and stuffing it in the basket, staying on her feet was what took attention. In the worst parts of summer, the sun could bake a negro inside out and put her on her knees, close to death, before she even knew she felt any kind of way.

Miss Beatrice's silhouette stood watch from her stoop, her Victorian hoop dress fanning out to the floor like roots. The evening sun sat right atop the Hairston mansion; the porch was covered in shadow, obscuring her slightly from view. Still Afiya could feel the missus's ice-blue eyes on her. They'd held nothing but hate for the negro, Afiya especially.

Harry the Overseer—a young white boy with more dirt in his pockets than money—pulled back on his horse's reins as he passed and circled around. His whip hung from the saddle, curled onto itself, the free tip flapping in the wind.

"I hate that thing," James said. "And the soul who made it."

"It ain't the whip that keeps us slaves," Afiya said.

"To them, the whip is everything."

"*We* is everything."

They went back to picking, because that's what they knew to do. The humid air was thick and hard to move through, but it was also good for conducting music. The crisp break of desiccated branches. The *slap, slap, slap* of worn brown palms chasing elusive gnats. The drone of crickets, shifting with the wind. The negroes fell into its rhythm. It wasn't the song of Afiya's ancestors, or even the song of freedom, but it took her places just the same.

...

The woodchucks built a smoking pit to roast the scraps Young Mister Louis left to them after taking two slaves hunting in the woods, something his father would have never done. They came back with two hogs and a deer. Mister gave them a quarter of one of the hogs to have all to themselves.

After the daily cotton weighing, the negroes gathered outside their cabins on the edge of the fields. They passed around a half-full bottle of whiskey made of soured corn. Just a swig made a negro forget he was a slave, if only for the moment he felt the burn in his throat.

"You gone keep us waiting?" James said to George.

The old negro leaned his head to the side. He was half deaf in one ear and all the way blind. He cradled a banjo made out of a hollowed gourd.

"I wait for the music," George said. But his fingers, their knuckles the size of grapes, started to strum at the strings. His grip found stead when he played, as if the instrument drank rheumatism in its notes. He plucked out a simple tune, low and sweet. The others jumped right into it. They made instruments out of whatever they could. Sticks resonated against cracked pottery jugs and glass bottles. Fork prongs scritch-scratched along the underbellies of rusted skillets. James even had a flute made out of reed cane. Its song, scraggly against the rest, simply belonged.

Music was everybody's thing, even if it wasn't. Cardplayers bobbed their heads as they brooded over their hands. The women hummed as they cut away the bottoms of pig feet, peeled potatoes, and shucked corn for the pit. When Sam, one of the field negroes, asked Afiya to sing for them, she only smiled and said her throat was dry. She instead went inside where two field negro girls were cleaning pig intestines in a bucket of foul-smelling water. Nothing went to waste.

"We almost done," Virginia said. Her gorgeous, glassy eyes floated in a sweet sea of mahogany. Her cheeks rose up tall when she smiled. She had hips Afiya secretly envied, with a backside that rested high and strong.

"You all right?" James said, trailing after his wife.

"Yes," Afiya said. "I just needed a change of air, is all."

The music started up again. Sam sang; his voice was like the rattle of a wind catcher.

"Your voice *got* to set us more free than that," James said.

"I wouldn't know what to do with freedom," Afiya said.

"You ain't got to do anything with freedom. You just be it. Be free."

James and Afiya shared a cot in the corner of the cabin under the one window, which gave them a shadow's worth more of privacy than the dozen other negroes they lived with.

"You going to become a Freeman, old Mister James?" Afiya teased.

"Naw, I'll keep the Hairston. Let them know I was born a slave but I'm not going to die one. Not by God, I won't."

This was a common topic with James, especially when he got drinking. Afiya knew well enough not to push it further, but Missus's slap still stung her cheek, even though her back felt nothing, not even an itch. Whispers were all it took to get a negro's ear cut off. Or worse.

"Imagine," he said, touching her belly. "Me, you, the children, on a big span of land down in Florida."

"We ain't got children."

"Not yet we don't." His hands found her neck. Her lips melded to his. She pulled away. "I got something to tell you."

"Tell me." He kissed her shoulder.

She wanted to share her music, introduce him to her Sanain ancestors. But she was afraid. Young Mister Louis was the last to hear her voice, back before their world had been torn into black and white, slave and slavemaster. Since then, she'd kept that part to herself.

"I love you," she said. And he said it back.

The music blessed them with cover. It guided them, as they were still unused to each other's bodies. Though James was always gentle, Afiya had to look past the pain left to her by a hasty childbirth to find pleasure. She didn't sing it away; she wouldn't dare. She wanted to be here fully for this, with him. His arms brought the only freedom she ever knew. No size chains could remove the memory they created, the feel of him inside of her, the smell of cotton and dirt and sweat that was somehow made sweet, the loving hurt so different from what she found on the tip of a whip.

They fell into each other, and in those moments, they were free.

...

I was there the day Afiya was born. I sat with her ma—her name Ella— while she labored, all through the night, and wrapped the babe in a towel. I swear she came out singing. She made baby sounds, she did, but they was different. She was different.

Ella kept the old gods, the ones that came with us over the water but most of us forgotten, while all the other slaves took up Jesus and the like. Even me. Pastor told us if we followed Jesus and our Master, we'd get to Heaven one day, and for us Heaven was freedom. Ella never believe that. When a negro got sick or in trouble, we all prayed over them, but Ella would sing.

Some say she sang to her ancestors and they spirits brought the healing.
Some say she called on the African gods by they names. Still others say her
voice so sweet the flesh had no choice but to get right. I like that last one myself.

She sang to Afiya all the nights. I knew 'cus it used to keep me up, and
being in the field, we needed all the sleep we got. That girl know how to
sing before she could walk.

Ella won't too good in the field and she won't fair enough for the Big
House, so Mister Jacobs was expecting her to give him nice, strong boys. He
thought taking her only chap away would help her get with child again, so
he sold Afiya to the Hairstons when she was six for ten dollars and a bushel
of corn. Ten dollars! The cost of freedom. Just ain't nobody know it yet.

—*Harriet Jacobs, former slave, 1836*

...

It had been years since Afiya had seen Young Mister Louis, and back
then he was only a boy, like she had been only a girl. She knew he
didn't have his father's stone heart or his taste for blood, but all men
live in their father's shadow.

The sun had just fallen behind the Hairston attic, which menaced
the field like an overseer, when Mister Louis came for her. She knew
his smell better than she'd like. She looked around. Her husband was
many lines down. Good.

"Miss Beatrice wants you," Louis said. "You got any idea why?"

"No, sir," she said. She looked for a sign of the boy with whom she'd
shared part of her childhood. If he was there, Mister Louis hid it well.
Not long ago those eyes gave her refuge. She'd felt special, in a foolish
kind of way, and when her belly was ripe with his child she let herself
believe things might change. He had been foolish, too. He talked about
running away together to some place they could *be*. When Old Mister
Charles saw Afiya's daughter came out mulatto, he gave the newborn to
Deborah, a young house slave rumored infertile, and drove them both
off to Alabama. He came back with three new slaves in their place; Afiya
never saw her daughter again. Mister Charles made Young Louis give
Afiya thirty strikes and then sent him off to Uncle Willy's plantation in

Virginia. The old man had sentenced Afiya to death by whip, she was sure, but she had her song. Even with that, she'd been close to death for weeks. James, a field negro, tended to her at night, when Old Lady Lilly was too tired to keep vigil.

The song had saved her body. James had saved her spirit.

She walked a few steps behind Mister Louis, head low like her mother had taught her. The last of the slaves dragged bulging bushels toward the counting shed. Afiya caught eyes with one of them. The slave's concern for her was infectious. Afiya returned her gaze to the dirt path and tried to quiet her mind.

"Did you weep when Pa died?" Louis said.

"Yes, sir," she lied.

"I didn't. What does that mean?"

"I don't know, sir."

Miss Beatrice waited on the porch under the shadow of her sun hat. Her face was mean and narrow. Her gaze chilled the summer air. With uneven teeth and a heavy brow, she wasn't the prettiest white woman Afiya had seen. By far, though, she was the most assured. A full head shorter than Mister, what she lacked in stature she made up for in a rigid back, long neck, and a determined jaw. Miss Beatrice stood from her rocking chair as they climbed the stairs. She knew; Afiya should have run off with James when Mister Charles first died, when no one would have cared about a couple of lost field slaves.

"Turn around," Miss Beatrice said.

Afiya did. Missus ripped the back of her shirt so hard, the lines of linen cut beneath Afiya's breast and across her ribs. Afiya scanned the cotton fields. Old and weary souls alike retired, spent, to candlelit shacks. She prayed no one saw. If James caught wind . . .

"You see?" Beatrice said. "Your niggers play you for a fool."

"I see a back that should be out in the fields," Mister Louis said.

"Harry gave her nine licks, and where is it? How she gone learn if she don't hurt?"

"Scars ain't the only things that hurt," Afiya said. She bit her lip. James would have scorned her for that, and he'd be right.

"There she is, sassing me again!"

Afiya backed down the first two steps and turned to lean against the banister. She needed an eye on Miss Beatrice. Her body knew to fear the woman more than the Mister.

"Not another word out of you," Louis said to Afiya. He turned to his wife. "If she got whipped, she got whipped. Ain't no more here to know."

"I don't know what kinds of tricks niggers got, but I know they tricks all the same."

"She was whipped once for foolishness. I won't do it again."

"She ain't learned."

"And that foolishness was yours!" Louis said. His wife stepped back, as if slapped. "My pa paid good money for *work*. You wasting work on feelings."

"Mister Charles would spit in his grave if he knew his niggers were running his plantation."

Louis looked ready to hit Beatrice, and for a moment Afiya thought he would. Miss Beatrice saw it, too. Her eyes grew as her posture shrank to fit the submissive role of a southern belle she surely despised. Any threat of violence fell away; Louis's face soured. He turned to Afiya.

"Go on out to the tree. Go on, now!"

Afiya pulled her blouse up over her shoulders and slipped out from under Louis and Beatrice. She hurried down the stairs, her feet against the floorboards a germinating beat for the low hum in her throat. Her skin prickled with the protecting fingers of ancestral spirits. Deep drums and percussions only she heard cooled her skin against the summer sun. She was of two minds when her arms fell into the man-made grooves of the whipping tree. In a few seconds Louis would unravel his whip and crack the air with its tip. Afiya was already deep in her song, her temporary place of freedom.

Somewhere far away, her flesh parted. The drums boomed louder. Afiya's pitch rose. Her song kept in her blood, kept out her pain, protected her.

"What in the hell are you doing, boy?" Louis's voice pierced her shell like no braid of leather could. She whirled around, her world half music, half gnats and crickets and heat and the stink of fear.

Louis stood over a fallen James, pointing a trembling pistol at him. For an impossible moment the two had traded places; Afiya's husband had the look of a crazed master, Louis one of a scared runaway. She rushed over, wincing at the fire spreading across her back as the power of her song faded.

"She ain't done a thing," James said.

"You done lost it, boy?" Louis said.

Miss Beatrice came running down the stairs, her dress pulled high about her ankles. "Once a nigger attack you, he like a rabid dog!"

"My pa say the same," Louis said without looking at her. His gun fixed, he nodded to Afiya. "One of you got to explain yourself. This your husband?"

"Yes, sir," she said. She steadied her voice. "He's just simple, real simple, that's all it is, Mister Louis."

"I never took you to marry simple," Louis said.

"Mister Charles—your pa—made it so. He's simple, but he's strong, and our children gone work these fields like none other."

This was the wrong thing to say. A flicker of the Louis she'd known came through after all, just at the wrong time. A small crowd of negroes and overseers watched from the edge of the field. Miss Beatrice stood waiting, her electricity hot on the air.

"Now you go on, nigger." Louis's voice broke as he said it. "You can clean her up after."

Afiya pleaded with James's eyes. He looked right back at her. He hated Louis, just for what he hadn't done to save Afiya from Mister Charles. He couldn't get over his hate. He was stubborn like that.

James turned and spit in Mister Louis's face.

Louis pulled a handkerchief from his pocket and wiped away the insult. His expression twisted into the old, angry ghost of his father. Anyone with a bit of sight—be they negro, master, or in-between—could see how badly the Mister's hands shook as he folded the cloth.

Louis sighed, long and deep. All eyes on him, waiting. The crickets held their song, waiting. The wind stilled, waiting. The whole plantation, it seemed, watched, waiting.

"Get him up," Louis told Harry the Overseer, who was eager to oblige. He dragged a fighting James over to the whipping tree and pulled on a thick, low-hanging branch.

"Put your hands up. Here, tie your fingers together." Mister Louis fastened James's wrists to the branch. He pulled up James's shirt and draped the bottom flap over his head. When James shook it off, Mister Louis whispered in his ear, and this time James didn't protest.

"Please, Mister, don't," Afiya said. "He's my husband. My *husband*. I ain't got nothing else."

"That nigger spit in my face," Louis said. "I ain't got a choice."

Afiya started to sing. Beatrice slapped her. Blood filled her mouth.

"You shush now, or I'll kill him," Mister Louis said.

That first crack of the whip broke Afiya more than any across her own back. She drew into herself with a panicked mind that sent her skimming lost and blind across the ocean, searching for the sound of her ancestors. The thundering beat of her own heart threatened her course. The part of her still on the plantation begged Louis. He didn't listen. Couldn't listen. She knew he couldn't, but she begged anyway. By the end of it, Louis himself screamed with each blow. Sweat soaked the slavemaster's shirt and vest. His face burned red under the blood-orange sun.

Thirty-nine lashes. Red dripped down James's buttocks, his legs, from his heels to mark the leaves and dirt and bits of torn cloth. He swung limp.

Mister left without a word.

Sam helped haul James back to the cabin. His teeth clattered together like the sound of twigs breaking, he shivered so bad. Virginia met them at the door.

"Oh, my Lord," she said. "What happened?"

"What you think happened, child?" Old Lady Lilly said as she limped out into the night. "Fetch me some salt and a wet rag. Make sure it's cold. Go on, now."

They took James inside. Old Lady Lilly, an eighty-year-old negro who never bore any children but had been the best cook until she was too old to hold the skillet, packed James's back with salt and kept a cold, wet rag on his head to run away the fever. She rocked to one side as she hurried across the room. Her hip had gone bad years ago. Sam and Virginia stood by, helpless.

"Protect him, Lord Jesus," the old woman prayed over James. "Heal him, Lord Jesus."

Afiya sat with her husband's head in her lap. She tasted the salt of her tears and smelled the metal in his leaked blood, mixed with the lingering stench of pig intestines from the night before.

"When I was real little," Afiya said as she rocked him, "Ma said we from a line of special folk from a kingdom across the ocean, called Sanai. When something terrible happened, like war or famine, they sang themselves whole again, rebuilt the tribe, kept our history. But they was more than one, you see, and after my ma's master sold me away, it was just me. I ain't know what to do with a gift like that. I used it to heal Louis one time, when he hurt himself climbing a tree and I was foolish and thought he'd think me special. I healed him and he went and hurt me. I swore to keep my song to myself after that."

James's eyes were closed in a shiver; his lips had gone pale. Afiya kissed his forehead and started her song. She could see her land in the tune, but James was too heavy to carry through. "Sing with me," she said. "Please, James. I can't do this on my own."

She pulled him close so some of the protecting warmth could spill over onto him, which wasn't enough. It had to be enough.

The land of her ancestors opened up; they stepped through. James was so much easier to carry now, though Afiya didn't know why. She didn't ask, only went forward, through a village of joyous spirits who gathered around her. The beat of drums, the hum of crickets, the click of tongues, all carried her past familiar faces she had never seen in life. Her mother was there, as she had been for some years now, painting the sky golden with her voice.

Afiya realized James was no longer in her arms; he'd walked forward along a path billowing dirt with the rhythm. He bent down and picked something out of the brown cloud and dusted it off; a flute. He tested its pitch, then began to play. Afiya wanted to call to him, to stop and stay and spend eternity singing to his tune, but the forward push of her ancestors was too strong. The flute's melody went soft and low, fading like a sunset.

"Afiya," a voice said. "Afiya, he's gone, child. He's gone home to Jesus."

She didn't open her eyes. She didn't want to see the color gone out of his face. Didn't want to lie and tell herself he looked like he was sleeping.

"Go with my ancestors," she said, quiet enough so only she could hear. "And be free. Sing for me, and for the rest of us."

Afiya laid James's head to rest on the dirt-caked floor as she rose on weak legs. His blood soaked her shirt and stuck cold against her skin, so different from the warm touch she'd now hold only in memories. She moved across the cabin.

"Where you going, girl?" Virginia said. She was young and full of thoughts. "We got to get him ready."

Old Lady Lilly slapped Virginia upside the head with a wet towel. "Shush you, child. We got enough hands."

Afiya grabbed the crusted knife used to separate pig entrails from the stomach lining and slipped out of the cabin.

The drone of crickets and the faraway song of bullfrogs walked Afiya across the short road alongside the field up to the Hairston house. She went around past the weed-infested shed where the house negroes lived, and up to the back door leading into the kitchen.

The click of the door behind her silenced the cacophonous night. She didn't dare sing or hum; just breathing felt enough to betray her. Being inside these walls made the comfort of her ancestors fall away. Afiya was alone.

The slaves in Afiya's quarters shared one rusty pot for preparing all their meals. Here, pans of various sizes, make, and utility lined the walls. She passed through the kitchen doors and into the dining room. While she had known crumbling brick and leaky rafters all her life, the Hairston mansion was polished wood, ornate decorations, and unapologetic decadence.

She floated upstairs and entered the master bedroom. The soft cotton rug under her blistered feet was a kinder fabric than she'd ever worn over her shoulders. The bed took up half a room the size of Afiya's entire quarters. Her own shared cot was a double layer of blankets over wires that pricked her in the night.

Of all the things foreign in Mister's inherited mansion, the sight of Miss Beatrice gave Afiya the most pause. She slept with her eyes covered with some sort of mask, which baffled Afiya. How could a slave ever hope to be free if she didn't even know what freedom was like? If she couldn't fathom being comfortable enough to sleep even more blind to the world than usual?

On the other side of Beatrice, Louis slept quieter than Afiya remembered. Back when they were teenagers, after the world had corrected ignorant childhood bliss, whenever he slept beside Afiya in his bed, the air would whistle through his nose, and she'd touch her own and marvel at their difference. She feared Old Mister Charles would string her up from the rafters for every negro to see if he knew, but somehow she felt safer with Louis than out in the field of cotton and bullwhips and sad song.

Part of that boy was here, but Afiya couldn't see him. She could only hear the chittering of James's dying teeth. She never felt more like a slave. Standing over him, knife in hand; even if she killed him, his whiteness would live to determine her fate.

She stood there for a long time.

...

A white sheet in the shape of her dead husband lay on the cooling board when she returned to the cabin. Afiya put away the knife, unused, wiped her face of tears, and went to him. He smelled of soap and leaves and wool.

"We going to be free," she said. "I promise."

...

Some of the niggers thought she was God walking among us. She won't much to look at, kind of scrawny-like with dull eyes and her lips tucked in 'cus she ain't have no tongue. But she had this fire no one could touch. Not Mister, not Missus, and certainly no nigger. Nobody wanted to touch it, neither.

This one time she stood up for this simple-headed field nigger—his name Gus, it was—who ain't return to the fields after noon break. Went up and sat by the river to catch crawfish and rest in the sun. One of Mister's dogs find him sleeping under his hat. Scared that poor nigger half to death!

Afiya walked up to the whipping post in that quiet way she had, took off her shirt, and put herself over him. She hummed so loud the birds sang back. Mister didn't like that, didn't like that at all. He ain't have no choice but to continue, with all us niggers watching. She didn't even flinch, just hummed this song. I couldn't tell you today where that song come from, only that it felt like her lips was on my bones. I swear by this—and some of the others would say it, too, if any of them still kicking—but her skin come together right after it ripped apart, like water.

Gus hated her after that. I reckon we had a big part in it, all the ragging we did on him about it. In truth, it made us all scared a little.

—Jimmy Ferrell, former slave, 1835

...

They buried James the next day in a coffin made from scraps of wood not yet set to fire. At sunset they laid him in an oxcart and pushed him on to his final resting place. When night came, after all the cotton was in and the overseers had wet their whips with the blood owed to the Hairston Plantation, negroes made their way over to the burial site.

Old Man George presided over the funeral. Before going blind, he'd taught Bible study Sunday mornings in a shack outside the white church up Chatham Road. He didn't know how to read any more than Afiya, but he knew his Bible.

"James was born free," George said. His fingers lightly coursed the strings of his banjo. "Just the world ain't know it. But he did. He made me this here banjo with his own hands. I reckon it'd be as good as any to send him on home."

George fell into a soft, slow song. Afiya came forward. She didn't say anything. She didn't warn anybody. All she did was tap her hand against her thigh to find courage in the beat. George tilted his head her way, smiled, and played on.

For the first time in years, she sang loud enough for others to hear.

Her voice poured from the spirits of her ancestors and out of her throat, warming around her as if they now carried James's arms in the beat of their drums. Some of the negroes stirred. At least two left. Others wept. Most looked at some faraway place.

Afiya shut her eyes to them and sang the song of her mother, the song of her mother's mother and all who came before, the song of healing, the song of Adesokash, the mother of Sanai.

...

Whispers in the dark. Low enough to leave a field negro to the little sleep she enjoyed, but Afiya hadn't slept a lick. Candlelight flickered dim on the wall, bringing the barrels and pots and small shovels to a dull life.

"I'm telling you, this here was the first," a woman's voice said. "Ole Mister Charles gave me that scar hisself. I never forget."

"You wake me for this?" another woman said. "I'm in no kind of mood for foolishness!"

"And I had another right here, right across the shoulders."

"You lie!"

"You ain't felt nothing like this?"

Silence.

"You has, hasn't you?" Laughter. "You sneaky old rattlesnake!"

"Shh, now, before someone hear us."

"How a thing like that happen? Huh?"

"Maybe it mean we free soon?"

"That's the dumbest thing I done heard all day."

"You asked."

Swimming in these new thoughts, Afiya found unexpected, sweet sleep.

...

I never believe for a second she was healing folk. You got to be a crazy nigger to think such a thing. That's what the white folk want us to think, that the only way we could have won that Rebellion War was with magic.

Well, let me tell you that might and heart won that war. We wanted our
freedom, and we took it.

But I see why people believe it. That's what slavery was. It was a bunch
of crazy. I'm glad to see it gone.

—*Cory Carter, former slave, 1840*

...

Whispers of healing rippled the plantation. Afiya kept her ear in
the tales. A burn mark that had been on Old Man George's left
arm since he was a kid, when Mister Charles's father caught him
taking some food from the pot and made him hold his arm against
the fire, had gone missing. That was George's playing hand, the
hand everyone watched and marveled at. Old Lady Lilly's limp was
still there, only lighter. Virginia had a tiny mark right under her
lip where her last missus had stuck a pin through it as punishment.
That, too, was gone.

The negro women were shucking corn for the next day's supper
while the men tied the logs together and got the bushels of cotton
ready for weighing when a whisper made Afiya's skin tighten.

"Afiya."

She turned around. It was only Sam, but he had something feral in
his eyes. He came over to her quick, looking around. He rolled up his
sleeve and turned his arm in the air. His grin was wide.

"See that?" he said.

"What I supposed to be seeing?"

"Your song was the best I ever heard." He leaned in close. His
breath stank of bad whiskey. "And I felt something down deep, like
you was singing to my bones."

"You been drinking? Don't let Harry catch you."

"I just wanted to tell you that." He slipped away, hands in his
pockets, whistling to himself like he was a free man.

She couldn't stop thinking about Sam's words. She cut herself three
times on her chucking blade, her mind was so gone. She couldn't deny
that her singing had affected the negroes at James's funeral. She had

sung for herself, and herself alone, as she'd been taught to do. Still, others heard.

Afiya found Sam sitting outside his cabin, wobbly on his stoop, whittling something out of a strip of bark.

"Can you sing?" she asked.

He looked up at her, first, bewildered. Then he smiled.

...

A cool morning breeze passed over the cotton fields the next Tuesday, moving the array of snow-white dots as if the land itself breathed. Hums joined each other as brown body after brown body came out into the field to start the day, bushel strapped over shoulder, mothers admonishing children flitting between branches, still too young to know misery. Some of the stubborn ones got whippings right there with a broken-off twig. Better that than the overseer.

Afiya's knuckles already ached. It was going to be a good day, though. Rain had come the night before, bringing up the worms to sweeten the soil. The birds sang to each other; already the field workers offered up their voices.

Sam shifted his bushel from one shoulder to the other. Without whiskey, he was docile, almost nervous. Afiya took his hand. It was trembling.

"Remember that song," she said. "You remember that, you'll be all right." She hoped she could believe that.

Sam nodded. He put down his bushel, adjusted his hat, and sat cross-legged in the dirt.

Afiya sang as she worked, something old and generic so that her mind could stay sharp in the now. It didn't take long for a curious negro to come up and ask Sam what was wrong. When they realized what he was doing, they stayed well enough away. Trouble on a plantation was like ripples in the water: best to stay out of it, else you end up in a wooden box as far in the ground as arms could dig.

Finally, the smell of chewing tobacco made Afiya look up. Harry passed by on his horse.

"You broke a leg or something, boy?" the overseer said. He called back over his shoulder. "We got a lame nigger over here!"

Afiya touched Sam through her gaze and turned away. She couldn't get caught up in Sam's ripple. Not yet.

John, an older overseer, galloped up.

"What's this fuss about?" John said in a stretched-out drawl.

"The sun done fried this here nigger's brains, that's what."

"He don't look fried to me. Rotten, more like."

The clink of metal, a grunt, and the soft sound of boots landing in damp soil. Afiya saw the tail of John's mare swatting flies. A basket woven of chewed-up bark and leaves tumbled into view. That's the farthest she dared look.

"You want to tell me why this is empty?" Harry said.

"Nigger don't work, nigger don't eat," someone spat. "Let Mister Louis deal with him."

"This here a defiant nigger if I ever seen one. Louis probably just give him a slap on the back."

"Let Mister Louis deal with him. And if he don't, he'll learn. We all do."

"Come on, get up!"

A scuffle. A pair of birds took flight. Afiya forced herself not to turn around. She willed calm over Sam. If they killed him out in the field, all would be for nothing.

Afiya was never so happy to see a negro walking beside a horse, his wrists tied to the harness. Sam glanced back at her. His eyes hung with fear. That was expected. *Remember the song*, Afiya mouthed. Sam nodded.

The wait was torture. She snuck by the whipping tree after supper. There had been no whipping that day. Ripped flesh had its own ghosts that lingered before moving on.

Back at the cabins, she found Elias, a field negro who often played cards with Sam. He blew over the top of a bottle while another field negro sang a tune and slapped his legs.

"Where'd they take Sam?" Afiya said.

"He in that nail box Ole Marse Charles favored," Elias said.

"Where at?"

"What you mean, 'Where at?' Wherever that nigger is, that's where at!" They burst into laughter.

Afiya grabbed Elias's ear and twisted. She could have torn it clean off, she was so mad.

"Behind the big house, where Marse keeps his towing tools. Now let off me!"

The nail box was a living man's coffin, only with nails penetrating every surface except the bottom, knocked in to press right up against flesh. A twitch, jump, or even a sneeze could be fatal.

Afiya lowered herself beside the box. Heavy breaths came through the cracked wood, along with crawling things that painted shadows in the dark.

"Sam," she said, real soft. "Sam, can you hear me?"

The breaths quickened.

"It's Afiya," she said.

She tapped her knuckle against the side of the coffin.

Tap tap . . . tap tap tap tap . . . tap . . . tap tap . . .

She kept rapping against the wood. Sam's breathing slowed. Afiya began to sing to their beat. By the end of it, her voice was not alone.

...

Afiya awoke to unfriendly voices, the new sun in her eyes. A faint but clear *tap tap . . . tap tap tap* still came through the wood. She quickly blinked out the haze. The voices carried from around the toolshed.

"Keep the song," Afiya whispered. She looked around. There was no clear place to go. She scrambled to the other side of the coffin and made herself small against the wood.

More footsteps. Closer. A shadow, stretched to the east.

"Wake up, nigger!" Harry shouted. The coffin rattled against her, then laughter.

"Dead?" Harry said. No one responded.

The lid opened and crashed to the ground, sending up dirt Afiya nearly coughed on. Her eyes watered.

"Not dead."

Afiya waited as they dragged Sam out of the box, waited until footsteps faded. She uncurled herself and peered around the side of the house as Sam hugged the whipping tree. He got twenty lashes. Afiya thought she could see his lips moving but couldn't tell for sure.

Harry spat in the dirt, coiled up his whip, and then mounted his horse to head back into the fields. Elias came forward from the gathering crowd to help Sam back to the slave quarters, but Sam shrugged him off.

"Make sure that nigger gets himself all right." Louis's voice drifted from around the house. Afiya frowned. Had Mister Louis stood watch that whole time? "He got to work in the morning."

Sam walked from the tree without a sound. He kept on walking past a sneering Harry, right up to the stoop of the slave cabin, picked up the flute James had made him a few days before he died, and began to play. He played loud enough for the field to pick up the tune. Its electricity flitted over the plantation like the promise of a sweet summer's storm. By the time Afiya made her way back to the cabin to grab her bushel and head out into the field herself, she thought the song would have died out, but it only grew.

Sam still sat on the stoop when the time came for all negroes to hang up their tools. He had a far-off look about him, as if he'd seen freedom.

"How you?" Afiya said.

"I been better. I been worse. A lot worse."

"You see Harry's face when you picked up that flute! Gah-lee!"

Sam smiled, weakly. He hurt, Afiya saw. "I reckon he never seen that before."

"I reckon none of us have," Afiya said. She sat beside him. "Did you see my ancestors?"

"No," Sam said. "But I felt you." He played a tune on his flute. She began to sing, but he stopped and said, "Now what?"

"Now we wait."

...

Nobody cared if she was magic or not, not really. I seen a lot of negroes get beat under the whip and not flinch, like they brains not connected to the rest of they body. When that happens, you know the white man got they soul. It's better that way, sometimes I think, 'cus you know they gone. Ain't no coming back once the white man got your soul.

It was the look she gave Marse that got us all going. That "I'm not yours" look. And he knew it, too. She was his, in a way, which made it that much more frustrating. Marse Ferrell had everything in the world, and a lot of his negroes loved him like they love theyselves. But she was the one that unwound him.

—*Conrad Ferrell, former slave, 1834*

...

Sam returned to the fields the next day, earlier than most negroes. He still hurt; his face grew tight when he stood upright. But he hid it well. He didn't look up when Harry rode by. The overseer's face was sour with grime and resent. The negroes who had seen Sam's blood run with their own eyes got close enough to make sure it was really him, but that was all.

The curious found Afiya under the night's blanket. She taught them her song and the ways of the Sanain people. She didn't know if they would be able to follow her, or what opening this door would bring, but when they sang together, the drums thrumming the air around them, the ululations of a thousand dead angels pouring over them, Afiya could feel nothing but hope.

"Is it true? Does it heal you?" one asked Sam.

"Yeah. Show us!" said another.

"You ain't got to," Afiya said to Sam.

He unbuttoned his shirt and gingerly slipped his arms out the sleeves. When he turned, Afiya gasped.

His back was mountains of old lines made new by fresh welts that still glistened in the candlelight. The song's effect had been little, if any.

"Sam," Afiya said. "I didn't know."

He pulled his shirt back on, turned around, buttoned, and then picked up his flute. He played a quick tune, low and sad, and then put it away.

"I was healed," he said. "Can you see?"

They could.

...

When Sam sat down in the fields again that next Tuesday, his empty cotton bushel discarded beside him like some dead thing, Elias and two other negroes sat with him. The next Tuesday, there were seven.

They didn't just sit. They sang. They sang the song of the old gods and legendary warriors, of first Osun and then Adesokash, the song of healing, the song of hope.

...

Afiya was never taught any formal math, but she knew Tuesdays were hitting Mister Louis where he couldn't deny it: his pockets. Afiya caught a glimpse of his worry one Wednesday morning as he loaded a town-bound cart with nothing but scant bushels of corn and firewood. There was a pang of guilt for the boy she'd grown up with. Afiya admonished that quick. She needed only remember her husband's still body, smelling of soap and oil.

Over a dozen negroes, some the most productive out of the Hairston Plantation on any other given day, sat in the soil, singing at the top of their lungs.

To his credit, Mister Louis made sure the whip sang right along with them. The young master spent much of his time watching the negroes from his porch, sipping more and more from his whiskey bottle. Each day he looked a little bit older, a little more like his father.

The next Tuesday, fourteen field negroes turned in empty bushels of cotton. The overseers didn't so much as look their way.

"We getting to them," Sam said that night. "They don't know what to do."

"Sure don't," Afiya said. But she couldn't share in Sam's joy. She was nervous.

...

Mister Jonathan Cole had a tobacco plantation with about fifty or so slaves, so he and Mister Hairston often did business together. He brought three of his strongest negroes to carry back whatever the two masters had agreed to barter on any given day. Nate, a tall negro with arms like tight branches, smooth olive-colored skin, and a white-toothed smile, fancied Virginia, who often came to hear him play on his panpipe as he sat waiting on the stoop for Mister Cole. When he finally asked to marry her, the two masters agreed.

Nate and Virginia's wedding took place in the Hairstons' backyard in a crop of dirt between the porch and the fields. Since marriage was a godly thing, all the negroes got a day off.

"I reckon Mister Louis just don't want to see us misbehaving when Cole is here," Sam said.

Afiya smiled at the thought. Her old friend was losing control. She just hoped he wouldn't get stupid about it. Or crazy.

While they waited for the wedding to start, the negroes passed around stories. From the way his slaves told it, Mister Cole was something fierce.

"One time, Marse Cole bought this young Virginia boy," Thomas said. His hands were calloused and thick, much like his body, but his face was soft and bright. "His name Albert. The negroes up that way a little bit more uppity, light-skinned type, you know. He sass-talked Marse Cole on his first day, feeling him out. Marse Cole smiled just like a devil. He gave him five hundred lashes himself, quick as lightning. Then he packed salt on his back, all by hisself. It was hot that day, and not a cloud in the sky. Mister Cole had him lay out on a rock where no tree's shadow touched until his back blistered just like eggs popping in hot grease. The poor fool lived, but he was never the same after that. Marse Cole sold him to some poor white trash for ten bucks."

"That's a bold-faced lie," Elias said.

"I seen it myself!"

"How's a nigger supposed to work after that? Ain't no white man that dumb."

"Mister Cole is," Thomas said.

Silence. Then they all laughed.

"Who held him?" Afiya said when it died down.

"What you mean?" Thomas said.

"I mean, which of you shameful niggers held that poor boy while Cole stripped him bare?"

Thomas's eyes went wide, as if she'd slapped him. "None of us, ma'am."

"All of you did," Afiya said. She shook her head. "You held him down by doing nothing."

Thomas sat forward. Afiya flinched, though there was no need. "You that girl, ain't you? The one with the voice?"

This surprised Afiya, but she didn't let it show. "Afiya," she said.

"We heard about you. What you got going here. Mister Cole always rumbling about another master's niggers and how they giving him trouble. That's here, ain't it?" Thomas licked his lips. "What you cooking?"

She opened her mouth to speak, the weight of hopeful eyes suddenly upon her. She hadn't expected an audience.

"Gone and tell him," Sam said. "We can't do this all ourselves."

"We don't get the bullwhip because we got control," Afiya said. Once she started, the words poured out of her. "We work the fields, we cook the food, we chop the wood. Without us, Mister would be as poor as that Johnson family that live at the bottom of the hill."

"Sound like you talking uprising."

"I'm talking control! This is our land."

"This ain't our land," Thomas said. "It's Mister Hairston's land. It's Mister Cole's land. They not just gone give it up. They'll hang us before they give it up."

"You right, they not. We got to take it. We got to hang them first."

Thomas shook his head. "You talking war."

This time, Afiya leaned forward. She hoped they couldn't see the way her legs trembled. "You sound like a house nigger."

Thomas bristled. Afiya didn't back down.

"You know I ain't no house nigger," he said. He looked at her right long. "What we got to do?"

...

If a slave could ever have a feast, they had one the night of that wedding. Boiled chitterlings and pig feet with corn on the cob and the edges of cornbread left over from Mister's kitchen. Collard greens and potato wedges and boiled pig fat. They drank whiskey and rum and sang and told stories and played cards and flirted.

Then Mister Louis walked out there, so quiet no one knew he was among them until he spoke.

"I didn't know you guys could play so good," he said.

It got real silent, as if the crack of a whip had torn through the air.

"Keep on playing," Louis said, gesturing with the bottle of whiskey in his hand. The liquid swirled at the bottom.

They did, their tune slower than before. George kept his fingers still. He didn't talk about it, but he'd been real messed up since James died.

"Play like before," Louis said. "Come on, now. I'm not going to hurt you."

When George still didn't play, he reached for the banjo. "Let me try at it."

George clung to his instrument. Mister Louis gave it a yank strong enough to loose it from the old man's fingers. George moved to get up but calmed at Sam whispering something in his ear.

Mister Louis strummed at the strings; the sound must have been like knives to what little hearing George had left. His fingers just didn't fit right.

"Keep with me," Louis said, gesturing for the others to continue playing.

Elias and Sam looked at each other.

"I like you," Louis said. He was out of breath. Sweat marked his brow. "I like all of you."

"Well, we like you, too, Mister Louis," Elias said.

"We're doing great things here. All this land, all this cotton, we build ourselves a good place."

Afiya slipped into the cabin while Mister was going on. She didn't want to hear him talk like a drunken fool.

"Mister's outside," she said. "Drunk as a skunk."

"What's he want?" Katie said. She had been Cole's house slave just the day before. Her skin was fair, her hair in loose curls. She knitted a blanket for the child in her belly, one Afiya guessed would come out even whiter than she. Afiya didn't know how much Louis paid for her and didn't want to know. Seeing as Cole's missus probably didn't take too kindly to mulatto children born to her land, Katie was most likely a bargain. Now she shared their cabin.

"Not you, child," Lilly said as she dragged in a bundle of clothes from the line. Her limp had gone back bad, but only slightly. "Mister be like that sometimes, right, Afiya?"

Afiya pretended like she hadn't heard. She took some of the clothes to fold. She tilted her head toward the door but couldn't make out more than rumbling voices and intermittent laughter.

She heard the footsteps too late. Afiya turned to make herself gone.

"Afiya," Sam said. "Mister wants you to help carry some of this pork and corn back up to the house."

"Can't someone else do it?"

"He specifically said you. He's in a good mood. I'm gone come."

Mister didn't so much as look her way as they walked back up to the Big House, carrying three bags of boiled corn and shredded pork meat between them. The sky was peppered with bright little angels. Meat and whiskey and the smell of laughter faded behind them. While it lingered, Afiya felt less alone.

"You was born under my pa, right?" Mister Louis said to Sam.

"Yes, sir," Sam said.

"You ever get to wondering what's outside the Hairston Plantation?"

"No, sir."

"You don't have to lie. We just talking."

"I guess sometimes I do."

"Well, I been a lot of places outside of here. Up high and down low. Places where they don't value stuff that should be valued. A nigger look at you the wrong way and they hang him from a tree, kind of places. My pa was like that. I always wondered what's the point in that."

"Don't seem like there'd be much point at all," Sam said.

"You're right about that, boy. No point at all."

They hauled the bags through the back door, into the kitchen.

Mister handed Sam a bottle of whiskey. "You niggers have fun with

it. Just make sure it doesn't keep you from getting up in the morning."
He smiled real big. "Good thing tomorrow's not a Tuesday."

"Thank you, sir," Sam said. He looked a little paler. He could almost pass for a house negro, Afiya thought. "Come on, Afiya." As he took her hand, she felt something cold and sharp slide against her palm.

Louis grabbed her other hand. "Stay. Help me wash this corn."

"We washed it already, sir," Sam said.

"I want it washed again."

"I wait here, then. It's a little ways back."

"A gentleman among beasts," Mister said with a smile. He rocked as he talked. The smell of whiskey poured off of him like water down a mountain. Afiya tasted the alcohol in the back of her throat. "But are you accusing me of being careless with *my* property?"

"No, Mister, nothing like that." Sam was already backing toward the door. Afiya tried to catch his eye, whether to tell him it was all right or to beg him to stay, she didn't quite know. As he disappeared, Afiya slipped what he'd given her down below her belt.

"You mourn quickly," Mister Louis said when Sam was gone.

"It ain't like that, Mister. Where you want this corn?"

Mister leaned against the counter and shook his head. "You used to look at me different. Have I changed?"

"I don't know, sir."

"My grandpappy had three plantations. This was one and, another my uncle Willy run down the road. After my pa sent me away."

"Sent you and our child away," Afiya said.

Louis held up a hand. "He sent me to Uncle Willy's plantation. My uncle is much different than my pa, and I'm different than both of them. We all see the nigger differently. My pa thought the nigger was no more than a mindless monkey with a price on his back. But he valued respect over money. My uncle just hates niggers, hates them so much sometimes I wonder if he should just sell the plantation and be done with them. He adopted Beatrice after his wife's cousin died of the bilious disease. So she hates niggers, too, I suppose."

"And you?" Afiya said.

"My uncle caught one of his nigger children under the steps, reading a book. It wasn't a big book, or an important one, just one of those books about shucking corn or geography. The boy wasn't even reading it right. He had it upside down and he was just saying words to this old song his ma used to sing. Still, Uncle Willy act like he had stolen gold. He held the boy by the back of his neck and whipped him with an iron poker. Broke both his legs.

"The nigger's father just watched. And when it was done, Uncle Willy turned to him and said, 'You got anything to add, nigger?' And you know what the boy's pa did? He yanked his son up—he had to do it twice 'cus I don't think he realized the boy's legs was broken—and yelled at him for being a dumb little nigger.

"When we was kids I used to sit and wonder how pa could treat another person like he did, but then I realized why. You ain't people. You ain't got the sense to stand up for yourselves and ain't got the sense to know when you got it good."

Afiya sniffed tears. Her mother, a field slave who had never seen the inside of a house, had told her before she was sold to the Hairstons that one day, one of the white children she liked to play with would hurt her. *You mean like they hurt Pa?* Afiya had asked. Her ma had said, *No, in a way deeper than that.* Afiya hadn't understood.

Now she did.

"And your child? What is she?"

"Forgotten." As Mister Louis stood, he had to steady himself. "Undress," he said.

"Mister Louis," Afiya said. She was past fear. "This what you really want?"

"I know what I want. Now, undress."

"Fine," she said and did as she was told. She slipped off her top first. The cold steel pressed against her thigh.

"What if Missus Beatrice come?" she said.

"Turn around." She did.

He came up behind her, the burning heat of his whiskey breath curling over her skin and crawling up to fill her nose.

"The devil's skin," he said. After having James, his fingers were like worms on her back. "Forgive me, Father."

He began to kiss her neck as he took off his pants. She felt him grow against her leg. She had known it before, when she was young and he was kind and gentle and the type of white boy that made her feel like freedom wasn't some abstract thing, but a loved one on the other side of the hill, waiting for reconciliation.

Her finger tapped against the wood. She parted her mouth just enough to let the click of her tongue send out the words she used to connect back home—her real home. Afiya floated over the cotton fields, the white bolls like constellations, over the trees and past more fields, over and over and over, faster and faster, until there was water and freedom and the steady beat of drums.

She slipped into the arms of her ancestors where she'd wait among the dead and the living and everything in between until the deed was done, until . . .

"I like that," Louis said.

When would it be over? When would she have freedom that was more?

Afiya stepped away from that sacred place. She reached behind her and clamped down on her master's cock. Whiskey stung her eyes and nose as she turned, the delicate force of her small body pulling her master slightly forward.

She brandished the knife Sam had slipped her and touched the blade to Mister Louis's tip. She meant only for him to feel its cold, but her hands trembled beyond her control. He spasmed a step forward; she held him firm.

"Afiya—" he said.

"Be quiet!" The two words surprised them both. He began to go limp in her hand. The change inspired her. "You listen to *me*, now."

"I'll have to kill you," Louis said, and began to sob it. "Dammit, Afiya, I'll have to kill you." His words rang so true she almost lost herself. Almost.

"Quiet, I said." He quieted, but his eyes still said the words. *I'll have to kill you.*

"Now I know you're thinking about stringing me up from that tree right about now, and there's not much keeping you from doing it as soon as I let go. But you're going to have to beat me bloody to get me off you, and I don't think Miss Beatrice will think too kindly of you having a naked slave girl in your kitchen. Especially one who held your child."

Afiya resisted the urge to look around. If someone—Beatrice, a house negro even—came and saw, her fate was sealed. She held more than her master's cock; she held her life. She couldn't lose hold of it. "Everyone will know. If you kill me, they gone know why. Beatrice gone know why. You think you losing respect of your slaves now, just wait."

She searched his eyes. Nothing but a scared little boy.

"What you want?" he said.

"Don't ever call me back here again. What we used to be, that's over. Got it?"

She jabbed the blade forward. He grunted, gripped the sides of his vest with strained fists, then nodded.

She let go. Quicker than he looked, the whiskey seemingly drained from his veins, Mister took her up by the neck and pulled her close. He swatted away her knife before she could get it halfway raised. His grip was shaky but strong.

"Don't you forget who owns who, here." He let her go.

"I won't, Mister."

...

Afiya cried all the way back to the cabin. She was thankful for each step where she didn't hear the crack of gunfire and a final, permanent weight on her back. Part of her wished for it. She'd spend the night pondering her chances in the woods with the dogs. She'd spend it pondering the noose she could make out of the pieces of twine they used to bundle the wood.

"You all right, child?"

Afiya hadn't noticed she'd stepped into the cabin. Lilly was waiting up for her.

"I'm fine," Afiya said. "Really, I is."

"Your eyes say you not. Come here, child."

Afiya went to her. Lilly no longer worked in the fields and smelled less of dirt and cotton and sweat and more of smoked meat and Sunday mornings.

"I told him no," Afiya said, loud enough for more than Lilly to hear. She wasn't the only one who stayed up when someone was missing.

"I know you did, child. I know."

...

A whisper came in the pitch-black of night: "Did you really say no?"

"I did."

Afiya sang to herself as she lay in her cot. It wasn't one of the old songs, or anything from praise and worship. There was no healing to be had or consult with ancestors. Just a song. And hope.

...

I went to all the meetings at Ferrell Plantation. Every single one. Mister Ferrell didn't treat us too bad, but he was still between me and my freedom, and that was enough.

Afiya, she showed us her pain through her song. She showed us not to be afraid. She didn't show us freedom, per se, but she showed us we could be free. If we wanted it.

Those meetings, they grew and grew and grew. Soon the whole cabin was brimful of negroes. It did me something to see so many black faces with freedom in their eyes. When talk of a real rebellion came, I wasn't sure about much, but I was sure about her.

—Jane Freeman, former slave, 1838

...

Mister Louis didn't so much as look at Afiya for days after that.

She continued to teach the negroes the art of singing. Some of the house negroes started joining, and then more still. They snuck out knives and steel, small gifts the revolution would need later, all to learn Afiya's song.

Mister Louis's passions had only swelled since Afiya's defiance. She taught the negro women her songs. They wouldn't help keep the act from happening, but they let them go to some far-off place.

Soon, they wouldn't need that place anymore.

...

Afiya woke to gunfire, and screams.

The shack bustled with the quiet panic of the enslaved. Many negroes had tried to run back when Old Mister Charles was living. Whenever someone did, all the negroes waited in the dark of their cabins, silent as a banjo without strings, praying for freedom. When the gunshot rang, which it did more often than not, prayers for freedom turned to prayers for mercy.

Scratch. A flame appeared somewhere nearby.

"If you here, say it," Lilly whispered.

"Virginia here."

"George, uh-huh."

"Afiya here," she said.

"Katie here."

"Where Sam at?"

"You there, Sam?" Afiya said. Her chest hurt.

The crack of gunfire made Afiya jump. More than one negro cried out. The shot hung on the air. And then another came. Dogs barked. Silence, then white, excited voices, then more silence.

Soft weeping, untouched by the weak light.

"Shut up, now," George said. "You going to make it worse!"

Whoever it was couldn't stop. She wept for all of them, too many tears for one poor soul to hold in.

...

Mister Louis sat on his porch all the next day, his eyes completely covered by shadow, as if the black skin he'd inherited reign over was slowly eating him up.

"Them two niggers I shot were runaways," he said. Afiya knew better.

Sam's and Elias's bodies hung from one thick branch, side by side.

Sometimes they swayed together. Then the wind would hit and they'd go in different directions. Most everybody—house and field negroes alike—bowed their head if they had to walk past the hanging tree, as if looking at the ground somehow made it less real.

Afiya walked right up to it. Sam's head was swollen. It would be easy to pretend he was someone else, that it wasn't the same high-spirited man she'd sang beside so many nights before. But she made herself look at him, at the eyes bulging under eyelids that wouldn't quite close, made herself see the parts of Sam's smile now hidden in death.

She hoped she kept her face stone the whole time she stood there. She hoped Mister wondered how the slave he'd played jump rope with as a child, the slave who'd birthed and then mourned over his daughter, how that same girl could look up at the horror of her reality and not flinch. Not bat an eye.

She turned away. The walk back to the fields was the longest walk she could remember in a long, long time.

...

More than twenty negroes came to that night's meeting.

When Tuesday rolled around, more than half of Mister Louis's slaves refused work. The whip broke in half before he could punish them all.

That night the negro song was so strong, the crickets took it up. Fireflies twinkled to the beat of drums no one really heard but felt all the same. The wind whistled through the branches, under the eaves. Mister Louis had nightmares of drums and giant goats. Miss Beatrice couldn't sleep and instead walked around the Big House, locking every door she could.

The night sang freedom.

...

Was she mute? I remember her leading all those meetings and getting us riled up. She must have been talking for that, right? My memory ain't shit these days. I took a bullet in the head during the Rebellion War, did I tell you that? During the Battle of Martinsville, where we won it all. I lived to see freedom, I tell you that much, didn't I?

Now that I think about it more, I guess she was mute, I remember now. Her old master Mister Louis take out her tongue. Now why would he do such a thing? White people did a lot of things I won't quite sure why.

—Jackie Freeman, former slave, 1853

...

Afiya's followers slipped into her cabin one by one in the black of night. Mister Louis's new curfew demanded all negroes be inside before the last of the blue left the sky. This had put an end to their singing sessions, which had gone from weekly to nightly, but the hunger for unity had only grown.

"Now?" Virginia said from beside her.

"Not yet," Afiya said. Not until the last negro was accounted for. She waited for a long silence without a newcomer's footsteps, then tapped Virginia's hand. "Now."

Virginia lit a candle. More flames around the room sparked illumination.

Afiya's breath caught. Black faces. Brown faces. Caramel faces. Young and old. Women and men. All sons and daughters of her ancestors.

They all looked to her.

"Mister Louis knows he lost control," Afiya said. "Now's the time to strike. Before he go and do something crazy."

"We got guns? They got guns," someone said from the crowd.

"No guns," Afiya said. "The less sound we make, the better. We want to win, remember, not die."

"Will the song protect us?" a woman asked.

"No. *We* protect us. We protect each other."

There was a grumble at this, to which someone spoke: "I felt it. My scars didn't go, but when I sang it, I felt it, in my bones."

"What do we do with the women and children?" a tall negro man asked. He looked like he could break a man in half, but his eyes held the sincerity of his question. "Missus is cold, but Harry's wife ain't never sent a bad word my way. They kids smile at me at times."

"Kill the women," Afiya said.

"And they children?" he said.

Afiya paused. She thought of Louis, running with her through the fields. She thought of how they pretended they were fairies and could fly to the moon and back. She thought of drowning in the lie of freedom behind his eyes.

"They children, too," she said. "Two nights from now. Be ready."

They began to disperse. Thomas came up to her after. From the looks of him, his mind was wary. He'd taken great risk coming all the way from Cole Plantation.

"We need Nate on board if we going to get Cole," he said.

"We got to work with who we got."

"He'll rat us if he knows. He'll be afraid for Virginia."

"You sure?"

"I know he will. His love for that girl is blind."

"She's his wife," Afiya said. "It's supposed to be. I'll work on that. You just get the rest of Cole Plantation ready."

...

Nate came nearly every day after laboring, with or without Mister Cole. He was smitten with Virginia. Afiya couldn't blame him. She was his freedom, in a way. A slave held on to whatever made him feel free. He had to.

Nate played his panpipe whittled out of old oak and strung together with horsetail hairs on the porch while Mister Cole did business inside the house with Mister Louis. Virginia must have been terribly behind on her cotton that day, because he sat alone.

Afiya slid up beside him and started to sing. He turned one eye up to her but didn't miss a beat. He played a chord higher to match her pitch.

"You think about what happen when that baby comes?" Afiya said when they were done. Virginia was young and one of eleven children. If she wasn't with baby by now, she wasn't going to be.

"He going to be a strong boy," Nate said. "Just like his pa, and his pa's pa."

"His momma live over here and you live over there. What you think they gone do if she get with child? How Cole think you gone be with a new son across the way?"

"I can come as long as I keep to his building when I'm supposed to."

"He say that now. But what the white man say and what the white man do is two different things. Mister Charles sold my daughter before I could even put her to nip. 'Cus I'm a good worker and he needed me working."

"I don't believe that for one minute," Nate said.

"Boy, look at me." He did. "Everybody lie in this world, but there's some things a mother don't lie about."

"What you getting at, Afiya?"

She told him what she was getting at. And he listened.

...

Gunfire broke the night.

Not yet, she thought. It was too early. Someone had gotten anxious. And she said no guns!

"Get up!" Afiya yelled. "It's now!"

She was halfway through the door when the horror of it dawned on her. Torches blazed like giant fireflies. White men with horses—men she'd never seen before—rode up to the slave quarters.

"Come on out, niggers," one of them yelled. "Y'all in a lot of trouble."

George went to the porch, his hands reaching for the old wooden banister that creaked and bowed under his weight.

"We Mister Hairston's property," he said.

"We know who you are, nigger." Afiya recognized the speaker as one of Mister Cole's sons. He stepped into the light of the torches, holding Virginia's husband by the nape. Though she couldn't see the negro's back, the pain in his face was enough to imagine fresh red lines parting the skin.

"Where's the nigger girl that spoke to you?"

Nate whimpered, then pointed. Afiya didn't turn away, only stood there.

"We been hearing talks of a rebellion," another white man said. "We can't have that round here, now can we?" It sounded like Harry the Overseer; his face was hidden in flame.

"If that's how it's gone be," George said. He sat down on the porch and picked up his banjo. He strummed a note and then stopped to adjust one of the strings where the root had broken through the flesh of the gutted gourd, which had begun to go soft. The white men looked at each other and laughed.

George played.

"I ain't never seen no blind nigger rebellion!"

George continued to play.

"Shut that up, boy."

George played louder.

"Take the girl to Mister Hairston. Kill the niggers in this here cabin, and the ones beside. That should be enough."

George played until he couldn't play anymore.

...

Afiya counted the hanging cookware to keep from passing out as she lay curled up next to the coal oven. Despite the pain, despite everything, she still couldn't imagine having so many options. Oh, the things Old Miss Lilly could have done with such a supply.

"You got to kill her," Beatrice said. She stood at the door of the kitchen, an angry fire set in her sharp features. Inside, Mister Louis stood over Afiya. The smell of seared flesh—her flesh—clung to the young negro woman's nose; they'd marked an *R* for "runaway" on her cheek with a branding iron. Louis's palm was red with her blood from slapping her quiet whenever she tried to sing healing over herself.

"I know what I got to do," Louis said. He wiped his hands on a gray cloth. "Now go on out of here while I do it."

Beatrice stepped forward. "You got back control of your pa's land. If you want to keep it, this nigger needs to hang from the rafters."

"I said, get!" Mister Louis glared at her. Beatrice stood before him a while longer, sneered at Afiya as if she were a rodent, and then left.

"I can't kill you," Mister Louis said when his wife was gone. He leaned against the kitchen counter and stared out the window as he spoke. "I love you." He banged the wood. "I love you, I love you, I love you."

Shots rang out. Screams. Shots silenced them.

"What we was," Afiya said. "That won't love. You can't own love."

"I was good to you," Mister Louis said. "I was good to all you niggers." When he turned around, he held a fillet knife. Though she tried not to, Afiya gasped. "They won't be so good down the road. Not to no runaway nigger that can't talk right. I was good to you. You'll see."

Mister Louis crossed the kitchen to the still-raging fireplace and held the ragged end of an old blade over the flames. Afiya thought of James as he turned to her, his tool glistening and smoky in his hand. Of Sam. Of Elias. Of George and Old Lilly and young, thought-filled Virginia.

"Sing for me," he said. "Sing for me the same song that turned all my niggers against me." Afiya readied herself for an overwhelming smell of whiskey when Louis pressed his body against hers, but none came. Her master was sober.

Mister Louis yanked her head back by her hair. "Sing!"

Afiya sang. She sang for her people. She sang even as the man she thought she had loved a long, long time ago grabbed her tongue. She sang as he sliced through flesh.

She sang through it all, until she couldn't sing anymore.

...

I fought in the Rebellion War, right up until President Jackson surrendered. I remember that day, because we was held up in Danville and we thought we was about to die. Then we heard that song. The song of legend.

I'd never heard it before. But when you hear it, you know. It was the song of healing. The song of Afiya. We all took it up, just knew the words, just sang and sang and sang.

I never believed in none of the superstition of it, but I felt something in the air that day. I don't know much about Afiya, or if she even existed, but if she did I liked to think she was there somewhere, listening. And smiling.

'Cus we was free.

—John Williams, Private, Company B, 18th Regiment,
Rebellion War, 1863

...

It felt like a thousand ants roamed Afiya's mouth; every so often, her phantom tongue would crackle as if containing its own little storm. She'd tried to find her song during the dark of it all, pushing air through her throat in ways that felt familiar, but anything of the sort only sent a blinding pain shrieking through her head.

The caravan came to carry Afiya away to Alabama two days after half Mister Louis's slaves were killed in the failed uprising. She didn't know what Mister Ferrell paid for her, but she imagined a mute runaway didn't go for much.

They hit a bump. Afiya lifted her head, tilted it. She thought she could—no, she *could* hear the faint beat of drums. Percussion.

And then, the voices. Coming from the plantation that was getting smaller and smaller.

Sweet wind passed over Afiya's throat. She pushed through the pain. Her hum lifted and swam with the song. Her song. Their song.

It rose. And rose. And rose.

The revolution was just beginning.

As much as she could, Afiya smiled.

Wellness Check

Jared

The virus had changed everything, even the way I ate. I laid out my meals for the day—yogurt mixed with whey and nuts, leftover hamburgers, an apple, and oatmeal—and poured dethawed mix into the waffle maker. I turned it on high and went over to my workbag to be sure I had all I needed. There'd be no coming back once I started my day.

I checked the time. Still another thirty minutes before the bus came. I sat back on the couch and scrolled through my phone's headlines, paused over a new outbreak alert long enough to confirm it was being contained in Houston by the coast guard and wouldn't affect my commute, and clicked on my notifications. Five missed video calls, the first four from Mom. I clicked on the last.

"You're up early," I said when Shanice's pixelated face congealed onto the screen.

"I couldn't sleep," she said. "You going in today, too?"

"I have to go in every day."

"Do you? I'm sure Darla and Greg would do just as well over FaceTime."

They wouldn't. We'd tried, but AquaZone's star seals were stubborn enough *with* an in-person trainer. Shanice's tone was playful, though, and it wasn't lost on me that she'd tuned in for more than one of my performances.

"Who would feed the fish?" I said.

"Drones?"

"You're one to talk. You got more contact points than I do."

"Only on performance days. And my theater is across the street. You take a bus. A full bus!"

Shanice's Love At Home profile had been the first and only one I'd "quarantined" after first downloading the app some weeks back. After three virtual dates I spent no less than one month's pay to secure a ticket and surprise her at her production's prerelease fundraiser showing. As I sat with nine other strangers in a theater with capacity for one thousand, I wondered if I should have bought her flowers instead. But within minutes of the lights dimming I could have been the sole spectator and it wouldn't have mattered. It felt like cheating, in a way, seeing her so much in her element, the passion that she put into her performance, the emotion that stirred up all the beauty and horror of my repressed feelings from the last few years. I realized a lot of things during those two hours, most of all how alone I had been. And when her eyes found me during the curtain call and a slight smile lit her face, I realized I didn't want to mess this up.

She invited me to "dinner" after, which meant us eating with our backs to each other and having to talk in code so algorithms wouldn't catch our unregistered meetup. I almost asked her to merge our pod circles. Almost. Instead, the night ended with a train ride home—ten feet apart, of course. Afterward, I couldn't decide if I had chickened out or come to my senses. Being alone was safe; being alone was surviving.

"One week until showtime, huh?" I said. "You excited?"

"Nervous. It's going to be weird without an audience. Even ten people make a difference."

"Just keep reminding yourself that I'm streaming and zooming in on your every move." She laughed. "You'll do great. It's basically like being on Netflix, but live, right?"

A harsh *beep, beep, beep* cut through my apartment and our

conversation. I looked up, toward the kitchen. A smoky haze billowed from the far counter, blotting the air like a bad video connection. I ran over, squinting against the smoke. I forked the blackened waffle skeleton into the sink and unplugged the maker.

"Shit," I said. "I almost fucked up."

"It's a sign," Shanice said from the phone. She donned an amused smile.

"That I should stay home?"

"That we should go out to eat again. Maybe we can even face each other this time." I nodded in response, focusing on cleaning up the mess I had made. "Well, I'll let you go. Tell Darla and Greg I said hi. I'll be watching. No pressure."

"Wait, Shanice, I—"

But she had signed off. I leaned over the sink, prodded the waffle to see if any of it was salvageable, and poured some cereal instead. After a bite or two, I checked the expiration date and put the rest of the bowl in the freezer. My appetite, it seemed, was still asleep.

I checked the charge on my Viral Detection Reality glasses and slipped them on for routine calibration. Faint green sparkles, like fireworks observed from aircraft, lit the air as I let out a breath and the particles from my lungs interacted with the glasses' UV rays. Once they had confirmed I was virus free, the security bolt on my front door snapped open and allowed me to leave my apartment.

The spring air, dry and crisp, felt good against my skin. I had learned to be thankful for every gust of wind since the string of viruses disrupted society almost three years ago now. So much had changed, and the things that stayed the same felt somehow new.

I tilted my head for easy VDR identification as I passed a foot patrol officer. When headlines and trackers of outbreaks across the globe weren't sufficient to feed my insomnia, I spent my nights consuming videos of pedestrians being stopped for not having proper RNA-identifying glasses. I couldn't afford a citation, not with Mom's medical bills. I'd rather keep my ten-foot distance.

I scanned my VDR at the bus stop and received my boarding ticket right as the 76 North arrived. I entered through the corresponding door; pine-scented disinfectant stung my nose. A faint but persistent beep tickled my ear. I pressed the side of my VDR to acknowledge that I had, in fact, checked my environment. Automatically closing out the alert without scrutiny was tempting; surely many did just that. But on one of my nightly scrolls I'd read about a housekeeper sued by a client after the family contracted one of the deadlier strains. VDR logs cross-checked with security cameras showed he'd dismissed an alert a day before when starting a job, despite there being clear viral remnants around.

I tried to relax. The uneven road below me was soothing, one of the few "sames" that reminded me of how things used to be. If I kept my gaze low enough, through the periphery I could almost forget the panes of glass separating me from the other riders. The illusion was short-lived, however. The bus exhaled pressurized air at every stop.

A familiar and unpleasant chime echoed through the bus. I shifted just enough to see red fog on the backmost cubicle's glass instead of the usual mint-green aura. Multiple groans rang out as the infected man took his seat.

"Door eighteen," a yell went up as the bus started to pull away. The passenger adjacent to the infected banged on the door of his own cubicle. My own muscles tensed at his tenor. "Door eighteen!"

"You can't catch it," the newcomer said as the bus pulled back to the curb.

The door opened. "Yeah, yeah, I'd rather walk."

The sick man was right, of course. His cubicle was hermetically sealed, just like the rest of ours. The bus driver was mandated to take him either to his documented home or the hospital, no place else. The policy prevented the recently diagnosed from navigating the streets on foot. Still, each red-tinted cubicle was a stark reminder that community spread still happened, even with all the precautions, technology, and sacrifice.

"The fuck you staring at?" the man said to me.

I came out of my thoughts. I *had* been staring, wondering. The man sat hunched forward, his arms resting on his knees. His angry features looked bullish through the red pane. He must have just found out. My heart went out to him. At the same time, I was thankful his dwelling was a few cubicles removed from mine.

I raised my hands in apology and looked out the window. Skyscrapers swallowed the sun as we entered the city. Passengers trickled off and quickly entered through the tall steel gates surrounding each of their respective buildings. Social workers and caretakers, mostly, off to meet with the city's once-homeless that now filled what used to be the financial district. Since the virus, the country had gone remote; virtual cities had replaced concrete ones.

My pocket buzzed. My heart welled with expectations of Shanice. It was my mother. I chose "audio only."

"Are you okay?" she said as soon as we connected. I didn't need video to know she was stressed; I heard it in the forced exhalation of her words.

"I'm fine, Ma," I said. "You know that."

"How can I when you don't return my calls?"

"You called me three times in the middle of the night. Where else could I have been?" I rubbed my temple with the back of my wrist. "What's on your mind?"

"I've been thinking, and I don't really need the home health aide."

"Ma—"

"No, hear me out." A pause. I saw her clearly in my mind's eye, shutting her eyes and taking deep breaths to quell the rising anxiety and keep herself from needing to grab her oxygen tank. "Nothing's really that high up, I can do takeout for food, and I've been practicing taking my own blood pressure. And the home health people, I just feel like I'm wasting their time."

"Insurance denied the claim, didn't they?"

Silence. Then, "It's not just that. Like I said, I'm not even sure I need an aide."

"This is ridiculous," I said. "I'll take care of it. You're keeping your home health aide, and that's final."

"But Jared—"

"No 'buts,' Ma!"

"Who's the parent here?"

Any other period in my mother's life, and that would have been a topic-ending yell. Now the words came out cracked and scarred. I waited. Labored wheezing filled my ear, and when my mother spoke, her voice was small again, defeated. "What time's your thing today?" she said.

I told her. "I'd rather you rest."

"Nonsense." Her voice had regained some of its texture. "I'll check the schedule on the website. You been eating okay? All alone in that apartment. Is your fridge empty? I know it is!"

"I can cook, you know."

"Want me to send you something?"

"Bye, Ma," I said. I could tell when she was gearing up to the topic of me still being single. "I'll keep you updated on what the insurance says."

I exited near the end of the line, a couple blocks from AquaZone. Though I saw no one, I knew I was surrounded by thousands, if not millions, of people. The towering windows felt like a labyrinth of eyes. Someone was watching me, I knew, curious to see where the young man was headed.

I scanned my ID outside the marine park. The gate's unmarked black metal was in stark contrast to the old building it protected.

A first beep indicated a facial recognition match. A second marked human confirmation from some remote, home-based station. That done, it was ready for my VDR read. The indicator buzzed red. I groaned, tried again, and on the third attempt the gates swung open.

Finally inside, I took off my VDR. I turned on the lights and let myself slow as I greeted the different tanks. The saltwater coral was my favorite. Thick glass ran from floor to ceiling. This was another of the "same." These self-contained ecosystems had no concept of any outside turmoil. Like when I closed myself off on the bumpy bus ride, I focused on the soft ripple of artificial current across psychedelic scales. The world, in that moment, was back to being okay.

I followed my usual path past all the exhibits and back to the locker room near the entrance, adjacent to my boss's office. My VDR beeped from my pocket upon entering; I tapped it quiet. Besides myself, only a handful of workers came and went every day. Though living alone wasn't a requirement for this line of in-person work, I bet that none of the others shared pods with a theater actor. In all functional units that I was aware of, at least one partner worked completely from home.

After changing into my wetsuit, I logged into my boss's computer, loaded the video communication software, and waited. Harry "Skipper" Murrain had already joined the meeting and muted his camera and audio.

"Morning, Skip," I said. I waited a beat. The microphone crackled.

"Give me a sec," he said. Someone yelled in the background, not unkindly.

"Take your time."

"Okay," Skipper said from the black. "I'm ready. Let's just . . . Ah, there we go."

His screen flickered on. My boss peered into his camera from in front of a bookshelf that looked artificially neat. More than anything else, seeing Skipper reminded me of how much things had changed, and challenged any hope of things ever being the same. He had gained back only a fraction of the weight he'd lost while battling the virus. His face, once full and rosy, was sharp and sunken, with more shadows than joy. Most devastating was the deep divot in his neck where a tube had once been inserted to bypass his airway; I couldn't help my eyes from going there. A low whine touched the microphone on every breath, much abated from the nebulizer treatment I knew he took in preparation for our talks.

"How are things at home?" I said.

"Same ole. Jameson just started algebra, so there's that. Did you learn that common code method?"

"Common *core*? Nah, it came right after me. Thank god."

"Whatever it is, I think we're about to retire it. Return to old-school math. How's our aquarium doing?"

"Good. Fish look healthy. Water's clean. We getting a big crowd today?"

Skipper chuckled. "Not unless you know something I don't. Ticket sales haven't been the best."

"Must be the traffic."

Skipper smiled. "Don't lose that sense of humor. I noticed something interesting in the sales."

"Oh?"

"The same person has bought a ticket every day for the last week, week and a half."

"You thinking hacker?"

"I don't know. Goes by this name." Skipper held a sliver of paper up to the camera with *Shanice* written in his barely legible chicken scratch. His smile, which was usually weak but withstanding, widened. "You know them?"

"The name looks . . . vaguely familiar."

"Your face says it all. I'm just glad they're not a hacker." Though some thought the tracking algorithms were always listening, any correspondence between employers and employees was particularly monitored. The practice originated to protect subordinates from pressure to bend containment laws. Societal implications soon proved broader. "They from one of those apps?"

"Yeah. We 'quarantined' each other."

"Quarantined? I'm guessing that's a good thing?"

"It means we're both interested. Kind of like we bought each other a drink at the same time."

Skipper waved a hand. "You're losing me. You like them?"

"Even if I did, there's only so much you can do these days. We went on a—" I mouthed the word *date*, and judging from Skipper's widening eyes, he understood. "If you could even call it that. I talked way too much and didn't know where to take it. This virus makes love impossible."

"You're young. Get creative."

"You sound like my mom."

"Maybe because I'm speaking some truth. I've seen our show. And while Greg and Darla put on one hell of a performance, this person has tuned in four times in a row. Four! Look, take it from me." Skipper paused to take a sip of water. Since the virus forced the whole world virtual, the average streaming quality had launched to former elite status.

I could see every detail of my longtime boss turned old friend. The way his chest heaved, the flare of his nostrils, the contraction of his neck divot as he swallowed. This conversation was longer than our usual. I almost stopped him, but I knew he'd resent me for it. "Life goes by too quickly to let this virus take any more than it already has."

I leaned back in my chair, rolled the back of my head against the wall, and sighed. Skipper's smiling, previrus face looked out at me from a grainy framed picture from the grand opening of the aquarium, back when I was still playing with dolphin figurines. I looked back at the screen. Skipper watched with patient amusement. His smile still had life in it.

"What?" I said.

He laughed. "You're what we used to call 'sprung.' What do you like about them?"

The question was born out of pure, mentorlike curiosity. There was no challenge to it, no trap in disguise.

"Ambitious. Passionate. Funny. Funny as hell. I saw them perform and for those moments it felt like before the pandemic. A lot of people let this virus define them. Not h— them." I almost slipped up. "They still doing what they love."

"You thought about merging yet?" Skipper said.

"They have a work situation. An important one. And so do I." I turned to focus on the security cameras. Darla and Greg lazed in the morning sun. "This is the only pod I need."

"It's a wet zoo, not a pod. If this place gave all a person needs, don't you think I'd be there?"

"If you could, you would be here."

"Semantics. Look, bottom line: if you needed to tweak your pod status, I'm sure we could make it work."

"How?" I said.

Skipper took another sip of water. We both knew he had to stop soon. Still, he leaned into the camera. "Are you letting the virus define you?"

"It's almost opening time."

Skipper stared. I didn't need high-definition to see the words writ in his gaze.

"Fine," he finally said. He muted himself and called to someone off-camera. I winced at the way the hole in his neck stretched. "Sorry about that. Kids. Gates open?"

"Gates open."

Skipper's eyes changed focus as he clicked away from the video chat. His smile bent, like a tree's branches under the burden of a night's sleet, and I glimpsed some of his daily discomfort underneath.

"One, two, three, launch." Skipper sat back. His smile returned, full, true, and, for at least that moment, without pain. "Here's to another day."

Shanice

Waiting made me anxious. There was no way I had the virus. I'd been extra careful, fully checking every space when entering, carrying two bottles of hand sanitizer in my purse, charging my VDR nightly, and only going from home to the theater back to home again. Still, every time I found myself waiting at a clearance station, I imagined that little indicator going red and changing my world. I was overdue for a personal disaster; things had been going almost *too* well.

The automated kiosk outside Ottoman's Theater went green. Of course; it was always green.

Another beat while the computer found a clean path, and then the door clanked open. The glass-walled hallway-within-a-hallway led to my changing room. I gave a half wave to a passing crew member, and it wasn't until I was at my door that I realized who it was. I looked back, but she had already gone. I double-checked the changing room to make sure it was mine, scanned my VDR, and stepped inside.

My pod partner Jeanie applied her makeup on the other side of the glass pane divider. Besides the preview a few nights before, I had physically shared the stage with her and only her for the last several months. The screenplay had been written specifically for social distancing, and most scenes were either monologues or pod partner couplets. While we kept our full distance offstage, we were allowed to break the ten-foot rule briefly to fulfill the purposes of a scene. All movements were tracked, analyzed, and a report was given at the end of the day reflecting compliance.

"Shouldn't Nell be back by now?"

Jeanie glanced over from delicately massaging her eyelashes and gave a genuine smile. "Hmm?"

"I just saw her understudy." Nell's violation of pod limits had grounded her for a crucial two weeks in the middle of rehearsals. At first, she continued in all the scenes virtually. Given the already established in-person pod-pair rotations, it wasn't much noticeable until a few days ago, when someone had forgotten to charge her kiosk. The understudy had been there, though, ready and willing.

"Nell's out," Jeanie said in her low, careful voice. She blinked her eyes, checked herself, and turned fully toward me. "But hey, don't you worry about that. You were so good the other night. Great to be back in front of a crowd, eh?"

I wanted to talk more about Nell, but Jeanie's maternal eyes advised me to let it go. I did. "Aren't you used to sold-out shows?"

"Ten or ten thousand, there's no beating the energy of people in a room."

"That's what I'm afraid of. How do we keep that same energy for the cameras?"

"The same energy? Impossible." She rolled her chair toward the divider, sat, and rested her chin on her arms. "But we do the best we can."

"You think this is going to be the game changer, like everyone says?" I asked.

"It'll be a change, all right," Jeanie said. "Broadway, from your home."

"There's supposed to be a live chat or something. How's that even going to work? Feels like a big experiment."

Jeanie held up a hand. "Let the producers worry about that. Our job is to perform. You killed it at the preview. After this, you'll be headlining your own sold-out shows."

"You think we'll get back there? Sold-out shows?"

"Yeah, eventually." The last word trailed with no clear ending as

Jeanie rolled back to the mirror to apply her finishing touches to the tracheotomy scar at the base of her neck. The goal was to enhance instead of cover. Her character had also beaten the virus. Sometimes I wondered if fiction had it easier than reality. But Jeanie kept that part of her close to her chest.

"So was that him, in the audience?" she said.

Some of that clearance-fear knocked against me. I retreated to my own mirror, though I always did my makeup at home. "I don't know what you mean."

"You know exactly what I mean. I thought he looked familiar. He watched you the whole time. So either he's a creeper or you like him. Which is it?"

"Well, I still don't think I know exactly who you're talking about, but if it was Jared—"

"Guy from the app?" I had downloaded the Love At Home app almost a year before, and in the beginning even tried to use it. But whenever I matched with anyone, I shut the app down, threw my phone across the bed, and didn't check again for a month. Jeanie had clicked "quarantine" on Jared before I could stop her. Her laughter and my horrified protests were both interrupted by the chime of his initial private message.

"Yeah, that's him. He may be possibly, maybe, inching over into the 'liking' category."

Jeanie pumped her fists. My cheeks warmed.

"So, what's he like? Tall, dark, and handsome?"

"Short, dark, and handsome," I said. "And really sweet. Really, really sweet. He told me his whole life story, you know? No guard, no games, just real."

"Was he drunk?"

"No," I said. "He doesn't drink, actually. He just opened up. I don't think he's dated in a while. We were both nervous. It was sweet."

"You're welcome," she said. "I'll send you a bill in the mail."

"Yeah, yeah, yeah." I straightened a wig that didn't need straightening and checked buttons that didn't need checking. "You had a lucky pick with this one."

"*You're* the lucky one. Or at least, hopefully you'll get lucky soon?"

"That would require merging of pods. Which is *not* happening."

In our banter, I hadn't heard the partition slide open. Jeanie's arms were suddenly around me. "I'm happy for you," she said. She'd made the premature silencing of her voice into something fully her own, soft and tender. "You need this."

"I got everything I need here."

Our sensors began to beep. Jeanie put her hands up and backed out of my cubicle. "I'll have you and whoever is listening know I remember exactly how I got the virus the first time, and it was from more than hugging. Speaking of, why no merging? He a doctor or something?"

"Worse."

I picked up my phone, scrolled through my email, and clicked on the link in my AquaZone access ticket. I showed her the resulting picture. She looked at it, raised her eyebrows at me, then back to the picture.

"I'm guessing that's not his backyard," she said.

"Nope. Definitely not."

Jared

A hum as the rolling kiosks came online. The air immediately filled with the incomprehensible chatter of the background noise from the remote aquarium-goers who still had their mics on. Mostly the sound of hyperactive children, more than ready to release their homeschooled jitters, and the futile pleas of their exhausted parents.

I watched on the security cameras as kiosks dispersed into the park. As far as we knew, we had been the first to implement such virtual tours. Skipper had taken great pride in being one of the only Black-owned and -run aquariums in the country. His life's work at risk, he had all but panicked during that first hard-hitting lockdown before the public had learned the appropriate fear of and respect for the virus. He had come into the park every day, even as his trainers and cleaners and managers began to quit, and I came in with him because I was young and single and wanted that paycheck that would liberate me from my mother's financial embrace, too naive to know the severity of what was to come. We worked on an email campaign informing our members of how we were keeping everything clean, what new species of fish we welcomed, and the updated show schedules. The city finally forced us to close by cutting off the electricity and water.

Skipper wasn't caught off guard a second time. By the time a new strain of the virus surged, he had already been in touch with several social distancing start-ups that had sprouted across the country. He'd found a solution.

The roving kiosks proved successful, but the price for our previous stubbornness was soon paid. Skipper came down with the virus during the second wave, his illness so severe that he was in the hospital for six weeks and needed home oxygen for a month after discharge. He didn't leave the house after that, and from talking to him, just the act of walking from one room to the other still left him winded.

But he still showed up every day in the way he could. He was still my boss, and I wouldn't have it any other way.

The next two hours were aquatic tours, feeding sessions, and question and answer. I capped it off with Darla and Greg, our main attraction. The jovial seals had grown sharper in their routine since the audience went virtual, delighting in new tricks and pleasing an audience of one: me. Today felt so good, in fact, that I went through two full routines, and by the end of it I was wet with enough sweat to look like I had spent the hour in the pool myself.

We bowed at the end of our routine. I found the kiosk marked with a red flower—Shanice's—and threw a wink in her direction.

Once I was sure the last camera was off me, I sat to catch my breath. I unzipped the top of my wetsuit to cool down and found little relief. Whereas the lingering chill of an aging California winter had greeted me that morning, the midday sun was a reminder that spring was moving in. The air, too, had thickened. I glanced at the sky, expecting to wince. Instead, there was full cloud cover.

I checked my watch for the weather and frowned. The temperature had actually dropped since the morning. With this dissonance came an increased awareness of self. My throat felt raw. My breaths were shallow and labored, not because of the air but the building pressure in the middle of my chest when I inhaled.

Like much of my life, before and after the virus, my next move was automatic. I double-clicked the crown of my watch for a quick read of my vitals and immediately regretted it. I had a fever—mild, but a fever. My oxygen scale dipped just below normal.

My phone began to ring. Wellness Check was calling. I considered letting it go to voice mail, but knew that was foolish. The call only gave the illusion of control. The CDC had access to my self-monitoring interface and would evaluate me, whether I participated or not.

I answered.

"Good afternoon, Mr. Rice," a wearied voice said. "Date of birth zero two, fifteen, ninety-five?"

"I think you have the wrong number."

"Please confirm. Jared Rice, date of—"

"Yes, it's me. I'm fine, okay. I was trying to open Candy Crush and hit the wrong button."

"I see," she said, but her mind was already focused on something else. I envisioned a woman in a lab coat, wearing a mask in a quiet room, typing away. "Low-grade fever, heart rate's a little elevated. If you could clench your fist for me—perfect. Oxygen is low. Significantly. Any cough—yep, there's one. Have you had any exposures?"

"Exposures? Look, I'm fine. I'm at work and—"

"Where do you work?"

The silence between us was short.

"AquaZone is what the GPS shows. What's your role there?"

"Animal trainer. How long is this going to take? I'm leading a tour for the kiddos in ten."

"Routing your commute. Scanning contacts."

"There's no way I could have gotten it. I check everywhere, for crying out loud."

"Your VDR is off. Is there a reason for that?"

Shit. "I'm at work, okay. It's only me here."

"Breathe onto the sensor, please."

"This is ridiculous. I just got done with a show with our seals, you see, and worked up a sweat. I'm not sick. I've done everything right."

"Look, Mr. Rice, it's much more likely that you have something benign, like the common cold. But once you enter into my care, it's my legal obligation as a licensed physician to make sure. I can't end this interaction and approve you going back to work without it."

"What if I hang up?"

"That would make both of our days a lot worse."

"Sure. Fine."

I puffed air over the face of the watch. The device recognized the gesture and told me it was uploading the sample.

"What's your name?" I said.

"Pardon?"

"Your name? You have one, don't you?"

"Dr. Fasika. Hana Fasika." A pause. "The test is negative."

"Shit yeah!" I stood. Behind me, Darla barked a response. "Sorry. That's great."

Dr. Fasika's tone disagreed with my assessment. "I have to talk this over with my attending."

"Why? You said it was negative."

"That's just one piece. I'm hoping to clear you, Jared, just sit tight."

"I can't go on quarantine. I'm at my *job*. I need this—"

One of the seals—Darla, most likely—plunged into the pool behind me. Water sprayed over the rim, sending a fine shower across my back. I looked up to see if anyone had noticed, but of course no one was watching. I was alone. The audience chairs were not only empty but covered with plastic to preserve the cushions in preparation for an actual reopening that might never come. If I walked out into the lobby and took it in—*really* took it all in—I'd notice the crushing void left behind by human absence. No discarded popcorn bags, lost tickets, or empty promises to litter the ground.

"Thanks for waiting," Dr. Fasika said. "We looked over your case, including your vitals over the last several days. We see you've been following protocol as well as anyone. There's a few places you didn't fully check—"

"I always check."

"I know, I know. You've done everything right. But this pathogen is resilient."

"Fuck. You said it was negative."

"The test for known strains is negative. But we can't just go off that. Not with its mutation rate. We look at four criteria to make a clinical diagnosis. Fever, cough, oxygen saturation, and loss of smell. This morning you almost burned your breakfast, correct?"

I was too shocked to answer. What else had they seen? Heard?

"Olfactory deficits. With fever and cough alone, that's enough to justify quarantine. Even with a negative test, we have to take your symptoms seriously. More seriously, even. This could be a new strain."

"So what now?"

I imagined her flipping through a manual, searching for what to say next. She must have sensed my angst and exhaustion and, blessedly, cut to the chase. "Thirty-day quarantine."

"Thirty? What happened to fourteen?"

"Fourteen is for known strains. If this is novel . . ."

"I can't. I just can't. You see where I am? Look at it. I'm the only one here. I run the shows, I clean the tanks. What else can I do? There has to be some workaround. I need this job."

"I'm sorry," Dr. Fasika said. And she was. Somehow that made it worse.

My VDR's status changed. The green blinking light that so frequently occupied my periphery that it had become invisible paused, then switched to red. My own scarlet S. I wanted to throw the glasses on the ground and stomp the red out of them. But outside these gates I'd be stopped within a block without my identifier. And if they thought I was dodging mandated quarantine . . .

"I want to appeal," I said.

"You have that right, Mr. Rice. After seventy-two hours you can send a request to the courts."

"Seventy-two hours?"

"Someone will be reviewing your case daily. We'll run more tests, see if we can identify the pathogen. The quarantine could be dropped at any time."

"How would you like it if someone did this to you?"

"Someone did. Twice. It sucked, but when you look at numbers and how many lives saved . . . it's why I'm doing this work, Mr. Rice."

"How long until I need to be home?"

Typing. She was reviewing my commute, which took about an hour.

"I'll give you two hours. I hope that's enough time to wrap up at work. But I need you to understand, you have to go—"

"Straight home. I got it. Anything else?"

"One last thing. Any contacts to report?"

"You have all that, right?"

"We do. But we realize tracking isn't perfect. If there are any contacts you have, now is the time to report."

I was suddenly grateful that this was only an audio call. My face would have surely betrayed me. "No. No contacts."

"Good luck, Mr. Rice. Someone will be in touch."

"Sure." I hung up. Before I could think, Shanice's profile picture floated to the surface of my phone. I answered it; she must have received the same news.

"That was great! How did you get Darla to flip like that? We should celebrate. What are you doing tonight?"

Or maybe she hadn't.

"I got quarantined," I said.

"Wait, don't tell me. Because your performance was so sick?"

"I'm not joking. Look at my sensor." I tilted the camera and looked at the ground. I didn't want to see her face change.

"It was that damn bus. Jared, I told you—"

"I don't think it was the bus."

"Then what?"

I looked at her for as long as I had to. If I said anything close to confirmatory, her Wellness Check would come through before I could even finish. The AI that had been listening all day was simple, not stupid.

She resisted, but eventually I saw the memory resurface in her eyes. That first and only in-person date. Per containment rules, we had to stay ten feet apart at all times or else we'd have to merge our registered contact pod, which would mean possible number violations with Shanice's theater. The dinner had been spent two tables apart, our phones on video chat so we could see each other. While the previous dates had been surface-level intrigue and attraction, the thrill of her performance seemed to open both of us up. By the end of the meal, I felt I had known her for more than half a season. She told me about the fiancé she'd lost to the virus early on, before anyone knew what it was, and how acting made the last few years worth living. We took the subway home, and deep in the tunnel the train stalled. Signaling across the car, I pointed out our VDR's lost service; she closed the gap between us. We whispered and laughed like schoolchildren passing messages behind the teacher's back. Her hands, light on my shoulder, sent sparks down my spine. I couldn't remember who made the first move, only the feel of her lips on mine, the first contact I'd had with another person in over a year. I wanted to ask her to merge pods with me right then and there so that we could do this all the time. But what if that put her theater in jeopardy? What if she said no? The train rumbled to life beneath us; the moment had passed.

I nodded at her realization now. And then the connection broke.

Shanice

I gripped the phone. Jared's terminated call stared up at me. I remembered well the night on the train and our violation: How could I not? I remembered all night shunning the absurd urges to break ten feet with him. There was too much to lose. And then the train had stopped. Well under the city, the virus, the quarantine, the pods, they all seemed so far away. And he was there, more real in that moment than all the rest.

Afterward, when the train had continued its slog through the tunnels, the anticipated worry and angst didn't come. No guilt.

No remorse. Only his warm shadow on my lips and the thought of more. I had spent three years surviving and abiding. I deserved that moment. I hadn't done anything wrong, laws be damned.

And yet here I was.

Would I survive? Would I do what was needed to survive?

I would call him back. Say that he was mistaken. He couldn't have gotten the virus from me. It must have been one of the other women he'd swiped on, someone a lot less careful than I had been. I would express empathy for his situation, which was hard as nails, but make it clear that it had nothing to do with me. I'd wish him well. He was younger than my fiancé had been; likely he would come through largely unscathed. We could even start back up once this whole pandemic thing blew over.

My thumb had migrated to the call button when Jeanie called my name from the stage.

"Damn it all," I said, pocketed my phone, and went to answer the call.

My partitioned section was front left centerstage. Jeanie was stationed six feet away, the closest she could be with the glasses between us. We exchanged our scripted banter during a scene that I currently had no conscious awareness of, just automatic beats under artificial light. I couldn't shift my gaze away from Jeanie's throat, the way the divot shifted and stretched with every word. How it looked like a bottomless hole . . .

The director, her hologram mounted on a central kiosk, had us repeat several scenes. She didn't call me out; she didn't have to. Every line out of my mouth raised Jeanie's eyebrows in curious prodding. I couldn't meet her eyes. Not with that notch in her neck, not after Jared's phone call.

"Let's call it a day," the director said, her voice amplified over the theater's sound system. We'd stopped just shy of the finishing number.

"No, I want to finish it," I said.

A beat of decision-making and then music filled the space. It did little to subvert the day's fatigue. Cameras turned off, microphones muted. We had all seen the play many times over. It was easy to mentally doze unless each line was infused with the spark of something fresh and new. Not today, however. Just lines. Just motions.

I began to sing. I, too, expected an uninspired rendition. But something caught as the melody passed my throat. Perhaps it had been the character's sorrow at knowing that her childhood was truly gone. Or was it the lament over my own career? My character spent the majority of the play making humor out of tragedy, and here was the moment meant to elevate the production above comedy. I had struggled with this number before. Not technically; I hit the notes and rode the cadence. Emotionally. Perhaps it was the transition from cheerily carefree. Or perhaps I hadn't been ready to tap into my own sorrow to give the song justice.

I sang, full of heart, as if this were not the performance itself, the rows filled with observers, but the last time I'd have this chance, on this stage. I lingered in the moment as long as my breath would allow, much longer than any vocalization coach would assign. I had seen all too well what the virus took from people, and in all cases it had been a little bit of air, lifted from their lungs.

It was at the end of the note that I felt the tickle in my throat. I cleared it—one small push of air across the flesh—and fought not to wince against the pain. My colleagues stared at me through a virtual lens. They erupted in staccato applause.

"Perfect," the director said. Her kiosk rolled forward. "Absolutely perfect."

"Save it for showtime, sweets," Jeanie said when the kiosks were powered off and stored. Their moving partitions were only a few feet apart. She cocked her head. "You okay?"

I shook my head, just slightly. Jeanie nodded and checked her control panel. "Feed's off. It's just us. What's going on?"

"It's about Jared. He called me right before I came onstage." And then, in response to her bemused look, "The guy you hooked me up with through the app."

A relieved smile. An "Oh, is that all?" smile that I immediately regretted calling up. "You know what? Fuck him. What grown man swims with seals anyway?"

"No, it's not that. He's been great. Too great."

"Thank god, because I really liked him. Most of the guys looking for love during this pandemic are a little . . . well, there's a reason some people are single, I'll just say that. What is it, then? Did he ask you to merge?"

"He's quarantined. Like, really quarantined. They think he has the virus. He just told me."

"Oh, honey. He's young, healthy. I'm sure he'll be okay."

I gestured toward her kiosk. Invisible to any casual observer, the kiosks allowed performers to pull up scripts or video in tandem with any other cast member. We could also text. Communication between same-level employees could be encrypted and become supposedly safe from surveillance.

Jeanie stood reading my message for what felt like a long time. Behind her, the theater stood tall and ready.

"We have understudies," she said. "It may delay us a day or two, and we definitely won't have someone who sang that song like you just did. I guess we weren't going to anyway, huh?"

"What if I don't have it?" I said. But I knew the answer. Even if my test came back negative, the fact remained that I had kissed someone no more than three days before he tested positive. I'd be quarantined for sure.

"Trust me, after that performance you just gave, they'll have you back in a heartbeat."

"Thanks, Jeanie." We both knew that was bullshit. Show business had a short memory. Either an understudy would create a chemistry that would be foolish to disrupt once the show was underway, or they would replace me with one of the many other talents waiting in line, their VDR log ready to show that they hadn't made contact with another soul.

Jeanie shouldered her purse and paused at the door, as if she sensed I had more on my mind.

"If I get tested," I said. "You want to know if I know?"

She shook her head. "Nah. I refuse to give any more of myself to this thing, even my mind space. It already took enough."

Jared

I made to call her back, then stopped. She'd hung up. This upcoming show was big for her; being under mandated quarantine would ruin it. But she had been my only true contact. And if she had it, her entire theater company probably did, too. If she wouldn't report our interaction, then it was on me. But could I? It would be the end of our relationship. Just two years before it would have been an easy no. Now, knowing how the virus had ravaged Skipper and my mother . . .

To take my mind off decisions still to be made, I focused on something I knew had to happen. I videoed my boss. He took it better than Shanice.

"It's a sign. You can do that thing you were too scared to do."

"I wasn't scared. And I'm not worried about them. I'm worried about this place. And you."

"Get home. I'll see you in two weeks."

"Thirty days," I said.

Skipper winced. "Thirty days, then."

"I'm sorry."

"Don't. Don't. You get better. The job will be here when you get back."

Skipper said this with such conviction that I knew he believed it. But belief didn't matter. Both the laws protecting sick workers and the insurance policies allowing small businesses to fund such protection had vanished after successful fearmongering around the last election cycle. He would have to hire someone else, and with the ticket sales, there wouldn't be enough room for two. Especially after he'd hired a deep-cleaning service before reopening to comply with state laws.

I looked up. A low whine filled the air as Skipper sent out a remote announcement about AquaZone's early closing. The kiosks rolled toward the entrance, their uniform speed and singular goal indicating that autopilot had taken over. The customers weren't happy. They'd be refunded part of the price of admission, if not the whole thing. That would hit Skip even harder.

I waited until they were all done, fully aware that I was eating up my time to get home. Still, I made sure the tanks were well fed, tested the pH and ammonia levels of the oldest of them, and added treatment to the ones that needed it. It kept my mind off the empty apartment awaiting me and the now-empty promise I had made to Mom about keeping her home aide services. When there was nothing more to do, I left.

The first bus slowed and then sped up at the sight of me. Another twenty minutes before the next would come. I could request a self-driving car to escort me home, but those scared me more than the disease.

I waited. When the next bus came, I stepped into the street and waved my hands.

"That's not helpful, you know," the bus driver's voice came through the special cubicle's speaker once I had boarded. "Good way to get hit."

"I'm mandated to get home. Wanted to make sure you didn't leave me."

"It's against the law not to service someone to quarantine."

"Tell that to your colleagues."

I buried myself in my phone. Surprisingly, the rest of the world hadn't changed much since that morning.

Mom called. I let it ring. I didn't want to tell her until I had to. *If* I had to. The virus had mostly ravaged her lungs, but I often expected it had hit her brain as well. Because even though I was relatively young, without risk factors, she would see my diagnosis as a death sentence and treat it as such.

Thinking of her, I pulled up my Wellness Check app. I went to the "Report recent contacts" section. I typed in Shanice's information and hovered over the submit button. Who had hesitated before reporting the person who would eventually pass the virus on to my mother? On to Skip?

A notification split the screen. Shanice R. has reported a recent contact with you and requests to merge contact pods. Click to see details.

I had barely finished reading when my phone buzzed again. A text. From Shanice.

Got tested. Looks like we'll be riding this out together. Netflix and chill?

I blinked and looked around as if to share my surprise with the other passengers. They didn't want to share anything with me, of course. The cubicles adjacent to mine were clear, and many glanced over at me warily every few seconds, as if I planned to escape and wreak havoc.

Being sick and quarantined was one thing; opening up one's pod was another. She had her theater company to think about. I almost texted *Are you sure?* and thought better of it. Of course she wasn't sure. Who could be?

Instead, I texted back, Only if we watch something where viruses don't exist.

Agreed. A pause. So you going to accept my pod request or should I reinstall Love At Home?

I accepted. The small panel beside the automated sliding door blinked, and "Alternative Home" popped up as a potential location in addition to "Home" and "Emergency Department." My VDR glasses went through some midlife crisis with rolling notifications and change in color palette. I ignored it. You deleted the app? You must really like me.

Or I thought it was worthless. Would you have reported me?

Of course not.

Liar, she texted.

I'm really sorry, I texted back.

For making the first move on the train? Don't be. I'm grown.

The virus is already messing with your memory.

?

You made moves on me.

She sent me an animated picture of a laughing emoji rolling across the screen.

Thanks for the laugh. You're officially a part of my pod. Dinner at my place tomorrow?

I'll bring wine, I texted. And Theraflu.

I put my phone away, sat back, and looked around. The aura filling my cubicle was noticeably red; the CDC had already registered and flagged whatever pathogen was present in my breath. People stared with curiosity, loathing, and fear, with many declining to board once they saw that my cubicle held a real live passenger rather than the more frequent seventy-two-hour stain of one.

My chest stuttered as the top of my breath caught my emotions. I realized I was afraid. But not of the virus. I looked down at my phone. It had been years since I'd been in a serious relationship, and for the last three I hadn't even had to think about it. What if she realized I was wrong for her? What if I realized she was wrong for me? Even scarier, what if we did stay together, and the resentment of quarantine and its sacrifices ate away at us? Because, in truth, who could say who infected whom?

I was afraid because at least being single meant no opportunity for an actively broken heart. No rejections. No judgments. No missteps. No navigating the pandemic with not just one soul to consider, but two.

My cubicle didn't offer me an exit until we arrived at the stop nearest my registered home. I stepped onto the empty street, coughed into my arm sleeve, and tried to file away the feel of the breeze on my skin—a memory I could readily access. It was going to be a while.

Spider King

A LONE SPIDER CRAWLED FREE ALONG THE HEAVY STEEL DESK, PAUSING TO taste the curious jailhouse air with its pedipalps. Inmate #8367 wondered how it had ended up in this hellhole. The damn thing would probably make it out before him.

The sharp click of a deadbolt drew the inmate's attention. The security door slid open. The guards ushered in a tall man in a neat but loose-fitting suit.

"Darnell Lee?" the visitor said without looking up from his tablet. He sipped water from a clear plastic cup as he sat across the table, just out of spitting distance.

"That's me. I'm Darnell."

"Possession of an unlicensed firearm, violation of parole, resisting arrest, and drug possession with intent to sell." The man finished his drink and rolled the cup between his fingers. "They have enough to put you under the jail. You didn't take the plea deal. Why?"

"I got a daughter. I can't sit and rot upstate while she's without her daddy."

The man looked up at the prisoner for the first time. "How's that working out for you?"

Inmate #8367 didn't need to be reminded how long he had been here, how many birthdays and milestones he'd missed. He focused on the carefree spider, slowed his breathing, and shifted his body as much as his chains would allow. Calm was better. Calm meant not being declared incompetent to stand trial.

"Look, I know what I did. And I know what I didn't do. I'm not suicidal, I'm not hearing voices or seeing shit. I just freaked out. I—"

The visitor dropped his empty cup top-down over the spider. It scurried in a panic from plastic wall to plastic wall. Inmate #8367's heart beat faster.

"Got him," the visitor said. "I'm not a psychiatrist. I'm here to give you a way out."

"Another plea deal? I'm no—"

"You're no snitch. I know. I'm offering all charges dropped and you go home today." He tapped the tablet. "I already have the signature from the judge."

"I'm listening."

The dealmaker's smile spread as he pulled a clear, capped syringe from his breast pocket and laid it on the table between them. The label read: *Freedom Rings.*

"We need volunteers. If this new medication helps convicts like yourself deal with the anxiety of returning to society successfully, everybody wins."

"I'll do it," Inmate #8367 said. "If it gets me out of here, today, I'm in."

The dealmaker considered him a moment and then signaled over one of the guards. As the injection passed hands, Inmate #8367 thought he saw something shift inside the vial, as eager to get out as he was.

"I think you'll do great," the man with the unsettling grin said. "I really do."

Darnell walked past that same holding room some hours later with a sore shoulder and freed wrists. He didn't think to look back. If he had, he would have seen that the cup was still there, forgotten, its lone prisoner scratching at the walls.

...

The burning itch of something foreign burrowing under Darnell's wrist came in the middle of his first job interview after being released from jail. He shifted in the undersized suit he'd bought from the thrift store the day before. The experimental medication had done little for his anxiety. This new sensation didn't help.

Joy Butler, the general manager of Delaney Street Restaurant, sat on the other side of the old, chipped wooden desk and asked him a basic question that sounded lifted from the same website Darnell had used to prepare.

Darnell had read that taking long, introspective pauses makes an applicant seem more thoughtful, trustworthy, and dependable. So he used the opportunity to look down at his wrist, where he'd been absent-mindedly picking at a scab. A piece of too-thick skin hung loose. The edges of the mottled flesh underneath quivered.

The itch deepened.

"Darrell?"

"Darnell," he said, looking up. He smiled, off cue.

"Right, sorry. Darnell. I'd asked what would you do—"

"I would first listen to the customer, see their perspective, and attempt to come up with a solution. If I'm unable to deescalate the situation, I would find the manager—you—or another senior member of staff."

Shit. Too verbatim.

Joy sat back, considering him. Darnell considered himself, too, but in a different way. The tip of his index finger rubbed his wrist. There was an obvious divot now. Around it, numb cold. He pressed into it.

Something pressed back.

"How long have you been out?" Joy said.

"Three days."

"You move fast. That shows motivation. You heard about how we work here?"

"Yes," he said. "I've heard a lot. Giving opportunities to people no one else will. Shit's dope." Heat filled his ears. "I mean . . ."

She smiled, and for the first time Darnell relaxed.

"You can be yourself. The customers come to see what you can become, not to feel like they're visiting a prison." She leaned in; Darnell resisted the strong urge to pull his arm to safe hiding. "Everyone here knows what it's like to be locked up. From the bottom up."

"Even you?"

"Especially me."

"But you're a . . ."

She threw her head back in a laugh. "Women can crime, too, you know. They have whole prisons full of them. Call them 'women's prisons.' Went away because I killed my husband."

"Oh," Darnell said. He looked back down at his wrist. Mistake. The skin moved.

"I'm just fucking with you. Drug charge." Her smile withered. "You doing okay?"

"I am."

"You clean?"

There was no judgment in the question. She understood what it meant not to be. He saw it in the thin skin beneath her eyes, the slight coat of grime on her teeth. Even the frequency with which she shifted positions, a sign of her subconscious continuing to rebel against sobriety.

"I am. I got a second chance. I'm not messing with that. I'm just . . . nervous."

"Don't be. You can start Monday."

Darnell forgot about his wrist. Had he just heard her correctly? Delaney—with its full benefits, decent salary, and flexibility for parole and court dates—was at the top of a long list of potential jobs, a list Darnell had planned to venture far down.

"I'll take that look as an acceptance."

"Hell yes. Sorry. Yes. Any way I can start earlier?"

She waved her hand. "I'll pay you through the weekend. Get whatever you need in order. I'd rather you rested and clearheaded. You got clothes?"

"I'll be ready, ma'am."

"Don't call me ma'am."

"Boss lady?"

She smiled, which was a relief. "Sure."

When they were done with the paperwork, he asked her to show him to the bathroom. Darnell waited long enough for her heel clicks to disappear down the hall before slowly turning the lock.

"You got a job, you son of a bitch," he said into the mirror. At some point during his interview, he'd broken into a sweat. Joy likely still withheld judgment on Darnell's sobriety, and this look wasn't helping. But he was clean—always had been—and he now had ample opportunity to combat any initial suspicions.

And then he felt it. The pressure.

Darnell inspected his wrist over the sink. The dried and curling flap of skin tittered. It reminded him of some unseen creature rummaging through an overturned garbage bin. For the moments before it revealed itself as a possum or a cat, it could be anything the imagination cared to conjure.

Darnell pinched the dead skin and pulled. It came off without pain. He'd uncovered what looked like a black-and-brown mole with rough, scalloped borders. Then, movement. Angled lines bled from the center, erratic in their dance. Antennae? No, too many of them. Legs? They tasted the air.

Darnell clamped his hand over his wrist and pressed it down onto the damp sink.

"Fuck," he said repeatedly. His skin tightened with each utterance of the word. What was that? A parasite? That fucking jail. He took a deep breath and lifted his hand.

A small bundle of legs sprang out of his skin. Darnell flung his arm hard enough to send a bolt of pain from shoulder to elbow. A black-and-brown dot scurried across the bathroom floor into one of the stalls.

What the hell? But Darnell knew the what, if not the why or the how: a spider had just popped itself out of his goddamn wrist.

He gave some attention to the divot left behind in his skin. Dry, hard, and many shades darker than the healthy brown surrounding it.

What. The. Fuck?

Darnell clenched his fists and gritted his teeth as his muscles stretched against themselves. His heart became vocal in his chest. He'd first experienced a panic attack in jail, and at the time thought he was having a damn heart attack. His screams for relief would have earned him a yellow coat if not for the meds. That little pill had helped. Oh, how it helped . . .

He reached in his pocket for the bottle he carried with him and chucked two capsules into his mouth. This experimental medication was different than the fast-acting pill that had squashed his panic attacks in jail. Still, the weight of medicine on his tongue brought some relief. With calm came clarity. He spit one of the capsules back into the bottle. Experimental or not, two could become four and four could become eight. He remembered the yellow-coats, lining up at bedtime for their meds.

He counted himself down. His hands relaxed. The thrum of his own heartbeat was replaced by the sharp drip of faucet water. He slowly moved to bring awareness to every muscle, every pain, every discomfort. The jail psychiatrist had given him that technique only after he'd begged for some alternative to more medicine. He turned from the mirror and leaned against the sink. Calm. Calm was better.

With calm came clarity. Being back on the outside was getting to him. He had to get it together.

And yet, beneath the stall door a tiny pair of eyes caught and reflected the wan light. Darnell stood straight. He vaguely remembered that spiders had many indistinguishable eyes. This standout pair, however, gave the spider a deep, curious look. As if it were trying to figure him out.

Darnell left as fast as he could.

...

"Weed is legal now, you know," Casey said before licking the edge of the cigarette paper and neatly folding it over. He extracted a long, arduous puff from his nicotine vape pen as he finished. Casey was a delicate blunt roller. Darnell suspected he enjoyed the craft more than the high. They sat just outside his apartment building, inviting the world to see.

"Legal for them," Darnell said. "Not for us. Craig caught a drug charge just last week."

"For real?"

"His cell was across from mine. He's up for ten years."

"Must have been more than weed."

"They can still bust you for selling it."

"We got to make money somehow. Good luck getting hired with a record." Casey glanced at him, ashamed, but Darnell pretended like he hadn't heard. Casey didn't owe him anything, even if Darnell had taken the fall for him.

"I might have a job," Darnell said.

"You fucking with me?"

"I'm not fucking with you. Got hired today. You heard of this place called Delaney Street—"

Casey jumped up, indicating that he'd very much heard of it. "Yooo! That place is legit. You get health care and everything." Casey brushed Darnell's shoulder. "Look at you. All employed and shit. We hitting the club tonight? Bottle service?"

"Slow down. I haven't gotten paid yet."

"But you're as good as paid. Live a little."

" 'Don't count it until it's in your hand.' "

"Your moms used to say that, right?" Casey handed over the half-smoked blunt. "You can count this, though. Three puffs, to celebrate."

Darnell took it, looked at it. Just then a black-and-white turned the corner and slowed. Casey took the blunt, pulled back on it, and let out a large cloud of smoke.

The cop rolled to a stop at the corner. The headlights weren't on.

"You wilin," Darnell said.

"They can't do anything to us," Casey said. Still, they went inside.

Casey lived on the third floor of a walk-up with one of his boy-friends. The burn in Darnell's legs and throat reminded him that he hadn't exercised since before the arrest. The itch in his wrist grew even still, demanding attention above all the rest. He fingered the divot there and thought of those curious, alien eyes.

"You ever been bit?" Darnell said as they entered the apartment.

"By a cop?"

"No, fool. You know, by a spider or some shit."

"Have I ever had a spider bite? You sure you not high?"

"I think I got bit. Bad."

"Let me see." Casey examined the wound with unexpected care. "Looks like an STD."

"On my wrist?"

"I've seen freakier. Doesn't look like a bite, though. It hurt? Looks like it hurts."

"No. It's numb, actually."

"Yeah, go to the doctor. You can go to a doctor, right?"

Casey threw his jacket onto the love seat that was already buried under an assortment of clothes. He had never cared much about straightening up. He kept the place clean, at least, if not easily navigable. Casey cleared an area of the couch of junk mail, inside-out tees, and a bottle opener.

"Of course I can. I was released, I didn't escape."

"Sorry, I'm not up on the rules." Casey looked at him, curious.

"What?"

"So, you fuck the judge or something?"

"What kind of question is that?"

"No parole meeting. No curfew. You didn't even see prison. You were found with a Glock and fentanyl—"

"Both yours."

"And I love you for it. But you already had the first two strikes. They should have sent you away. The prosecutor must have liked you. Or didn't give a fuck. Or . . ."

"Or what?"

"Or you made a deal you don't want to tell me about." Casey was scrolling through his phone, but his eyes watched Darnell. "You didn't sign up for one of them studies, did you?"

That's exactly what he'd done. "I can't talk about it."

"Or what?"

"Or they'll send me back."

Casey feigned looking around. "Who's going to hear you?"

Darnell shrugged. "They said if I talked about the details, they'd know and I'd go back."

"That's fucked up. They should have never passed that law."

"You don't even vote."

"Nigga, I know people who vote. My point stands. Who facing hard time wouldn't become a government guinea pig for freedom? I'm sorry, man."

"Don't be. They gave me some meds, that's it. Don't even have to take them anymore." He almost told him about the injection, but thought better of it. "I just have to stay out of trouble for a year. Then I'm free for life. That is, unless you take me on another of your . . . joy . . . rides . . ."

They both saw it at the same time. The spider was thick-bodied, much more so than the usual spindly-legged dwarfs hiding in bathroom corners or clinging to starved webs on plastic houseplants. The spider stood rooted in the middle of the table. Darnell was once again struck by the unconscionable depth of its gaze. How long had it been there, waiting to be seen?

"Look at that little fucker," his friend said. Thick smoke filled the room. Casey slowly grabbed his sneaker and lifted it high. The spider didn't move.

Darnell snatched the shoe from Casey's hand just as he was bringing it down. Casey stumbled into the table. The spider jumped back an inch, straightened its two front legs, and slapped them against the wood.

Casey whirled around, purple in the face. He reached for his shoe; Darnell pulled it away.

"Yo! What's good?"

"Nothing. Just . . ." Darnell grabbed an empty red cup and upended it over the spider. Casey stared at him as he slid a magazine under the cup. Darnell opened the front door, went downstairs with his catch, and freed it onto the curb. The spider chittered about, disoriented, and then faced him.

"Shoo!" Darnell said.

To his surprise, the spider immediately obeyed. It scurried into the grass. Beyond, the black-and-white was still parked across the street. Only now its headlights were on.

Casey was waiting for him inside, eyebrows raised in inquiry.

"Life is short," Darnell said.

"Okay, Captain Planet. I got to go, life being short and all. You trying to roll?"

"Nah. I got stuff to do. Get ready for Monday."

"Ole working-ass negro. You need clothes?"

"I'd look like a cancer patient wearing your clothes."

"Better than a convict. Hey, man. Thank you."

"Stop—"

"No, I mean it. I know we grew up with that 'snitches get stitches' shit, but I never expected it. Every nigga on this block would have ratted me out in a heartbeat. But you—"

"Get out of here with that shit."

"No, for real. That's ride or die shit, right there. And if you want me to love spiders, I will. I'll fuck the shit out of some spiders for you, man."

...

Ashleigh was asleep when he got home. Thank God for that. The hearings, the trips to the jail, the separation from their daughter, and the endless conversations with her disapproving family had all taken their toll. Only she knew the full details of Darnell's arrest, how Casey had run from the stopped car and Darnell had followed. He often wondered which would be worse: her family seeing him as a gun-wielding drug dealer or as a simp dumb enough to sacrifice it all for a friend whose stubbornness would likely land him in prison anyway.

Darnell showered and fought the urge to finish quickly. He wasn't locked up anymore. This was his time. He could enjoy the water for as long as he wanted, safely. Anxiety passed. His fisted hands relaxed. He let the warm water fall over him. The conditioned relief upon finishing pushed out any joy of success. Still, progress.

He left the bathroom slowly and maneuvered around creaky floorboards and tightly tucked sheets as he made his way into bed. An elusive sleep danced around thoughts of starting the new job, his record, and the black-and-white slowly rolling by as a reminder that freedom was a bastardly, borrowed thing. When sleep finally settled to bestow mercy over his battered mind, a burning itch in his wrist sent it away.

Prickles, up his arm.

Darnell sat up.

"Babe?" he said to the dark. Ashleigh didn't stir; her breath remained heavy. Who, then, was watching him? He waited for the sensation to pass. It only grew.

He shone his phone's light into the corner between the television stand and the wall. In a world of shadows, a tiny hole in the dark stood out.

A piece of lint?

Darnell slid his legs over the side of the bed, stood, and advanced in a half crouch. He just needed to be sure. Jail had taught him that small reassurances went a long way.

It wasn't lint. The spider was back.

The spider had doubled in size since that afternoon. Absurd to think of it as one and the same, yet here it was. Thicker than any house spider, its prickly legs tucked underneath itself in a neat show of etiquette. Darnell saw now the multiple smaller pairs of eyes flanking the main forward-facing duo. They added to the illusion of introspection.

Curiosity took over. Darnell knelt and touched one finger to the floor a few feet away. The spider shuttled toward him, stopped, and tapped the floor with what looked like a pair of dwarf frontmost legs. Without reason, Darnell tapped the wood with his own knuckle, twice. The spider continued forward, cautious but resolved, and climbed up and onto Darnell's palm. It stopped just before his wrist. It looked up, as if for permission.

Crazy? One way or the other. Darnell gave the slightest nod.

His wrist hairs bent under the spider's weight as it advanced. It tapped the divot; twin firecrackers resonated up Darnell's arm. The spider tilted up toward him, apparently satisfied at this response, and then backed into the hole. Darnell gasped as the flesh dilated to receive it. Soon only the fine hairs of its front legs extended past the opening.

Darnell kneeled there for some time, not caring about the acid building in his legs, before returning to bed. This was not normal; he housed a living spider in his wrist, like a damn kangaroo. But with his itch gone, sleep's alluring dance returned to focus. Any attempts to reason out what had just occurred devolved to meaningless word fragments. He floated down into darkness, welcomed the dance, and, finally, slept.

...

Darnell wore a tight, high collar to cover his few neck tattoos for his first shift at Delaney. Though the cheap cotton irritated the skin there from the moment he put it on, it became second to first-day jitters by the time he settled into the back of the bus.

As his mind predicted all the things that could go wrong that day, his finger went to his wrist. The divot was smooth now, cold, and numb. The spider hadn't stirred all morning, further suggesting that this was all in his head. He looked to his wrist for possible confirmation of this and sat up. This was new. The area had scabbed over. He looked closer, and quickly saw his mistake. While a scab was rough and dull in its transition back to skin, this smooth covering caught the light of the bus. Underneath, if he kept a still eye, movement. He sensed the motion, too, but not through his wrist; that was still numb.

Darnell started. Shit. Just his phone. He pulled it out and read the text from Ashleigh.

Missed you this morning.

Didn't want to wake you, he texted. Still getting Kaylee from your mom's today?

That's the plan. You good with it?

Of course. She into dolls?

She's a superhero girl. But don't stress about it. Worry about work. Love you. Glad you're home.

His stop. He pulled down his sleeve and got off. Whatever was happening with his wrist, he needed this job. Ashleigh's coding consultant contract with a gaming start-up provided good money and flexible hours; she assured him they were fine on finances. But Darnell knew his court proceedings had run up their credit cards. And he had no intention of making her work harder than she already had to support him.

The day started smoothly. The customers proved to be respectful, his colleagues supportive, and Joy proud of what she'd helped create.

The first hour he checked his wrist constantly; by midmorning he fell into a rhythm that felt a lot like content.

The itch from his shirt collar returned while he was picking up a young couple's order, halfway through his shift. It deepened to a throbbing pressure at the base of his throat. Attempts to clear it as he crossed over to table nine only made it worse. When he relieved his hand of one of the plates—the eggs Benedict—he quickly forced a finger below his collar.

A pop; felt, not heard. The itch erupted. Pressure spread into his face, threatening to expel his eyes from his sockets and cut off his air. And then . . . a release in his throat. A tickle tumbled down his shoulder and arm.

Fuck. Another one. He knew it right away.

He offloaded the second dish, forced a smile for the couple's benefit, and was about to retreat back to the kitchen when the man stopped him.

"Wrong," he said from under a faded baseball cap. Though he wore an ill-fitting hoodie, his watch and demeanor gave away his wealth.

"Sir?" Darnell said.

"Eggs Benedict's hers. I ordered the steak."

"Oh. My, uh, my apologies."

"And there's a lot of flies in here."

"We're working on it, sir."

Darnell switched the plates. The man watched his movements. His partner nudged him.

"So, what type of stuff you guys get busted for?"

"John . . . ," the woman said.

"What? It's a reasonable question. It's an interesting gimmick."

Darnell's forced smile was getting harder to find. He'd been oriented on the different kinds of customers. Most were respectful, if not a little voyeuristic. Others seemed to venture in out of offended curiosity.

"I killed a nontipping customer. This is my chance to set things right."

Darnell didn't wait to see the response. He returned to the kitchen and found an empty corner. He shook out his sleeves, untucked his shirt, anything to find the little—

"Hey, Fresh Out." Joy leaned into the kitchen. The label was without malice. "You got table nine? They're looking for you."

Darnell sprang up, fixing himself. "What they say?"

"Relax." Behind the desk, his new boss had been intimidating. Darnell wondered if that whole thing about being an ex-convict herself was just blowing smoke up his ass. Seeing her now, her hair pulled back in a neat bun, accentuating the wearing effects of years of incarceration, a serving tray balanced on one hand, he saw with new comfort that she really was one of them. "They probably just want some extra tea."

"He asked what I was in for."

She stepped fully into the kitchen. "I hate those. Want me to deal with him?"

"No, I got it. Hey, where can I find a toy store?"

"You want to buy him a toy?"

Darnell laughed. "I'm seeing my daughter today for the first time since . . . since too long. I want to get her something."

"I love that. There's a department store just across the street."

The wealthy man vocalized his displeasure as soon as Darnell was in earshot. "The steak's overcooked," he said, his eyebrows raised in expectation. Dissatisfied, he waved Darnell closer. "I want to show you, so you know. See how the pink turns too close to the center? Does the chef use a thermometer?"

"I'm not sure, sir," Darnell said. He didn't give a damn about how the steak was cooked. He did care, however, about the orange-red spot on the edge of the plate, too far removed to be food. It moved.

Darnell reached for the plate. The orange spot disappeared underneath. "I'll relay to the chef."

"Make sure you do. It's important." The man touched his arm. "Also . . ."

"Babe, let it go," his partner said.

"I didn't appreciate your joke."

"It wasn't a joke."

The man released his grip. Darnell was just about to pull away when another spider—all legs—scurried from his shirt cuff and onto the table. It went right under the woman's downcast, embarrassed gaze. She yelled, swiped at the intruder, and knocked the man's coffee into his lap. Darnell reached to help, and laughter erupted from inside of him.

"You think this is funny, fucker?" the man said, standing. He was taller than he looked. The restaurant paused. The man only now seemed to remember the other side of where he was. He averted his gaze to his soiled lap, happy to have his own ruin to focus on. His eyes paused at his sleeve, where something spindly circled the cuff. He yelped and threw the spider off.

"Let's go, okay?" his companion said. Her eyes traced movement up Darnell. He felt something shift between the buttons of his shirt, half-way up his midsection, followed by a faint tinge dragging up toward his neck. "This place is filthy. Let's just go."

By the time Joy came over, the couple was long gone.

"Those the rich folks?" she said. "Man look like he's carrying gold up his ass?"

"They didn't like the service," Darnell said.

"Fuck 'em. Congrats: an asshole on the first day. It's part of the job."

...

The rest of the shift held neither conflict nor spiders. At the end of it, Darnell counted his tips and stepped out into rain. He ran with his jacket pulled over his head and Kaylee's gift stuffed under his arm. He barely made the next Inglewood-bound bus. He still hadn't gotten his license back.

He found a spot at the very back, where nothing could surprise him. His mind replayed the incident at Delaney's. The now unmistakable sensation of something removing itself from him had come quick and easy. As if his flesh worked in anticipation of more.

Darnell unbuttoned his collar, rolled down the sweat-stained rim of fabric, and used his phone's camera to inspect his neck. A glistening black void replaced the tattooed eye of Kaylee's toddler face. The spot didn't leak. It didn't hurt. He undid his shirt further, traced his hand over his collarbone, and found another hole in the meat of his shoulder.

The flesh expanded to receive his finger, like a lover. There was no pain. He pushed in deeper, nearly to the first knuckle, and retracted when he realized he'd hit bone. Nausea doubled him over; he fought the urge to retch.

He remembered the shift of contents inside the jail's experimental syringe and pulled out his phone. He scrolled through the contacts and found the Freedom Rings number. Call here if there are any issues or questions, they'd said.

The phone rang six times before a young woman's voice filled his ears: "Thank you for calling Freedom Rings. We are not in the office right now but will return your call as soon as possible. As a reminder, all studies are confidential and any discussion of details outside of monitored sessions could result in legal action."

He'd first called the number moments after his release, when he was far away enough from Twin Towers to be sure no one would grab him and cite some mistake in his pardon. The message's warning made little sense then. Now, though . . .

Darnell hung up and just barely kept himself from hurling the phone halfway across the bus. That fucking jail. They had done this to him. And for what?

The bus announced his stop. Darnell ran the short distance home— happy for the cold rain to distract him—and took the stairs two at a time up to their third-floor apartment.

He began to unlock the door, then stopped. He counted himself down from ten and rang the doorbell instead.

I wonder who it is? he heard Ashleigh say. A lighter voice followed it and caught Darnell's breath. The sound cleared his mind of spiders and jail.

The door opened. Just inside, Kaylee hung on to her mother's leg. Darnell had seen hundreds of pictures of his daughter in the time he'd been away. Still, the cut of time stung. Her legs were confident in their stance, whereas before they had been thick and wobbly. She held a Marvel action figure in her free hand and eyed him with caution.

"Look who it is!" Ashleigh said. "It's Daddy!"

"Hi," Kaylee said, half her face covered by Captain America's shield.

"You've gotten so big!" Darnell said. "Have you been eating Nana out of house and home?"

Kaylee leaned farther into her mother.

"I got a gift for you." Darnell lowered to his haunches. His daughter had been well taken care of. Her hair was manicured in neat braids, her skin lotioned, her mouth unchapped. All this growth, all this change, had occurred without him. He had been the first to hold her after a thirty-hour home birth both horrific and beautiful. He'd never rolled away from her nightly piercing cries, turned his nose at diaper changes, nor chosen hanging with the boys over his baby daughter—all the responsibilities his own father had skirted.

Now, he was functionally a stranger.

"Go on, it's okay. He's your daddy," Ashleigh said.

The girl took this comfort and stepped forward. She initially smiled at the gift bag, but her face soured and turned as she pulled out the box. She scrutinized the toy through its plastic casing. Darnell's heart sank. What had he been thinking, buying such a thing?

Then Kaylee's face lit up. She opened the box, careful not to tear the packaging even in her excitement. Darnell had been just as meticulous with his own presents as a kid. For a moment it looked like the remote-controlled creature inside was emerging on its own accord. Darnell winced at the pain such size would cause.

She turned the mechanical spider belly up, counted its long, furry black legs, and delighted in how they shifted with gravity.

"What a . . . nice toy," Ashleigh said, her tone drawing his eyes. *A spider?* she mouthed. Darnell shrugged. He picked up the box and inspected it. He hadn't fully registered his purchase until now. Shortly after the incident at Delaney's, he'd spent his break drifting through the nearby department store's toy aisle, checking every itch and displaced hair for signs of the spiders. Turns out, he found one.

"Here, try it out." Darnell switched on the remote control and handed it to Kaylee. Her fingers adapted to the D-pad surprisingly well. A low hum began as the tarantula's legs crawled forward like drumming fingers. The eyes glowed red, a feature Darnell didn't remember seeing on the box. Kaylee giggled as she turned the spider toward Darnell. It lunged forward, its eyes burning a path. The creatures inside of him clenched into balls of fright. The sensation sparked a greater fear. Not because of the mechanical arachnid; it was just a toy, after all. But because he didn't know how many things shifted inside him, only that it was more than three.

...

Kaylee finished her dinner and quickly returned to her new toy while Darnell and Ashleigh watched, amused.

"She ate all her veggies," Ashleigh said. She ran her fingers through her locs, which had doubled in length in the last two years. "Rule is she has to eat them before she can play with her toys. Even then, I'll get a few bites at best."

"What can I say? The girl likes spiders."

Kaylee held on to the spider as her mother changed her into her pajamas, brushed her teeth, and read from her collection of comic books.

"Can I take it to bed?" Kaylee asked. "Please?"

"Yes. But it stays off." Ashleigh leaned into Darnell. "You want to tuck her in?"

"Can I?"

Darnell followed as his daughter yipped in glee and ran to her room. She floated the spider along the wall as she did, the click of its legs sending prickles up Darnell's arms.

Kaylee hugged her new spider through her covers, its legs spanning her little chest. Though Darnell remembered turning it off, the eyes continued to glow. He pulled the Avengers blanket up to her shoulders and stopped. Ice filled his fingers, his toes, and began to spread inward. The spider—the first one—was perched on the back of his hand. Kaylee saw it, too.

While Darnell considered what to do, the spider decided for him. In a quick pump of its legs, it teleported from the back of his hand to the edge of Kaylee's bed, just beyond where the covers began to rise over her. Kaylee propped up on her elbow to watch.

The spider drummed its two front legs, which were thick with fur.

The two main bulbous eyes lent it a chilling awareness. An intelligence. Darnell opened his mouth to reassure his daughter, but there was no need. Kaylee wasn't worried. Not at all. She was fascinated.

"Is it real?" she asked. Her hand crept forward, then retracted, considering.

"What do you think?"

"It looks real."

The spider chittered in his direction, then turned toward his daughter. It waved its straightened frontmost legs up and down, eliciting a giggle. It repeated in rapid succession, then thrust its thorax down in a quick motion. Kaylee offered her open palm. The spider's size became strikingly apparent as it considered the young girl's hand. The spider stepped toward her.

"Stop," Darnell said, only a whisper. Mentally, however, he'd lunged as if to catch a falling glass of water. Whatever interest this thing had in his daughter, he didn't like it.

The spider paused. Darnell grasped hold of that wisping mental connection and pulled. The resulting discomfort was like trying to break out of a dream that kept a paralyzing hold as the real world came back into focus. One of the spider's back legs clicked upward, then the other. It slowly moved backward.

"Are you controlling it?" Kaylee whispered.

Darnell nodded, not trusting himself to speak. The spider didn't like this new relationship; Darnell could feel its resistance. Still, it lifted its hind legs to mount Darnell's open hand. As if in retaliation, the spider sent a load of its sensorium to Darnell in return. He gasped as he felt the warmth of his own skin through it, the beat of his own pulse. The spider was a microcosm of instinct and sensations.

Darnell relinquished his control, his breath heavy. The spider could have used this moment to leap onto his daughter, and Darnell would have been powerless to intercept. Instead, it centered itself on his palm. Kaylee met it at eye level, inspecting its intricacies with innocent fascination. The connection of senses remained open; Darnell recognized the exhaustion of his own lifeblood through its legs.

"What's its name?" Kaylee said.

"It doesn't have one."

"Can we name her Portia?"

"I like that name," Darnell said. And then, before he could vet his words, "Do you want to see something cool?"

Kaylee nodded. A grin took over her face in a way only a child's could.

"You can't tell Mommy, though. It's just for us."

Darnell pulled up his sleeve and curled his fingers to coax the spider—Portia—back toward his wrist. It resisted at first, like a child being called in from play. Darnell flexed his fingers. They both wanted to avoid another mental effort. For now.

Portia turned, paused her cartoonish black eyes over Darnell's, and then approached her birth spot cautiously, as if stalking valuable prey. She prodded the wound with her feelers. His flesh parted to accommodate the matured arachnid.

"Does it hurt?"

Darnell shook his head and hoped his face didn't give away the lie.

"Can I do it?"

"Only grown-ups. If you see Portia or another spider, you tell Daddy, okay? Don't play with them alone. Promise?"

She nodded.

Darnell tucked his daughter back in and handed her the mechanical spider. She wrapped her arms around it, but not as tight as before. Her gaze was off to the side, thinking about something else.

...

Darnell returned to his bedroom with Portia tucked back in her home. There, scented candles sent golden shadows across their bed. Ashleigh sat against the headboard, dressed in her black lace lingerie; the same from their wedding night. She held two glasses of red wine.

"What's this?" Darnell said.

"First day of work, done. I thought—Nell, what's wrong?"

"Nothing, I just, uh . . . it's been so long, you know? Kaylee, she's gotten so big. I can't believe she's into superheroes now."

"And spiders, too, I see." She sat up to pass him his wine; the fabric of her silk shifted over her body. While a lot had changed, some things stayed the same. "You're here now. That's all that matters."

It wasn't that simple. He knew it, and she knew it. After the pain he'd put her and Kaylee through, no one would have blamed her for leaving. Especially her family. Ashleigh's decision to stick by him could not have come without cost. The adolescent joy he remembered had withered to adult worry while he was away. There must have been lonely nights soaked with resentment, anger, and doubt. Him being home couldn't make those feelings magically disappear. Whatever remained, she'd put them aside to allow celebration. But everything has its price. Especially freedom.

Darnell sipped the wine—the first alcohol he'd tasted since his arrest—and followed his wife's gestures to sit on the edge of the bed. She positioned herself behind him and began to massage his neck.

"Relax," she said.

After two years of constant guard, that was easier said than done. Let another inmate or detention officer get close enough to touch, and they were close enough to hurt. The soft hands on him now—the same hands he'd held at the altar all those years before—were safe, though, right? How could he possibly imagine them turning malevolent, imagine them moving around his neck? Tightening until life leaked out of him? Yet the image was there, burrowed deep in his mind like the spider in his wrist.

Her hands paused, just as he was beginning to relax. Her soft touch floated over his neck, abruptly disappeared, and then returned a few inches away. She explored further, down to his shoulder, and found the other numb spot.

"Who hurt you?" she said.

"How do you know I didn't hurt them?"

"Because you're my gentle giant. It looks like someone took a bite—"

He shrugged her off and pulled up his shirt. "It's nothing, alright?"

"Nell," she said. She moved to his side. "It's me. You can tell me anything. I just want to know if I need to go down to the courthouse and beat somebody's ass."

Darnell couldn't help but laugh.

"Because you know I will."

"I know," he said. "That's why I don't tell you. We can't both have a record."

"You don't think they'd hire me at Delaney?"

"You don't want to work there."

"Aw, shit. Bad day?"

Darnell rubbed his wrist; his neck and shoulder throbbed. He told her about the couple, leaving out the part about the spiders. Ashleigh began to kiss his cheek, and Darnell felt words slip away. As she made her way down, she stayed clear of the numb parts; he felt every bit.

"Sounds like they had your back," she said.

"They did. It felt good. This feels good."

Ashleigh's hands went down his shirt. When he remained stiff, she pulled back.

"You don't want to?"

"I do," he said. And he did. But doing so meant a full release. What if she saw one of those things crawl out of him? How would he explain it? He had already asked so much of her; would that be too much?

He turned to receive her lips, which fell over his. They lay back on the bed; she shifted to top him. It took him back to those solitary nights, still chained to the dark recesses of his captivity. He had imagined feeling her again: her lips, her hips, her weight on him. But it had never felt as real as this was now.

"They gave me something," he said as her kisses moved to his chest. "A medication. I think it changed me."

She grabbed him, just firm enough to make him shudder.

"Feels the same to me."

"Not that," he said. "They said it would help with anxiety. I think it just made it worse."

"Hey," she said. "Look at me. Whatever it is, we'll work through it."

It was his turn to kiss her. For a time he forgot about jail, forgot about the spiders, forgot that anything had been different. In the embrace of their intimacy, time had become immaterial. She was slow with him, and patient. He felt silly, like a schoolboy losing his virginity. Embarrassment, insecurity, all these stupid emotions that had no place in his bed, with his own wife. If Ashleigh noticed, she had the grace to pretend she didn't.

After mutual satisfaction, sleep came easily in her arms, which felt like home. But steel bars and intrusive legs pushed into his dreams. Back in his cell, spiders poured from under the bed and through the cracks in the wall. He yelled for help. The guard who came had large, soulless eyes under its cap and hairy feelers that reached through the bars to provide a comfort Darnell didn't want. His wrist, neck, and shoulder all pulsated. He woke in a gasp, breath heavy.

Darnell slid from under Ashleigh's arm, slow, listening for any change in her breathing. For many nights—most nights—over the last two years, sleep hadn't come until his cellmate's breathing had deepened and slowed.

Darnell scooted to the edge of the bed and onto his side. He found his phone under his pillow and turned the flashlight on low. He clenched his fist, concentrated on his wrist, and pushed. Three lazy legs poked through his skin. Darnell continued the effort. The spider emerged in a spray of dead skin and grains of flesh; the hole contracted behind its tenant. He willed the spider forward. It dipped to the side, fell off his wrist onto its back, and scrambled to right itself. It immediately made back for Darnell's wrist, but he stopped it. Mentally.

Easy, easy. Legs tight. Thorax back. Forward. Darnell's lip quivered.

Excited, he pushed again. This time was quicker. A second spider fell from his neck onto the bed beside Portia. It hit the sheets as a tight ball that sprang open to reveal long, spindly legs that dwarfed the pinpoint thorax. It scurried around as if avoiding being stepped on.

Darnell focused; the spider stopped. Its legs paused in a disarray, like a bundle of thick hair. Portia had resisted; this one fought. White flashed in Darnell's vision; he winced from the pressure in his head. When he looked again, the spider was gone, over the side of the bed. Portia tucked her legs into her body and made herself small.

Slow and steady with the third. He sensed the creature awaken, like a part of himself coming into focus. It shifted under his skin. The shoulder muscle spasmed. A minute or so later it was out. The orange, hairless spider circled his arm, deployed a silk anchor, and descended to the bed. It approached Portia. Unlike the eldest spider, this new one's exoskeleton had a plastic sheen to it that caught the light. It led with its frontmost legs, sending them out like walking sticks with careful purpose.

Portia reared up on her own legs in a wide warning. Darnell pushed for calm. Through this mental portal, a wave of alien fear and fury came in exchange. Only through bearing the spider's emotions could he maintain control. Portia stilled as the orange spider inspected her, tapping the pointed end of its legs on hers. Beyond them, the third spider crested the edge of the bed, curious.

Darnell felt the world uniquely through all three of them. For not the first time, and certainly not the last, he wondered how much of himself he'd relinquished to gain freedom. He had a feeling he'd find out soon.

Darnell must have dozed off watching the three of them discover each other. Dull, distant pains in his wrist, shoulder, and neck brought him to the edge of wakefulness, and then fell away. Soon enough, all was calm.

...

There had been nothing "normal" about jail. One couldn't fully adapt to waking up every day in a cage, to having every civil liberty stripped away, every bit of self-dignity challenged. But it became familiar.

In that same way, the spiders became familiar. His body's ability to produce autonomous eight-legged creatures seemingly out of nowhere quickly became a bizarre guarantee.

The itch of impending birth only deepened with scratching. By the time a new arachnid broke free—from his hip, the fatty area above his knee, his ankle, and several from the meat of his buttocks—the area around an eruption was usually raw with blood from Darnell's nails.

His experience with the three that night—Portia, in particular— gave him confidence of at least some control. Maybe he couldn't stop what was happening to him, but at least he didn't have to stand aside and watch. He practiced during his bus rides. Portia, the most obedient, he trusted to roam most of the commute. A section of his mind became increasingly tuned to experiencing the crosstown bus and all of its giant passengers through her senses while the rest of him worked on coaxing the others to his will.

Every connection with Portia left him wanting more. There was a primitive but potent thrill in how she saw the world. One morning he tuned in fully as she stalked a small orb-weaving spider that had nested between a chair and the window. Portia had taken position to drop death from above when a new passenger's long braids blocked her trajectory. She promptly changed course, crawled down the black lining between windows, and approached the web unseen. She tapped the web's silk anchors with the skill of a seasoned pianist, drawing the spider over for what it thought to be helpless prey. Portia had eaten well, and when Darnell snapped into focus to see the bus pulling away from his stop, he realized his own mouth watered. Even after running a mile to his shift, even as he took the first order of the day, he still felt the thrill of the hunt.

She enraptured him at work, too. More than once he asked a customer to repeat themselves because Portia had spotted some unsuspecting fly gorging itself on a dropped morsel. She was a patient stalker; her prey was alerted to her presence only after feeling her embrace.

With time Darnell felt comfortable letting more of the spiders roam and letting his mind roam with them. Most wove intricate webs in Delaney's many corners. He quickly learned to recognize floods of excitement not as unannounced panic attacks but as the vibrations of a successful catch. Likewise, he familiarized himself with the more intense alarm of human interference. He became a frequent volunteer to clear out a web, or to "take care" of a spider spotted by a customer or coworker.

Like a song stuck in his head, the spiders stayed with him always, their ubiquity felt most in his dreams. The worst nightmare put him in the throes of labor, with no appreciation of his incongruent anatomy or the fantastical dream setting. He shifted from the excitement of becoming a parent to the horrible knowledge that he was giving birth to something not human. A couple of monstrous legs, their fur dripping amniotic fluid, curled up from under his hospital gown and toward him—

Kaylee pulled him sharply out of his nightmare with an innocent knee to the stomach.

"Can we do it, Dad? You promised!"

"Not so loud," he said, suppressing the fear and pain encasing languid confusion. Kaylee's energetic joy alone told him he was safe, for now. Morning rays broke through the blinds and lit her braids brown. "You'll wake your mother. What did I promise again?"

He lay back and clenched his stomach against the roving pain that felt out of proportion to any trauma a four-year-old could inflict.

"Portia, Dad." To her credit, she whispered, albeit fiercely. " 'Spider King.' Our game. You said in the morning. Daaaaad!"

He remembered. Displays of emergence and obedience—mostly with Portia—had become part of their nightly father-daughter routine. Last night he'd been exhausted from a double shift at Delaney and promised to do it in the morning. Kaylee began to beg again.

"Kaylee, honey," Ashleigh said. Her locs half covered her face. "Let your dad sleep."

"But he promised—"

"Okay, I'm up, I'm up," Darnell said. Ashleigh's smile drifted back into slumber. To Kaylee's delight, Darnell rolled out of bed and followed her to her room. "We can play Spider King."

Whether it was the dream, the close call with Ashleigh, or the knot in his stomach, Darnell couldn't sit still during the ride into work that morning. He tried to set his mind on something he knew: facilitating a new birth. So far he'd met a total of nine spiders—two of which absconded from his pant leg shortly after emerging, never to be seen again—and number ten was proving the most timid. He had nearly conquered whatever was inside the uniquely uncomfortable cyst under his left middle finger's knuckle when the knot in his stomach burst lightning. The morning was cloudy and damp; the sudden pain forced out a puff of frost across the bus's window. Something shifted in his belly, threatening ruin to his pants. He remembered his dream: this was another one.

He reeled in his bicameral focus from the unborn knuckle spider and Portia—who had been plotting on a roach crawling along the rim of a sleeping man's hat—and demanded control over his midsection. The pain intensified; he broke into a cold sweat. He gritted his teeth to snuff out any sound that would bring unwanted attention. Something popped loose in his stomach. The relief was physical, its implications horrifying. Across the aisle, Portia paused halfway up her silk line anchored to the bus's ceiling. The writhing cockroach she held escaped in this moment of distraction. The cyst on his knuckle burst in a silent spray and many little spiders, each the size of a period in a book, circled his finger and dispersed over his hand. None of this mattered to Darnell. He pulled up his shirt.

"Fuck me," he said. All at once he remembered a passing moment a few days prior, while he was sitting with Kaylee, helping her put a Spider-Man puzzle together. A pang in his stomach had threatened to end their peaceful time. He had immediately and forcefully silenced the awakening of whatever new thing his body had conjured. The relief had been like suppressing a strong urge to defecate, and he quickly forgot about it.

Now it was back, swollen in constipation, a thing larger than Darnell could realistically birth. It visibly pushed outward against his navel. Flesh parted as the first thick, navy-blue leg tasted the world. It was as long as his middle finger and half the width.

Darnell pulled his shirt down. The leg scratched against the cloth, unhappy at this new barrier. The bulk of the emerging spider continued to persist against his flesh. He counted himself down, quicker than should have been beneficial. The spider was coming, he couldn't help that, but letting it go at its own frantic pace meant sure maiming, or worse.

The leg stopped scratching. It retreated back into his stomach. Darnell imagined an abdomen and thorax thick with age, imagined the many legs tucked inside the body. The form shifted so that its smallest part faced a dot of light in the dark. Forward. Too fast, too big. The spider was eager to be free not only of this space but of the mind violating its autonomy. There was no reversing; Darnell risked losing control if he did that. Forward, slow, controlled. His skin and sinew stretched to accommodate. The first half was free; excitement welled. Slow still, not too eager, the largest part was next.

"End of the line, kid."

Two things happened simultaneously. Darnell opened his eyes to the bus driver standing halfway up the aisle, and the spider freed itself of his flesh and mind. Under the cover of his shirt, it scaled his body, around to his back, leaving wet trails with heavy legs.

"I said, end of the line. Everyone off."

The driver's firm expression demanded serious attention. The bus's engine was off; they were the only human souls aboard. Out the window, other resting buses lined the parking lot.

"I missed my stop. Any chance I could . . ."

She was already shaking her head. A hard "no."

"Are the police on their way?" Darnell said.

"Maybe. If you leave now, there shouldn't be a problem."

"I'm getting off. Just fell asleep, that's all."

The driver knew this was bullshit. But she wasn't about to dispute it, as long as he did as he said and left without any trouble.

Darnell leaned forward, ran his hands over his face, and rose slowly, as if drunk. The bus driver watched him closely while keeping her distance. When Darnell felt Portia's light legs on his skin and her body slip back into his wrist, he straightened with sobriety and exited. According to his phone, Delaney was two miles away. He began to jog. Judging by the way the newest spider gripped into his back—he could feel every leg—it didn't like the running. Connection with the newcomer was weak, but its panic was enough to push Darnell to run faster. The spider's legs progressively dug into his back before suddenly dislodging itself and circling around to Darnell's belly. He tried to stop it from entering, but it was too late. The day turned a sick, red hue and tilted on its axis. Black clouded his periphery. He hit the stale dirt of an untended yard shoulder first. It jostled him back to full awareness. He sprang up as if by a string and ran faster.

Darnell paused just outside Delaney. Sweat ran down his face and wet his already dirt-streaked uniform. Through the window, Joy took an order from a table—his table. Fuck. Her customers considered their menu. Seeing a chance, he slipped into the restaurant and bee-lined it to the public bathroom.

He closed himself in an empty stall, wiped his face with his sleeve, and began a text to his boss. Bus broke down! Jumping in an Uber and will be there as fast as I can!

Darnell hesitated. A better solution didn't present itself. He could always leave through the back and resign, tell her it just wasn't working out, save them both the embarrassment.

Then what? Who else would take him? And what would he tell Ashleigh? The spiders made me late, so I quit?

He pressed send and exited the stall. He wiped his face again, this time with a towel, and raked his hair with overgrown fingernails.

Darnell grabbed an apron from the kitchen to cover most of the dirt stains. He'd just finished adjusting it as Joy nearly hurried past him before stopping in a double take. She gestured with her phone. "You're here. I just got your text."

"Weird. I sent it over an hour ago. Really sorry for being late. Bus broke down and the Uber got lost. I saw you got my table. I can take over, tips go to you."

She studied him. Her eyes went to his arms; in his hurry, he'd forgotten to roll down his sleeves. His collar was also unbuttoned. There was no use covering up the many scars now. Doing so would just further cement him in guilt.

"Everyone needs something," Joy said. "Some needs are predictable, some are not. Some are easy to relate to, others not so much."

"Boss?" Darnell said.

"If you're not getting what you need here, we can work it out. But only if you tell me, okay?"

"Everything's good," he said. "I won't be late again."

She nodded. "Don't worry about table nine. I get a 'I don't believe in tipping' vibe from them anyway."

The spiders stayed quiet the rest of that day. Darnell spent his lunch break crouched behind a recycling bin in the alley. It took nearly the full hour to coax out the newcomer. Flecks of dried blood fell from its legs as it oriented itself in Darnell's palms. The spider had already nearly outgrown his hands. Its abdomen and thorax were substantial. The shiny fur shifted from a light blue to a neon green as it moved.

The legs lacked this effect but impressed with their own deep blue checkered with silver. He watched the spider take its first independent steps. The sensual feed from it was faint, barely there, not like the others. At the end of his break Darnell called the spider back inside. It didn't move; it wasn't bothered.

Darnell tried again. Connecting with the others was like moving his own arm or leg, any difficulty akin to a limb that had fallen asleep. Now he felt as if he were trying to lift a rock with his mind. He nudged the spider with his fingers, harder than he meant. The spider reared up and hissed, a sound like air escaping from a can. Its fangs unfurled from under its feelers; drops of venom accentuated each.

Fear; all his own. Not of those fangs, which were substantial, but of the complete lack of control. Only with this understanding did the spider step off Darnell's palms and begin to ascend his forearms. He lifted his shirt so it could step onto his belly. The spider paused, then entered its burrow on its own accord, as if to say: I'm complying. This time.

...

Over the next week, Darnell's control over most of his cluster strengthened. He continued to practice on the bus and used his phone's alarm to keep him from missing any more stops. He became a punctual employee once again. Joy's observant eyes eventually fell off him, and Darnell felt the beginnings of trust.

The ability to suppress a new birth came in most handy during working hours. He strategically saved this power for particularly exposed moments, like handling food or taking a customer's order. The mental fortitude such a feat required left him vulnerable the rest of the day, allowing his cluster to come and go freely. Some tested boundaries more than others. Darnell watched helplessly as one chittered around the base of an unsuspecting customer's soup, and almost had a heart attack as another ziplined from one table's edge to another in an attempt at a web.

The spiders became skilled in dodging human eyes. They were uniquely crafted, a sight one expected to see on the Discovery channel, not in an American restaurant. They were also light and quick of leg, and any sighting was never more than a fleeting glance. Darnell witnessed some of these moments himself. A customer would pause mid-order. Their eyes would shift to something in Darnell's background, something that elicited an instinctual fear. Some acted unfazed, while others seemed to lose their appetite.

Ironically, the few days when none of the spiders emerged proved to be the hardest. There was something about having those eyes out there, watching over him. It eased his mind better than any pill. Without them to worry over, his mind let in old foes. A customer walking too closely behind him, a black-and-white slowing down outside, the fear of going back behind bars.

Darnell took more and more of his breaks in the dingy alley behind Delaney. While his coworkers used this time to feed the nicotine addiction they'd picked up in jail, he repurposed the recycling bin as a desk and sketched pictures of his new companions from memory. He drew Portia the most, with her keen, doll-like eyes and reserved demeanor. Another was jet black with a thick, rectangular body and legs thick with branching hairs. The largest one—he called her Charlotte—offered the most detail to work with, though she hardly ever stayed still long enough for proper inspection. She spent the most time of all his spiders out in the wild, but always returned. He only drew the all-legs spider once, as it was the most unpleasant to watch emerge. Its legs sprouted out of his skin like some terrible parasitic weed.

One night while Ashleigh was working late on a new game launch and Darnell was making dinner, Kaylee's sobs drifted into the kitchen and lifted above the pop of grease. He found her in her room, balling up a paper in apparent frustration. A few of his drawings lay nearby.

"Hey, what's going on?" he said, sitting beside her.

"I can't do it like you," she said.

Darnell unballed her attempt. Her ovals weren't as even as his, and the legs were all bunched together rather than spread evenly apart over the spider's body, but it was better than anything he would expect from a four-year-old. She thrust the crayon into Darnell's hand. "You finish it."

"I like yours," he said. He pointed to the red streaks that she had put on its body. "This part is so cool. It's Portia, right?"

She nodded.

"This one is all wrinkled," he said. "You want to help me make a new one?"

He summoned Portia, who was a little sleepy but otherwise happy to oblige. She stalked a daddy long-legs in the corner while Darnell sketched and Kaylee colored.

"What kind of spider is she?" Kaylee said as she added the finishing touches—lightning bolts coming out of the spider's eyes—to their art.

"Portia spider," Darnell said.

"No, Dad, not her name! What kind is she?"

"I don't know," Darnell said, and realized he didn't know what kind any of his spiders were. "Want me to find out?"

Later that night, after Ashleigh had fallen asleep ten minutes into a movie she'd let him pick, he searched the web for an enthusiast forum, registered, and started a thread with the subject Anyone know the species? After a half hour or so someone responded to his description with Got any pics, dude? He yawned, snapped a picture of Portia, and uploaded it. He reloaded the page a few times before falling asleep himself.

The thread was forgotten until well into his shift the next day. Some self-claimed arachnologist had emailed him, asking if his photo was the real deal. If so, they wanted to connect because he may have found a new species of spider. Darnell almost dropped the phone. He put in his tables' orders, ducked into the employee bathroom, and went to his thread. Thirty replies. There had been a substantial argument over the identification. Finally, the consensus was that either this was a completely new species, or the original poster was both adept at Photoshop and full of shit. What's more, his hand was in the picture with the marks on his wrist and knuckles. Any average internet-goer wouldn't think much of it, but if the right person saw it . . .

Shit. How could he have been so careless? Could this be considered a violation of his hush-hush agreement? Suddenly, he felt watched. He peeked out into the hallway, just enough to assure himself he was alone. No one from Freedom Rings had contacted him. No one had checked in on him. Which meant they knew exactly how he was doing. And if they were that close, would they know of this blunder?

He closed the door, locked it, and spent the next hour deleting his post and his profile and searching the internet to see if his photo had made it anywhere else. It hadn't. He was vaguely aware of his cluster entering under the door and returning to their homes. Their bodies vibrated with nervous energy.

Somebody knocked.

"Just a minute." He nearly yelled it.

"It's Joy. You okay in there?"

"Yes! Sorry, I'm just—coming right out!"

He stepped out into the hallway. Joy raised her eyebrows in surprise. Hopefully showing himself quickly squashed any presumptions of paraphernalia laid out on the bathroom counter.

"I didn't mean to rush," she said. "You need someone to cover you?"

"No, no, I'm fine. Just lost track of time. I'm good."

He kept his phone close for the next couple of days, startling at any message or call. He kept the spiders even closer. That email unsettled him. What if one of them was caught? What if someone took interest in an exotic new species found in the middle of Los Angeles? His eyes wandered to Delaney's front door whenever it opened, expecting to see men in uniform coming to lock him back up.

Charlotte was the only one that didn't fall in line. Just the opposite, she began to stay out for days at a time. He found himself hoping she had been eaten by a cat, or squished under someone's shoe. But no matter how long she was gone, she eventually returned. Not to enter him—she'd quickly become too large for that—but perhaps to just let him know she still existed, that she was still something to worry about. Worst of all, she began to leave presents. One morning, close to opening, Darnell found a dead mouse under a booth he serviced. The meat had been sucked from the poor animal; only skin and bones and teeth remained. He'd cleaned it up quickly, before anyone else could see.

As with all things, time took the edge off. The forum called to him. They had responded so quickly. And was it true? Was Portia a new species? What about the rest of them? He went back onto the site, started a new alias under SpiderPencil, and made sure to use a fake email this time.

He uploaded his and his daughter's drawings to spark debate over identification. The speed and abundance of replies caused his hobby to spill over into work. He constantly refreshed the page on his phone, drawing ire from customers and coworkers alike who assumed he was on social media. The small but vibrant community of arachnid enthusiasts delighted in his drawings, which resulted in rich, detailed discussion about species. None resulted in consensus. The thorax, for example, most aligned with this species, while the length and shape of the legs fit another entirely. Someone commented under a drawing of Portia that it looked a lot like the forged picture posted some weeks before. Thankfully, the comment didn't catch on. Most praised him for his creativity. They confirmed that what he was experiencing was something new.

...

Some weeks passed, and things fell into rhythm again. No one had come through the door of Delaney's looking for him, and his control over most of his cluster had become second nature. He continued to hold them close and limited their hunting to Delaney's and his apartment. He hadn't given in to letting them out on the bus again yet. The risk of being spotted was too real.

Just before his punctuality started to decline again, Joy made a fleeting comment that made Darnell realize how hunger had crept into his daily discomforts.

"Don't forget to eat," she'd said toward the end of one of his shifts.

He had lost some pounds, which likely struck Joy as particularly odd. Usually ex-convicts gained weight with freedom. Darnell's own cousin had gone from being stick-thin to a butterball in just the few months after his five-year stint in prison.

Darnell's own appetite had certainly increased. But that was the thing: no matter how much he ate, when was the last time he felt satiated?

He woke ahead of the sun from a twilight dream the next morning, Joy's words still echoing in his mind. What's more, a dull, hungry ache sat in his stomach. His hand went to his navel; Charlotte's hole had nearly closed, but would never fully heal.

Darnell slipped out of the sheets, careful not to tug at the end wrapped around Ashleigh, and went into the kitchen. The cabinets were well stocked. Cereals, pancake powders, rice cakes. Most important: ample sugar, flour, and honey. He bent a blind to peer out the window. Still dark with only the beginnings of morning spreading over the horizon. He got to work.

Some hours later, footsteps, the creak of their bedroom door, light giggles, and Ashleigh's half-asleep response.

"Nell?" came floating out of the room.

"In the kitchen. Take your time!"

Ashleigh rubbed her eyes with one hand and hugged a yawning Kaylee with the other. She blinked at him, bemused, and then shifted focus to the kitchen.

"Whoa, babe, what's the occasion?"

"Pancakes!" Kaylee yelled.

"Lots of pancakes," Ashleigh said. She plucked the empty bag of flour from the top of the overflowing trash. "Who's going to eat all this?"

"It's a breakfast feast." Darnell tore off a corner of a pancake he'd just added to the finished stack and dipped it in syrup. "I was hungry. Thought I'd make us all something."

His wife and daughter enjoyed the breakfast. Darnell had started nibbling while cooking and went back for another serving when his family threw away their plates.

Ashleigh did little to hide her concern but said nothing. Kaylee came over and gave him a hug.

"Thanks for breakfast, Daddy! You're not chopped!"

"She's been watching some TV," Ashleigh said.

"Anytime, sweetie. You like my famous recipe?" He smiled, and she smiled back. Then she cocked her head to the side in that curious manner of a child.

"What happened to your face?" she said.

"What happened to *your* face?" Darnell said.

"No, I see it, too," Ashleigh said. "You're breaking out. Bad."

Darnell's hand went to his left cheek. There, above his cheekbone, the flesh was solid and numb. No itch. He pressed the area, cautious.

"Must be the weather," he said. And then, to Kaylee, "Or perhaps I'm . . . turning into a fly!"

"Portia will eat you!"

"Who's Portia?" Ashleigh said.

"Her spider. King of the Spiders, actually. And you tell Ms. Portia King Spider she can't eat me." And then, to his wife, "How bad is it? Should I cover it up for work?"

"Maybe just some cream. You working the late shift tonight?"

"No, why?"

"It's just, usually you'd be gone by now."

Darnell paused mid-chew and turned to the window. The morning sun had taken its place high in the sky. He yanked up his phone.

"Shit. Shit shit shit."

"Language! Relax, Nell. You're a hard worker. They know that."

The angst of tardiness got Darnell dressed and to the bus stop in just a few minutes. Once on board, hunger quickly resettled. Breakfast had done nothing to satiate him. Though Darnell's belly was engorged to the point of nausea, he still hungered. Every little spider pod was like a heartbeat. He felt the new one on his face the most. His face . . . that felt sacred. What other areas had he assumed were safe but really weren't?

Well before his stop, Portia and the others—at least a dozen now, each easily distinguishable—awoke all at once. While he was still pondering what he was going to do about his face, they took him off guard and poured out under his work clothes, scurried frantically to find light, and crawled off the bus. A man with headphones stared at him, his expression twisted into *What the fuck?*

Darnell didn't want to see this play out. He got off with the spiders.

"Hey," he called, looking around. They were still in Inglewood, a section ripe with gentrification. "Hey!"

One of the younger ones was slow but confident in its path. Darnell followed. The size of a pea, this new spider was a brownish red and without mark. Its hairless legs spread out wide as it navigated the cracked concrete and turned onto a walkway leading to someone's porch. Darnell felt the presence of the spider's siblings. Metal touched his tongue. The air stank of sour decay. His teeth ached with the pull of adrenaline. His fists clenched in a primitive reflex to grip and grasp at . . . at what?

Darnell opened the waist-high gate and approached the quaint two-story house. Finally, he saw, though sight at this point was only supplementary. The young brown spider ascended the rotting stairs, scaled the porch's column, and joined its older siblings on a long, exhausted strip of wax paper. The fly catcher curled under the weight of its victims. Some of the doomed insects still moved and quivered. The spiders—his spiders—were feeding.

Darnell stepped forward, dimly aware that his mouth had begun to water.

He saw what had drawn his curiosity all too late. A wasp freed itself from the wax and stung him on the left side of his face, right above the cheekbone. The already swollen area filled with an immense pain that peaked in seconds and culminated in a burst and spray of organic material. Something different fell onto the grass. It writhed as Darnell clutched his torn face. The creature's drying wings caught the air, and it took flight. Its abdomen was thick with red-and-blue-striped fur, its many legs hanging off its body like weeping willow branches.

Darnell snatched up the wax paper, stuffed it in his workbag, spiders and all, and went to find a pharmacy.

...

Joy waited for him outside Delaney's staff entrance. Darnell was a full three hours late. She gasped at the site of his bandaged face, composed herself, and invited him into her office. He had no rebuttals, no apologies. He'd thought of many excuses on the bus ride in, but none of the lies seemed worth telling.

"I like you, Darnell," she began.

"I like you, too, Boss Lady."

This got a smile, but not the reassuring kind he'd come to look for.

"The staff likes you, and I've seen you with the customers. You work hard and are honest."

"I feel like this is where I would normally say 'Thank you.' But there's a 'but' coming."

"But . . . when you're here. Not just physically. It's becoming increasingly clear to me and others that you're preoccupied with other things."

"I'm fired?" Darnell said.

She blinked at his frankness, then recovered. "We don't fire people. We give them 'opportunities.' Your spot will be here. After you take the 'opportunity' to work on yourself." She handed him a list of rehab centers.

Darnell flipped the one-sided resource over, numb. Then he began to laugh. "This won't help," he said.

She started to reply, but nothing got through his laughter.

"I get it. I get it. You think I'm a junkie. Why wouldn't you? I'm late, distracted, always itching. I mean, look at my fucking face. But I'm not. I swear to you, I'm not."

"The time out in the alley?"

He laughed harder and pulled out his phone. "You know what I'm doing in the alley? Drawing. See, look."

"I know the signs." Her eyes, full of pity, flitted to his arms.

"These marks?" He pulled up his sleeve. Faint, swollen lines connected the three exit wounds on his forearm. He stuck his bandaged cheek forward. "You think I'd do this to myself? You think this is, what? Heroin? Meth? Okay, can either of them do this?"

Darnell put both fists on Joy's table, wrist-up. He gritted his teeth and pushed. Weak veins pushed over wire-thin muscle.

"Come on, come on, comeoncomeon." He sat back, defeated. "I need this job. Please."

She drummed her fingers on the desk. She was considering him. For a moment he thought she might give him another chance. Then her face hardened. She sat up, steadied her hands. "And it's yours to have. After you work on yourself first."

"I don't know how," he said, more to himself than to her.

Joy straightened the resource sheet and pushed it toward him. "Prison changes everyone it touches. Everyone. But it doesn't have to define us. You'll be back. I know you will. And we'll be waiting for you."

He thanked her and left. Joy was wrong about the cause, but she was right about him. He did need to focus. He had changed since jail. The question was, how much?

···

Darnell entered every Downtown Culver City restaurant or bar along the long walk home. The horrified looks he received relayed a clear reticence to have him as a customer, much less an employee. He wondered what it was, cycling through hypotheses of prejudice, class bias, racism, and disdain. The more he walked, receiving the same responses in Black-owned venues in Inglewood, he realized the truth of it.

The jail had marked him in a way people couldn't identify. It would have been better to have a thousand spiders canvassing his body; at least then people would know what to make of him. As it was, he represented unrecognizable unease, one that pulled at each person's own unique fears.

Defeated, he called an old friend, one he knew would always be there.

"D! I thought you lost my number."

"I been trying to get myself straight."

"Don't I know it." Casey laughed. Darnell could hear the smoke in his voice. "What's good?"

"I need a favor."

···

It was well into the night when Darnell came into the apartment. He'd texted Ashleigh that he'd picked up a late shift, and now she and Kaylee were sound asleep.

He sat in the dim kitchen and scrolled aimlessly through his phone. He found himself searching the web on recidivism rates and predictors. Somehow, he came upon a statistic for suicide amongst ex-cons. Killing himself had crossed his mind while he was waiting in jail for a trial that could put him away long enough to miss Kaylee's prom, if not her wedding. Suicide was the only surefire way to achieve freedom. Sitting here now, free but still in chains, he let his mind wander back to that place.

His breath quickened. Heat flushed his face, neck, blurred his vision. A weight crushed his chest; the walls closed in on him. Something terrible was about to happen.

He gripped the kitchen table. He ran to the bathroom and vomited in the sink. He threw open the medicine cabinet, desperate for anything. His fingers found the nearly forgotten pill bottle given to him by the tall man with the baggy suit after the injection. He turned it in his fingers.

Darnell untwisted the childproof cap, tapped out a pill, and frowned. One of them—the one he'd spit out, judging from the faded coloring—had doubled in size. He inspected it. The capsule walls bulged; something shifted inside. He squeezed it. Eager legs, the size of eyelashes, tasted the air through a crack. He squeezed harder. The capsule burst. A hundred spidery parts scattered onto the sink, writhed around as if frying in oil, and skittered out of the light to find shadow.

"What. The fuck." Then, "I fucking knew it."

He'd always suspected that Freedom Rings and their injection had done this to him, somehow. Seeing it with his own eyes, though . . . knowing that they'd kept doing it through these pills they'd pitched as boosters to quell any breakthrough anxiety. Suddenly the world felt small. He looked around. Eyes, on him. Someone had done this to him. Purposefully. Were they watching him now?

Darnell flushed the rest of the pills down the toilet, went out into the kitchen, and opened the oft-forgotten storage closet. He planted his feet and focused all his mental energy. Out! He felt his flesh pull apart and the pain of his once dormant inhabitants springing forth in violent protest. Darnell persisted. Blood trailed down his arms and thighs as more than a dozen spiders scurried down to the floor, adrift in their sudden exile. Portia was the last to leave. The full width of his wrist now, she clung to him even as he flicked his arm. Finally she lost her footing, fell, and stopped midway down. Darnell swiped through her silk anchor. She hit the ground, rolled, and retreated into the shadows. Darnell shut the closet and filled the crack with the kitchen rag.

This done, he backed against the door and slid to the floor. Behind him, a faint chattering made him think that the spiders were searching for a way out. But it was his own teeth. He was shivering all over and ached with tension. As if he'd just run for his life way farther than his body could handle.

He began to cry. Thankful, sorrowful tears.

It was time to take back control.

...

Work with Casey proved both anxiety-inducing and lucrative. As a mid-level heroin dealer, he sold mostly to middle-class millennials who were deceptively functional in their addiction. The transactions Darnell assisted with were sporadic; he worked odd hours. His many wounds had begun to heal, and soon the spiders seemed a distant memory. His anxiety, however, was in full force.

He dreamed of being back in jail nearly every night. He woke in a cold sweat. When he couldn't immediately go back to sleep, he ambled out to the kitchen closet and spent most of the rest of the night fighting with himself not to open it. He could feel them, their helplessness, their incarceration. Like him, they understood little of what was happening to them.

"Can we play Spider King?" Kaylee would ask him, night after night. He closed the book he'd been dozing off to while reading to her. Casey had him working until five that morning. And since Ashleigh thought he still worked at Delaney's, he'd spent the day getting shitty sleep on any bus that would take him.

"Sure," he said. He plucked her mechanical spider from the bottom of her toy chest.

"Not with that, Dad," she said. "With Portia."

"Portia's gone," Darnell said. "Remember? She went back to her family."

"When is she coming back?"

"I don't think she is, honey."

"Well, I think she's coming back." Kaylee played with the toy spider's legs, then put it aside. "And when she does, I'll make her Spider King of the whole world!"

One more week, he thought the next day as he walked up to their apartment after another aimless trip around the city. He'd have enough money to focus on looking for work. Maybe even Delaney would take him back if Joy thought he was clean.

He stopped outside their door to catch some calm. He counted backward from ten, willed his heart to slow. His fingers found his wrist, where Portia had been born. The portal—all of them—had closed.

"That smells good," Darnell said when he entered. Ashleigh and Kaylee were rolling homemade pizza dough. "Are you getting chopped tonight?"

"Daddy, look what I drew!" Kaylee jumped off of her stool, hands white with flour.

"Wash your hands first, sweetie," Ashleigh said. "You'll get powder everywhere."

Kaylee ran her hands under the sink quickly, ran to her room, and came back with a drawing.

"Oh, this is a beauty," Darnell said. He was able to muster joy and pride for his daughter's benefit, but inside he felt the floor of his stomach pull away. The spider took up the whole page. Kaylee had gotten quite good at drawing; she had an eye for detail. The long, thick forelegs tipped with serrated fangs, the twin spinnerets extending from the backside, not visible in any of the smaller spiders. The blue, the silver.

"Charlotte," Darnell said.

"Go in your room while Mommy and Daddy talk," Ashleigh said. The tone of her voice grabbed onto the fear Kaylee's picture had hooked into his stomach and yanked it up into Darnell's throat. Any smile on his wife's face was only for their daughter's benefit. She knew. Fuck, she knew. "I'll tell you when it's ready for the oven. Go on, now."

"When did she draw this?" Darnell said. As casually as he could, he checked the cabinets and looked under the dining room table. Then he saw it. Someone had removed the towel from beneath the storage closet door.

"We need to talk, Nell," Ashleigh said. She leaned against the fridge, her arms folded.

"Oh?"

He opened the door. A dozen dead spiders lay on their backs, their legs curled into their bodies. Darnell instinctively reached for them, as one might at the passing of a loved one's casket at the end of a funeral. He felt nothing. The largest of them was an unmistakable blue and silver, her fangs curling toward her own underbelly. Charlotte had come in here to die with the rest and leave him in peace.

"I have something to show you," he said.

"I went by the restaurant today," she said.

He turned to her. She did know. But not what he'd thought. "Oh."

"To surprise you. You know what the manager asked me?"

"Babe, I have something to show you."

"She asked me how rehab was going. Rehab, Nell?"

"Let me explain."

"I'm listening."

Darnell licked his lips. He'd rid himself of this "experiment" more than a week ago. No one had come for him. No one was watching. He'd gone through this whole fiasco alone, for nothing. "I'm clean now," he said. "It's over."

"So it was drugs? Meth?"

"Hell no. I'd never use that stuff. It wasn't drugs."

"What, then? Gambling? Sex?"

"Only with you."

"That's not funny."

"Something I got when I was in jail," Darnell said. "But I took care of it."

"Took care of what, Nell?"

He swung open the closet door fully, turned on the light, and lowered to his heels. "Come, see for yourself."

She leaned in over him, let out a stifled scream, and retreated into the kitchen.

"What the hell?"

"Come. Please. This is what they did to me in jail. I want you to see." She inched forward, skeptical. "Some injection somehow. And in the pills, too. They're dead."

"All of them?"

"All of them."

He moved aside so she could take his place. She bent over and went for Portia.

"She was the first one. She came out of my wrist, and I didn't know what to do. They told me not to tell anyone."

Ashleigh stood, her face stone. "I'm taking Kaylee to my mom's for a few days."

"Wait, why?"

"I can take you doing a little meth. I can take you needing time to work on yourself. Hell, I can even take you throwing away two years of our life for some bullshit."

"Casey's my boy—," Darnell began, automatically.

"I can't take you lying to my face. Really, Nell? Fake spiders?"

"What? These are the real deal." He moved past her and into the closet. He scooped up Charlotte's body. "See—"

Charlotte was light as paper. He turned it over. Hollow holes circled the thorax like an antique rotary dial. The abdomen had shrunk into a pitiful tail. He picked up another spider, and another. They were all the same. Light. Hollow. Discarded.

"They molted," he said. He looked at his wife. "That fucking jail."

"Whatever, Nell," Ashleigh said. She called for their daughter. "Kaylee! It's time to visit Nana. Help me get your stuff together."

Darnell leaned against the fridge and knocked his head against the door. He hit it hard enough to wince and, when he opened his eyes, he noticed a single spider—the runt he'd followed the morning he got fired—still struggling with its old skin. It freed itself and scurried out of the closet, only now the size of a small mouse. It went into the hallway and toward the back rooms. Curious, Darnell followed.

From the bedroom, Ashleigh screamed.

Darnell broke into a run. When he got there, Ashleigh held Kaylee on her hip as they backed toward the far wall. Their daughter still clung to her drawing paper in one hand and a jumbo pencil in the other. Charlotte—now the size of a cat—reared up with wide legs and hissed as it closed the gap. The spider reached one leg forward. Kaylee screamed as its hairs grazed her own shin.

Darnell ran up to the thing, raised his knee, and brought his foot down with enough force to eviscerate. At least, that's what should have happened. The spider instead jumped sideways, turned in midair, and sank its fangs into Darnell's leg, right above the ankle. White flashed; stars spotted Darnell's vision. He was on the floor. Charlotte reared over him. Fangs the size of a meat fork dripped onto his clothes.

A blur, and suddenly Portia clung to Charlotte's underside. She buried her own hidden fangs into the giant spider; one of Charlotte's legs came clean off. She shook Portia off and stumbled backward.

Before it could recover, Ashleigh brought Kaylee's jumbo pencil down on the spider. The first blow elicited a sickening angry hiss. Charlotte began to rear up, but Ashleigh brought the makeshift dagger back down on its ring of eyes, which smeared together in glistening shards. She stabbed again, and again, and again.

Darnell rose, slow, his head pounding. Blood marked his temple. Around him, he saw that his other spiders were present. They crawled along the frame of Kaylee's bed, hung from the ceiling, and peeked out from inside the hamper. All watching.

"It's okay," Darnell said to Ashleigh and to himself. "We're okay—"

The runt of the group entered the room. Bright red and hairless, it tasted the air with excited feelers. Ashleigh was all maternal instinct. She crushed the late comer under her foot before Darnell could even register what was happening. White flashed and tore his headache open, bringing him down to one knee.

Ashleigh didn't stop. The spiders scattered as she brought down her foot without remorse. A light of Darnell's world flickered and died. Not Portia. He hoped it wasn't Portia.

"Mom, no!" Kaylee said. "Please, stop! They're my friends! Daddy's friends."

But she wouldn't stop. The heel of her shoe found another.

"Stop!" Darnell yelled. He meant to grab Ashleigh, to give her at most a little shake, only enough to get her to listen. But the combination of her forward motion toward her next victim and his mistiming caused her to lose her footing.

She fell headfirst in excruciating detail. Darnell had the fleeting, cogent thought that perhaps this was how Portia saw the world.

Slowed, deliberate. She'd passed on to him her evolutionary gift of time manipulation. Only it did nothing to push Darnell further toward his goal. Instead it cursed him with the perfect clarity of his downfall. All that he'd done to escape from jail, both the one in Twin Towers and the one he'd brought home with him, to regain his family's trust, in this moment, erased.

Ashleigh's shoulder hit the wall. Her yell began in pain and ended in shocked anger. Fear quickly joined as she took in the remaining spiders, which had stopped scurrying and started to reassemble. The spiders were clearly on his side, whatever that meant.

Kaylee rushed over to her mother.

"Babe, I didn't mean . . . ," Darnell began.

Ashleigh stiffened at his approach. She clutched their daughter as if Darnell himself had eight legs.

"Stay away," she said.

"Show her, Dad," Kaylee said.

"Hush, baby," Ashleigh said. "It's okay."

"Show her! Dad, please."

Darnell held his hands up. "It's fine. It's safe."

The spiders crowded around him, a mosaic of flesh colors. Their signals distorted his thoughts. Had he missed them? Yes, he had.

"Dad controls them," Kaylee said, as if it were the simplest explanation in the world. "I told him they'd be back."

"Is this what they did to you?" Ashleigh said. "In jail?"

"I wanted to tell you. I really did."

Ashleigh stood. She inched along the wall, around to the door. Darnell's cluster watched her without threat. "I'll come back for our things tomorrow. I want you—and them—gone by then."

Darnell didn't argue, though his daughter certainly wanted him to. Ashleigh carried her kicking and screaming down the hall. Darnell let them go. The spiders didn't move to stop them, either.

Sometime after the front door slammed and his daughter's wails faded, Darnell went into the bathroom, ran the shower, and stepped in without waiting for it to warm. They followed; he could hear their many legs across the linoleum. He closed his eyes.

They came all at once. Crawling up into him. Agonizing pain as the largest of them squeezed back into their atrophied nooks. Darnell's knees buckled. His right leg shot out at a peculiar angle to catch his fall while his left foot slid on the wet porcelain. The compensating knee cracked, a sound like muffled thunder as the shower beat ice on his back. Scratching at the walls slowed his descent. He planted one palm on the floor of the tub and found the faucet with the other. He rode out the wave in this contortion. Finally, the tendons around his joints relaxed; he tucked his legs underneath him and turned his face up to the spray. When he looked down, flecks of skin circled around the drain.

He cut the water and stepped out. He checked his wrist. Portia's camouflage was so complete that he had to touch it to be sure he hadn't imagined the reunion. The difference in texture was unmistakable. As if in confirmation, the spot of skin-colored exoskeleton shifted under his touch, temporarily revealing the rest of the arachnid underneath. The spot of camouflage shifted back into place.

When he returned to his room, he had a text from Casey. Feeling both whole and desiccated, Darnell got dressed and went to make some money.

...

Darnell paused outside his apartment complex three hours later; the living room light was on. He climbed the stairs, in no rush to see what else awaited him tonight. At this point, after that awful blowup with Ashleigh and narrowly escaping an undercover cop after the deal Casey sent him on turned to shit, he expected anything. Police. Freedom Rings. A million angry spiders. Even Ashleigh coming back was a fleeting possibility. Still, seeing her waiting in their apartment was a surprise.

"Hey," he said. She sat on the couch. She still had on her jacket and shoes. "I thought you left."

She approached in two quick strides and slapped him across the face hard enough to ring his ears. Emotions welled; he swallowed them.

"That for not telling you?" he finally said.

"That was for pushing me."

Darnell nodded. "I can see that. You know I didn't mean to, right?"

"I know. You're not crazy." She sat back on the couch and folded her arms across her chest.

"What made you come back?"

"I promised Kaylee I would. Only way to get her to stop crying. That, and I don't think I'd be able to sleep tonight without knowing what the fuck has been going on."

Darnell sat down beside her. Ashleigh got up and went over to the love seat. Darnell nodded at this. He rested his forearm on his leg, wrist skyward, and clenched his fist. Some of this was theatrics, he knew, but perhaps showing the pure ease with which he'd surpassed his own humanity would be too much to share all at once.

Portia played her role well and came out elegantly. She stood on his wrist, turned toward his wife, and waved her legs as if in greeting.

It was a long time before Ashleigh spoke. "How many are there?"

Darnell sighed. "A lot. Not more than twenty. But, a lot."

"And the one that attacked Kaylee?"

"Charlotte. She was rogue. I never could control her."

"You can control the others?"

He nodded. "Promise you'll be cool."

"I'll be cool."

Darnell connected to Portia in that visceral way that he had never experienced with another sentient being before. He became acutely aware of several aspects of the environment that were previously unavailable to him in his human skin. The hidden insects that vibrated within their apartment walls, the fear emanating off Ashleigh, even his own angst. Darnell pushed through this all to get to his goal. Like a loaded spring, Portia jumped from his wrist to the love seat's armrest. Ashleigh started, but there was also a smile there. Portia tucked in her feelers and extended her frontmost pair of legs. She waved them back and forth, spun around, and then slapped these legs onto the fabric. She lifted her back legs, too, and shuffled forward two beats, then back two beats.

Ashleigh looked from the spider to him. His forehead had gone damp.

"You never were a good dancer," she said.

"Oh, thank god," Darnell said. He released his hold on Portia. The spider put all eight legs on the armrest, regained its bearings, and then jumped back to Darnell.

"You should have told me." Ashleigh shook her head. "Does it hurt? When they come out?"

"Not anymore," Darnell said.

"Can I see?"

He let her. He hadn't taken the time to take inventory. Scars marked his arms, his chest, his legs, and neck. Ashleigh touched where his navel used to be. His abs contracted, though he felt nothing.

"That was Charlotte," he said. "The big, scary one."

Ashleigh leaned in and kissed his stomach. He heard the sound, felt her warmth near his chest, the pressure of distant touch. Otherwise, numb. She went on to kiss his arms, his neck, his face. When she was done, she settled beside him.

"Did they tell you . . . if it's permanent?"

"They didn't tell me anything, only that it would get me home to you. You know I never read the fine print."

"Whatever this is, however long this lasts, we'll get through it together."

Ashleigh frowned and looked past him out the window. Red and blue flashed slivers across her face. Then he heard it.

The whir of police sirens.

...

Not twenty-four hours after arriving at the county jail, Darnell was transferred to Twin Towers' psychiatric unit for a suicide attempt. His intent, in fact, hadn't been to kill himself. The tin cup top he'd pocketed from the dining hall had proved sharp enough to do the job. The guard had found him, weeping hysterically, calling out for Ashleigh, Kaylee, and someone named Portia, splattered with blood, surrounded by dead spiders.

They removed the suicide vest after five days. On the seventh, he had a visitor. He sat at a large steel table, both ankles chained to the floor.

"Are you my lawyer?" When the tall woman in the suit jacket didn't respond, he tried again. Her apparent comfort in this environment unsettled him. "New psychiatrist?"

"I'm from the court."

"Can't talk without a lawyer. I know that much."

"Listen, then. I read your psych forensic report. It won't hold up in an incompetence plea. While on parole, you were caught in possession of a Schedule 1 controlled substance with intent to sell and fled from the scene."

He remained tight-lipped.

"As your first offense on record, this won't get you much. But if old charges were reinstated . . ." She tapped her tablet; Darnell felt the walls close in around him. "You're looking at a long time in prison. Your daughter's high school graduation, her prom, probably her wedding."

"Why are you here again?"

She placed a familiar syringe in front of him. "To get you back in the study."

Darnell sat forward, pulling his chains taut. She was not the man who'd first offered those words what seemed a lifetime ago. But in many ways, she was the same. The same neatly pressed attire, vacant gaze, and detached impatience.

The woman caught his recognition and smiled.

"You're from Freedom Rings," he said. A second's pause, then she nodded and waved her hand in dismissal.

"We have many names. Your control of the spores was remarkable. Better than we've seen. You obviously connected with them. Cared for them." She looked over her shoulder to see if the guards were watching. They weren't. Her eyes sparked. "Tell me, where is the one you call Portia? Can you feel it now?"

Darnell shifted. So they had been watching all along. "I killed all the spiders."

"No, not Portia. We checked every single spider in your cell. Is it back with your daughter? Kaylee?"

"She has nothing to do with this." Darnell blinked, and in that time he reached out to the one link he had left in the world. In that split second he sensed his daughter's blood through Portia's legs, felt her glee. She was safe. She kept that part of him safe.

"Did you teach her how to control it?"

"Guard!" Darnell yelled. When no one came, he gestured to the syringe. "You know the definition of insanity? Doing the same thing twice and expecting a different result."

"That's not insanity. Besides, I'm not asking you to do that same thing. Not exactly."

She pulled a glass box from her briefcase and placed it on the table. Though the creature inside had grown and developed far beyond what it was when Darnell had last seen it, he immediately recognized what he'd hoped was a nightmare among nightmares. It had, after all, come from his own face. The hybrid didn't have room to fly in the glass cage, but its large wasp wings were rivaled only by its long, thick legs. Its abdomen elongated into a pulsating double tip. Darnell, despite himself, squinted for a better view. Clear liquid dripped from one of the needles; fine lines of silk stretched from the other.

"Tell it to fly," the woman said. No sooner had she spoken the words than the abomination beat its wings to a blur. Darnell stilled it as quickly as he'd excited it. He lifted one leg—an exact leg—and then another. The control was fluid and complete. "We've learned a lot about you and your connection. We can perfect it."

"You want to use me again? Then tell me what's this really for? Some weapon? Bioterrorism?"

"That's classified."

Darnell scoffed.

"Does it matter if it gets you out of here? Arachnids are independent creatures. It was a mistake to think they could be fully controlled. The incident with the tarantula shouldn't have happened."

"If not spiders, then what? This mutant shit—"

Buzzing. So faint at first Darnell thought it was just another of the jail's many unexplained moanings. A bee passed overhead, trailing sweet fermentation. His cavities itched in fearful anticipation. The bee hovered in front of him. Beyond, the woman grinned.

"Six months. Your job would be just to stay out of trouble, otherwise do what feels natural. We'll take care of the rest."

"And after the six months?"

"No more. Enjoy your wife. Your daughter. Your life."

He sat back. She did the opposite. The bee retreated behind her and the buzzing stopped. Her brown eyes glistened with the anticipation of the day's catch.

"Fuck you and your shot," he said.

This time she called the guard. As she got up to leave, he grabbed her arm.

"Can you make it four months? And get my job back?"

Half her mouth curled into a smirk.

"I think we can manage that."

One Hand in the Coffin

DESPITE EVERYTHING, FOR HIS NINTH BIRTHDAY COREY WISHED HIS BROTHER Michael back. Part of this was Corey's best friend Patrick's fault. When one of the older boys called Corey retarded, Patrick yelled, "He's not retarded, he has Asperger's!" sparking the kids to chant "Ass Boogers, Ass Boogers, Corey's got Ass Boogers!" Now that same boy was about to get a slice of his birthday cake. Michael would have done something.

Corey repeated the wish in his head as his twin sister Alisha blew out their birthday candles. He pictured the warrior woman in the book his mother had left in Michael's room. The woman named Adesokash, the Healer of People, who wore eagles as a helmet and carried an elephant as her sword. He started the "Happy Birthday" song, high and pitchy, because the book said she healed through music. Though the text warned him to "let the dead rest," maybe Adesokash would make an exception?

Alisha joined in his singing; their guests took up the song and tried to drown them out. Corey knew they weren't supposed to sing it, but he had Asperger's, not Ass Boogers, and maybe singing would help that kid learn that for good.

The song ended; Corey's aching hand told him his wish had come true. He searched the smiling faces gathered around the orange cake, grimacing at the way the sound of their clapping scratched his skin. He avoided the itch of their dark and intruding eyes. Instead, he looked for Michael's half-smiling, full lips, his braided hair with the escaping curls, his sparkling black earrings. Corey's gaze landed on his therapy puppet, sitting in the corner of the cramped apartment. With its loose white T-shirt, faded blue pants, and Brillo-pad black hair, it looked nothing like Michael.

And yet . . .

"Michael's here," Alisha said.

Corey turned from the puppet. The sound of Alisha's voice had become a rare and missed treasure since their brother's death. Only he heard it; Mom had started off the encore with what she called the Black happy birthday song: Hah-pee birth-day to ya! Hah-pee birth-day to ya! Hah-PEE biiiirth-DAY!

"Kids in the living room, adults in the kitchen," Mom said as she stood on a cracked wicker chair to grab a knife hidden in the shelves above the stove. Her gaze flitted to Corey; he looked away, and Mom began to cut the cake. "Corey, why don't you do a puppet show for your guests?"

Corey looked at Mom in that way she didn't like. He hated the puppet, but Mom had worn a big smile when Dr. Adelman found one that was "brown like him." Puppets, he said, were good for "high-functioning spectrum kids" like Corey.

"Michael?" Corey whispered as he picked it up. Nothing. Just hollow wood and a dumb, wide smile. He took it to the couch and dangled it over his lap. It smelled a lot like his school's arts and crafts markers with their faded color names and missing caps. Only Mrs. Wright didn't let Corey draw during arts and crafts anymore, not since Michael died, not since the tub and the red water and his older brother's dead eyes had made it onto the construction paper. Corey had so much more to draw, like football skins and mousetraps, but Mrs. Wright never gave him the chance and Mom never said anything, so when drawing time came around he just laid his cheek on the cold wooden table. The puppet smelled a little like that, too.

Corey swept his gaze over the half-dozen kids Mom had invited to his and Alisha's ninth birthday party, avoiding their eyes. They sat cross-legged, waiting for his show. The cartoon characters on their shirts wore encouraging, excited expressions. Anthony, the boy who'd called him "retarded," sat right up front. Large and round, he stuffed his face with Corey's cake. Michael would have stuffed his face with something else.

But Michael was dead. *Let the dead rest*, his mother's book had warned.

Who, then, would protect him?

Off to the side, Alisha and a boy from her special school—the school Corey was "too smart" to attend—lined up her dinosaur toys. The two weren't playing together, not really. The other boy plucked one of the dinosaurs from the middle of the line to inspect it. Corey's twin sister didn't seem to notice. Sometimes—most times—Corey wished he was more like Alisha. People knew what to expect from her. With Corey, trapped between two worlds, people always expected the wrong thing.

Corey slipped his hand into the puppet's back, like he had done many times with the doctor who made him talk about Michael and bathtubs and redness. His breath and stomach squeezed whenever he reached into dark, invisible places. He waited for pain to light his fingertips, like Michael's favorite game: catch the mousetrap. Sometimes Corey won, and it hurt and it burned, but most times he lost and he only had the wait, the not knowing, the promise that metal teeth or cold, furry rat parts were still under the bed for him to find.

The world went fuzzy. Corey let out his breath and his worry. His fingers found the familiar soft pillows opposite each other. He brought them together; the puppet's mouth closed. The fear of his wish seemed far away now.

"Hello, Ladies and Gentlerats," Corey said. The room hushed.

"Hello, Laddies and Paddies," the puppet said, but really Corey had pushed the words out the side of his mouth, like on television. It made for a voice low and not his own. "Hello, boys and girls. Toys and whirls."

Patrick laughed louder than the others. He lived three floors below, close enough that Corey could reach him on walkie-talkie just about any time of day. Patrick had a good sense of humor. A Corey sense of humor.

"I just flew in from Vancouver, and boy, am I tired! Want to hear a joke?"

"Sure," Corey said.

"What do you call someone who lets his friend get bullied?"

"I don't know."

"Fat-trick." The puppet's head spun; Corey's wrist cracked and sent a dull line of pain to his fingers. The sharp, sudden smell of grease stung Corey's nose. "Isn't that right, Fat-trick?"

Anthony laughed so hard, Corey smelled carrots.

"Don't call him that," Corey said to the puppet. "His name is Patrick. His mother gave him that name."

"It's either Fat-trick or Titty Monster. Pick one."

Patrick's head dipped low, and a second later Corey's walkie-talkie crackled. He kept it with him always, even at night. Patrick did the same.

"Falcon." *Crackle.* "Come in, Falcon." *Crackle crackle.* The vibrations tickled Corey's hip. "Warthog is going down."

The puppet turned to the audience. "Hey, Fat-trick, get off the phone. McDonald's doesn't deliver." The crackling stopped. "Your friends are making you soft, Corey."

"Michael," Corey whispered. The puppet looked at him. "I'm telling Mom."

"Tell her, and I'll shave Alisha's hair again. And you'll watch, you weak little shit."

"Awww," Anthony said. "He said a bad word! Ma! Corey said a bad word!"

The carrot-cake-stuffing, name-calling kid ran around the corner toward the roaring grown-up laughter. His tattletale wails soon drifted up and over. Mom said something Corey couldn't make out. Patrick was already to the front door. Corey swallowed. His tongue tickled the roof of his mouth. He rubbed his puppet-bound fingers together. His scalp itched. Someone's watch kept ticking. In between breaths, Corey's stomach thrummed with the beat of his heart. Onetwothreefourfive, onetwothreefourfive, onetwo . . .

Corey focused on the puppet and disconnected from the stress bubbling in the small room around him.

"Why did the chicken cross the road?" he said, finally.

"To K-I-L-L me," the puppet said.

"You're supposed to say 'Why?' "

"Why? Why did you K-I-L-L me?"

"To get to the other side."

Instead of laughter, Corey heard Mom call his name. She sounded angry. Corey would worry about that later.

"Why?" the puppet said.

"I didn't kill you," Corey said. He sniffed. "The knife did."

The puppet began to shake. The wooden parts of its mouth rattled. A hot pain spread around Corey's wrist, keeping his hand stuck as the puppet's insides shrunk around his fingers. The whir of a hairdryer made Corey turn. A white crack lit his fingers, one he felt more than heard. He cried out, yanked his hand free, and the puppet fell to the floor. Lying there, it was light, dead wood. The hair had lost its glisten. It didn't look like Michael.

When Corey looked up, Alisha was the only kid left at Corey's little show. She stood a foot or two away, staring at the puppet. She bent to pick it up; Corey pulled it back. This was his problem, not hers.

Corey crossed the living room in three steps and stuffed the puppet in a trash bag hanging from a doorknob. He pushed until cake-smeared plates and paper towels buried it.

"I didn't mean it," Corey said to Alisha. She had returned to her line of dinosaurs. Alisha didn't answer, of course. She hardly ever did anymore, not even in the special way she had, not since Michael died. "It's better with him gone. We're better."

"Corey Daniel Green!"

Whenever Mom said all three of his names, she was angry. He didn't know exactly what he'd done wrong. Singing Michael back, the puppet show, scaring away all the other kids Mom hoped would become his friends. The way Michael died. All the things Corey wanted to take back.

...

"Corey, you can't say stuff like that," Mom said. Everyone had gone home. Lazy balloons with cursive celebrations drifted in the cigarette smoke. Large, fading pieces of artwork Mom sometimes called their ancestors watching over them from across the ocean hung luminous and condescending over the apartment's disarray. Paper plates, soiled utensils, plastic cups with drinks the colors of the rainbow. Mess upset Mom in the mornings. Still, she likely wouldn't get to it tonight; she wiped her eyes with the back of the hand holding a brown drink with loud ice.

"Why not?" he asked.

"You just can't. Patrick's mom called and said you made him cry. Cry! It's already hard for you to make friends as it is. This is why—" She stopped herself, shook her head, sipped her drink, and sat back. Corey heard the words all the same. *This is why Dad left. This is why Mike left. I'm alone because of you.*

"I killed him," Corey said to an abandoned ash-smudged playing card on the carpet.

"Oh, baby. I'm so sorry you have to go through this."

Corey pulled away from her hug.

"You miss Mike," Mom said. "We all miss Mike."

"I wanted him dead," Corey said. "It's better now."

Mom held up a hand, then put it to her face. She began to sob; her tears smelled like the glass she held.

"He was a good kid," she said.

"I'm sorry."

"You didn't know. You'd take it back if you could. I know you would."

Would he? He'd thought about it the hardest at the funeral, standing there just outside his brother's coffin, so close he could smell the grease they'd used to soften his wild hair before braiding it in tight, thick rows. Corey hadn't looked at his brother, even as he stuck a hand in the coffin to feel his stiffness, because that's what he'd heard about the dead, how stiff they were, and he wanted to be sure. He'd looked over, though, expecting something of the same from Alisha, but she was staring right at Michael. In all his life—her life, too—Corey had only seen Alisha look one person in the eye, and that was their older brother. That moment more than any other, Corey would have taken it back.

"He loved you. He loved Alisha, too. He was just such a knuck-lehead, just like his father." Her face stretched sideways. As Corey watched, tears pulled at his own eyes. Whatever anger or scorn had prompted his wish had vanished; now there was only fear. The fear of Michael coming back. The fear that Corey wouldn't be able to send him away again.

Mom hugged him. She understood him less than he did her, but he welcomed the hug. This close she smelled like Mom, not like brown drink.

Corey pulled away and wiped his eyes. His mother leaned forward and picked up the book with the African warrior queen in it. She flipped through it. Corey read the title over and over as she did: *The Sanain Empire: History, Culture, and Mythology.*

"Corey, did you move this?"

"No," Corey said. That was the truth. He had left it where he'd found it, in Michael's room.

"I don't like when you lie, Corey." She showed him the picture he'd drawn on the blank page opposite a profile of Adesokash. His brother Michael, X's for eyes, balanced the therapy puppet on his knee. Opposite the pair, Corey had drawn Anthony, the kid who had called him retarded, crying his eyes out. Corey said nothing. Mom wouldn't understand. She looked at the picture again, closed the book, and stuffed it in her pocketbook. "We're going to go see Dr. Adelman soon. Real soon."

Sensing that their time was done, Corey went to his room. Before their talk and after she'd finished yelling, Mom had quietly taken the puppet out of the trash bag hanging in the living room, wiped off the orange streaks and stains, and returned it to their lives. Alisha played with her toy dinosaurs while the puppet sat against the wall.

Corey took a step forward, paused, reached out to the puppet, then pulled his hand back as if his fingers had found an invisible flame. Black sparkled at both the puppet's earlobes; they hadn't been there before.

Who had pinned on Michael's earrings? Mom? No, she kept Michael's things perfectly in place. Then who? Alisha? Corey looked back at his sister. When she did things even he couldn't understand, the world grew and he shrank.

"You were supposed to help," he said to the puppet. Michael. "You just hurt. You always hurt."

Nothing. Corey kicked the puppet's shoulder. Lighter than it looked, it slumped over on its side, its puppet face kissing the floor.

Why couldn't Michael just leave them alone?

...

Corey was almost asleep when a dot of cold pricked his cheek and made a wet line to his ear. He looked up at Alisha's bunk above him. A small orb of water swelled between the planks, catching a little bit of light from the hallway. Another drop was about to fall when Corey felt the eyes.

Drip.

Mom's sobs continued to drift from the living room. Michael had cried like that, back when Corey was five and Dad left for good. "Why he don't want me, man?" Corey hadn't known the answer, and Corey hadn't cried. Maybe he should have; after that night, Michael turned mean.

Drip.

Mom in the living room. Eyes on him. Alisha, who never looked at anybody now that Michael was gone. Another drop of water. Eyes on him.

Corey turned, wiping his cheek dry. Alisha was across the room, her back to him. She touched the head of a spindly red dinosaur to the tail of a shaven green one, adding to a long line stretching across the room. Beyond her the puppet sat against the wall, its eyes sparkling more than its ears.

Corey shot up, hitting his head on the top bunk. Crackling white spun his world. Water ran down his face and pooled in his lap. He clutched his forehead as he edged over the bed.

"Did it move?" he said. Thinking was hard against the pain, but Corey remembered. The puppet had been facedown when he drifted to sleep. Had his sister propped him back up?

"Do you see these horns?" Alisha said, holding up the toy. "These horns make triceratops the king."

Corey's stomach wrenched with Michael-fear. Michael was dead. Corey had seen the bathwater darken with his blood. This puppet was just wood and paint and chicken wire. That twist in his stomach, though, he only ever felt that . . .

Acorn eyes. Had they moved into focus? Maybe.

. . . when Michael had his hungry look, that you-can't-protect-Alisha-forever look. The look presently in the puppet's eyes. Eyes that were no longer dull plastic, but glistening. Fleshlike.

"Did you know that triceratops had three horns?"

"I don't understand—" Corey had begun, when Alisha turned and looked at the puppet. His eyes—Michael's eyes—stared straight back at her. No . . . no, no, no, no, no. They had been on Corey just a moment ago. He rubbed his own eyes, gritted through his pounding head, and willed the puppet's gaze back to him. It remained on his sister.

Corey put the puppet outside the room and closed the door.

...

"Warthog, this is Falcon. Come in, Warthog."

Corey waited. Besides studio audience laughter leaking from Mom's room, the apartment slept. "Warthog, we're coming in hot," he said into the walkie. "We need your guidance. Do you copy?"

Silence. The walkie always woke Patrick up. Always.

"Warthog, we're sorry."

Silence. Corey turned in bed, squirmed his shoulder until his skin was comfortable against the cotton, and then found the familiar paper-cut-thin line of unbroken light under the door. How many nights had he stared at that line, well past when Mom went to bed, waiting for Michael to break it?

...

Mom's body changed when Corey brought home bad grades. Usually in history, English, science—anything where words could break apart on the page and swim around each other. Sometimes Mom's eyes would melt; sometimes she shrank a little; sometimes she just sighed and handed the report back to him.

Math was the only thing in school that made sense. No matter how far apart the numbers drifted, he could always link them back together. If he focused.

Today he couldn't focus. His mind was on those acorn eyes, those black earrings, the memory that the puppet moved clashing with the knowledge that wooden things don't move, not by themselves. These thoughts left him vulnerable to the full sensations of the room. The scratch of erasers, the sniff of wet nostrils, the flat of the metal seat against his backside, the whispers of kids cheating, the *click-clack* of the novice substitute teacher's broken heel against the floor as she sought, unsuccessfully, to weed them out.

When the math quiz was over, Corey rushed out into the hall.

"Falcon! Corey! Wait up!"

Patrick. He'd been just outside the door. Relief slowed Corey to a walk. He had to look up at his friend, where a year ago they'd stood level. He was wider than Corey, too, but he'd always been that way. Patrick wore a smile. Corey knew the name of the expression, but not all the meanings. A smile could mean joy, or fear, or—as Michael had taught him—menace. Was there one for hate? Corey didn't know.

Maybe Patrick's smile was a warning.

"We're still friends?" Corey said.

"Why wouldn't we be? What I do?"

"You weren't on the walkie last night."

They quieted as Anthony came out of the bathroom and crossed the hall in front of them. When he was gone, Patrick leaned in and whispered.

"I was asleep. Did I miss anything?"

"I said some pretty mean stuff." Fat-trick. Titty Monster.

"It wasn't you."

"It wasn't?" Corey said. It had felt like him. Once, Corey rode in Uncle Junior's front seat on the highway, even though Mom had told Uncle Junior to put him in the back, but Uncle Junior didn't listen because Uncle Junior did whatever the fuck he wanted, and Corey had pumped his arms and bicycled his feet and it had felt like he was running, faster than anyone had ever run, and passing joggers—sweating, suffering joggers, going so slow—made him feel like the most powerful thing in the world. His words, coming out of the puppet, had power; they made Patrick change. Not a good change, but a change. That's how Michael must have felt most of the time. Corey knew that now. It gave him a headache.

"The puppet said it."

"You read the book, too?" Corey said. He ran his fingers along the grooves of the brick wall. The texture soothed.

"What book?"

"The one with the woman and the elephant sword. The one that said music could heal." *And to let the dead rest.*

"Elephants can't be swords," Patrick said. "Wait, did you give it a name?"

"It's for therapy. It doesn't have a name."

"Mr. Wiggles, then. It's Mr. Wiggles's fault."

"That's a dumb name."

"Duh. Dumb 'cus he sounded like your brother. Your dead brother, I mean."

"I only have a dead brother. And he wasn't a puppet. You sure you're not mad at me?"

Patrick patted him on the shoulder. "Mister. Wiggles."

"Thanks," Corey said.

"Yeah, yeah. Are you going to get rid of it?"

They stopped at a water fountain, but it didn't work. They waited for one of the kindergarten classes to pass by. Corey picked at his nails to balance the sound of them.

"I want to," he said. "It's supposed to make me feel better."

"Does it?"

Corey thought about that Michael feeling, even as his head continued to softly throb. "I don't know. It's not Asperger's anymore. I'm autistic."

"Like Alisha?"

"No," Corey said. "Yes. Maybe."

They stopped outside Corey's homeroom. Patrick was in Mrs. Koenig's third-grade class right across the hall.

"How was the quiz? What are the answers?" Patrick held a pen against his palm.

The numbers floated by in a beautiful matrix. "Thirty-five. Seven. Six hundred. Zero. Eighty-five."

"Slow down, Speedy," Patrick said. "Say it again."

...

After a cereal breakfast, Corey leaned on the wall by the door. Last night's sleep had played a grueling game of hide-and-seek, and when it finally tagged him, the thought of Michael's voice coming out of the puppet took its place. The living room's mosaic of potted ferns and painted landscapes hanging like windows into a luxuriously unobtainable past was heavy around him. Mom stuffed papers, cards, and scraps of money into her scaly green purse. She reached into the pocket of her hanging raincoat, pulled out a balled-up hairnet, and stuffed that in, too.

"Don't forget to do your therapy today."

Insurance kept Corey from seeing Dr. Adelman every week, so home therapy consisted of Corey pretending the puppet was Michael. Therapy was the opposite of math. It made no sense; Michael was dead, and the puppet had never been alive. Mom was supposed to help, but she was already clipping her hospital ID to her cafeteria uniform. She yawned, long and painful. Her eyes were red. Had sleep taunted her, too?

"With you?" Corey said, despite knowing the answer.

"You know I have to work, Corey. Give Alisha some time with it, too. She loves that puppet."

"She hates it."

"Let her decide. She might surprise you. Just spend some time, okay?" She paused to look up at and then past him. "Have you been watching Mike's TV?"

"No."

"I don't like it when you lie, Corey. No going into his room when I'm not here. You know better." Mom looked at her phone, cursed, and opened the door. She turned back and held up a finger.

"Number-one rule?" she said.

"Don't open the door for anyone," Corey said. "Even you."

"Good. Number two?"

"Watch Alisha."

Mom kissed his forehead. The cold of her lipstick made Corey squirm inside, because squirming outside would chase away Mom's joy, and he liked her better when she smiled. He pressed the tips of his fingers together as he waited for the door to close. When she was gone, he wiped his sleeve across his forehead. He wiped and wiped and wiped until a deep, building itch gave way to relief.

Then he went to find his mother's book. He checked the kitchen drawers, behind the trash can, under the bathroom sink, even under his mother's bed. Nowhere. He stopped outside Michael's room. Since the birthday party and the song and the puppet, he didn't know if it was safe anymore. What did he want the book for anyway? To send Michael back away? To see what other songs he could sing?

Back in their room, Alisha was bouncing the velociraptor on Mr. Wiggles's head, the puppet's short, tight curls acting as foliage. Her velociraptors didn't sound like the ones on television, but Corey had never heard a real velociraptor, and Alisha knew things through ways he couldn't access. Mr. Wiggles stared straight ahead, seemingly fascinated with the toy chest against the opposite wall.

"Would you have stayed if Dad stayed?" Silence. "Mom hates me. Because of you."

It didn't feel like talking to Michael anymore. Corey turned away as tears burned his eyes. What had he been expecting? An answer? Some truth?

The puppet fell forward. Its head knocked the floor. Corey rose and stepped back. Alisha bent to continue bouncing the velociraptor on the back of his head, then moved down his spine. The plastic dinosaur dipped under the puppet's white shirt. Alisha's arm began to disappear.

"Don't do that," Corey said. He thought of the catch-the-mousetrap game. Once Corey had refused to play, so Alisha took his place. Although she'd won, she hadn't cried. She walked around the apartment for the next week, hitting her fingers on the edges of things, over and over and over, until they were raw red. Michael's laughter was short-lived. The fourteen-year-old wore the look of a worried child who had likely broken his favorite toy. Corey had slept with Dad's switchblade after that.

Corey grabbed Mr. Wiggles by the sleeve, pulled, and almost tripped from the thing's weight.

"It's time for a puppet diet," he said. Patrick would have liked the joke, but Patrick wasn't there. He considered going to find his walkie-talkie but chose focus. He dragged the puppet out into the living room, moved a pile of magazines and unsorted mail out of the way, opened the closet of stored winter coats and toolboxes and bags of nails and Christmas lights, and stuffed Mr. Wiggles inside. Corey wiped his eyes. Had the wood been softer? Heavier?

Almost . . . warm?

He moved to close the door and paused. Mr. Wiggles's sleeves had scrunched up; hair-thin cracks lined the puppet's forearms. Corey had spied Michael carving lines into his own arm once and tried it himself, but he must have done it wrong because it hurt and the result made Mom scream. Michael kept carving and carving after that; Corey never got the courage to try again. Soon Michael could only wear long sleeves because short sleeves made Mom cry. Even worse, she thought Michael got the idea from Corey.

He looked over his shoulder, past these memories, and back to the window. They lived on the fifth floor. One two three four five. It was a long way down. If Corey pushed hard enough, Mr. Wiggles would land in the street. Corey could see it clear in his mind.

His heart raced. Why did you K-I-L-L me?

He'd panicked. If he got rid of his brother without water and rage and fear, then what?

Corey closed the door. Back in their room, Alisha was crying.

"It's better without him," Corey said. He sat across from his sister and picked up a pterodactyl. His fingertip brushed the dull plastic beak once, twice. The winged dinosaur dove to knock over the middle of Alisha's line. Exactly three dinosaurs remained standing on each side. Corey smiled.

Alisha smiled, too, in that way she did without moving her lips. Tears drew parallel lines down her face, one slightly longer than the other. Corey imagined the invisible diagonal line connecting the two tears as a dino-slide. He brought the pterodactyl up and flew it parallel to this line. Alisha laughed without looking. It was nice to hear her laugh again.

She reached into her dinosaur jar and produced a *Tyrannosaurus rex*. She looked at it sideways, then placed it down.

Corey pointed to the dinosaur. "Michael's gone," he said. Air pushed apart his tongue and the roof of his mouth as he said different parts of both words. He silently repeated the movement a couple more times, the air tickling the back of his tongue.

Alisha roared. Corey had never heard a real life T-rex roar, either. He liked hers. He touched her arm; she was warm where he felt cold. The small hairs just below her wrist curled up and tickled the side of his pinkie, making his own hairs stand.

"Michael's gone," Corey said again. "Sometimes I think he shouldn't be." Sometimes.

Alisha slipped her hand from under his, pinched his wrist, and made his palm tap the apatosaurus's backside. She pushed his fingers closed and he picked it up.

She roared. And roared. And roared. Corey dropped the dinosaur—threw it. Alisha continued to roar until flecks of spit flew from her mouth.

Corey looked at the door. Someone had let the dark in. He wished he'd turned on the hallway light while the sun was still out. Now it belonged to the shadows. He imagined Mr. Wiggles or Michael—it didn't really matter which—standing hidden there, his earrings reflecting black light, silently roaring like the Tyrannosaurus he was, or had been, or still wanted to be.

He wrapped his arms around Alisha's waist. Her breath and heartbeat synced with his. This was normal. He expected it like he expected a sidewalk bordered by choked, yellow grass when he walked outside their apartment building, expected two uniting numbers to form the same new one every time. With Alisha, consistency was the rule.

They rocked until their breaths slowed, until their hearts beat to the rhythm of a slow song. He imagined they had been similar in Mom's belly, where there was just sleep and heartbeats. Corey swallowed, and felt his heart slow as the aching in his hand faded.

Then he slept.

...

Cold. Bone cold.

Keys jingled. Fine carpet needles itched. Drool stained both arm and nostril. Wet stung at thighs and crotch. Ammonia. A door opened, a sigh, a door closed.

Corey awoke slowly, remembered, and sat up. Someone had let in the dark.

"Alisha?" he said.

He was alone. Lying on the carpet in front of him was his drawing, crudely ripped out of his mother's book.

Corey jumped up and sprang out of the room. His foot burst through the pile of magazines he'd moved and sent them sprawling. He swung open the closet door.

"Corey! You scared me!" Mom's voice.

He ignored her. Mr. Wiggles was gone.

"Why are you up so late?" Mom said. Her eyes went to his pajama pants. "Corey, you're all wet. Did you—" She shook her head as she drifted over from the front door and onto the couch. She pulled her hands down her face and looked over her fingers at him. She smiled the type of smile Corey knew meant something the opposite of happiness. It matched the smell of hospital meat and subway sweat.

"I fell asleep," Corey said, pleading with Mom. Only she didn't know it. He could see it in the way her eyes narrowed, the tilt of her head, the constant reminder that they were of two different worlds. He tried to use his words, but sometimes his words weren't the same as everyone else's words; when that happened, words didn't help anybody. "I fell asleep! I fell asleep, I fell asleep, Ifellasleep!"

Mom held up a hand. "What's that noise?" she said. He heard it, too. He'd felt it before he woke up, because, somewhere, Alisha felt it. It was the sound of running water. "Where's your sister?"

"I fell asleep!" Corey said.

"Oh, Lord," Mom said. She rose quick enough to send Corey stumbling, but he caught himself and hurried after her, into the hall's shadows, around the corner to the bathroom.

Mr. Wiggles sat outside the door, a dark shadow covering his small chest. Just before Mom swept him aside, Corey thought he saw the golden-brown chin fall. The shadow disconnected and bounced noisily down the hall.

"Alisha! Alisha!" Mom jiggled the handle. Locked. "Open the door. The key. Where's the key?"

Muffled sobs. The door blurred; Corey blinked down his tears, which pushed heavy on his cheeks.

Mom yanked Corey's arm. "Tell her to open the door!"

Corey couldn't tell Alisha to open the door, not like this. He opened his mouth to explain, but all that came out was "I fell asleep!"

Mom rushed away. Corey moved toward the bathroom. The sound of water faded. He touched the wood. It was warm.

Mom came back with the key. She kept missing the slit in the doorknob. Corey gently took it away from her. The metal was cold and hard and felt different in his fingers. He slid it into the lock.

"Hurry up!" Mom said. He did.

Alisha sat in the middle of the tiled bathroom floor, her head jackhammered between her hands, rocking back and forth. Tears sparkled her cheeks under the light, like porcelain. She wailed, long and high, until she had to gasp for breath, then wailed more. Dad's pocketknife lay along thin lines of blood beside her. Water began to slick over and down the sides of the tub.

In seconds Alisha had her arms wrapped around Mom's neck, hands pressed back against her own ears. Mom turned off the water, and they were gone.

Corey walked up to the knife. He hadn't seen it since the day Michael died. He tried to pick it up, but it burned his fingers. His hand ached as he went out into the hall and found Michael's basketball. He hadn't been able to make it out sitting in Mr. Wiggles's lap in the dark, but under the low hallway lights he could see the faded Spalding brand and a nickel-size splash of white from when it had bounced into the street and his older brother made him crawl under an old, leaking pickup truck to retrieve it. Part of Michael's things, it belonged in his room with all the rest, hidden and forgotten.

The puppet lay sprawled a few feet away, one arm forward, the other twisted back, cheek to the floor. He was in just the right position to have one eye on the bathroom. Wisps of his hair flattened against the cracked, black-scarred wood, some long enough to curl onto themselves more than once. Something caught the light. Corey dared a step forward, kneeled down, and picked it up. A button. T-shirts didn't have buttons. He looked at Mr. Wiggles, but the puppet was mostly on his stomach, and the shirt looked white. Unchanged.

Corey ran to Michael's room and paused. The door was open. Dull light flashed inside. The smell of cigarette smoke floated along the beat of high-pitched, muffled voices. He recognized one of them from *South Park*, Michael's favorite show. A laugh cut the air—Michael's laugh. Corey looked back at the puppet. How long had that awful grin been there?

Corey threw the basketball as hard as he could through the gap that wasn't supposed to be a gap because Michael was dead and his door stayed closed and dead people don't smoke and dead people surely don't watch television. Something shattered, but Corey was already running away. From the room, from that wooden smile angled against the floor. He didn't stop until he was at the hallway light switch. He flipped it down, waited, and felt some relief.

The dark, and whatever it might bring, was safer than having that smile on him.

...

Alisha finally fell asleep after a long run of broken sobs. Mom fumed into the living room. Blood stained her uniform. She sat at the table with a glass of amber liquid, ice clinking inside. Each clink needled Corey's side.

"Come here," Mom said.

Corey sat in the chair next to her. His feet dangled beneath him. He rubbed his fingers together.

"What happened?" she said.

"I fell asleep," he said.

"How did your sister get locked in the bathroom?"

Corey thought about it. With math, he found solutions for combinations of two new numbers by looking at the dance of other familiar numbers. Michael had locked Alisha in the bathroom before. He was supposed to blow-dry her hair while Mom was at work, but he wanted to play basketball. They had yelled about it and many other things, including Michael dropping out of school, why Dad left, and the new mountain ranges of scars erupting along his arms. In the end Mom had won because she was Mom. Corey dedicated a close eye to his sister, but he lost a Michael game, and by the time he made it back into the apartment, it was too late. He grabbed Dad's knife and assaulted the bathroom door with his fist. Bang! *Alisha*! Bang! *Mike*! Bang! He couldn't find a key, and banging wasn't helping, so he shoved the blade into the side of the door like he'd seen in a movie, and when he finally got in Michael was standing over the tub, one hand on the curtain, the other wielding the blow dryer. Alisha thrashed faceup, fully submerged in the filling water. Every time she came up, Michael gave her hot air straight to the face. Back under. Corey didn't think; he lunged. Michael turned around just in time to move out of the way. But Corey wanted him to pay. Even as Alisha scrambled out of the now overflowing tub, he needed his brother to pay. Dad's knife sliced Michael's thigh. His brother grabbed at it, missed, and Corey stuck the blade again. It folded backward; a line of fire fell over his own fingers. But only Michael yelled. Then Corey's world went all red and blue and black, spreading from hot pain in his nose. When he could see again, Michael held the blade in one hand and wore Corey's blood on the other. Corey remembered yelling something, something so bad that when the colors cleared on the other side of it, Michael had the blade against his own wrist. *You want me gone so bad? I'll do it, you know I will.* And Michael did. He dragged the knife across his wrist. Corey was supposed to call a number and the police would come and Michael would go away and get better, like last time. But something in the red dripping from his brother's wrist into the water inspired an alien rage in Corey. He didn't want it to be like last time. Didn't want there to be another time. The rage propelled him forward, and Michael fell back into the bathtub. "You little shit! You little shit!" Corey ran out into the hall, closed the bathroom door, and waited. He waited for angry splashing to give way to the sound of wet footsteps, a string of curses, something to forewarn him of approaching repercussions. What came instead was distant, muffled crying. Somehow that was worse than the promise of more black-and-blue pain, worse than the thought of his brother dying, because Michael needed help and Corey didn't know how to help him. Didn't know if he wanted to help him. Why wasn't he getting the phone? Why wasn't he *doing* something? He didn't know. The sobbing stopped, eventually. Cool touched his toes, soaked his socks; dark water crept into the hall. Corey creaked the door open. Time slowed. Michael lay back in overflowing pink water. Not asleep, no. His eyes were open. Glass. Corey sloshed over and turned off the water because it was the only thing he could think to do. Then he closed the door and went to find his sister. He held on to Alisha until Mom's screams filled his ears, and then he held her tighter.

Sometimes he wondered what would have happened if he hadn't gotten into the bathroom. Maybe Alisha would be dead instead of Michael. Maybe they'd both be alive. Maybes were hard for Corey. They weren't like numbers.

"What happened?" Mom asked again.

"I don't know," he said. *Mr. Wiggles.*

"Corey, I'm going to ask you again, and I want an answer. How did Alisha get locked in the bathroom? She's never locked a door before."

"Maybe Mr. Wiggles—"

She slapped him. "Don't lie to me."

Corey tightened his face. If he cried, Alisha would cry, and that was the last thing he wanted. His breaths were quick, hard pats that whistled out his nose.

"Don't ever do that to her again." Mom pulled him in for a hug. "Ever. Ever. Ever." She burst into tears.

...

Corey dreamed as Alisha spoke. His nightmares had gone down since Michael died, but they still came. He woke in a sweat from one of them and would have gone back to sleep if not for Alisha being awake.

He knew this the same way he knew the sun was out without having to look up at it.

"It's Michael," she said.

"Where?" Corey asked. He waited, staring at the underside of her bed. He repeated the word, over and over, its whistling sound swirling into the wood above him. He was almost back to sleep when he heard a thumping sound. His body remembered it before he fully could. His butt cheeks squeezed together. It was the sound of a flat basketball hitting the wood.

Thump. Thump. Thump.

He turned to the door.

The line of light—his line of comfort, of safety—was split in two.

"Mom?" Corey said. The answer that came wasn't Mom. Cartman, Stan, and Kyle, paper voices rising in static. Laughter rose between them. The splash of shadow under the door quivered.

Corey closed his eyes. A dream. Had to be.

"Alisha?" he said.

"It's Michael," Alisha said.

Drip.

"Stop!" Corey yelled. Quiet now. No television. No laughter. No basketball. Just the sound of his own breath. The line of light was whole.

"It's Michael," Corey agreed. That was clear. Now, what was he going to do about it?

...

While Mom got ready for work, Corey hauled the ever-thickening Mr. Wiggles into the closet. The cracks on the puppet's arms had blossomed into moist chasms. The day's heat conquered their apartment's one window air conditioner, and by the time he'd leaned a chair under the handle, his face itched with sweat and his back throbbed like a heartbeat. He waited, put his ear up to the door, and when there was nothing, walked away. He stopped by Michael's room. The door was open just enough for Corey to put his hand through if he wanted. A warm breeze touched his cheek. It smelled of cigarette smoke. The black inside was complete, but he could still see his brother's room in his mind all the same. Video-game cords, basketball shoes, the old television, the intricate puzzles Michael had assembled with Corey back before Dad left, back before things got complicated.

Corey crossed the hallway to the bathroom, found the hair dryer stowed away under the sink, and came back to Michael's door. Mom never knew the role it had played. She had never asked. Corey threw it into the dark, grabbed the knob, and pulled. A sharp, dreadful whir rose from the black as angry cigarette air pushed forward and wedged between the door and its frame. Lights flashed against the static-chopped voices of excited cartoon characters. Corey grunted, dug his feet into the floorboards, and yanked.

"No more, Michael," Corey said when the latch clicked closed. "No more."

The doorbell rang. Even still, Corey waited. He waited until the last of the Michael-room sounds faded away. It wasn't hard to wait. He had the numbers in his head, always adding together to make something else.

...

"You sure you don't want them downstairs?" Patrick's mother stood a head taller than Corey's. She was wider than Patrick, but not as wide as the kids at school said.

"Alisha . . . doesn't take to new places," Mom said.

"Is it the autism?"

"Maybe," Mom said. She turned slightly away from Patrick's mother, who had moved to look at the art hanging on our wall.

"This is nice. Oh, and this one's real nice."

"Sanain art," Mom said. "My dad's side of the family swears we can track our roots right back to West Africa. He left me these. I like to think of them as our ancestors watching over. Lord knows we need it."

"One of my cousins—the one who went to be a doctor—got the whole 23andMe thing done. I was thinking about doing it. I'm sure wherever we from got to be better than here. Now, Patrick, you come right downstairs if you need me. Otherwise, have fun and respect Ms. Green's house."

"The boys will be fine." Mom smiled big and bent her knees. She pulled down the sleeves of her sweater as she spoke to Patrick. "We have two rules. First, watch Alisha—"

"I watch Alisha," Corey said. They all turned at the same time. Patrick's mother's face twisted. Patrick waved so hard, his Spider-Man backpack looked like it was shaking its Spidey head. Corey almost waved back.

"You both," Mom said carefully. "You both do. It'll be nice to have a friend over while I'm gone tonight, right, Corey?"

"A babysitter," Corey said.

"A friend. Patrick's your friend."

Mom came over and kissed his forehead. He didn't resist wiping. It chased Mom's smile away, like he knew it would, but he couldn't care because he watched Alisha and Mom knew that. A piece of her smile came back when she turned back to Patrick's mother, but it wasn't the same.

"Be good, boys," she said and opened the door.

"What's the second rule?" Patrick said.

"Don't open the door for anyone," Corey said.

"Except me," Patrick's mother said. And then, as she and Mom left together, "You going to be okay with that sweater? It's hot as all get-out."

"Freezing in the hospital, though. And it's cute, ain't it?"

"I watch Alisha," Corey said again when the door was closed. He turned to his friend with a look he hoped was serious. Even when Michael was alive and Mom left him in charge, Corey watched over Alisha. He'd messed up, he knew, but still wasn't quite sure how.

Patrick lifted his hands. "I know. I thought I was just here to sleep over."

"Mom thinks I'm like Michael."

"Are you?"

"No. You bring the knife?"

"Oh." Patrick dug a white-handled knife from his backpack. It was twice as big as the other.

"I said a small knife."

"Only one I could find. What's it for?"

"We're getting rid of Mr. Wiggles. We'll call it Operation Trashcan."

"I like it." Fear touched Patrick's eyes. "Are . . . both of us doing Operation Trashcan?"

"Yes. Come on."

They went over and removed the protective chair from in front of the closet. Corey grabbed the doorknob, ignored its warmth, and was about to pull when Patrick's fingers dug into his arm.

"Are we going to get into trouble?"

"I don't know."

Patrick let go. Corey opened the door.

"You changed its clothes?" Patrick said. Instead of a T-shirt and jeans, Mr. Wiggles wore a collared button-down and black dress pants. This made sense to Corey but puzzled his friend. Why? He searched his memory, found it. Patrick hadn't been to Michael's funeral.

"No," Corey said. He slipped the knife into his pocket, careful not to stick himself with the blade. "You get the legs. I'll get the arms."

Patrick looked at him sideways, bent over, grabbed one of Mr. Wiggles's legs, pulled, and nearly fell from the unexpected weight. When his friend looked back up, his eyes were wide.

"Yeah," Corey said. Mr. Wiggles had thickened: that was apparent. Still, he weighed more than any toy his size should. "We have to deal with it."

The throbbing returned to Corey's back as they dragged Mr. Wiggles out, legs first. Patrick's eyes burned the side of his face. Corey didn't have to look to know his friend's fear; he felt it, too. Heat pulsed through Mr. Wiggles's cotton pants. The wood beneath had gone soft and thick. The puppet's head thumped out of the closet and onto the floor, sending a vibration up Corey's legs.

Corey squatted down and reached his arms under Mr. Wiggles's armpits. Patrick took his feet. When they lifted him, the middle of his body curved down in a U.

"He smells like gym class," Patrick said.

Mr. Wiggles's cheek brushed against Corey's as he tried to get a better grip. He flinched away, but the stinging stubble had already hooked a memory. Michael had been trying to teach him how to shoot a basketball so the boys at the normal school would see him as more than a punching bag. Frustrated, Michael passed the ball so hard Corey's fingers hurt for a week. Corey didn't cry, not then, but rather turned to the basket and forgot what his brother taught him about lining up the ball or pushing off with his right hand. He watched the ball and the rim and his hand like only he knew how and let the quiet part of himself take. The ball went in. Michael hugged him. A real hug, like back before Dad left. Not a fake hug, or a dangerous hug, but the type of hug that made finger pain go away. Michael had just started growing face hair. Its prickle was warm and scary and tipped with love.

Halfway out the door, Patrick dropped Mr. Wiggles.

"He looked at me," Patrick said. "I swear, he looked at me."

"Pick him up," Corey whispered. He looked over his shoulder. Had Alisha heard? "Come on. Please."

They carried Mr. Wiggles out into the apartment building hallway. His back rested against Corey's leg as they waited for the elevator. They laid him inside.

"Where's the knife?" Patrick said. His eyes were as wide and as deep as his breathing.

Corey checked under his arm. Not there. "I'll be right back." He turned before Patrick could respond, ran across the short hallway to his front door. There it was, resting on the welcome mat. His heart slowed a little as soon as his fingers touched the handle.

Patrick screamed.

Corey whirled around. His friend had fallen against the elevator wall. A dark line fell down the side of his head, like a tear. A black ashtray rolled across the floor. Mr. Wiggles sat upright, firmly holding one end of Michael's silver chain, the other wrapped tight around Patrick's wrist. He turned his head. Teeth that hadn't been there before shone through the puppet's wide, wild smile. As the old metal doors slid closed, Mr. Wiggles turned back to Patrick.

Corey crawled, ran, stumbled to the elevator. He banged the flat of the knife against the metal. "Patrick! Patrick!" The water, was it running? No. That was another time. Another failure. He didn't have to fail again. He forced himself to step back, take deep breaths. Think.

He ran down the stairs. *Onetwothreefourfivesixseveneight, Onetwothreefourfivesixseveneight, twofoursixeight*, three flights. When he got to the bottom the elevator gears were still grinding inside the walls.

"Patrick!"

Patrick's own yells grew louder and louder as the elevator came to a stop. What would he see? Mr. Wiggles—Michael—hitting Patrick with the ashtray, over and over again, until his face was all red? Or Patrick sitting on the puppet's lap, a wooden hand extending into his back, making his lifeless jaw work as his eyes rolled back . . .

The doors opened to Patrick's black moon eyes. Michael's chain tied his wrist to the elevator banister. His yells solidified into words: "He got back off!"

Corey's hand ached.

He ran up the stairs, two, three at a time, so fast that the counting part of his mind couldn't keep up. Falling, shin against metal, the cold railing burning the palm of his hand, pulling up and up and up . . .

Their front door yawned open. Corey flew to Michael's room.

Alisha sat in the middle, playing with her dinosaurs. She sang the Black "Happy Birthday" song as Mr. Wiggles stood behind her, combing her hair with Michael's yellow pick. He was as tall as Corey now, if not taller. He turned his head, continuing to lace the pick through Alisha's thick curls. The puppet's own hair was half braided, half wild. He wore a black suit jacket—Corey recognized the yellow flower in the pocket from the funeral—but no tie.

Lying on the floor beside them, torn to shreds, was Corey's mother's book. An elephant's eye stared up at him from one of the ripped pieces.

"Core-eee." Mr. Wiggles's mouth flapped like a cow chewing grass. Somewhere in the black, Corey thought he saw a tongue trying to figure out how to work.

Corey lunged at him, knife raised. The thing smiled its cow smile even as Corey flew through the air. Contact. Pain entered his shoulder and spread like fire. It felt like trying to tackle a tree. He fell back, dizzy and empty-handed. Mr. Wiggles, unshaken, stood over him.

"Tuffen up, Core-ee," Mr. Wiggles said. He grabbed Corey's neck. Mr. Wiggles's blood might have already begun to run hot, but his fingers remained cold. They clamped down.

The world went red. Then gray. Corey scratched at Mr. Wiggles—at Michael—scratched until his nails splintered against both wood and flesh alike, thrashed against the hate he'd collected for his brother, a hate planted in the disdainful way Michael looked at his sister, sprouted in his games, and ripened by the knowledge he'd won even in death. Because of him, their lives would forever be miserable.

Color came back. The pressure left his neck. His buttocks hurt. He was on the floor. Mr. Wiggles hovered there, eyes wide, unbelieving.

Behind him, Alisha stood, one hand floating a dinosaur across the air, another lodged into the puppet's back.

"Alisha," Corey said. He shook his head, tried to regain thought. "Your hand, Alisha, your hand. Get it out."

"She's good, bro," Alisha said. Only it wasn't Alisha. The words came from her mouth, but they were somehow lower. Older. Mr. Wiggles's jaw mimicked them. "She's with her brother now."

"That was my wish. Not hers. She hates you."

"She wished me here because you're shit without me. You both sang the song. You both need me."

"No, we don't." He knew now why he'd wished Michael back. It wasn't to beat up a kid for calling him a name. It was because talking to painted wood and a fake smile only made his skin warm. He wanted that puppet to be Michael, so that he could say what he hadn't found the courage to tell him in life. "I wanted you gone. Everything was harder with you."

Corey scooted backward. If he was going to get up, he'd need more room. He looked around. Michael's basketball rested in the corner. One of Michael's trophies—the last before Dad left—stood tall on his dresser. The hair dryer lay plugged up near his video game system. Patrick's knife was lost.

"You never liked us," Corey said. "You wished we weren't born.

Dad left because of us, remember?" Michael had said this so often, it had become one of those truths Corey didn't think to question.

"He did, and I hated him for that. Who took care of you after, huh? Me."

"You tortured us. You tortured Alisha."

"I helped Alisha! Every time I tried to be her big brother, you acted like her savior. I made her stronger, and you killed me for it."

"I didn't kill you."

"You did, you little shit! You let me bleed out. Your own brother."

"Shut up," Alisha said, this time in her own voice. Mr. Wiggles's head turned toward her. "Shut up, shut up, shut up!"

"Alisha," Corey began. He had to get her to take her hand out of Mr. Wiggles.

"Listen," she said to Corey, drawing out the last syllable. She turned to Mr. Wiggles and repeated the word. "Listeeeen."

"Okay," Corey said. "Okay. I'm listening."

"I loved you, Michael. Corey loved you. You loved us." But. The lingering unsaid *but* made the room smaller. "You left us. Like Dad."

"I didn't—" Michael's voice was different. "I was teaching Corey a lesson, but he left me there. He should have called nine-one-one. He did it."

"No," Alisha said. "You left. You did. You're better dead."

Mr. Wiggles's head turned toward their sister, his jaw hanging open. Alisha's dinosaur floated through the air in diagonals.

"You helped us, but you hurt us, too. Don't hurt us anymore."

"I won't, Alisha. Corey. I promise I won't. What can I do?"

"Go away."

With this said, Alisha pulled her hand from the puppet's back and moved away to fly her wingless dinosaur around the room. By the time Mr. Wiggles turned back around, Corey was in a wide stance like in the movies, pointing the hair dryer at his dead brother. His imagination had no answer for what might happen when he turned on the power, but the apparent fear in those glistening, wooden eyes was enough encouragement.

And then Mr. Wiggles did something Corey didn't expect. His

bronze face distorted. Lines split in the wood where the transition to flesh was incomplete. His knees buckled. A low hiccupy whir rose from his mouth.

Michael was crying.

"Why . . ." Michael spoke through his wooden sobs. "Why no one want me, man?"

Corey had heard this cry before, when Dad left. He hadn't known what to say or do. His brother's tears weren't from falling down or not getting his way. The hurt was there to stay; how could words fix that? So he'd stood there as his older brother wet his palms with tears.

He wouldn't stand by silent again.

Corey lowered the blow dryer, took two long strides, and hugged his brother. Michael's skin was still hard in places, and the puppet was skinnier than Michael had ever been. But the scratch of stubble against Corey's cheek erased any doubt.

"I love you," Corey said, and he meant it.

Michael hugged him back. "I love you, too, bro. I'm sorry I left. I just . . ."

"I know."

Corey stepped away and raised the blow dryer again. He forced himself to look in Michael's hazel eyes. For maybe the first time, they understood each other.

Corey flipped the switch. Michael let out a single grunt that could have been outside branches scratching against the apartment. Mr. Wiggles shrank. Shine spread across its hardening skin. Teeth slid back into their holes. The buttons disappeared; the black suit melted and faded into the white T-shirt of before.

The last thing to go was the eyes. Corey never got to see them change.

A guttural, high-pitched wail cut the room. Corey turned to see Patrick run at a full sprint through Michael's door, across his carpet, and throw his shoulder smack into the middle of the puppet's chest.

Mr. Wiggles sprawled through the air as if made of paper. Wood clicked and cracked against the far wall and crumpled to the ground in a misshapen heap. Corey tossed the hair dryer aside and rushed over.

Any sign of Michael was gone. Just Mr. Wiggles. Just a thin pile of wood and paint.

"Did I get him?" Patrick said.

...

Things happened quickly after Michael left again. Mom came into the kitchen as they tried to find mattress bags to clean up all the mess in Mr. Wiggles's wake. Her talking turned loud and fast when she saw the blood on Patrick's face. Corey couldn't remember all he'd said, how much he'd told, but it had been enough to land him in Day Glow Psychiatric Hospital.

The young doctors there asked him the same things every day. If he was hearing voices, seeing things, or had any thoughts of wanting to hurt himself or anybody else. One asked him about Dad leaving, then Michael leaving, and if he had any thoughts of leaving himself. Not anymore, he'd said. Corey wasn't the best at reading expressions, and he couldn't tell if they liked his answers or not. They sent him home after a week, and life went on.

Mom got rid of the puppet and the therapist. He heard her tell people on the phone that it made things better. He didn't tell her otherwise.

Corey still saw Michael, sometimes. In dolls, passing faces, photographs, even in his sister. Sometimes in the rare moments of silence in his house, he could hear faint laughter, the buzz of an old television, and the smell of smoke. It never lasted; just long enough to cause Corey's hand to ache.

"Is Michael here?" he asked Alisha one day before he could stop himself. A faint, familiar laugh had come and gone like a breeze. The babysitter—someone old enough that Mom needed to work an extra shift a month to pay her—slept in the living room.

Alisha didn't look up from her line of toy monster trucks. Corey couldn't remember when she had stopped playing with dinosaurs. As long as she was happy, that was okay with him.

"Yes," she said.

Corey nodded. She was right. And that was okay, too.

Customer Service

The following e-mail chain was presented as evidence in the case of *Janet King v. Two Places At Once* on Monday, January 18, 2038.

Satisfied customer reporting small issue.

49 messages

Jason King <jmarlonking@gmail.com>   Thur, Jun 11, 2037 at 9:38 AM
To: Customer Service <info@tpao.com>

To Whom It May Concern,

I don't want to come off as ungrateful, as I have very much benefited from your services. In fact, I haven't been this productive in years (really, that's an understatement ... I don't think I've ever been this productive, but don't quote me on that)! I went to my daughter's football game last month. She had five sacks. Five! When I asked her which one was her favorite, she said the one where she saw me cheering from the sidelines.

So, don't get me wrong. Two Places At Once has been a godsend. It's everything you advertised, and more.

But I can't help but question whether the last part of our agreement has been properly upheld. I am referring to, specifically, "Help Disposal." I have read our contract multiple times and it says under Article 13b:

If, at any time, the customer is dissatisfied with the performance, appearance, eating habits, cost, energy expenditure, philosophy, upkeep, or virility of the help, customer may request replacement, enhancement, or disposal of said help at no extra cost. If customer decides to discontinue his or her membership with *Two Places At Once*, customer will be responsible for the full amount of last month's payment. Disposals are taken care of within two weeks. All traces, correspondents, offspring, waste matter, identifications, emergent viral/bacterial/fungal infections, outstanding medical/bar/hotel/extracurricular bills will be eradicated and will be the sole responsibility of Two Places At Once, not the customer. [Note: highlight added by me.]

I filed the request for disposal two weeks ago and even received a notification on the mobile app that it had been taken care of (that's a nice touch, by the way). I haven't seen him since. So, naturally, I thought all was well.

However, some peculiar things have come up in the last week. Without getting into the details, I suspect that disposal may not have been complete. Could you please look into this for me and let me know when it's been taken care of?

If you need any further information, don't hesitate to ask.

Best,
Jason King

PS: Your customer service line seems to be disconnected. :)

Customer Service <info@tpao.com>   Thur, Jun 11, 2037 at 12:19 PM
To: Jason King <jmarlonking@gmail.com>

Dear Jason,

I am sorry to hear that you wish to discontinue your service.

Could you please describe your reasons for ending your membership with

Two Places At Once? We are rolling out many promotional packages that may be of interest to you, given your specific needs.

Sincerely,
Bridgette Hannity, Assistant Director of Customer Service
Two Places At Once: When Failure's Not An Option

Jason King <jmarlonking@gmail.com>   Fri, Jun 12, 2037 at 3:44 PM
To: Customer Service <info@tpao.com>

Dear Bridgette,

I apologize. I explained why I chose to end my membership to customer service a couple weeks ago over the phone. I shouldn't have assumed you already had that information.

In short, your service worked so well that I don't need it anymore! At first, it was great. The help handled my work meetings while I was able to spend more time with the wife and kids. I went from feeling like a constant failure to finding happiness both at home and at work. As you know, my firm was in the middle of a merger that has since been finalized. With that out of the way and some extra hands around, I've been able to slowly get my own rhythm going.

I just haven't had that much need for the help lately. I enjoy his company from time to time, though now I see why people say I can talk the ears off a rabbit! All in all, I thought it was unfair to have him just waiting around in the basement all day for something to come up. Occasionally I would call on him in the middle of the night to do the dishes, but what kind of life is that?

You know, *that's* the real beauty of this service you've created. I think it would be very effective to run a campaign offering a six-month package with the promise that, at the end, you'll be so organized you won't need help anymore. I think it could open up your market to a lot of people who don't think paying for such a service long term is realistic. I majored in marketing, if it means anything.

That all said, would you be able to look into the aforementioned issue? A few days ago the best man from my wedding, Brian, called me in a panic to tell me he'd seen me out to lunch with another woman and that I need to be careful. It took me a while to convince him that it wasn't me. Obviously, it would be best to avoid these types of misunderstandings occurring again in the future.

Also, my wife was *very* happy that I had breakfast ready for her when she woke up this morning. But I slept in. I don't ever remember giving the help a key.

There's no rush on this, just whatever you can do. But the earlier, the better, if possible.

Thank you,
Jason

Customer Service <info@tpao.com>   Fri, Jun 12, 2037 at 5:12 PM
To: Jason King <jmarlonking@gmail.com>

Dear Jason,

I'm glad you enjoyed the service. It sounds like Two Places At Once has really had an impact on your life!

We're willing to offer **50% off** for the next year if you choose to keep your membership with us. In fact, we'll throw in a free signed copy of *Living With Help: How to Maximize the Other You* by Charles Dicker, MD, CEO and Founder of Two Places At Once.

Sincerely,
Bridgette Hannity, Assistant Director of Customer Service

Jason King <jmarlonking@gmail.com>   Mon, Jun 15, 2037 at 8:45 PM
To: Customer Service <info@tpao.com>

Dear Bridgette,

I appreciate the offer. Really, it's a hell of a deal. But I just don't need it anymore. Also, I thought I had already ended the service and just need help on this one issue.

I think Janet (my wife) is on a date with him right now. She texted me three times today about how excited she was to go to French Laundry, that awfully expensive restaurant in San Francisco. She's been hinting at going for years. We're supposed to meet there after work, apparently. I hadn't made any reservations. I'd show up there myself, but if she sees me and the help together, it could be a disaster.

Would the help do that? Schedule a date without telling me?

Hey, by the way. Do you think he knows I want him disposed of? Do they care about stuff like that? I'm sure you guys have thought this out already, though.

Please let me know if there are any updates on my case.

Best,
Jason

PS: Would that French Laundry bill count as something covered under 13b? I just looked at their website and they have a fixed menu of $350. $350!

Customer Service <info@tpao.com>   Mon, Jun 15, 2037 at 9:06 PM
To: Jason King <jmarlonking@gmail.com>

Dear Jason,

Per our guidelines, all *outstanding* medical/bar/hotel/extracurricular bills at the time of membership termination are covered. If a bill is paid, it is no longer considered outstanding.

Sincerely,
Bridgette Hannity, Assistant Director of Customer Service

Jason King <jmarlonking@gmail.com>   Thur, Jun 25, 2037 at 11:29 AM
To: Customer Service <info@tpao.com>

Dear Bridgette,

   I just wanted to say thank you. It's been a week and there's been no sign
of the help. I apologize for the back-and-forth earlier and hope I wasn't too
much of an inconvenience! And don't worry about the restaurant bill. I took
care of it. Besides, French Laundry was something I should have done a long
time ago. I just wish I got to taste what I paid for, but that's water under the
bridge.

   I will definitely spread the word. If you ever get a page up on Yelp, let
me know, and I'll write a review. In the meantime, you should be receiving a
call from Brian. If there are any promotions available for him, that would be
great!

   Best,
   Jason

Jason King <jmarlonking@gmail.com>   Wed, Jul 1, 2037 at 11:01 PM
To: Customer Service <info@tpao.com>

Dear Bridgette,

   I tried calling your offices multiple times in the last few days. In fact, I used
my one call after they booked me to try to reach you. Your number is still
212-555-0961, right?

   And, yes, I said "booked me." I was in jail. Police officers barged into
the middle of a meeting with Johnson & Becker. It was like a movie. I think
someone even said, "What's the meaning of this?" I calmly told the officers
that this must be some kind of mistake, and they slammed my face against
the wall.

   Needless to say, things didn't go well. My wife bailed me out (that, French
Laundry, and the monthly maintenance fee that I still seem to be paying are
starting to drink me dry . . .). Thankfully, I was able to explain to my boss that

it was all a misunderstanding. They're not going to fire me. At least, not yet. They put me on paid administrative leave.

They think I murdered a hooker. A hooker! They have me on security camera entering a hotel with her in Harlem. They said I slit her throat and cut off her hand. Who does that?

I want to work with you here, but at the same time *they think I murdered someone*. I can't help but think that I have no choice but to go to the authorities and tell them everything. I know I'm contractually obligated to consult you about such incidents before reporting to the police, so please advise.

Best,
Jason

Customer Service <info@tpao.com>   Thur, Jul 2, 2037 at 8:53 AM
To: Jason King <jmarlonking@gmail.com>

Dear Jason,

If you are going to have extramarital relations with sex workers in public, we advise you to utilize the help.

Sincerely,
Bridgette Hannity, Assistant Director of Customer Service

Jason King <jmarlonking@gmail.com>   Thur, Jul 2, 2037 at 10:01 AM
To: Customer Service <info@tpao.com>

Dear Bridgette,

You're kidding, right? I didn't take the hooker out! The help took the hooker out!

Customer Service <info@tpao.com>   Thur, Jul 2, 2037 at 10:32 AM
To: Jason King <jmarlonking@gmail.com>

Dear Jason,

   Would you like to change your extracurricular activity settings?

   Bridgette Hannity, Assistant Director of Customer Service

Jason King <jmarlonking@gmail.com>   Thur, Jul 2, 2037 at 10:54 AM
To: Customer Service <info@tpao.com>

   No. No. No. I don't want to change any settings. This helper isn't supposed
to be around anymore at all!

   But first things first. Is there any way for you to call the authorities and
tell them it wasn't me? Technically, this wouldn't be a homicide since the
individual died by fault of a company product. At worst, you'd be hit with
a wrongful death lawsuit. That's assuming this woman had any family at all.
Even then, lawyer fees are expensive and we could make a case for reckless
use on the part of the victim.

   I'd be willing to represent you. It'd probably be better to talk over the
phone. Please call me at 415-555-5704.

   Best,

   Jason

Customer Service <info@tpao.com>   Thur, Jul 2, 2037 at 3:12 PM
To: Jason King <jmarlonking@gmail.com>

Dear Jason,

   Under section 2f, Two Places At Once is not responsible for any illegal
activities conducted by the help while under the management of the customer.

   Best,

   Bridgette Hannity, Assistant Director of Customer Service

Jason King <jmarlonking@gmail.com>   Thur, Jul 2, 2037 at 4:16 PM
To: Customer Service <info@tpao.com>

Figures.

Okay, fine. That's fine. Just please … please, please, please dispose of the help. I'll figure something out with the legalities of it all. I'm a lawyer, after all.

His DNA isn't an *exact* replica of mine. Right?

Customer Service <info@tpao.com>   Fri, Jul 3, 2037 at 11:05 AM
To: Jason King <jmarlonking@gmail.com>

Dear Jason,

Have you filled out an official termination request? If not, please fill out the attached form, print it, sign on the dotted line (a wet signature is required), scan it, and return it to this address.

Your request should be fulfilled within 5–10 business days.

Annie Raines, Assistant Customer Service Coordinator

-----Disposal Request.pdf
101k

Jason King <jmarlonking@gmail.com>   Fri, Jul 3, 2037 at 11:07 AM
To: Customer Service <info@tpao.com>

Dear Annie (?!!),

Are you ducking kidding me? Where's Bridgette?

Check your files. I've already put in a request.

Best,
Jason King

Sent from my mobile device. Please excuse the typos.

Customer Service <info@tpao.com>   Fri, Jul 3, 2037 at 1:37 PM
To: Jason King <jmarlonking@gmail.com>

Dear Jason,

Bridgette only works Monday through Thursday. Today is Friday.

I do not see any past requests from you in our record. Please fill out the attached form, print it, sign on the dotted line (a wet signature is required), scan it, and return it to this address.

Your request should be fulfilled within 5–10 business days.

Best,

Annie Raines, Assistant Customer Service Coordinator

Disposal Request.pdf
101k

Jason King <jmarlonking@gmail.com>   Fri, Jul 3, 2037 at 2:03 PM
To: Customer Service <info@tpao.com>

I worked late last night when I was called in to consult on a project. Being on leave, I had to play ball. I'm on thin ice, here. I missed Nikeila's championship game. While I was still at the office, their coach sent out pictures from the postgame celebration. There I was with my arm over Nikeila's shoulder. We both had the biggest smiles on our faces.

I never let him around my daughter. Never.

This was supposed to be taken care of TWO. FUCKING. MONTHS. AGO.

If you ask me to file that request one more time, I'm going to the cops.

Customer Service <info@tpao.com>   Fri, Jul 3, 2037 at 2:50 PM
To: Jason King <jmarlonking@gmail.com>

Dear Jason,

   I'm sorry that you are upset. We at Two Places At Once put utmost value in our customers' satisfaction.

   I have bypassed the need for a termination form and submitted your request for expedited processing.

   Best,
   Annie Raines, Assistant Customer Service Coordinator

Jason King <jmarlonking@gmail.com>   Tue, Jul 7, 2037 at 8:54 AM
To: Customer Service <info@tpao.com>

   Brian's dead. He's fucking dead. What the fuck did you make?

Jason King <jmarlonking@gmail.com>   Tue, Jul 7, 2037 at 9:30 AM
To: Customer Service <info@tpao.com>

Dear Bridgette/Annie/Whomever,

   I apologize for the harsh words. It was unprofessional of me and I apologize.

   I told Brian about the help. Normally, this would be a breach of section 7c, but Brian signed up for one of your Calendaring services and technically was a customer. Anyway, I had him follow the help after one of the dates with my wife (they do that a lot lately) and update me through text. He followed the help to the Bronx and saw him meeting up with a small group of people outside a warehouse. Then Brian stopped texting.

   I hadn't heard from Brian in two days. They found him floating in the Hudson River this morning. They think it's suicide. But I know Brian. He was the happiest guy on the planet.

   You did this. You, you, you.

Jason King <jmarlonking@gmail.com>   Thur, Jul 9, 2037 at 5:20 PM
To: Customer Service <info@tpao.com>

Dear You,

   I received a package today. Brian's hand. The note said: "Dearest Original,
Your life gives me tremendous joy. Please accept this gesture of my
appreciation. With warm regards, Help."

   I think the bastard was trying to make a joke with "gesture" and hand. I
don't know. I don't know, I don't know, I don't know.

   PLEASE ADVISE!

Jason King <jmarlonking@gmail.com>   Thur, Jul 16, 2037 at 9:07 AM
To: Customer Service <info@tpao.com>

Dear You,

   My wife left me. Not that you care. She took Nikeila and just . . . left.

   I thought the murder allegations would get to her sooner or later. They
didn't. What finally did it, then? She saw me kissing some twenty-year-old
outside a restaurant. A restaurant two blocks away from her job.

   I told Janet everything (yeah, yeah, yeah, I breached the contract, so
shove it). I really poured it all out for her. And you know what? She already
knew. She said the help told her three darn diddly fucking months ago
and she was just waiting for me to come out with it. He told her that I'd
purchased him so that I could sleep around without my family finding out.

   She threatened to call the cops if I try to contact her.

   Would you mind calling her for me? 415-555-7656. If she hears it from you,
maybe she'll believe me. Maybe she'll come back home.

   She's with that monster. Her and Nikeila, with that monster.

Customer Service <info@tpao.com>   Thur, Jul 16, 2037 at 10:30 AM
To: Jason King <jmarlonking@gmail.com>

Dear Jason,

Only those who have signed the agreement may have formal correspondence with Two Places At Once. I checked over your record and do not believe Janet King is part of your plan.

Would you like to add her for an additional $199 per month?

Bridgette Hannity, Assistant Director of Customer Service

Jason King <jmarlonking@gmail.com>   Thur, Jul 16, 2037 at 10:49 AM
To: Customer Service <info@tpao.com>

I've decided you're a robot. Yes, definitely a robot.

Best,
Jason King

Sent from my mobile device. Please excuse the typos.

Jason King <jmarlonking@gmail.com>   Mon, Jul 20, 2037 at 12:31 PM
To: Customer Service <info@tpao.com>

Dear Bridgette or Annie or Whomever,

I went into the office today. The boss looked at me, said "How's it hanging?" Being the fool that I am, I thought maybe a small portion of my life was still intact. I said, "I'm surviving, Carl. You?"

Next thing I know two steroidal guards are throwing me out the back.

A code phrase!! Who says "How's it hanging?" anyway?? Your damn abomination must have told them everything, but he's pretending to be me.

You'd think a bunch of lawyers would consider that "Hey, maybe the impostor got there first." What's up with your policies now, huh? Isn't the help breaching all kinds of codes by telling everyone?

At least I still have the house. But without Janet and Nikeila, it feels so empty.

Would he hurt them?

Jason King <jmarlonking@gmail.com>   Wed, Jul 22, 2037 at 4:26 PM
To: Customer Service <info@tpao.com>

I messed up. Nikeila saw me. I just wanted to see her, to make sure she was all right.

I waited for her after school. But the help was there. She saw both of us. She was so upset. Janet was upset.

I didn't know what else to do. It was all out there. I confronted him. I called him a liar. I made a big scene. You might even hear about it on the news.

He's strong. He broke my jaw. When they were leaving, I heard him tell Janet he'd take care of me.

Damn, he's strong. Please advise.

Customer Service <info@tpao.com>   Wed, Jul 22, 2037 at 5:03 PM
To: Jason King <jmarlonking@gmail.com>

Dear Jason,

Damage of Two Places At Once property is strictly prohibited under section 3c!

I have looked into your request and we have been very patient and accommodating. The disposal process takes up to 5–10 business days. May I remind you that weekends are not business days. Also, please factor in holidays.

Still, we at Two Places At Once highly value customer satisfaction. If your helper is not performing to your standards, you can always utilize the code phrase to deactivate him or her.

Sincerely,

Bridgette Hannity, Assistant Director of Customer Service

Jason King <jmarlonking@gmail.com>   Wed, Jul 22, 2037 at 5:06 PM

To: Customer Service <info@tpao.com>

There's a code phrase?!
You fuck!

Best,

Jason King

Sent from my mobile device. Please excuse the typos.

Jason King <jmarlonking@gmail.com>   Wed, Jul 22, 2037 at 5:16 PM

To: Customer Service <info@tpao.com>

Dear Bridgette,

I am kindly requesting the code phrase to disable the helper that I ordered on Monday, April 6 of this year.

I will be more than happy to cover any costs associated with prematurely disabling the model.

Thank you,

Jason

Jason King <jmarlonking@gmail.com>   Wed, Jul 22, 2037 at 8:27 PM
To: Customer Service <info@tpao.com>

Shut. Shut shut shut shit. He just pulled into my driveway.
What's the code phrase?

Best,
Jason King

Sent from my mobile device. Please excuse the typos.

Jason King <jmarlonking@gmail.com>   Wed, Jul 22, 2037 at 8:39 PM
To: Customer Service <info@tpao.com>

He went next door, to Maureen and Joe's house. He's knocking on their
door right now.
They have our spare key.
Please don't be home. Please don't be home. Please . . .
Shut, they're home.

Best,
Jason King

Sent from my mobile device. Please excuse the typos.

Jason King <jmarlonking@gmail.com>   Wed, Jul 22, 2037 at 9:29 PM
To: Customer Service <info@tpao.com>

He killed them. He ducking killed them!

Best,
Jason King

Sent from my mobile device. Please excuse the typos.

Jason King <jmarlonking@gmail.com>   Wed, Jul 22, 2037 at 9:41 PM
To: Customer Service <info@tpao.com>

I called 911.
What's the damn code phrase?

Customer Service <info@tpao.com>   Wed, Jul 22, 2037 at 10:01 PM
To: Jason King <jmarlonking@gmail.com>

Dear Jason,
Code phrases are reserved for absolute emergencies. Are you experiencing an emergency?

Sincerely,
Bridgette Hannity, Assistant Director of Customer Service

Jason King <jmarlonking@gmail.com>   Wed, Jul 22, 2037 at 10:03 PM
To: Customer Service <info@tpao.com>

YES!

Best,
Jason King

Sent from my mobile device. Please excuse the typos.

Customer Service <info@tpao.com>   Wed, Jul 22, 2037 at 10:03 PM
To: Jason King <jmarlonking@gmail.com>

Dear Customer,
Our offices will be closed until Friday, July 24th for professional

development. For urgent matters, please call and leave a voice mail at 212-555-0961.

   We will get back to you as soon as possible.

Best,
The Two Places At Once Team

Jason King <jmarlonking@gmail.com>   Wed, Jul 22, 2037 at 10:04 PM
To: Customer Service <info@tpao.com>

   Duck you!

Best,
Jason King

Sent from my mobile device. Please excuse the typos.

Jason King <jmarlonking@gmail.com>   Wed, Jul 22, 2037 at 10:05 PM
To: Customer Service <info@tpao.com>

   *FUCK you!

Best,
Jason King

Sent from my mobile device. Please excuse the typos.

Customer Service <info@tpao.com>   Fri, Jul 24, 2037 at 9:01 AM
To: Jason King <jmarlonking@gmail.com>

Dear Jason,
   The code phrase is "silk pajamas." Saying this within hearing distance

of the help will immediately disable his motor, speech, mental, and reproductive abilities.

Please let us know if you need any further assistance.

Sincerely,

Annie Raines, Assistant Customer Service Coordinator

Jason King <jmarlonking@gmail.com>   Fri, Jul 24, 2037 at 11:20 AM
To: Customer Service <info@tpao.com>

I just woke up. That fucker knocked me out. He cut open my arm and stitched it back up. I think he left something inside. It just started beeping. Literally. My. Arm. Is. Beeping.

What did he do? What should I do? There's something in there. It burns. Please advise.

PS: Silk pajamas?! Really?!?

Customer Service <info@tpao.com>   Fri, Jul 24, 2037 at 1:01 PM
To: Jason King <jmarlonking@gmail.com>

Dear Jason,

We are happy to inform you that your disposal request has been processed. A Dismantle Team is currently being dispatched and will track down and dispose of the help within an hour.

Please let us know if you have any questions or concerns.

Sincerely,

Annie Raines, Assistant Customer Service Coordinator

Jason King <jmarlonking@gmail.com>   Fri, Jul 24, 2037 at 1:05 PM
To: Customer Service <info@tpao.com>

Wait! He put his tracker in me! Abort disposal!

Jason King <jmarlonking@gmail.com>   Fri, Jul 24, 2037 at 1:11 PM
To: Customer Service <info@tpao.com>

Call them off! Their coming to get the wrong guy!

Customer Service <info@tpao.com>   Fri, Jul 24, 2037 at 1:20 PM
To: Jason King <jmarlonking@gmail.com>

Dear Jason,

A disposal request cannot be rescinded once it has been processed.

Many of our customers discover they made the wrong choice in getting rid of their help. After all, how can you be in Two Places At Once without help? We will be more than happy to discuss replacement options with you once disposal is completed.

Sincerely,

Annie Raines, Assistant Customer Service Coordinator

Customer Service <info@tpao.com>   Fri, Jul 24, 2037 at 2:01 PM
To: Jason King <jmarlonking@gmail.com>

Dear Jason,

Your request has been completed. We apologize for the inconvenience.

Sincerely,

Annie Raines, Assistant Customer Service Coordinator

Jason King <jmarlonking@gmail.com>   Mon, Jul 27, 2037 at 10:41 AM
To: Customer Service <info@tpao.com>

Dearest Customer Service,

   I sincerely thank you for taking care of this issue. This resolution should put an end to all other complications. I look forward to being able to continue on with my life's work.

   That being said, I will be in need of much more help. I believe you have my DNA on file, yes?

   Also, how would I go about enrolling my wife and daughter? I would very much like them to be a part of this experience.

   With warm regards,
   Jason King

Customer Service <info@tpao.com>   Mon, Jul 27, 2037 at 10:51 AM
To: Jason King <jmarlonking@gmail.com>

Dear Jason,

   This is great news! We'll get your order in right away.

   Bridgette Hannity, Assistant Director of Customer Service

Jason King <jmarlonking@gmail.com>   Mon, Jul 27, 2037 at 11:01 AM
To: Customer Service <info@tpao.com>

   Perfect.

Now You See Me

GOOD ART CHANGES YOU. AND THAT WAS THE POINT, RIGHT? THAT'S WHAT the social media ad that caught my attention wanted me to believe: *Our Shoes: You couldn't understand our struggle . . . Until now.* I had read the line over and over again during a rare downtime in the on-call room and was still mesmerized by it when Danny messaged our Allies 4 Life group. I got three tix to that new BLM exhibit in Brooklyn. Who's rolling?

As the timely one of our little group, I had the privilege of holding our place in a line that almost circled the block. I looked around; I was the only White person. A young obstetrician in East Harlem, I was no stranger to Black spaces. My patients were Black, my nurses were Black, and I had gathered more than a few Black friends through college, medical school, and mutual gatherings. Still, I couldn't help but wonder what they thought of me, the quiet White woman in line for an exhibit about them.

Finally, I saw Pam and Danny at the edge of the parking lot. They were an odd pair. Danny was easily spotted with her long, confident legs, wide smile, and asymmetric red hair that reached past her shoulders on one side. Pam, on the other hand, was your typical near-term pregnant woman with the easy ponytail and slow waddle. I rose up on my tiptoes and waved them over as if signaling a lifeboat. I rocked back on my heels and tried not to cringe at the sight of Danny's brown-and-black BLM hoodie. She'd always been extra with her ally-ship, especially considering she had come late in the game. I sometimes remembered the things she'd said in high school, the jokes she had made, and wondered if they stayed in the back of her mind or if she had shut out that side of herself completely.

"Wow, this is quite a crowd," Danny said. She made a point to flash her big grin to the group adjacent to us. "A beautiful day, beautiful people. I can't wait. It's going to be fucking awesome."

"I hear it's hard to stomach," Pam said. She rubbed her pregnant belly as we rounded the last corner. The line seemed to move quicker now that I wasn't alone. We'd likely be on the tail end of the next batch.

"That means it's powerful," Danny said. She quickly brushed her hair to the uncut side, leaned back into us, and took a selfie with the *Our Shoes* sign in the background. The optics of three White women posing outside an exhibit about Black suffering seemed to be lost on her. My gaze caught Pam's. She was just as uncomfortable. "We need something every once in a while to shake us up, you know? Speaking of . . ."

Danny pulled a dark-blue newborn shirt from her fanny pack and leaned down to coo at Pam's belly. "Godmommy got you something special. I can't wait to meet you, little one."

Pam unfolded the shirt, laughed, and held it up.

" 'I fuck with godmom'?" I read. "Really, Danny?"

"Damn right. We have to show her love. With Pam as the mom, me as godmother, and you delivering, that's the dream team right there."

"Don't jinx it," Pam said. She pulled her peach-colored shirt down around her wrists to cover her many tattoos. Any close friend of Pam was familiar with the intricate sleeves of professionally colored vines and flowers intertwined with stylistic quotes. Looking at her now, with her straight black hair, subtle makeup, and conservative dress, a stranger would be none the wiser. There were no regrets, as Pam expanded her body art regularly, but she hardly ever showed it off in public. "She could come at any time, on any shift."

"I'll be there," I said. I had arranged my month's schedule to be exclusively labor and delivery for the weeks surrounding Pam's due date. Even if she did deliver overnight or on one of my mandated off days, as chief resident I could easily make sure I was there without anyone making a fuss about duty-hour violations.

"Shit," Danny said. "'No food, no drinks' type scene. I have to finish this. Want some?"

Danny pulled out a half-eaten chocolate bar with tattered wrapping and broke me off a piece. The chocolate had an earthy taste to it that I couldn't quite place.

"Spread the love," Pam said.

"Here, have mine."

Danny slapped my offering hand. "No THC for my godchild. You should know better, Doc."

I spit out the chocolate. Danny was already laughing. "Weed? You gave me weed?"

"THC."

"Are you fucking kidding me? What if they drug-test me?"

"Why in the world would they test you? Little Miss Perfect, chief resident no less. Live a little."

I wiped my tongue with my shirt. I hadn't swallowed. A little would be absorbed under my tongue. A minuscule amount. Still. "What if I'm working tonight?"

"Are you?"

"That's not the point. You have to tell someone before you give them weed—THC, whatever. What if Pam went into labor and I was stoned?"

"Good point," Pam said.

"All right, all right," Danny said. "More for me. Check it out."

Right inside the entrance was a small poster: a Black woman in intricately decorated tribal dress who carried a longsword and a broad shield. She rode atop an elephant with thick, curved tusks and war paint across its head and ears. A caption ran underneath: *This exhibit is dedicated to the memory of Adesokash, the long-forgotten Sanain Queen of Healing and Music. Though her voice is no longer with us, her music lives on. May it heal you.*

"I wonder what happened to her," Pam said.

After a brief check of our bags, we entered a dark, cramped space. In front of me, Danny's excited light dimmed to a silhouette. My breath whistled as heat rose through my neck and settled around my eyes and ears. I slowed just enough to let Pam lean into me. I could almost feel her vibrate in pace with her racing heart; she sought the same comfort.

"It's like the underground railroad," Danny threw back in a whisper.

"Not funny," Pam said.

"No, she's right," I said. Perhaps that was the artist's intention. A lack of control in the darkness of America. Probably bullshit, but I needed to hang my hat on something to keep me from turning around and pushing through the too-quiet line until I found sunlight. In the hospital, I was in charge. Even when the patients crashed, I knew my role and everyone else's. Here, there was only darkness and a quiet chaos. An uncertainty without form.

The corridor ended. We suddenly had space and room to breathe. My heart eased itself back down my throat but still sat high and loud in my chest. Darkness continued to cling to the air even as pockets of art illuminated the distant walls around the room. I could hear the other visitors milling about, but besides the shadows passing in front of the exhibits, could see no more than an arm's reach in front of me.

"Pam? Danny?" Where had they gone? I felt silly calling for them. I wandered toward the light of one of the pieces and soon found myself leaning into the art. A vibrant and colorful restaurant, its patrons in the middle of good conversation and good food. Hanging in someone's home—Danny's parent's, perhaps—I wouldn't have given it another look. Here? Yes; White. All of them. I searched the less-defined features of the waitstaff. Also White. Next, I searched for meaning. I was missing something.

I moved on, unsatisfied. The next were similar. A packed subway train. A board meeting. A garbage truck making its rounds on a residential street with overlapping trees shedding autumn leaves. All White, from the kids running in the grass to the men collecting trash.

Reading the reviews, I'd expected something like the National Museum of African American History and Culture in DC, which I'd been to twice. A walk through the perils of the slave trade, the Civil War, and Jim Crow as a reminder of history's dark side. Here, there was none of that. The paintings were all modern. How they would help me understand "the struggle" was beyond me.

A bit of light caught Pam's pregnant figure. Her frozen expression blunted any relief I felt as I walked over. She was either on the verge of tears or a scream, paused so perfectly between the two that she could have been part of the exhibit. She cradled her swollen belly. I followed her gaze, felt my mouth part, and just barely stopped myself from collapsing into her.

What the fuck was this?

I'd seen worse in my training. I'd handed a healthy, crying baby to his mother's arms for the first time a few hours before passing another pale and near lifeless one to the pediatric ICU team on standby. Though when documenting later that night I entered the same measurement for both—seven pounds—the perceived weight of life wasn't lost on me. The dying newborn was simultaneously lighter and harder to bear than anything I'd ever held. I'd rolled a screaming mother from the emergency to the operating room to find that her uterus had slowly necrosed and died over the few days following an otherwise routine C-section. I'd informed families who had come to celebrate new life that instead they'd now have to plan a funeral. My heart had grown hard enough to do the job.

Still . . . what the fuck was this? I didn't know. Not at first. The scene was relatively routine. The laboring mother. The monitors. The hospital staff. All familiar. And yet . . . Was it the mother's distress? Young and Black, her mottled hospital gown tipped with sweat and the slightest hint of blood, her belly rose like a stone, indicating the painful contractions of active labor. No, I had seen that face as well, in all shades and colors. I frantically searched the scene for some blatant horror and the source of whatever fingers wrapped around my lungs. If I didn't find it, it might undo me—

And then, I saw. It wasn't the mother, or the surgical kit open and ready for an inevitable emergency C-section. It was the response of the medical team. The doctors looked on with something that wasn't quite amusement, but it wasn't concern, either. They could have been the waiter taking an order or the trash collector signaling the driver to move to the next block.

"They don't care," Pam said. And they didn't. One watched the fetal heart monitor like one might watch the pump at a gas station. Another leaned against the doorway, drinking a coffee and browsing his phone. I blinked; the doctor checking his watch must have been my imagination.

"Come on," I said. "This is too much."

"No," she said. "I need to see this."

The sisterly thing to do would have been to nod and stand by her. But it *was* too much. That wasn't how things were. The hospital was a place of healing, heroics, and miracles. In that painting was a place of indifference and silent contempt. I moved away; Pam didn't notice me go.

I found Danny with her arms crossed over her chest and her shoulders hunched as if taken by a chill. She had a serious, somber look I hadn't seen on her since her father's funeral that first year out of college. The piece was of a young slave woman fleeing across a field, her masters in hot pursuit. My eyes drunkenly rolled over the canvas. I focused on the center for stability, where two German shepherds snarled and tugged on their chains. Wait—I'd had a German shepherd growing up; they were relatively modern breeds, only a century or so old. I stepped back. The woman wasn't a slave at all. How could I have thought so, with her tight-fitting jeans, neatly braided hair, cell phone in hand, and brown hoodie ripped at the sleeves? She was running from two police officers, obvious in their blue uniforms.

"She's been running for a while," Danny said. "See?" And I did.

I moved away, and as soon as I did, the memory of the painting was hazy and incomplete. *Had* she been a slave? Were the dogs nineteenth-century hounds or modern breeds? Whispers from the other people in the display room rose from the quiet ashes. The shuffle of feet, the soft wheeze of someone who likely had untreated asthma, they all told me I wasn't alone, even if it felt that way. Only the art accompanied me.

I wouldn't say that the painting caught my eye so much as it caught *me*. There was nothing particularly special or remarkable about it. An empty city street, the cars and buildings exaggerated in their cartoon appearance. The grit of the city lay in contrast to the golden sunset sky that showed between the gaps in the skyline.

I don't know how long I stood there, taking it in. My eyes went to every corner, every mark, as if some clue or insight into the creator's mind lay about, ripe for the taking. It was there, I just couldn't see it. It gnawed at me like an absent word on the tip of the tongue. Thoughts of being lost and undecided in medical school flitted by. The lack of purpose, the desire of fulfillment. That was before. I'd worked to establish myself now, to be rigid and proud in my profession. If I could . . . just . . .

A hand on my shoulder. I screamed, stifled it with my fist, and turned to find Pam.

"I'm leaving," she said.

I began to ask why, but I knew.

"All right, okay. Let's find Danny and—"

My hand went to my mouth. I'd sent a glance back that was supposed to be a fleeting thing, but . . . there it was. The purpose. There was a woman in the picture. Not hidden. In fact, the picture was *of* the woman. She was smack in the middle, standing on the sidewalk beside an intricately painted car. Even as I wondered how the hell I had missed her, I found it difficult to see her fully now that she was exposed. My gaze rolled around her like clumsy fingers trying to catch a piece of ice. I focused; she came to clarity. Spandex pants, a loose-fitting tee. Skin the color of birch and with the shine of obsidian. An elephant pendant hung prominent around her neck. Everything was defined. Everything was clear.

Except for her face. Of that, she had none.

...

I found Pam pacing outside the gallery as she spoke into her phone. Her free hand steadily circled her midsection. A natural movement for any expecting mother that I'd come to recognize, in its excess, as a sign of mental distress. But she was okay. A ridiculous thought, but a real one. We'd survived something, even if we wouldn't be able to say what it was.

"You sure I shouldn't come in?" Pam said. "It's been almost two hours, and I've been moving the whole time."

"What's wrong?" I began, but Pam held up a finger and shook her head. I quelled the urge to push further. Despite the ethical and emotional complications, I had essentially become Pam's ob-gyn. I had counseled and guided her through the initial in vitro fertilization process and had been with her ever since. She and her baby, they were my responsibility.

"Right, okay. Lots of water. I will, Doctor."

"What's going on?" I said again once the call was over.

"I haven't felt her move since before the exhibit," Pam said. "One of the doctors on call—a man, low voice—said I should drink cold water, but I don't have any water. She's supposed to be moving, right?"

"She's probably just a little sleepy," I said. Behind what I hoped was a reassuring smile, my mind went through all the more serious explanations. "Why didn't you ask me?"

"I would have. I just couldn't find you. And you shouldn't have to work on your day off." She jumped a little, placed both hands on her belly, and then closed her eyes. "There you are, big girl. You scared momma."

"I'm never off. Not when it comes to this."

Pam nodded, though her mind was elsewhere. "Where's Danny?"

Behind us, the entrance to the exhibit sat cold and bare. The line was gone. No one had emerged after me. Shit. I'd have to go back. Why would Danny do that? Why would she stay in that awful place and make me come after her?

And then my friend walked out of the art exhibit, her face lit in laughter.

"Whoa, what happened?" she said when she saw us. "Baby girl coming?"

"Not today," Pam said, pocketing her phone. "Let's get the fuck out of here."

...

On the drive back into Brooklyn after leaving *Our Shoes*, Danny's need to evoke laughter ran up against our temporary inability to laugh. Her jokes did little to cut through the thick and stifling silence. She even pulled out an old racist one from high school. The irony of her allyship gave it a levity that would have forced guilty laughter any other day. Now I just felt uneasy.

Thoughts of the faceless woman had eaten up the last of my reserves. So when Danny spoke again after a particularly long silence, I took in a sharp breath to yell at her to shut up. But what she said was without humor. Her voice had the same cold quality I had heard back in the exhibit.

"The pictures changed for you guys, too, right?"

Danny's words sucked all the unclaimed emotion from the car.

Laughter, safer than tears, sparked between the three of us. What we had just witnessed had stirred something we didn't want to share with ourselves, much less each other. Allies have to laugh every now and then so as not to go crazy.

"That shit was insane," Danny said. "Damn near thought I'd lost my mind."

"How do you think they did it?" I said.

"A hologram. Some lighting tricks. Unsettling, huh? My painting, it kept changing. I swore it was a runaway slave at first. And that must be what it was. Then I saw the dogs, and when I looked at her again she wasn't a slave at all, just a woman running from a mob."

It wasn't lost on me that Danny had referred to it as "my painting."

"That one was intense. It's why I couldn't live in the South. Still so much is backwards down there." Danny mouthed *The South?* I ignored her. "I saw one where the woman was invisible, but not invisible, you know?"

"Yes, I know exactly what you mean by that cryptic-ass sentence."

"It must have been the hologram." But what about the face?

Danny slapped the steering wheel. "Fucking great. I love great art. My take? It's a metaphor of how things change today."

"Maybe," I said. "I didn't get a lot of it, to be honest. I just felt kind of . . . out of place."

"What do you mean?" Danny said.

"Like, where do we fit in, you know?"

"You wanted us in it?"

"No, that's not what I'm saying. Just, all the White people were in these regular paintings. I don't know what the artist was trying to say, is all."

Danny framed her hand as if imagining a billboard. "Maybe they should have called the exhibit *White Women: It's Not About You*."

"Fuck you, Danny," I said.

Danny laughed. "What did you think, Pam?"

I locked eyes with Pam in the rearview. She had laughed, too. The hint of it still lay across her lips. "It was powerful. Just not my cup of tea."

"What was yours?" When Pam raised her eyebrows, Danny went on. "Come on, I know something spoke to you."

Before Pam could speak, flashing red and blue lit our world and brought back our silence. Danny cursed through the rearview mirror, hit her steering wheel, and cursed again.

"Last thing I need," she said.

"How fast were you going?" I said.

"The speed limit. They ran my plates at the light."

"You got expired tags?"

"No! My shit's up to date."

The police wouldn't just run a random person's plates. There must have been a reason.

Danny put on her blinker and slowly changed lanes, so formally and carefully that it would have been fitting for her to put her arm out, too. Instead of speeding up to pass and apprehend someone more deserving of his energy, the cop fell in line behind us.

Danny continued to curse softly as she pulled the car onto the side of the highway. I touched her shoulder. She started so badly that she hit the horn.

"You got a dead body in the back or something?" I asked. "You look stressed."

"I'm just . . . my ID, it's in my purse." She reached into the back, rummaged through it, and then gripped her license against the wheel. She thrust her cell phone into my hand. "Here, put this away."

"Your phone?"

"I'm not taking any chances."

A dead body in the trunk was a joke, to be sure, but other thoughts began to fill the space. Did she have something worse than weed? I knew she dabbled, maybe even sold. These thoughts led to others. Had I seen this car before? It did look new. Stolen? Wild and frightening notions, not only in their absurdity but also in how they manifested in my mind less as fantasy than as a call to caution. I pushed them aside.

An unsteady glow approached the driver's side. Danny rolled down her window. I squinted against the officer's high-powered flashlight. The beacon fully blocked his features.

"Do you know why I stopped you?"

Danny stared straight ahead, hands gripped to the wheel, mouth set. Her undefined angst bled over and into me. *What the fuck?* Pam mouthed when I looked back at her. I shrugged in response. Danny had been one to find trouble all throughout high school and college. The number of run-ins she'd had with the police was second only to the times she avoided them. If there was anyone I'd want to talk to the police on my behalf, it would be her.

"What seems to be—" I raised my hand against the light as it shifted to me. "What seems to be the problem, Officer?"

The light continued. The officer said nothing. The flashlight's circle grew in my vision, dreamlike. The cop was leaning in.

"Was I speeding?" Danny finally said. The light immediately left me, bobbed, then clicked off. I could see his face now. Young, soft. There was even the hint of a smile.

He looked at Danny for a while, then behind him as if to check where he was, and finally spoke. "Sobriety checks. Just want to make sure everyone is all right."

Danny's grip loosened. Her shoulders fell. "We just came from the most sobering place ever. You need me to get out? Take a breathalyzer? I could use the fresh air."

"No need," he said. "You all have a safe evening."

Danny adjusted and eyed the rearview to make sure the cop was fully in his car before pulling back onto the road. We barely crawled a silent mile before fresh headlights lit our interior. They weren't the flashing red and blues of before but had a seeing quality to them.

"Why's he still trailing us?" I said.

"Fuck if I know. He can't stop us again, can he? Isn't that double jeopardy or something?"

"Shh, not so loud," I said.

"He can't fucking hear us," Danny said in a fierce whisper.

The headlights angled; the cop turned the corner behind us.

"Fucking cops," Danny said. "I know we said we'd get drinks after, but—"

"Let's just call it a night," I said.

"Good idea. I'll drop Pam first. You cool with that?" Danny leaned into the rearview. "Hey, girl, you good back there?"

"It scared me," Pam said. Her voice was low and weak. My eyes instinctively went to her belly, as if I could somehow sense the parameters we relied on in labor and delivery.

"Me, too," I said. "Danny, what the fuck?"

Danny was nodding in agreement until she caught on to my tone. "Wait, you think that was my fault?"

"He had to pull us over for some reason. Maybe you sold his kid a joint or something."

"Really? I slip you one little edible and now you think I'm a dealer?"

"You were spooked. I saw you. Something's going on."

"Stop. Damn it, stop. You're upsetting the baby. And I wasn't talking about the cop." Pam looked out the window as she rubbed her belly. "It's that damn exhibit that scared me. Did you see those doctors? They just didn't give a fuck. What if I lose the baby?"

"Fuck, Pam," Danny said. "Don't say that."

I adjusted my seat belt and turned fully toward her. "That painting fucked me up, too. They could have left that one out. Shit like that is why people don't trust doctors. It's just a painting. It won't be like that."

"You can't promise me something won't go wrong."

"Yes, I can. You're my sister, and I'll be there. You're as good as one of us. VIP care."

"That's kind of dark," Danny said.

"Just drive. Before you get us thrown into jail."

"What about you?" Danny said as I turned back in my seat. "You haven't said anything about the exhibit."

"I told you. Invisible woman. Some type of hologram."

"Yeah, yeah, but how did it make you *feel*?" Danny's hands, which had finally relaxed, went to ten and two on the wheel as she peered into her sideview. She let an SUV pass. "Just someone in a rush."

"Like I said, I didn't get it. I don't know what I was supposed to feel."

"Maybe because it wasn't for us," Pam said.

Despite the silence that followed, I didn't agree with Pam. Quite the opposite: I thought the exhibit was for us specifically. And I knew exactly how my painting made me feel. I just didn't know how to tell them.

...

I slept a deep, dreamless sleep that carried me past my morning alarm and didn't break until the sun through my window was strong across my face. I checked my phone and had almost gone back to sleep when my day brain took over.

Shit.

I jumped up, washed my face, and grabbed my phone to summon a rideshare while I got my workbag together. The phone's facial recognition kept jamming, and it had been so long since I used my code that I was almost locked out with my attempts. Finally I got through, called a nearby car, poured Othelia fresh kitty litter, and double-checked that I had everything before stepping out the door.

A red Prius slowed to a crawl halfway up the block. I checked the app; the tags matched. I waved. The driver looked right at me and then away. I groaned and walked forward, already committing to a three-star review. He rolled down the passenger window and leaned over.

I told him my name and gestured with my phone. "Heading to MacArthur Hospital, right?" That and my tone should have been enough to convey that I was in a rush.

The driver frowned and sped away. I stood there, half in the street outside my apartment, and for a moment I didn't care that I was late. I looked around, suddenly ashamed. Had I done something wrong?

I swiped at my phone to see if there was a glitch on the app or to call another ride, almost threw it into the gutter when it stuttered in recognition error, pocketed it instead, and headed down the block to the nearest station. I took the train and used the extra thirty minutes of commuting time to email the clinic and file a complaint to the rideshare company. I was *never* late.

Once that was done, I opened up our Allies 4 Life group, started to type, deleted it, started again. I stared at the blinking cursor hovering over the send button, sat back in the cheap, cushioned seat, closed my eyes, and desperately tried to bring up the woman's face in the painting. I saw the tight-fitting pants, the dark skin, and the elephant necklace. These aspects remained as clear as standing in the exhibit. I even noticed the chipped end of the elephant's right tusk. Its small eyes were narrow and menacing. As for the woman's face, nothing.

No matter how hard I tried, I couldn't see what I knew was plainly there. I abandoned the image and returned to my phone. My painting made me feel powerless. The text to my fellow allies, waiting for me to make a decision.

I hit send and got off the bus.

I entered Building 200 and, as I took the stairs to the fourth floor, went through possible scenarios of what I would say to Dr. Ernst, the hospital's director of labor and delivery and the attending supervising today's clinic. In residency there were no excuses, only outcomes. And I was chief because I had some of the best. But my reputation was only as good as the outcome it promised. Being late shouldn't matter as long as I got the work done.

Why, then, did I feel like an intern that just fucked up on the first day?

I entered MacArthur's Family Healthcare Clinic through the back and slipped into the resident's workroom. A resident was presenting a case to Dr. Ernst on the far side. Neither of them looked up. I hung up my workbag, put on my white coat, and set up at a sleeping computer.

"Pressures are good," I heard the resident say. I recognized him as a second-year. We'd been on labor and delivery a few times together. He emitted a nervous air around the team, like he had something to prove. I got a chance to see his bedside manner, however, and he was surprisingly warm and empathic with his patients. "I put in for a fasting glucose."

"What's the main thing you have to watch out for in her, given her age, number of pregnancies, and her last three pressures?" Dr. Ernst said. "This is a 'read-my-mind' question, but I want you to read my mind."

I tapped my finger as the electronic medical health records system loaded. I was used to playing catch-up secondary to a late patient or two. Even if the first three were roomed and waiting already, I could skim their charts for the crucial pieces, order routine labs so the phlebotomist could get started, see them in rapid fashion, and be back on track by lunch.

"Huh," I said when my schedule loaded. No arrivals yet. What's more, the day looked thin. I counted; definitely more than a few cancellations. The most I'd ever had, to be sure.

"Lucky me," I said to myself. I sat back in the soft, borrowed comfort of a salvaged day and stifled a laugh. What a shitshow. I absentmindedly opened Allies 4 Life and began to type out my morning when I saw the message I'd sent during the bus ride to work. My painting made me feel powerless. Still unread. I sent what little I'd written about the odd day and refreshed my schedule again. Nothing. Had everyone forgotten about me? Perhaps all my patients had canceled because . . .

Because what? I shook away the thought. Medical school and

residency taught me first that insecurity would always be there, and second what to do with it. I instead checked the online schedule to see who'd be on the floors with me over the next week.

My cursor ventured to Explorer's search bar. I typed *Adesokash* and got only a few results. I scrolled the images, found the illustration from the exhibit, and hit a dead end of broken links. I tried another search and came across a few short paragraphs on what looked like an old, abandoned site. The narrative presented itself as fact without a single reference. After inheriting the throne of Sanai, a dying West African kingdom ravaged by the slave trade, Adesokash's attempts to slow the sale of her people into bondage ultimately failed. When the Portuguese came for her, she fought and sang until her last breath. One slaver was so haunted by her song he later ended up throwing himself into the Atlantic. I sent the link to the group. So much for being healed, huh?

I closed the window. The second-year resident's presentation drifted over. Something about it piqued my interest and tugged with familiarity.

I clicked through a few tabs in the electronic medical records, found the source of my intuition, and sat up fast enough to cause the front of my chair to lift a little.

"That's my patient," I said. And it was. I'd delivered her baby three months ago, and this was her second postnatal follow-up. I skimmed the notes quickly to see if there was any reason she'd appeared on a schedule other than mine. I didn't have any missed-page alerts. They would have told me she was here, waiting, before shifting her to another resident.

"That's my patient," I said again, standing.

The resident slowly stopped; his eyes shifted past our supervisor and onto me.

"Oh," he said. "Are you sure? I don't think so."

"Positive. I delivered her baby right before sign-out, and I was there two hours later because I wanted to get everything in. Gestational diabetes, right? G-two, p-one, didn't want the epidural. Had to observe the baby for hypoglycemia, almost sent him to the PICU."

The resident frowned. "That's a lot of our patients."

I caught myself soon enough to make it look like I was just turning to engage better in the conversation. If the attending wasn't in the room, I might have said something more. I knew what our patient population was like. Hell, I had taught his "Intro to Harlem" lecture on it more than a year before.

"She's definitely my patient," I said instead. I watched the attending out of the corner of my eye without actually shifting my gaze, a skill I'd picked up early in residency. That brief sliver of a second of direct eye contact put all your insecurities out there on the table. "I don't know how she got off my schedule and onto yours."

"I've already talked to her and put in the orders."

I nodded and, on my own terms, turned to Dr. Ernst. "I can see her with him. None of my patients are here yet. I'm familiar with her, and it can save you some time."

She waved a hand. "I have to see the patients anyway."

"If you want to just eyeball her, I can sign the note."

Dr. Ernst leaned back in her chair to look up at me. Despite our respective roles, I hadn't the pleasure of seeing firsthand how she gained her infamous reputation amongst the residents in and out of the operating room. I was spared this side of her for the same reason I became chief: I was too good to criticize. She regarded me now as if I was an ever-elusive treasure, finally within her reach.

"Are you suggesting I jeopardize my license by committing fraud?"

I hadn't expected that. Dr. Ernst's eyes lit in enjoyment; her mouth remained rigid. "Because that's what it would be, right? Signing something that said I met with and assessed the patient, when I didn't at all?"

I really had nothing to say. The practice I suggested wasn't only widespread, it was encouraged. Most of the attendings had private afternoon clinics, wanted to be done as soon as possible, and the autonomy was good for the residents. It was like I'd just gotten a citation for being wet outdoors during a thunderstorm.

"Also, it might be worth considering that the patient requested a different doctor."

The resident turned his back to me and continued with his report. He recounted a patient history that I had already gathered, the type of history that sticks with you and doesn't require notes.

I retreated to my computer and, for the first time since contracting senioritis, hoped for a patient to pop up in my waiting room. I'd never had a patient fire me. I called the front scheduling desk. No one answered. I hung up, tried again, gave up sooner, and went out to the front. Gloria, our longtime patient coordinator, was dealing with a patient's insurance issue. I stood off to the side, tried to make eye contact, and ended up scrambling in front of her before she could beckon over the next patient in line.

"Name?" she said without looking up.

"Jane Doe." I quickly saw that someone had already soured Gloria's day. That wasn't an easy task. "Has anyone from my schedule showed or canceled?"

"The app isn't working?"

"No, or else I wouldn't be out here."

Gloria's key-tapping stopped. She looked at me over her glasses. The other assistant, in the middle of checking in a patient, paused to turn our way as well.

"Sorry," I said. "Just a bizarre morning. Can you check my schedule? It's not working in the workroom." Out of habit, I told her my last name.

"I don't see any appointments."

"Is it blocked off? Maybe I made a mistake and today is my vacation or something."

Gloria frowned, typed. "It doesn't show up as blocked. Let's try scheduling a new one. Weird. See?" She turned the screen. "Appointment made, in the system, wait a second, hit refresh and . . . it's gone."

"Has that happened—"

The next in line came up beside me; I had to move out of the way. Gloria smiled at her and took down her information. I waited a moment for her to politely pause with the woman and finish with me, saw that she had no intention of this, and doled out a weak "Thanks" before returning to the workroom.

Dr. Ernst and the resident were gone, likely out seeing my patient. I dropped behind my computer and woke it from sleep. As it booted, I checked my group messenger. There was a flurry of activity. I scrolled up, thinking it stemmed from my earlier messages. But they were still unread.

PAM: I'm having these strange stomach pains. They're sharp.

DANNY: Sounds like gas.

PAM: Funny. This might be it.

DANNY: Isn't labor supposed to be painful? You can handle it, you're strong. How far apart are they? I typed.

PAM: Thought maybe I should call the hospital.

DANNY: How far apart are they?

PAM: Every three minutes or so. But sometimes just a constant pain. Any bleeding?

DANNY: They'll just send you home.

PAM: You think so?

DANNY: Def. It's probably just your nerves. Besides, I might need you to come pick me up. Can't get in my apartment and my neighbor just called security on me. #kiddingnotkidding

I imagined Danny cursing out her landlord or trying to break into the window and began to type What'd you do to make them do that? I stopped myself and instead sent an emoji with its tongue sticking out. Then I typed, Pam, call me.

"There they are," I said when I looked up at the screen. The day's schedule, albeit thin, was as I had seen it before. I habitually reloaded the page.

"What the fuck?"

All the patients were gone. Only they hadn't simply disappeared. They had loaded with the page and then dissolved just slow enough to leave the impression of a spreading disintegration.

I leaned in close enough to feel the screen's static hum against my nose. Some of the names were still there, faint and likely illegible to anyone not familiar with them. I shifted the screen with the arrow keys. No, not an artifact burned into the LCD monitor. Each letter faded at its own pace, seeming to ripple as its edges blew away into nothing.

And then, only white.

...

I took the bus home. I dropped my medical bag at the door and called for Othelia. She was usually somewhere close when I arrived. I checked her nook by the couch, the kitty litter, and finally found her dozing on the back windowsill. She opened a feline eye toward me, yawned, and went back to sleep.

"You too, huh?"

I changed out of my clinic clothes, checked to make sure my pager was signed out to the overnight team, and logged into my work email. The last time stamp was from the day before. I checked the internet connection and reloaded. Still nothing. I switched over to social media and began a mindless scroll.

I woke to the vibration of my phone. The day's emails were finally coming through. This had happened before; some connection problem with the server or my phone. I expected upward of fifty emails from hospital administrators, program events, and patient inquiries. Except, there was only one. A notification.

I opened it, sat up, and read it over again. Dr. Ernst had filed an incident report against me for poor professionalism and lapse in clinical duties. What's more, the department requested a drug test. It was my first grievance in my nearly four years of training at MacArthur. And for a chief resident, it was unheard of.

...

I woke a full thirty minutes before my alarm the next morning and immediately reached for my phone. The residency program director hadn't yet responded to my acknowledgment of the incident report and request to meet. I refreshed my email a few times, checked the Allies 4 Life chat, and stopped myself from going down the social media hole. Today was a hospital day. Twenty-four hours of labor and delivery, no less. For the first time I'd be walking into the hospital with a scarlet *I* on my back. Being late—being *anything* other than perfect—wasn't an option.

I entered the hospital earlier and more anxious than I had in years and considered it a mercy when the busy, serious nature of the work took over. Still, little things that usually left me unfazed stuck. The patient that forgot my name or thought I was the nurse. The junior resident who didn't inform me of a significant clinical change in one of our patients. The *other* junior resident who didn't come grab me when our patient went into active labor. The nighttime attending tapping the other residents for a learning case, when I had been right there. The near constant pushback from my team, as if they had all somehow witnessed my previous day's failure in clinic.

Thankfully, the work kept the speed.

Things quieted as night turned to dawn. After two deliveries and one emergency C-section after midnight, the floor was finally calm. My hospital checklist was done. No patients were near fully dilated, and I had thirty minutes to spare. I went to the resident lounge, poured some coffee, and set a mental reminder to later check the day's notifications from Allies 4 Life. I'd gotten one email my whole shift, informing me of an important package in my mail. Something that needed immediate attention. I saw the small, square package in my cubby, opened it, and almost laughed. I looked around, read the notice that came with the package, and laughed again. Unfuckingbelievable.

The small workroom where we signed out smelled of coffee and pastries. I thought I'd have to wait a few minutes, but the second-year from the previous day's clinic was already here, set up at the worktable. I pulled my list from my back pocket.

"I got seven to sign out," I said. "I suspect all but two should deliver during your shift."

"Oh, I already looked them up. Straightforward. You don't need to sign out."

"A good sign-out is important. I hope the senior residents are teaching you that."

He sighed with impatience. I didn't remind him that he was a second-year and I was chief. I could have. As a junior resident I had been reminded of such things for much less. Instead, I took extra time reviewing my patient list. For his benefit and the sake of patient care. Overconfidence—especially in junior residents—scared the shit out of me.

"Her pressures have been good overnight," I said about the last. This was her third pregnancy. First two she had preeclampsia, one of which ended badly. "I really hope she delivers before change of shift. She's been here a minute. A trooper, too."

"Looks like she was a little hypertensive here," he said. "I already put in for a diuretic."

I frowned. "That was one occurrence, and she was laying on the cuff. If you look at her other reads, they're all normal. I had the nurse redo it—see, here. Did fine."

The resident didn't say anything, only continued to click through her chart.

"You'll dry her out and put the baby in distress," I said. I could have let it go. I'd signed out, and it was the end of my shift. What the resident chose to do now was between him and the attending.

"Better than letting her get HELLP," he said.

"She's nowhere near that. I just told you—"

But he continued to frown at the page with that vital sign. He picked up the nearest phone and called the patient's nurse. "Hey, can you check vitals on twenty-three B again?"

I waited for the retort. The nurses had yet to change shifts. She had already rechecked the pressures, and waking a sleeping woman during labor was not fun.

But the nurse actually sounded relieved. Her voice drifted over the phone. "I'll get that right now. Overnight doc wouldn't let me. You never know with these GD cases, though."

"You done?" The resident turned to me. I noticed for the first time that he had a lazy eye with an unsettling, off-balance gaze.

"Sure." I wasn't. "Here's my overnight notes. Page me if you need anything."

The week went on like this, and by the end of it I was looking back at that no-hitter in clinic and thinking of it as the best day in the world. Even if the universe balanced it, a busy clinic day was still better than the floors, and I looked forward to my next one on Thursday. However, a resident called in sick and the automated jeopardy system selected me to cover their inpatient shift. This was obviously an error, as the chief wasn't usually available for staffing needs, but I was too tired to raise the alarm.

Finally came a two-day break, mandatory for the stretch I'd just had. I fingered the package in my locker after sign-out. I'd considered not doing it at all out of principle.

I went to the restroom, filled the cup, placed it in the sample bag, and put it in one of the collection baskets for clinical labs before leaving.

...

My legs are swollen. Is that normal?

One foot was still in a dream as I checked my phone. The last two days had gone by in a blur of restless sleep. Even as a senior resident I worked upward of seventy hours a week, with usually just enough rest to give the obligatory morning coffee something to work with. Being on this sudden, forced vacation, I'd crashed. My body rejoiced in the rare opportunity to slow down.

The message was the latest in a days-long string between Danny and Pam in our Allies group. Until now, I had completely forgotten about them.

Another from Danny popped up. They sent you home, you're good. You know you're dramatic.

I read through the whole conversation, and by the end of it I didn't need coffee. Me missing Pam's trip to the emergency room shouldn't have mattered. Based on what I'd just read, she should have still been in the hospital. Headaches, blurry vision, long bouts of little to no movement from her baby. Just one of those warranted an overnight stay to rule out preeclampsia.

I called Pam and almost broke my neck tripping over my scrubs as I pulled them on. No answer. I paced my small apartment for my workbag as I dialed the resident workroom on the labor and delivery floor. No answer. Shit. I found my bag under a sleeping Othelia, who was not trying to move. She hissed as I pushed her aside. I'd reflect later how her hairs stood all over her body, how her back arched, and how her teeth bared in a defense usually reserved for the unknown.

...

Pam lived alone in the West Village in a nice two-bedroom that her parents owned. The crosstown bus stopped right in front of her building, but the back doors were jammed. I pushed and kicked them to no avail. The bus began to leave, and I screamed.

"Back door!" a man yelled from his seat behind me. The bus stopped; the doors opened. The man gave me a half nod as I stepped off. Then he and the bus were gone.

Pam dropped her phone when she saw me. This initial surprise gave me pause. Instead of sisterly recognition there was bemusement and fear. Some of it I'd seen in that rideshare driver before he drove off. I might have left to wander the streets in a lost daze if not for her eyes. Beyond the red streaks of tears and insomnia, her sclera was tinted yellow.

"It's me," I said. "Pam, it's me."

Her expression softened. Her hands, which had been habitually covering her many tattoos, fell to her side. She smiled, then gripped my arm hard enough to leave a bruise as a contraction went through her. My experience held a healthy inventory of women in the beginning parts of labor too early to start the epidural but far enough along to solidify my decision to never have children. As for those who chose to do the whole thing natural—God bless them. I knew normal labor pains of all intensities. The sharpness of Pam's grit, the rigidity of her body, and the pungent odor that grazed the air would make me nervous even at a hospital. Outside of one, I was terrified.

And her eyes. Damn it all to hell, her eyes.

I picked up her phone from the floor when her painful episode had passed.

"We're getting you to the hospital. What's your password?"

I checked her blood pressure with my cuff on the ride over. Fuck. I checked it again.

"That bad?" she said. Pam was between contractions that thus far proved as irregular as they were concerning.

"It just means they'll get you roomed quick," I said. "We should call Danny. She'd want to be here."

"She's probably busy. Up to no good. She's going to get herself killed."

I nodded. This made sense, even if I couldn't place why.

"They won't see you," Pam said. She laid her head back. Sweat matted her head. Her eyes shone with the sharpness that labor pains brought to the mind. In between the contractions, I'd heard some patients say, was an eerie comfort and clarity. "We shouldn't have gone to that exhibit."

The contraction came. I offered my hand to her grinding grip and rode it out. I watched the buildings pass by in a blur as the abnormally long contraction came to an end. We pulled up to the back of the hospital near the emergency bay. I helped Pam out, got her into a wheelchair, and scanned my ID at the physician entrance. The sooner I could get her upstairs to the unit—and probably the operating room—the better.

My card didn't work. By this point I wasn't surprised. I rolled Pam to the check-in desk.

"Patient's name?" the receptionist said.

"Pam Hunter. She's thirty-five weeks pregnant, is having irregular contractions about three minutes apart, and hypertensive with systolic in the low two hundreds. Jaundiced, fatigued. Classic preeclampsia. She needs an OR."

The receptionist typed at the same speed she had before. After what felt like another hour she looked up and at Pam. "Hunter, is it? What's going on?"

"What the fuck?" I said. "I just told you. She needs to go to the OR."

"You're scaring me," Pam said.

"No need to be scared," the receptionist said. "We'll get you set up and you can talk to a doctor. How's that sound?"

A nurse came to roll Pam back past triage and into a single room.

"I'm an ob-gyn resident here," I said to the nurse. Slow, careful, as if a misstep might cause her to ring the alarm and bar me from coming back with them. "I think she might be in fulminant liver failure. We need to get gyn surgery and liver here as soon as possible."

"We're putting you in bed eight," the nurse said to Pam. "Your doctor will be with you shortly."

She helped Pam into a hospital gown, set up the baby monitor, and then left us. Alone and waiting. I paced the small room and tried not to go insane with each of Pam's contractions, which I could do nothing about. Intensity aside, I noticed that they grew more frequent, more concrete. I rang the bed alarm for the fourth time and was about to walk out to the nurse's station when the door opened.

Finally, my favorite second-year resident came in.

"Is the OR ready?" I said. "Where's the attending? Is Ernst on?"

"Hi Pam," the resident said and walked past me. He sat on the edge of the bed, put on a fresh set of gloves, positioned Pam's legs, and quickly checked inside her. Pam sucked her teeth from the pain. The resident was slow and deliberate. Still, he had made an awful misstep. I know either myself or someone else senior in the residency had shared the importance of asking the patient every time before doing a vaginal check. Finished, he took off the gloves. "Close. About six millimeters, moderately effaced."

"She's got late decels all throughout her read." I pointed to the baby monitor. "Where's the attending?"

My coresident stared at the monitor. He saw the decelerations. Recognizing that pattern was a key part of his training, as unavoidable as learning how to walk. Yet his features did not reflect the horror of it, the urgency. He almost looked . . . uninterested. Nausea poured over me. I'd seen this before. At the exhibit. A doctor looking on as a deadly medical event happened.

This wasn't going to turn out well. Both Pam and her baby were in serious danger. I knew that. I had been trained for that. From the very first week of medical school, where our first patient had been a cadaver, I expected death to be an integral part of my career. But no one had trained me on losing a friend.

One of the emergency technicians came in with the ultrasound. He rubbed gel on Pam's belly and started projecting to the screen.

"There's a lot of fluid," the resident said. "Some outside of the gestational sac." He touched the screen. "And where is this collection coming from?"

I watched with growing angst. The junior resident was still too green around the ears to recognize what I could. Pam's liver had burst. I logged into my paging software and paged Dr. Ernst. She came within minutes.

"Thank god," I said. I began to rattle off the details of her condition. "G one P one, mid-thirties—"

"You can't be here," Dr. Ernst said.

"What? Okay, any other time, but now—"

"Your drug test came back positive for cannabis. You are barred from clinical duties, until further notice." She looked up from me. I felt erased. "Let's take her to the OR."

Everything moved fast after that. They gathered Pam's lines and monitors and began to roll her out of the room. She was just coming down from a contraction and began to call out for me.

"Pam, I'm here!" I grabbed her hand. Someone else pulled it away. Pam continued to call for me and looked around, frantic and frightened, everywhere I wasn't. "Pam, I'm right here. I'm not leaving you. You're going to be okay."

The medical team piled around the bed, pushing me back. I slipped and fell. My knee cracked against the floor. I scrambled up and followed them out into the hall. Other hospital personnel, technicians, rushing doctors, and even patients walked the halls without notice or regard for my existence. I fell twice more and tasted blood in my mouth.

I ran to the elevator, holding Pam, and wedged my foot between the closing doors. They didn't acquiesce like they usually did. I yelled out in pain as the heavy steel pinched my foot. I yanked back; it came out with a pop. I banged on the metal, but it was too late. I could hear the machinery rising.

I took the stairs three flights up. The door was locked. I searched my many pockets for my ID, found it, and used it. The indicator flashed red. Again. The same. I banged on the door. Residents, surgeons, nurses, and technicians in blue surgical scrubs passed just inches away from the door's glass window. None of them turned. None of them saw. None of them heard.

I began to scream.

...

Hours. I was in that damn stairwell for hours before a scrub nurse at the end of his shift decided to take the stairs. I pushed past him and onto the floor where I'd spent half of my training performing C-sections, both emergent and planned.

I heard the steady cry of a newborn as I rounded the corner and entered another long hallway of operating rooms. The sound should have brought me joy, but I was too good, too experienced. The sound was singular, cutting, and without any of the comfort that came with the immediate bonding with mom after birth.

Two pediatricians rolled Pam's newborn down the hall in a hospital bassinet. They chatted with each other as if discussing the weather. The newborn's initial wail had withered to a pout. I didn't look at her as they passed. I couldn't. God, I couldn't.

I opened one of the double doors to the operating room. I saw my friend's rosebud tattoos before anything else. Pam's limp, blood-spotted arm extended from under the sheet and hung off the side of the table. That's all it took.

I pushed down the public stairs, out of the hospital, shielded my eyes from the golden sunset peeking through a break in the skyline, doubled over, and vomited into the gutter. Passing legs knocked into my side and I stepped forward into the mess of puke, leaves, and the trash of New York. My offender wasn't blind or oblivious or preoccupied. Only indifferent, as if he had casually kicked a can lying in the middle of the sidewalk.

The roll of tires. I moved just in time to avoid the approaching car claiming the empty parking space. No horn blare. No screech of the brakes. Only the squish of the front tire moving casually into my vomit. I stared at the driver as he got out. He didn't pause at the woman still doubled over by his car, drool dripping from my mouth. If he even saw me, that is.

I screamed. Hot bile burned my throat. The man briefly looked up from his phone, as if he'd overheard the beckon of someone else with his same name. Distant and faint, more of a cursory glance than a real curiosity.

I straightened myself, leaned against the man's car for a second as a mild dizziness passed like a warm wind, and went to stand in front of the parking meter. Even in New York, the city where I could stroll the streets naked and not get a second look, I should have been more than remarkable. Spittle dripping down my chin, hair disheveled, a mottled pair of scrubs that looked stolen. What's more, I was fully blocking the meter, so he'd have to acknowledge me.

He stopped just short of me without looking up. What was he waiting for? Did he even know?

"Excuse me," I said, soft at first. "Say 'Excuse me.'"

The man's eyes flickered, but not my way. Whatever crossed his mind had nothing to do with me.

"I'm right here," I said. "I'm right fucking here! See me!"

My voice climbed to a yell that rattled my throat. The world shook and blurred until I saw not a man but rather the gray representation of everyone shutting me out. The residency, the demotion, that fucking drug test. All the blood and sweat and sinew had done nothing to stop my own friend from dying in front of me.

I'd heard before of the world going red, of the hot blood pulsing behind the eyes in the fit of rage. I thought it was all colorful nonsense. Not anymore. The gray sky turned to blood.

"See. Me!"

I punched him. I punched everything. My knuckles cracked across the bridge of his nose, which began to spurt blood almost immediately. He yelled out and cradled his assaulted face, looked down at his bloodied hand, and then at me.

"Now you see me. Ha!"

Any triumph fell into a hollow dread. He looked at me, but not in the way I wanted. If he had yelled, or cursed, or hit me back, or fled as if I had meant to kill him, any of those would have been better than this dead stare. I stepped away; my back hit something soft. Another stranger, this one tall and lanky, just standing there, staring at me. I took in more of my surroundings. The hospital's revolving door had stopped midturn; its occupant stared at me from inside the glass. A car stopped in the middle of the street. Its driver leaned across the passenger seat to let me know that he, too, saw. A group of young interns, scurrying back after grabbing a quick lunch to go, paused to stare.

I pushed past the man. His fingernails dug lines into my arm, drawing blood. I swatted him away; someone's shoulder collided with mine and knocked me to one knee. They were all still staring, closing in but not moving at all. I saw all their grief, their sorrow, their disappointment in life aimed toward me, blaming me.

The worst of it was the silence. All of New York admonished me without words or reason.

I pushed myself up and ran. I lived in Tribeca, miles on foot from my hospital, which bordered Central Park. I ran the same and didn't stop. Every conversation paused, every stride slowed, every eye I passed turned toward me. Never at me, not directly. I ran even as my legs wailed and I felt the overworked thrum of my heart in my skull. If I stopped to rest, that dead gaze would be there, and it would eat me alive.

I almost collapsed when I reached my building. I took three big breaths and pulled out my key. It didn't work. I tried to buzz myself up, but the call wouldn't go through to my phone. One of my neighbors—an older woman with three dogs—appeared on the other side of the door. I quickly rehearsed an explanation for my lost key. The door opened; my neighbor came out and didn't acknowledge a hint of my soul. I slipped inside.

I yelped. A warm, strong grip on my arm. My neighbor, her body only halfway through the door, held me tight, decisively. She continued to look toward the street; sweat coated her brow.

"You don't belong here," she said.

I yanked away, ran upstairs, and kicked up the mat outside my apartment door. I almost laughed as the spare key slipped into the hole and turned. I'd gotten one up on it. Whatever *it* was.

I slammed open the door hard enough to bounce loudly off the coil. My roommate—usually staying over with her boyfriend—lifted her eyes from her phone for no longer than a second. I screamed frustration and kicked over the trash can. The sound of metal against wood and the tumble of domestic trash was sucked into the walls. My roommate didn't even flinch. She would find the mess later and imagine she must have bumped into it in the middle of the night or blame Othelia, even though my cat had never done such a thing before. That's how this worked, I was realizing. The world corrected for my absence.

The inside of the bathroom was darker than usual. My fingers paused on the light switch. What if I saw nothing in the reflection? Would I cease to exist? My hand fell away. I moved close to the mirror, trying to see myself in the darkness. Small bits of light leaking in from the hall played silhouettes in the reflection. I swayed from side to side but couldn't quite sync up the movement with mine. I lit my phone.

Any angle I tried, the glare went right into my retina, blinding me. Where was I? I could just make out what seemed like the outline of my body. Finally, I swept the light in rapid ovals. What I saw in the mirror set my heart to thrumming inside my throat.

Matted hair beat down by a surgical cap. Below that: blushed, featureless skin without shape or nuance. A face blank, like a canvas.

I slammed my phone into the mirror. It shattered into spiderwebs. The slivers caught better what little light there was; a thousand faceless monstrosities stared back at me. I picked up a fallen shard and ran it across my face, sparking fire. I ran another line, then another, and another.

As I left, I briefly saw my roommate, still scrolling through her phone.

...

I called a car using Pam's phone, made sure I stayed clear of the driver's rearview as I approached, and buckled myself in before he could object. I dialed Danny as we crossed over into Brooklyn. No answer. I called her again, left her a voice mail that I deleted before it could save, and gave up. Tears began to fall.

"Damn you, Danny," I said. "Pick up."

The driver turned up the radio. I tried Danny, again and again and again.

"An unarmed woman was shot and killed this morning during a domestic dispute in Chinatown," the radio said. I scrolled through my texts with Danny and the group to make sure I wasn't missing any clues to where she could be. "Witness reports say the woman approached the police officers, pulled out what they feared to be a gun, and she was shot eight times in the torso. It was later confirmed that the woman did not have a gun but was holding a cell phone. She was pronounced dead at the scene."

Pam's phone dinged to inform me that I was at my destination. I looked out the window. The parking lot was empty. The signs were gone. There was no line, no buzz of anticipation. The entrance was bare and uninviting. I entered, slow. The air was so still and quiet that I wondered if my transformation had been complete. That's what this was, right? A transformation? Had I passed on to where no one could see me and I could see no one else? I stopped to listen for any joy or laughter coming from some parallel existence, where the exhibit was still running and still attracting a crowd.

Nothing. I went inside because I had nowhere else to go. The same claustrophobia met me as before, only now I had no shoulder to lean into. I stopped at the creeping sound of sobbing and realized from the sting of tears on my torn face that it was my own.

The door to the exhibit yawned open. No one checked for tickets. I paused at the entrance. The dedication poster was gone, replaced by a placard that simply read HEAL THYSELF. The dark, narrow corridor was no more. Paintings hung in neat order around the exhibition room. A few people mingled about, passing from one piece of art to the next with stoic expressions. None of the few White people seemed uncomfortable in their whiteness.

I entered. If this was the place that had stolen myself from me, what would I be inside? Invisible? An intolerable monster? A failure for everyone to see?

But no one noticed me. One man frowned at the picture he'd been admiring as I passed behind him, as if the art had suddenly revealed itself as offensive in some visceral way.

I almost passed it: Danny's picture. There were no dogs. No chains. No fear of imprisonment, mauling, or the whip. Just a Black woman talking casually to the police. Beside it was the delivery room, only now it was postpartum. The mother smiled as she cradled her newborn daughter. In the background a nurse rested one hand on the mother's shoulder while she waited for the blood pressure read to show.

And then, the one of me.

Me? Why did I think that? The one like me. Either way, I'd come prepared to focus, like before. But that wasn't needed. I could see her immediately. She stood smack in the middle of the street, fully facing the viewer with her hands on her hips and chin high in a stance of confident pride. Her face was clear, detailed, and pleasant.

She smiled, because the world could see her.

The World Wasn't Ready for You

MOMENTS BEFORE SHE PASSED, MY WIFE WINCED FROM THE STILL-RAW PAIN OF a long labor as she tried to rise from the couch. I assured her that our newborn, asleep in the other room, was fine. Jordan's entry into this world had been far from normal; we all needed time to rest.

"You were so good," my wife said as I settled beside her. She squeezed my hand, but her gaze was off elsewhere. "The world just wasn't ready."

It was a lifetime before I knew what she meant.

Twenty-Five

I can't breathe.

I place my hand on my son's chest to sense a rise and fall. Nothing. Cold. Soft. Unmoving. I try to put Jordan over my shoulder, but he has grown heavy somewhere along the way. Inhaler; I need his inhaler. He's going transparent, fast. I pat his muscled back. He waves me off. I kneel down beside him and try to help him to his feet, but something keeps him down . . .

I can't breathe.

. . . I try to pry merciless fingers from stifled locs.

I gasped up and out of the fog of sleep, remembered myself and where I was. When I was. My room was empty, quiet, just like the house that had felt ten times too big ever since Jordan left home a few years back, when he turned twenty-one.

Jordan . . . Something was happening. I reached for my phone while trying to remember if he would be working on the *Reliance* this week or next.

No answer. Maybe he was on the ship. Then I remembered the travel ban, how I had just seen him a couple days before for dinner.

Calm down, Drew. I was freaking myself out. Quickly, I saw that wasn't the truth, not completely. These emotions weren't mine; they were Jordan's. His despair stretched out unmitigated across whatever distance separated us. I fought an old urge to run into his room.

I focused. *I can't breathe.* An asthma attack? Lung failure after years of overworked compensation for the scarring during birth? No; this was different. Something was keeping him from breathing. I felt his struggle, almost as if that oppressive something were me. Something—someone—was doing this to his body.

I called to him. Our *iunctio* had grown weak from the years of estrangement and had only begun to strengthen under our recent reconciliation. It was like trying to communicate through a thin crack in a soundproof wall. Would I sit there, screaming helplessly, as my son died from something I couldn't even see?

No, I wouldn't. I couldn't save him—that truth came fast and strong, like the cold realization that his mother, lying dead still in our bed two decades before, was beyond helping. I could either act or spend the rest of my life regretting what I did in that lonely room in the last moments of my son's life.

I reached across the *iunctio*, past the force oppressing him, past his gasping locs, and stroked his head in the same way I had first done in the neonatal ICU and for many years after that. The texture of his locs was real on my fingers, the warmth of his life as cogent as the fear of losing it.

Jordan felt me as I felt him. He stilled long enough for me to catch some of his perspective. Hot concrete scratched against his cheek. Something hard and blunt pressed into his back; dark words barked into his ear. A threat of death. It was the tight grip on his locs, however, that was killing him. I had let them grow thick and long in his childhood to act as a second set of lungs, just as Marlena and I had discussed while watching over him in the hospital. Often peace officers tied up a Keplan suspect's locs during a detainment because they were considered weapons.

With this connection I felt my own throat close; I swallowed against it to show myself I still could breathe, despite the sensation.

With everything in me, I began to sing:

"Down by the river, where the kids play . . ."

Serenity coated my son's mind as his labored breathing slowed. He struggled against his captors enough to get in one last breath to call out for me. I nearly unwound. I didn't have to tell him I couldn't help; my silence was enough.

And then, all was still.

Five

A mild cold was a poor reason to keep a five-year-old out "sick," but Jordan's school had already sent him home three times that month. My only son had woken up that morning with enough energy to fuel the sun, oblivious to the slight discoloration rippling across his skin. A mild runny nose should have earned such a vibrant kid a decongestant and a lollipop from the school nurse.

Jordan, though, was not like other kids. He brought with him the irrational fear of another Keplan virus outbreak, still ripe in old and young minds even after a decade. It didn't matter that he had never set foot on the Keplan mothership *Reliance* and likely had the best immune system of anyone in his school.

So instead of being present for my own product's launch meeting, I packed Jordan a quick lunch and we went to his favorite park. He unclipped his seat belt before the car came to a full stop.

"What's the number-one rule?" I asked him as we climbed the hill.

Jordan thought about it. A light orange flickered over his skin, with darker sunset spots touching the surface like fish. His locs, infused with the memory of his mother's people, sparkled. "Have fun?"

"Jordan . . ."

He sighed. "Don't mind-talk to strangers."

"That's right. Only with Daddy."

He broke into a run as we came to the playground. While most of the other parents sat in tranquility, I walked along the perimeter, watching. Jordan was a sweet kid, and a mindful one, but at times he would get excited and forget he wasn't the only one trying to have fun. Though he was neither, a large swath of the Earthbound population saw Keplans as aggressive and unruly. Marlena and I had somewhat protected ourselves from this by putting roots down in one of the most progressive cities in the country. Still, seeing as how I hadn't met any other interstellar families in our neighborhood, I didn't trust anyone to give Jordan the benefit of the doubt he deserved.

My mind began to wander—How was I going to get my company's Keplan marketing initiative done? Had I taken any meat out to defrost for dinner?—when I snapped back to see a kid pushing past Jordan up the ladder. Though the kid looked similar in age, Jordan was thin and light. His hair was the biggest thing on his body.

"Take turns, let him go up," I said.

Jordan did, and I could tell by the decolorization of his skin that he wasn't happy about it. The other kid waited at the top. When he blocked the slide entrance, Jordan instead spun the adjacent toy steering wheel. The kid lunged forward to turn it the other direction. I looked around for a potential parent. A man with short, wavy hair and folded arms sat on a nearby bench. His enhancement glasses blinked a dull orange to indicate that he was mentally somewhere else entirely. His lips moved wordlessly. Perhaps he was also balancing work with an unreasonable sick-child policy. Still, his kid was being a jerk.

Jordan abruptly abandoned the battle over the steering wheel and went for the slide. The other kid failed to beat him to it. I almost cheered until I saw him zipping down behind Jordan and just miss kicking him in the back.

"Hey! Play nice!" I said. The kid's father didn't stir.

Jordan ran back around to the ladder. The other boy was there a moment later; his shoulder sent Jordan stumbling. Jordan bounced up, and we both ran forward. I wouldn't let my five-year-old son roll around in the shaved wood with some stranger asshole kid. But Jordan had other things in mind. He grabbed the metal of the ladder and—

—it disappeared. Just like that.

The boy, who had been halfway up, stopped as if someone had pressed life's pause button. He looked at his hands impossibly gripping air, his feet, standing on nothing.

Naturally, he began to yell.

"Daddy. Daddeeeee!" Finally his father came back to reality. Other parents began to stare; some gathered up their children. Though the kid bawling on the invisible ladder had been the aggressor, they would see my son as the danger. Because of what he was.

Jordan backed into me, the ladder reappearing with his release, and pulled my arms around him as he looked up at the boy. I wasn't sure if Keplan genes coded a skin tone for self-admiration, but this had to be close.

"You ready to get some ice cream?" I asked. He was. After we were well on the road, I asked another question: "Did you do that on purpose?"

Jordan looked out the window. I asked again. "It was an accident," he said.

"It's okay if it wasn't. He deserved it." At the next red light, I turned to match eyes with him. "But don't do it often, okay? Some people might not be too happy about it."

"Like the mind-talk?"

"Yes, just like that."

"Because it's bad?"

"No. Because people might not understand it. People don't like things they don't understand."

"Okay." He picked at his fingernails, a childhood habit of mine that had somehow been passed down.

"Did you see how he froze in place?" I said through the rearview. Red giggled his skin. "I thought he turned into a statue—"

Red and blue lights popped into our world. My heart pumped with preparatory fear even before I recognized the unwelcome blare of peace officers.

"Are they coming to arrest me?" Jordan said. He sat up. His tones purpled. "Because I did the bad thing?"

"No one's going to arrest you," I said.

"How do you know?"

"Because I just do, Jordan."

Where had he picked this up? I remembered my father's unspoken angst whenever a police car approached. How it had poisoned our car's air and made it unbreathable. I never wanted that feeling for my own son and had worked to hide my unease. Maybe he felt it anyway, through our *iunctio*. Maybe he sensed that a primal part of me had, for a second, wondered if they were coming for him.

The patrol car passed us, and I let out a breath I hadn't realized I was holding. The vehicle it pulled over was low to the ground, slim, and tubular. With their mental connection to the technology we had appropriated, Keplans had no need for steering wheels, which made them easy to spot. I rubbernecked as we passed, saw that the peace officer was Black like me, and felt deep guilt for wondering what the Keplan had done wrong.

I smiled through the rearview. "See, I told you—"

Jordan's locs curled like dead spider legs over his increasingly translucent face. His chest heaved in forced jerks. His nostrils flared.

"I can't breathe!"

I pulled into the next driveway, parked, and emptied Jordan's bag. Shit; I must have left his inhaler at home. I climbed through the middle into the back, unbuckled his seat belt, and maneuvered him into my lap. His locs expanded against my fingers as I untangled them. The wheezing lessened. His digging fingernails relaxed on my thigh.

"Breathe," I said. "Breathe." I still had quite a bit of untangling to do but found my own breathing calmed from the relief. And so, sitting there in the back seat of the car, cramped against his booster seat, I began to sing for both of us:

Down by the river, where the kids play
Laughter and sunshine, till the new day . . .

I ran my fingers through his locs; they curled around me lovingly, full again. Jordan was fast asleep. Translucency fell over and lifted from his skin in rhythm with deep breaths. I wondered, not for the first time, if he dreamed of the future.

Seventeen

Another Keplan had been killed by peace officers for "reckless use of telepathy" not three days before. Jordan had seen the videos, had read the reports. I knew because I had shown them to him. How, then, could he be so stupid?

I began to wash the dishes, something my own father would do when he was mad. Even if everything was clean, he'd grab something from the cabinets and run it under the water. He told me once that it was so he could have something to do with his hands.

I turned to look at Jordan leaning against the wall. At seventeen, my only son was a head taller than me. His muscles were still wiry and tightly strung, a testament to the years of physical therapy I had hounded the insurance to pay for. Passing in a crowd, my son was no stranger to the curious glance or two. Lately, however, glances were turning to stares. People were noticing.

"Well?" I said, a single word right out of my father's playbook. How many times had I told him to be careful?

"Well, what?"

"Jordan!"

"He talked bad about Mom, Dad."

Jordan's skin changed as the fragmented words came out of him. Pockets deepened around his eyes and sent a shadow extending past his nose. A single tear fell during this transition, and for a split second an intricate network of pumping blood was visible along the surface.

I sighed, rinsed the chipped blue dinner plate I had been lathering, and found a crack in the overstuffed washing machine for it.

"Then you come to me. You don't go trespassing into someone's mind—"

"He challenged me! It was my right."

"Oh, really? Is that what they teach you on that ship? These people don't care about your Keplan rights if they think you're a threat. Who else saw this kid bait you?"

"Nobody."

"So you have no proof? Just your word against his?" I held up a soapy hand before Jordan could rebut. I wasn't finished. "What do you think would have happened if he called the poh? What would they have seen?"

The answer to my question flashed briefly through my mind as Jordan remembered. My legs weakened; I leaned against the kitchen sink. Though the telepathy was brief, its memory lingered. It was a wonder Harris Magnet High hadn't expelled him.

"Oh, Jordan. Did . . . did anything break?"

"No."

"And what about the boy? Is he hurt?"

"You're worried about him? Do you even care what he said about Mom?" Though his voice stayed level and well within his age, bluish-purple spots checkered his skin.

I slammed the table hard enough to make Jordan jump. A faraway, unimportant pain cut between my fingers. My son's skin spots bloomed.

"Watch. Your tone," I said. The spots lessened, but not completely. "I know what he said. Because I've heard it before. I don't give a shit about him. I care about you going out there and making a target of yourself. Now, is the damn boy hurt?"

"I'm not stupid," he said. "But he won't be talking about Mom anymore."

My son. Was he smiling? I had been that same teenager. Sneaking out to joyride, playing hooky, doing drugs, naively thinking I could be as carefree as my white friends. Dad's warnings that I would be seen as different because of my brown skin fell on deaf ears. That is, until he made me listen. I'd avoided the jail and the grave, thanks to him. I was determined to do the same for Jordan. Even if he hated me for it.

"I'm pulling you out of the *Reliance* this semester."

Jordan looked at me so quickly that if I hadn't been prepared for a reaction, I might have flinched. A sharp buzz touched my mind; a glimmer of metallic yellow flicked across my son's skin like sunlight reflecting off a morning tide. The air suddenly felt warmer.

"I know, son, I know. But this is serious. You could have been arrested—"

"I didn't do anything wrong."

"They're not going to react to what you did do, but what you could do."

"If I don't pass the spring exam, it'll be another year before I can claim citizenship."

"You should have thought about that before." Another phrase lifted from my father. Though I vowed he'd never meet Jordan after his treatment of Marlena when she was alive, here he was now, somehow still able to reprimand his grandson.

Something shattered behind me. I didn't turn to look. That didn't bother me; most in the small condo was Jordan-proof. A therapist had suggested some years ago that I keep a precariously stacked set of cheap plates, offering real-time feedback to help calm his most intensive anger.

"You're trying to trap me here."

"Earth is your home."

His skin, which was already glowing a faint blue, flickered as if there had been a change in lighting. I ignored the foul language.

Something else broke behind me. While the one before sounded like a glass accidentally tipping off the counter, this one held a fierce, intentional quality. A light wheeze that hadn't been present a moment before cut the air. His locs, usually thick with highlights, thinned and curled.

"You're working yourself up," I said.

His breaths were heavy now, past the point where he could self-soothe. His locs congealed into clumps.

"I can't breathe," he said. The phrase heard throughout his life had never lost its ability to induce fear. I was at his side immediately, the air gone out of my anger. I began to undo one of his hair ties; he shrugged me off with a force I understood but didn't expect.

"Remember if they get air, you get air," I said. For a moment Jordan only stood there, tense with wheezes. I moved to step in, his will be damned. But then his hand went to his hair. He raked his fingers through freed locs.

"You alright?" I said.

"Can I go to my room now?"

"Are you alright?"

"Yes! Now can I go?"

I stepped back and gestured the way. His first couple of steps were soft. He straightened himself to his full height and stopped outside his door. For a foolish second, I thought he was going to turn to make a joke and dissolve some of this useless tension between us.

"I wish you had died and not her."

My hand gripped the counter for balance, Jordan's door slammed behind him. The house rattled with more than its force.

"Well, you know what?" I yelled. "That makes two of us!"

I rubbed my bald head, retreated to the sink and, when there was nothing to be washed, started scouring my bedroom and the living room for dirty clothes. I left Jordan's. He didn't like me to touch his stuff.

"Nice comeback, Andrew," I said to myself. He was right, of course; we didn't understand each other at times. As if my son were from another planet or something. I laughed at this and paused to look at a holograph I'd taken with a pregnant Marlena a few weeks before her death. She would have appreciated that joke.

When things were quiet again, when the thermostat read normal, I went to stand outside my son's room. A faint melody bypassed my ears and rose to life inside my head. Jordan used headphones whenever he could. Pure Keplans were near deaf, but Jordan could hear almost as well as me. Jordan told me once, though, that without headphones the sounds leaked out into the world and he wasn't able to enjoy them as much.

I lingered there for some time, missing Marlena. I remembered the last look she'd given me as she retired to bed that first night back home, seemingly exhausted from Jordan's birth, just a couple hours before a blood clot silently took her from us. She had known of her own mortality, like every other Keplan, but had said nothing. What's more, being so close to death would have given her sight over all of Jordan's lifespan. I spent many nights after wondering about that last look. What of his story had she seen? What was so important to protect me from, that she left me completely in the dark?

The world just wasn't ready.

Wasn't it my job, then, to bend him to that world?

Though my late wife never divulged the future to me, her experience of time had offered a comfort I didn't fully appreciate until she was gone. Like having a navigator who could see through the fog all the way to the horizon. Being able to look at her now, to see the calm scarlet tones of her skin, would be all the comfort I needed to go and talk to my son, to know I wouldn't make things worse. Instead, I was left to make the decision blind.

A warm pressure on my temple. Jordan sensed me. He regarded me in that special way he had gained from the stars. That *iunctio*, the neuronal connection that made Keplans both fascinating and frightening. Since that rolling tide of puberty, this intimate line of communication had thinned between us. I cherished a moment like this; it brought me closer to his mother.

The music from his headphones filled my ears. I laughed; it was the same melody I'd hijacked many years ago to sing for him at bedtime.

Daddy loves chocolate, daddy loves stew, I sang in my head, and knew he could hear it. *More than this all, son, daddy loves you.*

Reliance? The question entered my mind as soon as the song had finished.

Next year, I thought.

The line went dead.

I let my hand fall from the door handle. It was done. Jordan's dual citizenship for the Keplan mothership would be delayed. Jordan had it wrong, though. It wasn't leaving Earth that I was afraid of. It was the coming back after fully embracing his Keplan heritage that worried me. I couldn't help that, but perhaps through this consequence he'd learn to be quieter, so I could enjoy him longer.

Thirteen

The stratovator rumbled as we passed through thick ozone. Below us, the cloud-streaked countryside dissolved into a shower of faint rainbows. A metallic grid replaced our view of Earth. Awe lit Jordan's skin; he'd never been on this side of the Tellurian Divide. And then, as if our minds were one, we both looked up.

Debris littered the dark space above. The *Reliance*—an oblong behemoth once alive with colors vibrant enough to ripple still photographs with life—now floated in the middle, its outer hull dull and gray. The Tellurian Divide ensured that most terrestrials would never see how a generation before us had nearly decimated the Keplan people and left them to rot in our orbit.

Little of this history was taught at Jordan's school, where he had recently been suspended for going invisible after a classmate pulled his hair. My naive hope of raising Jordan to pass as terrestrial dwindled with each incident. Once considered adorable, his telepathy, his chameleon skin, and even his locs slowly became symbolic threats. By trying to protect him from this truth, I had made him oblivious and careless. The *Reliance* and its Keplan-run academy could teach him how to control his abilities. They could teach him how to placate terrestrials. That was the hope, at least.

"Did we do this?" Jordan said with his tongue. He hadn't used telepathy with me since I'd grounded him for going invisible. Talking shifted his filtering mask; he quickly adjusted it, as if its malfunction would prove fatal. I had assured him that his natural locs would welcome the nitrogen-rich Keplan air and take from it whatever his body needed.

"Decades ago, yes."

My son stood silent for a long time. I found myself wondering what he was thinking. In just a few hours he'd know a lot more about his history.

"Will it hurt?" he said, finally.

"What?"

"The download."

"You mean, emotionally?" My smile was audible through my own mask.

"Dad!"

"It won't hurt, son," I said. Marlena had told me about the passing down of history through experience. There was no storyteller, no interpreter, just the raw experience of being there. They revisited the good and the bad, from the glory days before the need for generation ships to the most recent terrestrial mandate that all Keplan-human pregnancies in the first and second trimester be terminated. "You were made for this."

I could almost see the words forming on his lips. *Half made for this.* But he kept them in.

The stratovator docked, the airlock hissed, and we crossed over into one of the *Reliance's* thin loading hallways. We went through processing, weapons scans, and telepathic probing before being cleared to pass through to the alien city. A shuttle that extended from the inner ship's transparent walls slowly made its way around to us. While I expected awe at the Keplan technology, I did not anticipate discomfort. The vehicle felt alive, from its glistening walls to the breathing rhythm of its expansion and contraction. It also felt slow, old, and sick. In fact, the whole ship did. The shuttle dragged us along the ship's perimeter through the elevated strip of residential areas that housed the city's terrestrial investors, scientists, and the voyeuristic wealthy. A clear demarcation lay between this and the bustling city that filled the ship's expansive center.

Jordan and I both looked out the window, through the transparent ship hull, and marveled at our blue home, rotating silently on its axis. The moon, half shrouded in darkness, loomed large at the edge of our view. This side of the *Reliance* faced away from the debris, aesthetically acting as another Tellurian Divide for the comfort of the gentrifiers who enjoyed this view.

The elegant, Earth-designed homes peeled away as the tram closed in on the abyss-facing end of *Reliance*. No Earth. No moon. Just stars decorating space. We unloaded at a row of identical hutlike structures that seemed to shift with the breathing of the ship. I checked my navigation device and located the main learning center where Jordan would begin his studies to eventually achieve citizenship.

"Come on, so we can get good seats," I said.

Jordan stopped. "We?"

"I can't sit in on your history lesson?"

"Dad!"

Once my favorite word, I was starting to resent it.

"I'm kidding. I'll wait while you're, uh, enlightened. You may want to lose the mask, though. You don't need it."

Jordan's neatly bundled locs shifted as if to test this. My son then removed the apparatus, more slowly than I would have liked. Panic welled as his lungs fought to extract adequate oxygen from the air. He nearly put the mask back on. Then the tips of his locs defied gravity and curled up toward the sky. He smiled—I'd seriously questioned if he'd lost the ability recently—and even had a touch of confidence in his step as he made his way toward the center.

A couple of teenagers—full Keplan by the length of their locs, the twine of their muscles, and the mental hum around them—stood blocking the entrance. I hung back but felt my body tense. Jordan removed the mask still hanging around his neck in response to one of their gestures. After a brief exchange, he made to move around them. The shorter one pushed him back.

"Hey," I said, loud and more confident than I felt. "Leave my kid alone."

They turned their attention toward me and shrank a little. I was ready to rail into them about harassing my son, that he had as much right to be there as them, when Jordan's skin gave me pause. My son filled my mind with a single, weighty image of myself, standing there in my terrestrial mask and ID badge, exerting my power over the Keplans. Marlena had told me how *iunctio* was stronger on board the Keplan ship. Now more than ever, I believed her.

I backstepped to keep my balance. Understanding came immediately, but too late. The damage was already done. The teenage Keplans held up their hands in submission. One of them, however, shot Jordan a look. He winced.

"What did he say?" I said after the two had gone inside.

"That my father's a Colonizer. Now can you go? Please?"

I waited under the shuttle stop and wondered again if I had made the right decision. The world just wasn't ready. Had Marlena meant my world, or hers?

I had been a baby when the Keplans first appeared outside of Earth. That initial welcome had been peaceful. Cousins, from across the stars! Biologists marveled at the implications of our common seeder intergalactic humanoid ancestors. They remained skeptical at the nearly identical nature of Keplan DNA until the first mixed child was born, which didn't take long. Engineers craved understanding of their organic-based tech and how it linked telepathically. The Keplans, depleted by their multigenerational trip across the stars, readily traded this science for a docking station to replenish with hopes of a new home. Extreme purists, disgruntled with the integration of alien tech into their lives, snuck aboard the ship disguised as Ambassadors and attempted mass terror. The mothership *Reliance* emitted a burst of mental energy in panicked retaliation, giving every living human on Earth a mind-splitting headache and vivid, often traumatizing, hallucinations. World leaders launched a crippling assault, bastardized versions of Keplan technology filling the night sky on this side of the Tellurian Divide with debris.

Both sides broke for peace. The terrorists were turned over to Keplan authorities for punishment, and Earth imposed all types of restrictions on telepathy. The lasting effects on the *Reliance* and its people, however, were devastating. More resource than life was lost. It took years to get the ship's main power grids back online. In that time, the higher classes sought refuge on Earth, often crossing over illegally to quickly outrun the poverty flowing through the mothership, like water filling a sinking ship.

Past the towering schools and housing complexes, I could almost see all this etched into the cosmos. My son would know all that and more. What else would he learn? Would it bring him closer to me or push him farther away?

The view became accidentally spectacular as the *Reliance* rotated to catch the sun's rays on its solar panels. When Jordan finally came out, the sun looked to be in a slow dance with the moon.

I stood to greet him, my apologies ripe on my tongue, primed in my mind to enter our neglected *iunctio* space.

It took me a moment to recognize the deep anger in Jordan's skin. I'd seen this Keplan intensity only once before, when Marlena had been rejected by her dream birthing center because she was "high risk." Jordan held that same glow now; raised welts lifted and flattened throughout his body. Whatever they had shown him in there had left an indelible mark.

I waited until we were in a private two-seater transporter that would take us across the city to process Jordan's application for citizenship. "What part got to you?"

"All of it."

I squeezed his shoulder. What could I say? That I had loved his mother? That I had been different? That I would have never done those things if I was in charge?

I said nothing. It was his right to be mad. I felt all that shame, and more, in Jordan's look. As if I had been unmasked.

Two

Jordan's birthday was a bittersweet reminder of Marlena's sudden passing, just hours after the joy of bringing him home. We went to a petting zoo for his first, and I fell into tears in front of the tour guide and my largely supportive but unmarried group of college friends. No one knew quite what to do with the widower holding an equally inconsolable toddler.

His second was low-key. We went to BubbleLand, which turned out to be a lot more fun than I had anticipated. Most of all, it was just the two of us.

We warmed up with small attractions. Giant bubble machines, sprinkler parks, and a bubble-gum exhibit. Jordan finally tugged me toward the Bubble Master's live performance. The wraparound line quickly ate up his short attention span. I had to carry him inside, he was so mesmerized by stray bubbles passing overhead. The diabolical line continued; it curved the perimeter of the small room where a short man with a top hat and colorful face paint used a hula hoop to lift a cylindrical wall of bubble up and over a young volunteer. Jordan trotted forward, hands poised and ready to pop the bubble tower. My attempt to stop him was too late. The bubble disappeared in a spray of magic.

"Someone's excited," the Bubble Master said and waved away my apology. He dipped the hula hoop back into the kiddie pool of soapy water and gestured for Jordan to step inside. My son's face and skin lit with their respective smiles as he did so.

The Bubble Master covered Jordan in a cylindrical wall of shimmering, pliable glass. Though my son hadn't yet said his first words, his skin spoke volumes. Usually light and easily interpretable, his tones had taken on a sophisticated quality as of late. Jordan jumped up to press his palm against the ceiling of the successfully enclosed bubble. The wall bent to receive his touch; his skin lit its own rainbow.

This joyous display was short-lived. Jordan's skin shifted. The contours of the bubble master's smiling face passed my son's like a projection. At only two years of age, Jordan was starting to turn invisible.

Invisibility had recently been made illegal in response to a group of young Keplan trespassers who snuck into the Vatican and made a dance video that quickly went viral. Some saw it as an isolated stunt, and others saw it as a signal to a larger movement. Now, any of-age individual could be detained for going invisible. Jordan was well below that cutoff. His violation was still seen as cute and adorable. When would that change? When would society decide he was old enough to fear?

I popped the bubble. Jordan's glee paused mid-smile, mid-tone-shift. His whole body began to cry. I winced at the building headache that often came with his distress.

"Come on, Jordan," I said. He sat on the ground in protest and poked at a hemisphere of remnant bubble. It oscillated in waves. I picked him up. He didn't make it easy.

"Oh my god, his skin."

A static-skinned woman with jet-black hair and a hungry grin was there when I turned around. The path leading out of the small showroom was too narrow to easily slip by her.

"He's completely adorable." The woman leaned forward, covered her face with both hands, then pulled them apart. Jordan laughed; fireflies of raw, not yet matured emotion played across his skin.

"We're kind of in a rush . . . ," I began.

"Oh my god, so cute. Come look at him, Carl."

"Careful," came a man's voice beside her. Then, lower, "Going to get your mind screwed."

"You're too cute for that, aren't you?" the woman said. "And look at that hair!"

She reached out to touch either his hair or his skin. I didn't care; I slapped her hand away all the same.

Hair had been a thing for my two sisters growing up, but not so much for me, as I kept mine cut short and wavy. *Don't you let them white girls touch your hair*, my mother would say as she got them ready for school.

Perhaps there was some of that here now. Perhaps it was that the oil from this lady's fingers could react in some unforeseen way with his, cause an allergic swelling, and his version of anaphylaxis.

Or perhaps I just didn't want this stranger feeling like she could touch my son's hair.

The shock in her eyes lingered between us. Jordan turned his curiosity toward her. The woman seemed to shrink, her gaze downtrodden. She realized, at least, what she had done. And for that, I almost felt sorry for her. Almost.

"What's your deal?" Her partner—Carl—had been partially hidden in the shadowy corners of the showroom. When he stepped into the wan light, I saw that while he wasn't the stereotypical muscled boyfriend, he gave no indication of being a pushover either. He stood a few inches taller than me—just enough that I had to lift my chin to meet his gaze—and was definitely in better shape.

"She was touching my kid," I said. "This isn't a petting zoo."

"It's no big deal, Carl." The woman grabbed his arm, but he stood firm. "Let's not make him upset."

"I'm upset." And then, to me, "She was being nice. Apologize."

I held Jordan tighter. I laughed, shook my head, and made to walk past. "Sorry."

He blocked my path with a hand to the chest. Pushing him back would have been easy enough, but his agitated energy gave me pause. Jordan felt it, too; his joy had dissipated. Whatever had happened in the last few minutes, hours, days, in this man's lifetime leading up to this moment, he seemed set to take it out on us.

"I would watch yourself, especially with that half-breed—"

The stranger's face abruptly twisted in agony, and he doubled over. I blinked. Had I hit him? I'd certainly primed myself to. No . . . This had been faster than me. From my arms, my son stared at the man with more focus than he gave even his favorite television shows. I shook him and whispered, "Stop that! Right now!"

Jordan whimpered and turned to bury his face into my neck. As if released from an invisible hold, the man sprang up, his eyes red and wide with fear. To my knowledge, I had been the only one to ever receive Jordan's mental energy, and they had all been mild pushes. This man looked like someone had set off a grenade right by his ear.

The Bubble Master came over. The hula hoop hung on his shoulder. "Is there anything I can assist with?"

"He needs to learn some fucking manners," Carl said. "Him and his kid."

"He's right," I said. "I'm going to see if we can find some in the giftshop."

I hoisted Jordan up onto my shoulders. The tendrils of his hair, already thick with weight, curled down to commune with my neck. I still didn't quite understand it, only that it gave him access to a part of me I would never consciously know. And that it soothed him. I stopped to put him down when we were far from the Bubble Master's house. He took my hand.

I tried to untangle his locs, but they curled around each other as if for comfort. My naive fingers couldn't find hold.

I began to sing, because I didn't know what else to do. To my surprise and intense relief, his locs softened at my words. I loosed them as I sang, and his breath became full.

> . . . *Till the new day, son, till the new day.*
> *Laughter and sunshine, till the new day . . .*

"Don't cry, Daddy," Jordan said.

I began to joke to compensate for my tears, then remembered my son's speech delay. He hadn't spoken at all. Not physically. I rubbed the spot where my neck still tingled.

"Do that again," I said.

He did. Something akin to laughter filled my head. No pain, no fear, just connection and love. The last voice I had experienced in this way had been his mother's. Now I really was crying.

And that was okay, too.

Twenty-Five

In the few years following my son's departure from home, before the Keplan uprisings and terrestrial response had brought us close, I thought our connection had dwindled or even completely faded. How wrong I had been. The deep and new emptiness I felt now, in the bed alone, the shadow of my son's last breath going cold on my cheek, I had not felt since before Marlena decided to *iunctio* with me and let me into her world. I had been able to feel Jordan since birth, even when I didn't know it. The nothing now was deafening. I knew without question that my son was dead.

I was still in bed when I received the call.

"This is Peace Officer Candy with—"

"He couldn't breathe," I said.

A substantial pause.

"He resisted arrest. We had to restrain him, and . . ." The voice on the other end stopped the explanation, because there was none. "He did not survive."

"Where—"

My voice broke. I bit it back. Emotion choked me. I couldn't breathe. This would all have to come out, but not now. There were things that needed to happen.

"Where is he?"

"He was a registered Keplan and was traveling outside the usual area—"

"Where is he?"

"The *Reliance*, per protocol. Look, I'm sorry for your loss. If he would have just—"

I hung up.

Nothing felt real. Most of all, I wouldn't be able to say a proper goodbye. With tensions rising to the brink of war, transatmospheric travel was temporarily suspended except to transport remains of deceased Keplans back to the *Reliance*. Which meant that if Jordan had a funeral, I wouldn't be there.

When Marlena died, she'd left behind a calming shadow of herself, ever-present in our son's eyes. The way his locs' many sensors tasted the air, the way I'd come to know his inner feelings from his skin tones better than any facial expressions or words could ever convey. He had been a living beacon of hope. Now what was there?

"You knew," I said to my wife's memory. Of course she had seen. What else would a new mother do, faced with her own mortality, besides look to the future of the one she had just birthed to see if she could rest in true peace? She must have seen this moment, this failure. Twenty-five years, and he was gone. "I'm so sorry."

The mental void left by my only son's death filled in a sudden, exuberant rush that pushed me up and out of bed. Rough, shaggy carpet pressed between my toes. My arthritic knee moaned in protest.

I listened to the unmistakable signal of someone I had only been able to imagine for the last several years. She had given me this message right before her death. A simple sentence, so quickly disregarded and forgotten then but now so clear:

You were so good.

I couldn't deny it as a memory, but I couldn't remember accessing it any time before.

I lay there, quiet, my dead wife's words clinging to the air. They didn't comfort me. In that moment, how could anything? But they gave me a sense of clarity in an otherwise obscure world.

And then I began to weep, heavily and without shame.

Seven (Days)

Marlena labored for nearly a week. We were well prepared for the differences in a Keplan birth. The hospital, however, wasn't. After a full twenty-four hours of stalled progress, they offered increasingly aggressive interventions. We successfully refused them in the beginning. But none of the anesthesiologists felt comfortable placing an epidural because of a lack of Keplan anatomical knowledge, and they were conservative with the pain medication.

So when the pain became unbearable, Marlena agreed to the inducing medication and had a bad reaction. Clots formed throughout her body, including the umbilical cord. She had an emergency cesarean. I remember hearing her pleading screams from outside the operating room. And then, silence. I was sure they were both dead. Not quite. Toxins had flooded little Jordan's lungs, someone explained to me afterward. He likely would have died quickly if not for his Keplan hair. They took him to the NICU and her to urgent post-op recovery.

Now we were home. I cradled Jordan's head; the entirety of his small body lay along my arm. Beneath translucent skin, networks of blood vessels gave insight into the intricacies of life. His tiny mouth puckered for food; when none came, he began to whine. Marlena was in the bathroom; she had been concerned about bleeding.

I tried to hum a tune to soothe him. None worked. I put on the radio in desperation, flicking past the channels, and stopped when Jordan began to coo. The song, unfortunately, was just wrapping up.

I picked back up the melody and began to improvise.

Down by the river, where the kids play
Laughter and sunshine, till the new day
Till the new day, son, till the new day.
Laughter and sunshine, till the new day
Daddy loves chocolate, daddy loves stew
More than this all, son, daddy loves you.

By the end of it he was asleep, his tiny arms hanging off his side, his small mouth agape. I carefully took him back to our room.

My finger cradled the light switch, and then fell away. I didn't want to wake him. I felt my way forward, grabbed the cold, fabric-laced rim of the bassinet, and placed my son down into it. A creak; I froze. Jordan stirred, then was still. The soft whistle of his breath touched the night air.

Marlena was in the living room, waiting for me. I gestured for her not to get up.

"He's fine," I said. "Sleeping."

"Well, aren't you superdad."

"Only on weekends," I said. I slumped onto the couch, the collective exhaustion of the last week hitting me like a brick. "How're you feeling?"

"Tired." She was looking out into the dark hall, as if she could see the bassinet through the walls, and something about it unnerved her. Something was wrong. "You were so good. The world just wasn't ready."

"You did all the work," I said. "I was just there to support."

She nodded, still looking off. Then she took a deep breath that seemed to bring her back from wherever she had gone. She smiled a smile that wasn't reflected in her tones, not from what I could see. "I'm going to get some rest, okay?"

"Of course." We kissed. "I'll be here."

Less than an hour had passed when I realized the whistling had stopped. I went to Jordan's bassinet. His infant face was twisted in silent anguish. I'd already screwed up. Jordan wasn't born with the same vocal abilities as other terrestrial children. The physical show he gave now was an instinct passed on from me without the equipment. Marlena must have been too exhausted to feel his *iunctio* wail. I had been disappointed and more than a little jealous when his mind hadn't also immediately connected to mine. Give it time, my wife had said. It'll come. I hoped so.

I lifted him from the bedding, took him out to the living room so as not to wake Marlena, and saw that some of his hair had twisted into his swaddle. I undid this and waited. The whistle returned, long, low, and steady. I walked him for another half hour, at least. He was on the edge of sleep when his midsection gurgled.

Jordan's eyes blinked open. He looked at me with what could have been the beginning of a grin.

In that moment, my newborn son awaiting his first diaper change and my wife resting in the back room, ready to start our new lives together as a family of three, I couldn't imagine where else I'd rather be.

Author's Note

AS A CHILD, I ENJOYED A GOOD COUCH ADVENTURE AS MUCH AS ANYBODY. MY love for genre fiction started with R. L. Stine's *Goosebumps* series. I devoured the fun little stories about evil dummies, cursed cameras, and monster's blood. As an anxious kid who worried about death and dogs and the dark, I looked forward to being "safe-scared." It felt good to exhaust my fears on something I knew couldn't actually harm me. Did I notice that none of Stine's main characters were Black like me? No. At least, not consciously.

As I grew, so did my tastes. Horror was my first love. *Gremlins, Arachnophobia, Child's Play.* Stephen King, Clive Barker, Peter Straub. Surviving a horror novel or movie was like conquering the big-kid rides at the amusement park. But it also brought me face to face with some difficult truths. An uncomfortable self-awareness crept in while watching *Scream 2*. I instantly aligned with the opening scene's young Black couple. When they were killed off in the first five minutes, it left me feeling like "Oh . . . this wasn't made for me." Suddenly, I wasn't "conquering" the ride after all. I was the kid crying inconsolably from just outside the gate as the real participants readily stepped past me and onto the loading platform. For years I protected myself from this by inserting my brown skin into the written narratives. Now, in full color on the big screen, it was undeniable: I was either a prop for white entertainment or watching from the sidelines.

This epiphany tainted my previously blind joy. Where *were* the people who looked like me? I wouldn't like the answer. All too often speculative fiction has been a tool to reinforce the principles of white supremacy. The Magical Negro trope (something I was mindful of when drafting "Afiya's Song"), where Black characters live solely to help a white protagonist reach their goal. "Exotic" characters in epic fantasy are used to represent an "other," usually less sophisticated people, in need of either a white conqueror or a white savior. Monsters in fiction and film—from King Kong to Xenomorphs to Freddy Krueger—represent the unknown and the misunderstood, stripped of history or context, there only to frighten and justify any measures required to defeat them. They allow the irrational but ubiquitous fear of Black people to fester unchecked in society's imagination without triggering white guilt. Once the monster is suppressed, once the "white savior" rescues the poor, marginalized character, once a person of color's special abilities are shown to be a reliable and friendly tool, society can return to a "normal," safe existence. Representations of people of color—whether metaphorical or explicit—reinforce us as inferior tools of white domination.

Lacking this crucial understanding of race in speculative fiction at the beginning of my career left me stranded in its genres. Although I had grown up in a Black home, went to Black schools, and lived in Black neighborhoods, when I sat down to write my first novel halfway through college, the protagonist was a blond, blue-eyed boy. The next novel, my attempt at horror, centered on a white family. I crafted what I thought was a standard haunted house tale, replete with gruesome ghosts and capped off with the mandatory twist at the end. Only it wasn't scary. As I reflected, I wondered how I had written hundreds of thousands of words and multiple drafts without incorporating my Blackness. No Black main characters. No inner-city setting. No community pride mixed in with societal fears. Fiction writing can be a window into one's psyche, revelatory in what's put on and left off the page. What exactly, then, was I trying to escape?

I've grown into embracing the Black experience (i.e., my experience) as the default in the fiction I create. I never set out to "write

Black," and I still don't. I write to understand my own perspective and, in that understanding, share that perspective with others. "The World Wasn't Ready for You," for instance, was written in response to an anthology call about parenting. What does parenting mean for me? The universals: bullies, restless nights, the rebellious years that may or may not last past adolescence. But it also means society's view of Black boys. It also means fear of law enforcement, fear of stereotypes, fear of punishment for being the "other." Speculative fiction has allowed me to explore xenophobia in a way I hope is relatable to everyone.

The Black experience is ripe for speculative fiction. Simultaneously horrific, unexplainable, and spiritual, its many joys, triumphs, and unique difficulties will likely exist in some form, for some group of people, far into our future. The spectacular allows the reader to experience these situations outside of the very politicized and polarizing nature of today's debates on race and racism. Why make up monsters when there are so many to fear in real life? What magic systems and lore are already rooted in my own culture and lineage? How does the journey that began in 1619 continue alongside seemingly unrelated sects of society, like space travel, pandemics, and medical education?

I also have the privilege of being a health-care provider. My writing has naturally gravitated toward more science fiction as I've gone through medical school and residency. The Black experience, however, was not separate from this. It was always present.

Medicine is a high-stress, high-stakes, highly hierarchical environment. Four years of medical school followed by three to ten years of residency (depending on the specialty), and every day is spent working one's way up the totem pole. This is made more complicated and stressful by being a person of color trying to navigate a system made in America and steeped in its history. I regularly witnessed minority colleagues reprimanded heavily for the same things our non-POC counterparts did without fear. I myself felt a constant pressure to be squeaky clean for the entirety of my training to uphold my peace of mind. "Now You See Me" explores this dynamic in a way that non-POC may be able to understand. In my protagonist's last year of residency, being a leader is a crucial part of her identity. The horrors she experiences as she slowly loses her autonomy are reflective of the real fears and experiences of Black and Brown people in this country.

It wasn't possible to write "Now You See Me" without thinking of a Black pediatric resident who recently died in childbirth, Chaniece Wallace, MD. Fiction allows art to relieve us from the hard truths of our reality by juxtaposing the supernatural with the macabre. They warn us in "safe-scared" spaces what humanity is capable of—what *racism* is capable of doing to Black and Brown bodies, legacy, and mental wellness.

For some readers, these stories reflected lived experiences historically underrepresented on the page. For others, it was partly a bait-and-switch, to be sure. Maybe I hope you learned something about my experience, because a world with a little more understanding is a little less scary for those who are historically and chronically misunderstood. Fiction, in a sense, was my way of luring you onto this faulty plane and giving you something familiar as you buckled your seat belt and settled in for the ride. And during that flight I attempted to give you a little bit of me through some tough-love turbulence.

How was it? I hope we landed safely on the other side, together.

Acknowledgments

WHEN PEOPLE ASK ME "WHAT'S YOUR SECRET?" I INVARIABLY TELL THEM, "I surround myself with good people." I—and by extension all the stories in this collection—am a culmination of my community. Where would I be without you? All of you?

First and foremost, I'd like to thank my wonderful wife, Johanna, who knew I was an aspiring writer and decided to go out on a first date anyway. Despite a bumpy front-row seat to the ups and downs of a difficult and arduous marathon, you've always been my biggest cheerleader. If a true representation of love exists in these pages, it's because of you.

I want to thank my children for pushing me every day to be a better father and human. Jackson, Jonah, and Juniper, my greatest lessons have been from fatherhood. I look forward to all you have yet to teach me.

I'm eternally grateful for my mother, Pamela Hairston. Your supply of books was surpassed only by your abundance of love. You taught me curiosity, kindness, and, as the first writer I ever looked up to, the mighty power of the pen. I love you. I thank you. Thank you to my stepfather, Adrian, a fellow Stephen King fan. Your nod of approval throughout the years meant more than you know. Thank you to my cousins, Neil, Jamila, T. Jr., Kim, Melissa, and Chip, for making this only child feel loved and supported.

I love my tribe and say thank you to my forever first-reader and lifelong friend, Marcus McLaughlin, for your years of excitement and wisdom. To John Dryden, for your encyclopedic knowledge and willingness to discuss ad nauseam all the most important things in life, like whether quantum immortality exists. To my best friend Robert Watkins, for your *unwavering* friendship and letting me be all versions of myself, and to Justin Turner for believing in me even when I didn't. To all my friends who have supported me over the years, emotionally, professionally, and intellectually: Jared Murphy, Obinna Emenike, Ryan Boles, Warren King, Jason Salim, Terrell Holloway, Michael Mensah, Evelyn Nelson, Liz Fisseha, Andrew Levette, Sonya Shadravan, Katrina DeBonis, David Muller, Ann Crawford-Roberts, and Jacob Appel. I thank you all for sticking by this weird kid who had big dreams.

Thank you to the Clarion West Foundation and specifically my 2015 instructors for seeing the value in my work and motivating me to chase my potential. To Andy Duncan, Eileen Gunn, Tobias Buckell, Susan Palwick, Nalo Hopkinson, and Cory Doctorow, I thank you. To my 2015 classmates—Tegan Moore, Leo Vladimirsky, Evan J. Peterson, Rebecca Campbell, Christine Neulieb, Margaret Killjoy, Nibedita Sen, Michael Sebastian, Jude M. Wetherell, Thersa Matsuura, Elise Johnston, Mimi Mondal, Nana Nkweti, Laurie Penny, Jake Stone, Samuel Kolawole, and Dinesh Pulandram—you will forever be a collective voice in my head. Thank you for teaching me about life, perspective, and friendship.

I want to thank my writing groups over the years for teaching me the importance of critique and growth. And to my writing friends and mentors—Sam J. Miller for reading my Clarion West application, Cadwell Turnbull for your collaborative spirit, Maurice Broaddus for helping me navigate the landscape as a black man, and S. B. Divya for letting a simple short-story sale grow into a rewarding mentorship—I thank you.

A very special thanks to Howie Sanders (and my UCLA mentor Dr. Wayne Sanders for introducing us). You took a chance on a psychiatry resident with a pen in his back pocket. You've opened so many doors and continue to push me to dream outside the box. Thank you to Ryan Wilson and the rest of the Anonymous Content team. To Adam Eaglin, my rock-star agent who made me believe a short-story collection was possible, you've been a great creative and professional partner. I thank you for handling this beginning to my career with such care. And I thank Sarah Ried, my editor, for your attention, thoughtfulness, and above all *excitement* for not only these stories but also for me as a writer. Without your vision and prowess, this book would not exist.

I want to thank all the editors who pulled one of my stories from the slush pile. Thank you to Kelly Jennings for being my first pro-sale, to C.C. Finlay for encouraging me so much in your rejections that I kept trying until I got your acceptance ("Afiya's Song"), to Diana Pho for helping me bring the best out of my stories ("The Perfection of Theresa Watkins" and "Spider King"), to Wendy Wagner for giving me a chance to be in a magazine I'd adored for years ("Now You See Me"), to Catherine Krahe, Lila Garrott, and Vajra Chandrasekera for indulging my take on the age-old possessed puppet, and Tonia Ransom for bringing it to audio life ("One Hand in the Coffin"), and to Jaymee Goh for inspiring me to ask the tough questions about parenthood ("The World Wasn't Ready for You").

And lastly, I want to thank my cousin Michael "Douggie" Hairston for loving me unconditionally like a brother. May you continue to Rest in Peace and I hope to make you proud.

About the Author

JUSTIN C. KEY is a speculative fiction writer and psychiatrist whose short stories have appeared in *The Magazine of Fantasy & Science Fiction*, *Strange Horizons*, *Tor.com*, *Escape Pod*, and *Lightspeed*. Born and raised in Washington, DC, Justin had an early passion for bridging the gap between medicine and communities of color. His love of narrative and the ability to connect patients to their personal stories led him to psychiatry. He received a BA in biology from Stanford University, an MD from the Icahn School of Medicine at Mount Sinai, and recently completed his residency in psychiatry at UCLA. He developed his own practice in Southern California and specializes in treating psychotic and mood disorders, anxiety disorders, and addiction. Justin is humbled at the opportunity to connect both with the patient through his medical training and with the reader through the page. When Justin isn't writing, working with patients, or exploring Los Angeles with his wife, he's chasing after his three young (and energetic!) children.